DOOMED CITY

Also available in the *Berlin Gothic* series

The Beginning

BERLIN GOTHIC 2

DOOMED CITY

JONAS WINNER

TRANSLATED BY EDWIN MILES

amazon crossing

Text copyright © 2011 Jonas Winner
English translation copyright © 2014 Edwin Miles
All rights reserved.

Doomed City was first published in 2011 by Berlin Gothic Media in four parts originally titled *Der versteckte Wille*, *Nachts bei Max*, *Die versteckte Bedeutung*, and *Gottmaschine*. Translated from German by Edwin Miles. Published in English by AmazonCrossing in 2014.

Published by AmazonCrossing, Seattle
www.apub.com
Amazon, the Amazon logo, and AmazonCrossing are trademarks of Amazon.com, Inc., or its affiliates.

ISBN-13: 9781477820254
ISBN-10: 1477820256

Cover design by Edward Bettison
Library of Congress Control Number: 2013922580
Printed in the United States of America

PROLOGUE

TWO YEARS EARLIER

Dear Till,

You've probably already seen it, since I've included the invitation with this letter: Betty's getting married next month! You can imagine how happy that makes me. For her . . . and because I hope you can finally come and see us in Berlin. Do you know Henning? Betty met him through Max, and she's head over heels in love. This means the youngest of us will be the first one to tie the knot. Who would have thought?

No doubt you've heard from Max. He's been back in Berlin since last fall and has found an apartment here. I love visiting him, sitting on the balcony and drinking coffee. He's doing . . . well? I guess you two probably keep in touch and that you know more about him than I do. It was never easy with Max, and last summer . . . well, he spent the summer traveling, maybe you heard about that? Something must have happened on that trip, but when I ask him about it, he just sidesteps the issue.

As for me, things couldn't be better. I'm just about to finish my internship at the newspaper, but I haven't really made up my mind what I'll do after that. I've still got a few weeks.

Enough about me. How are you, Till? I take it you're slowly building a life for yourself over there? Meeting a lot of people? One hears so much about Toronto—it's supposed to be such a lovely city! Will you be staying in Canada for the next few years? Or do you have other plans? How long will you be able to visit us in Berlin when you come for Betty's wedding? Just a few days? Or a little longer? Max will be over the moon . . . me too . . .

Me too, Till. I would be so happy . . . I know I shouldn't be telling you this, but I find myself thinking about you a lot. I even dream about you at night. Should I say that?

My life . . . I hinted at it just now, didn't I? Everything's great. Wonderful! Fantastic! It's just that sometimes I get the feeling that everything is somehow already . . . predetermined? IS THIS WHAT I EVEN WANT? To work for the paper? Why? What does it mean? Who does it benefit? Me? How?

Don't get me wrong, I'm not complaining about anything. Maybe I should just get away from Berlin for a while. I've been living here for so long, and I've never spent more than a few weeks in any other place. Sometimes it seems to me that every building, every tree, every paving stone is saturated with the memories I carry around with me here.

But I'm beating around what I really should be talking about, Till.

Will you come to Betty's wedding? That's what I want to know. What I have to know! Now that you have my letter in your hands, there in Toronto, at your desk . . . will you write me a few lines? "Dear Lisa, lovely to hear from you, but . . . but unfortunately, I can't make it . . ."

Is that what you'll write?

So much has happened in the last few months. Things I can't or don't want to even mention, let alone explain. All I can think is, can it go on like this forever?

I miss you . . .

No! I'm not going to write what I wanted to write. I'm NOT going to!

Nothing seems to have changed here in Berlin. But the truth is, nothing stays the same. The truth is, everything is in flux, in motion, and sometimes it almost feels like this change is rolling over me, burying me, and I don't have the strength to defend myself.

How can I say something like that?!

You're right! I take it back! It's not true. I'm doing wonderfully well! In case you can't make it over to Betty's wedding . . . I can understand that, Till. Have fun in Toronto. Enjoy your life there. I hope you have a lot of friends, nice people around you, and maybe even someone there you love.

Lisa

TODAY

Butz presses the phone to his ear and shoves the car door open with his foot. "Hello?"

"Something's . . . Konstantin?" Claire's voice.

"Still here."

"Something's happened," she says.

"Uh-huh?"

"Let's talk about it tomorrow morning."

Anything could happen by then! Butz slams the door behind him and heads for the entrance to the building where he's double-parked. Three more vehicles are already standing in front of his: his assistant Micha's, a forensics squad van, and a patrol car, its blue lights illuminating the dark street.

"Claire . . . we don't have to spend hours . . ."

"Konstantin, really, it's complicated."

"I don't want to go through every detail, Claire. All I'm talking about is . . ." He wants to say "Frederik Barkar, the boxer"—but she's right, it's not that simple.

"Are you even listening?" Claire sounds upset. "Are you trying to *force* me to explain it on the phone?"

Explain what? That she's . . . what? What is she doing? Leaving me?

"Tomorrow morning. Just the two of us," she says.

Butz would like nothing more than to cave in, let Claire have her way . . . but *can* he do that? *Dare* he do that?

"It can't wait until tomorrow, Claire. It's not just about us. It might be connected to the case I'm working on."

He reaches the building as they talk. He leans against the front door, the latch clacks, and the door swings open. Butz crosses a narrow corridor and then walks up a narrow stairway that leads to the front building. Third floor, Micha said.

"Where are you?" he asks.

He hears Claire breathing on the line.

Why did this happen *now*? Is it just coincidence? Coincidence that Barkar has come into their world just *now*—while Butz is investigating a series of murders unlike anything ever seen before in Berlin?

"I'm switching my phone off now, Konstantin." Claire's voice sounds unfamiliar. "I'll try to be at the apartment tomorrow morning."

"Wait! Don't you get it? You're in danger."

Butz stops on the landing outside the front door to Fehrenberg's apartment. *Did Fehrenberg actually live here with his girlfriend and her kid?*

The door is ajar, and he taps on it.

"Claire, I spoke to Ms. Bastian today. The chief's secretary." The door swings back, giving Butz a clear view of the hallway inside the apartment. "She showed me some pictures from a boxing fight."

Is she still on the line?

Butz holds one hand over the phone and calls down the hallway. "Micha?"

He steps into the apartment.

"Are you still there?" Back on the phone to Claire.

"Yes. Yes, I'm still here."

"I saw you in the pictures, Claire." *Why wasn't there a cop stationed at the door? Anyone could wander in!*

"*Micha!*" Loud, sharp.

"What?" Claire's voice is slightly distorted.

"Sorry, Claire, no, not you . . . I just called out for Micha, I'm still here . . ."

Then he sees it.

"I have to hang up now, Konstantin." There is a click in his ear. Claire is gone.

Butz has reached the door leading into the first room.

He has the impression of time stretching.

The head is thrown back. The lower jaw misaligned. The eyes are directed straight at Butz. But they stare at nothing, and a large hole gapes in the cheek. Butz can see the back teeth through the hole. Blood-smeared and smashed. The hole makes the corpse look like it's grinning.

Butz still has the phone pressed to his ear. His lips move but no sound emerges.

Micha.

It is his assistant, Micha. Lying in the room, grinning lifelessly at him.

TODAY

"Whoa! Where did that thing come from?"

"Haven't you been here before?"

A greenish light fills the room. It's very dark, but Malte can still see the tank shimmering at the other end of the hall. It looks like some kind of complicated lighting system has been installed inside the tank.

"Wild!" He takes a few more steps toward the massive tank. It has to be at least twelve feet high, maybe fifteen. The glass is so thick and the light refracts so strangely through it that moving his head almost makes him dizzy. "Have you given him a name?"

The man with him, who brought him here, gives him a mocking look. "Cap'n Ahab, something like that?"

The movements of the creature in the tank are intoxicating. Elegant. Majestic. Composed. Stretched out, Malte guesses it must be twenty-five feet long. But it doesn't stretch itself out. It flows through the water, gliding and circling, moving forward in wavelike bursts. It approaches the glass wall but doesn't touch it, changing direction instead, swimming away, disappearing into the blue of the tank, reappearing a moment later, and then sweeping forward again with a stretch of its arms, its flowing body, the limbs unfurling.

"Is she already in with him?"

The man nods to one side and Malte follows the nod with his eyes.

"Wow!"

Her body shimmers brightly in the dark water. The thin beams from the lights mounted inside the pool meet her body, casting a shimmering, golden net across her skin. Malte watches as the woman eases away from the edge. Her head is above the surface of the water, out of sight to him, but her legs, her arms, her belly, and her feet are drifting through the gigantic aquarium in front of him. With slow strokes, she makes her way to the middle of the pool.

"What's it doing?" Malte instinctively takes another step forward and lays one hand against the glass. It's pleasantly cool, though the air in the hall is warm, almost hot. As if the heat of summer has been stored up in here.

One arm stretches out, curling from the rear part of the tank, in the direction of the woman. The tip of the tentacle seems to literally be feeling its way through the water toward her. Malte wants to see the face of the woman with the eel-smooth body, but all she does is lower one arm into the water, opening up her hand, while she goes on paddling slowly with her feet, just enough to stop her from going under. Enthralled, Malte sees the tentacle nearing her hand. It brushes it gingerly—recoils without her having moved—advances again, touches the hand.

But this time the tentacle does not shy away, gliding instead between her hand and the side of her body, around to her back, encircling her . . .

Malte holds his breath.

The woman arches her back, her breasts straining the bikini top. Oozing around from behind, the tentacle reaches her belly, curls . . . wrapping more tightly around her, pulling her down.

Air bubbles rise around the woman's face and her hair streams back as her head breaks through the silvery surface and submerges. Her eyes are open, fully focused on the creature, which still does not move from its place in the back of the pool. But now it unfurls a second arm in her direction . . . while the tip of the first cautiously winds under the sheer cloth of her bikini bottom, sliding in and—it seems to Malte—going deeper and deeper.

The woman's hair has fanned out, flowing around her shoulders like spreading smoke. The pulling and thrusting movements the animal is using to move her through the water are reflected in the delayed movement of her hair. Malte glances at the man beside him. *How does she do that?* he wants to ask, wondering how she can hold her breath so long. But then he turns back to the tank again and sees the woman's fingers, seeming very small, wrap around the powerful tentacle between her legs. He sees her try to push it away from her; her neck is arched, her legs crooked. Then the second arm reaches her, gliding under and past her chin, along the straps of the bikini top, sweeping the skimpy cloth aside, baring one breast, obviously aroused by this game.

In the same moment, she has freed herself from the tentacle between her legs and swims up again, her head breaking the silvery film of the surface, which dances in the light. But the arm follows her, undulates along her hip, grasping the bikini bottom, tugging, jerking it free and sweeping it aside in one motion, giving Malte a clear view of the woman's body, her smooth, fluid skin, now completely naked. The bikini bottom sinks in slow circles to the bottom of the pool.

Malte turns his head to one side.

A dull rumble fills the room.

What was that?

"Shall we get going?" his companion asks, glancing at his wristwatch. He must have heard it too.

Malte looks back at the pool. The swimmer is holding tightly to the far side of the pool. He can still see her through the water, but only just.

She must have felt the rumbling too. From the play of light on the surface, Malte realizes that the water is rippling. His hand reaches out to the glass in front of him. It is vibrating. Then another deep rumble hits.

Shocked, Malte looks over to his companion. "Feel that! The whole thing is shaking!"

The crack comes so hard and sharp that for a moment Malte feels like his skull has been split open.

A sharp beam of light hits him—probably one of the spotlights in the pool, he thinks, knocked askew by the shaking.

He doesn't even have time to close his eyes. Everything happens at once.

In a second, the room is hip deep, then shoulder deep in water.

The wave that surges from the breach in the glass sweeps his companion away. Malte is thrown backward, his legs over his head, his shoulders slamming onto the floor, then the wall. The torrent of water is so strong that he can't control the movement of his arms. The roar and rush of it goes right through him. His head hits an edge, and he feels himself blacking out—but he knows he'll drown if that happens. He twists and rolls, is washed into one corner of the room, and manages to hold on there for a moment before the water rips him away again and flings him across the floor.

Malte did not hear the glass breaking. Only the surge and roar of the thousands of gallons pouring, falling out of the tank and into the hall—and then plunging through the massive, grated openings covering the floor.

Malte's ear is burning from where he hit the wall. A chill shoots through his drenched body. The water rumbles through the drain that opens beneath the grates. The entire hall is filled with the noise of dripping, trickling, gurgling, and slopping, as if a cloudburst had just hit the neighborhood and stopped as instantly as it started. For all the power of the deluge that inundated the hall, just a few seconds later, the water has drained away through the grates in the floor.

Malte blinks. He is lying in the corner where the water tossed him. The tank is empty, the glass wall shattered. A few steps away from him, a damp black mass trembles on the floor—sunken in on itself, limp and slimy. Farther back, he can see the woman's naked body, her arms stretched out above her head. She's rolled partly on her side, one hip curving upward.

Malte stands up. The heat in the hall is once again gaining the upper hand; the dampness is evaporating, the air is clammy, and the coolness of the water is gone. Without a second glance at the fishy mass, which seems to be falling apart, Malte ducks his head and lopes over to the woman. He kneels on the ground beside her. She is both cool and warm, her skin moist and smooth. She seems to stir at his touch, to straighten, stiffen . . .

Malte can't stop himself. Mechanically, unconsciously, he peels his sodden pants down over his hips and lays one hand gingerly on the woman's pelvis. Slowly, she turns onto her back in front of him. His hands explore her sides, her thighs, still glistening from the deluge—and he lowers his body on top of her, in the iron grip of desire now, enslaved by her beauty, by what her curves, her lips, her hair, her breathing . . . by what all of these trigger in him and promise him.

There's no more turning back, there's only one direction—straight ahead. There is just the craving for a release from the lust and the hardness raging in him provoked by the sight of the woman. He sees her eyelashes flutter, her eyes opening in front of him, her pupils at first dilated, then contracting, looking at him.

She exhales.

Malte's hand moves down. He feels the contact between them, the way her thighs glide across his hips. They close around him and he feels her legs urging him forward from behind, forward and inside her in one long, seemingly endless motion . . .

"MALTE!"

His stomach twists.

"MALTE!"

He jolts upright.

Her breasts . . . her thighs . . . the motion . . .

"Goddamnit, Malte! Come on, it's time!"

Half sitting, he presses his fingers to his eyes, digging his index fingers into the hollows right and left of the bridge of his nose.

And the weight of his loins on her hips, the seemingly endless motion . . . ?

"It's happening!"

What's happening? Is that what made the tank burst?

Someone snatches away the blanket still wrapped around him. Dazed, Malte looks around. He is in a vaulted room the size of a gymnasium with two dozen people around him, maybe more. Like him, some of them still look half asleep. His back is stiff from the camping mat he's been lying on.

Tank? There is no tank!

His guts cramp again. The disappointment has left him speechless.

"You okay?" someone asks.

The others are pulling on their clothes.

He'd been just a heartbeat—a blink of an eye—from finishing the dream! Why didn't they let him sleep just one more minute?

TWO YEARS EARLIER

Lisa headed for the edge of the forecourt, where a long table was set at a right angle to the red brick facade of the church. Guests were still walking from the parking lot, from the bus stop, and along the narrow side street where the church was located.

"Thank you," said Lisa, accepting the flute of champagne a waiter handed to her across the table. She took a sip and, over the rim of the glass, swept her eyes across the forecourt. She estimated that there were nearly a hundred wedding guests.

Everyone was dressed to kill. Max was wearing a tuxedo and stood with a small group of young men just beside the church entrance. Most of the women had opted for sophisticated outfits, some of them skintight, mainly in black or white. Lisa's gaze settled on Felix, who was wearing a pale-beige linen suit and had just then extricated himself from a group.

She set the empty champagne glass on the table and weaved a path through small knots of guests toward him.

Felix's eyes flashed. "There you are! I've been looking for you."

Lisa immediately took him by the arm and drew him a few steps toward the church. "Do you have a moment?"

Felix laughed. "Don't you want to say hello to your friends first?"

But they were already entering the dim nave of the building. The air smelled of mortar and wood. A shiver ran down Lisa's spine.

"You can go back out again in a minute." She bundled Felix onto the rearmost pew and sat down next to him. He wrapped one arm around her waist and pulled her close.

"Hey!" Lisa pushed backward and jabbed him sharply with her elbow. "It's about the speech!" she hissed and, with relief, felt his arm retreat. "I still don't know what I'm going to say."

Felix leaned back against the back of the bench. "Isn't it a little too late to be thinking about that?"

Lisa took a deep breath. She hadn't counted on a more useful response. But it still made her queasy to think that her little sister might get married today with nobody to deliver a speech.

"I *have* to say something. I promised I would, and I can't go back on my word now. It's bad enough that Claire can't be here today."

"How's she doing, by the way?"

"Very well, actually. But the doctor says she can't travel just yet. She's stuck in Malaysia crying her eyes out because she's missing Betty's wedding. And all because she just *had* to do an internship with that photographer!"

Felix looked at her. "You really think she wanted to work for that photographer so badly? Or was it more about getting as far away from Julia as she could—"

"So, now you're blaming *Mom*?" Lisa interrupted, glaring indignantly at Felix.

Felix raised one hand and took hold of a strand of Lisa's hair that had come loose, sweeping it back behind her ear. "Hey, it's okay. I don't want to fight with you." He smiled. "As for the speech, all you need to do is stand up and smile at the guests. That is definitely the loveliest thing they can imagine." Lisa again jabbed him with her elbow, but Felix tensed his stomach muscles in time and her elbow glanced off.

"Come on!" she snapped at him, half laughing, half desperate. "Think of something, Felix!"

He leaned forward slightly, ready to intercept any additional incoming jabs with his left arm. "How can I tell you what to say about your sister?"

"What would you say if it were *your* sister getting married today?"

He thought this over for a moment. "All you have to do is think about what *kind* of speech you want to deliver," he finally said, his eyes gazing into the depths of the nave. "Something mischievous about Betty's weaknesses, for example. Or a speech about how you racked your brains about the speech? If I were you, I would talk about the special relationship you and your sister had growing up without a father. Didn't you become a kind of stand-in dad for little Betty?"

"Lisa?"

Lisa spun around and saw her mother coming toward her through the church entrance. She sensed Felix edge away slightly.

"There you are! Betty just arrived."

"Good!" Lisa stood up. "Time to get things started."

"She wants to see you." Julia stopped beside them and nodded to Felix, who was now standing also. "She came into the church through a back entrance and she's waiting in a side room." Lisa's mother's concern was plain to see.

"Has something happened?"

"She doesn't want to speak to anyone else." Julia smoothed one eyebrow with a finger, obviously making an effort to stay calm. "Will you go to her please?"

TWO YEARS EARLIER

Betty was sitting on a wooden chair and staring out the window. When Lisa pushed the door open, her little sister turned to face her. Her eyes seemed larger than usual. She had thrown back the veil and the sprawling wedding dress looked slightly disordered. Lisa barely recognized her. She hadn't been with Betty in the early morning, when the beauticians had come to get her ready. Everything about her looked different. Her eyelashes were dark with mascara, her hair styled, and her fingernails polished. For a moment, she reminded Lisa of a wax doll.

"Lissi, I . . . I . . ."

Betty stood up from the chair and moved toward her. The dress dragged on the floor.

Lisa threw her arms around her.

"I'm not allowed to cry. I'll get all smeary," she heard her sister whisper in her ear. "They can't fix it up anymore now. Everything's ready, everyone's waiting, I . . ."

Lisa felt her seventeen-year-old sister's strong, slim body shaking in her arms. Everyone—her mother, Max, even Felix—had asked Lisa if she thought Betty was old enough to get married. "The only one who can decide that is Betty herself," Lisa had answered. But now she wasn't so sure. Maybe Betty just wanted to prove to everyone that she really was old enough to go through with it.

Lisa held her sister by the arms and pushed her back gently. "Betty, look . . . nothing has happened yet. If you want me to, I'll go out and tell everyone." Lisa smiled. "Then they can mothball all their stupid tuxes and outfits for the next five years."

Betty looked at her uncertainly. "What about Mom?"

"Forget Mom! It isn't Mom who's getting married. You are, Betty. And if you don't want to do it anymore, then I can understand that perfectly well. There's only one thing that matters, and that is that you *don't* go out there and say 'I do' *because they expect you to!*"

Betty's arms dropped to her sides. She already held the bridal bouquet in her hand. She took a few steps back and flopped onto the wooden chair. The stress she was feeling was clear.

"Is everyone waiting? Is the church full?"

"Let them fidget a bit longer. And I haven't seen Henning yet, either."

It was as if her husband-to-be's name was a needle pricking her skin. Betty's head drooped forward. "What's he going to think?"

"Who *cares*?!" Lisa couldn't stop herself from raising her voice. "Seriously, Betty. The way I see it, up to now you've done everything right. But if you let Henning or anyone else force you into taking a step that you don't want to take, then that's something else. I do *not* want to find you on my doorstep tomorrow telling me it was all a mistake."

Betty lowered her head and stared at the toes of her white shoes.

"Do you love him?"

Betty didn't move.

"You don't know if you love him?"

Lisa's sister shook her head imperceptibly . . . but it was impossible to miss.

"Hmm."

That, of course, was a problem. If Betty scuttled the wedding and figured out later that Henning was the right one *after all* . . .

Betty looked up apprehensively, as if she feared having to read in her sister's eyes that she really was stuck in a hopeless situation.

"Henning's a . . ." Lisa started. She wanted to say *a nice guy. A good man, a good friend* . . . but none of that was what Betty wanted to hear. Or marry.

"Yeah, I know," murmured her sister. "That's why I let it go as far as it has. But he . . ." She looked at Lisa, her eyes burning. "You know, if it were Felix, that would be something else. But Henning? I can't shake the feeling that he . . . I mean, I like him, he's always been good to me, but when he asked me if I wanted to marry him, I was so surprised. It seemed like such a crazy idea that I thought . . . I thought, maybe it could work out for us! But now that everything's come so far . . . I don't know. It's like I'm suddenly not so sure."

What does Felix have to do with this? Lisa thought.

"I tried to talk to Henning about it," Betty continued, both hands wrapped around the bouquet tightly. "I hoped he'd be able to just sweep all my doubts away with a word. Maybe I even hoped he wouldn't take it all so seriously, you know? That he'd stay as crazy as he was when he asked me to marry him. But Henning seemed really shocked. He said we'd have to cancel everything, and he went on about his parents, and Mom, and our friends . . ."

Betty's eyes seemed to be searching Lisa's face, looking for something to hang onto. "He didn't say a word about how we'd be able to make it work. I got the impression that he thought the only reason we should still go through with it was because it would be embarrassing for him to have to call it all off."

Lisa nodded. That was just like Henning.

"If it had been Felix," Betty started again, "well, he knows what he wants; he doesn't have to talk himself into anything. But Henning?" Now her eyes filled with tears. "How could I ever get it into my head that I wanted to marry Henning?!"

Lisa hesitated. "Well, you might the have wrong impression, Betty. Felix . . . maybe it's actually good that it's Henning and not Felix. Not someone like Felix."

Betty looked at her, her forehead creased, as if waking from her own thoughts.

"Felix seems so on top of things, so cheerful . . . but . . ." Lisa searched for words, but gave up and left the sentence unfinished.

"But *what*?" Betty was leaning forward slightly.

"There are days, nights . . ." *Don't breathe a word about that!* barked something inside Lisa. Not on Betty's wedding day!

"What?" Betty turned all her attention to Lisa, as if she had completely forgotten her own worries.

"Sometimes, a kind of impatience takes hold of him," Lisa murmured. "Something untamable, or discontented." *No!* "It's like he's not himself, as if he . . ." Lisa swallowed. Didn't she have to tell her sister? Betty didn't know what to do. She had asked Lisa to come to her, she had asked her for advice . . .

"It just hits him," Lisa whispered, her voice hoarse. "He gets wound up and furious. He doesn't hurt me, but it's like something's tearing him up inside, and he has to call on all of his strength not to savage me or rip me apart."

Betty stared at her, pale as chalk and totally confused.

"And I never know if his strength will really be enough to keep him in check."

Spent, Lisa paused. *She doesn't need to know any more*, she told herself. *She* can't *know any more*.

"Henning isn't like that, Betty. You should be glad of that." Lisa forced herself to suppress such suffocating thoughts of Felix.

"But isn't it nice too?" Betty held the bouquet before her face, as if to make sure no one would hear her. "It is nice, isn't it . . . too? Or you would have dumped him a long time ago."

Nice? As nice as plummeting to the ground from a clear-blue sky. As nice as being churned up by a tidal wave. As nice as the certainty that one day you'll die. It was so nice that every time he dragged her down with him in his madness, in one of his episodes, she felt that she would die. So nice that after he raged with her through the night, she usually couldn't get out of bed for a week. So nice that she sometimes wondered what she would give to find a way out of her relationship with Felix. But the truth was she could not free herself from him.

Lisa shook her head and looked her sister in the eye.

"No, Betty. Nice it is not."

"So, why don't you leave him?"

Because I can't, Lisa heard herself saying—but only to herself. Instead, she reached a hand out to Betty. "So, what's the deal? Have you thought it over?"

Betty smiled. With relief, Lisa saw that her sister seemed to have rediscovered her old self-confidence.

"I'm doing it!" Betty laughed and stood up. "Isn't this crazy?"

The two women embraced. *Yes*, thought Lisa, *it is*. And suddenly, she knew why she had been nervous the whole morning. Not because she didn't have her speech finished. But because she still didn't know if he was going to come to the wedding.

Till.

He had never answered her letter.

TODAY

Micha's right shoulder is sticking up in the air. He is still wearing his overcoat, but the material is twisted under his legs.

When Butz puts a hand to the jutting shoulder, the thin body slips and collapses onto its back. One of the handmade English shoes that Butz's assistant was so proud of has come loose at the heel, but Micha's toes are still inside it. His legs are crossed, his arms half outstretched on the floor.

Micha's eyes are open, gazing past the top of Butz's head at the ceiling. The jaw hangs open, the chin—once so striking—hangs slack.

The bullet hit him in the cheekbone, shattering it and ripping open the throat below.

Butz hears himself exhale.

Every breath seems to take five minutes.

Thoughts shoot into his brain like fireworks in the night sky, and then burn out again.

Nothing holds, nothing locks in place.

Butz reflexively grasps his assistant's coat collar and pulls him up, as if he could get him to stand.

Breathe out.

Breathe in.

The photo.

The photo that Micha had sent him.

Butz can see it in his mind's eye.

A bedroom . . .

His eye wanders to the doorway that Micha's body is blocking.

Breathe out.

Breathe in.

He carefully lets the lifeless body sink back to the floor.

He can already see the next one, lying in the adjoining room. A colleague from forensics.

The bullet had hit him in the forehead, jolting his head and body back. He had fallen backward onto the low glass table in front of the television, and was still lying there, his legs bent under him and his feet askew on the cheap carpet.

Butz's head is buzzing.

His breathing drones in his ears.

Is he still here?

The one who shot them?

Breathe out.

Breathe in.

The window is open in the room where the forensics specialist is lying. From the courtyard out back come the sounds of neighbors. Someone pulls a cork from a wine bottle.

Women's voices. Just talking.

Butz's shirt is soaked with sweat and clings to his skin between his shoulder blades. He silently moves his hand to his shoulder holster and he draws his gun. The knurled grip settles into the palm of his hand.

Butz holds his crouched position. He wants to listen, but his senses are grotesquely distorting every sound he hears.

The clack of a window from the courtyard. The dripping of blood from the glass table into the black pool on the carpet.

And . . .

It's not in his head.

Breathe out.

Breathe in.

It's a kind of crackling, or a humming noise. An insistent buzzing, in motion, polyphonic.

Noiselessly, Butz straightens up a little, and moving catlike, takes one long, smooth step over Micha's body and into the living room, where the forensics guy's body is lying on the glass table. He scans the room. Two doors lead off it.

One of the doors goes to the corridor. Butz sees the torso of a third man lying in front of it. One of the two uniformed cops. His back is turned to Butz, and he isn't moving.

Butz feels his right hand stiffening. He's been holding the pistol far too tightly.

The second door.

He hears steps cross the courtyard outside.

No one in the whole goddamned building heard a thing.

A drop of sweat trickles down Butz's side.

The second door is ajar.

The buzzing—that's where it's coming from. Back there.

Butz takes a step toward the door, reaches out one hand, and touches the door. It swings open silently.

A warm, sweet, stinking stream swirls to meet him.

Flies. Dozens. Hundreds.

Butz's eyes sweep the room. The ceiling light is on.

The fourth officer. He is lying in the corner between the bed and the wardrobe, must have been thrown back against the wall by the shot. His upper body is bent forward, hanging a hand's breadth above his outstretched legs.

The wardrobe is open. The officer had probably been searching it. But that isn't what draws Butz's attention.

It's the bags and packets, bits of paper and crumbs. The scraps of chocolate bars, plastic bottles, stale chips, cheese puffs, ice cream tubs, clumps of gummy bears, drink containers . . . The entire bedroom floor is inches deep in the remains of a junk-food orgy that must have gone on for days, maybe weeks.

It isn't the first time that Butz has seen this sea of garbage. He already saw it on the photo that Micha sent him on his phone.

But something's off; it still feels to Butz as if he has to orient himself in Fehrenberg's bedroom.

Because . . .

Okay, he already knew about the bags and packets and chips and cheese puffs. But . . .

The bed . . .

Fehrenberg's body . . . bloated and grotesquely distorted. In the photo it was easy to recognize. And it had been lying on the bed.

But now the bed is empty.

The flies are still here. Their buzzing fills the air. They are already landing on Butz's hands, his face, his lips. But the body—Fehrenberg's body—is gone.

TWO YEARS EARLIER

"No sweat, it opens from the inside too."

Max jumped when the door slammed closed behind him with a solid bang.

Quentin waved him inside. "It'll just take a second—we'll be out again soon enough."

Max stuffed his hands into the pockets of his pants. His breath was steaming. Quentin stepped over to a shelf in the cold room and set the two water glasses they had brought with them onto an insulated box with a transparent lid. Through the lid, Max could make out several fish covered in a crumbly layer of ice.

Quentin reached behind the box and when his hand reappeared, it was holding an ice-cold, frost-covered bottle. Without comment, Quentin screwed off the cap and poured four fingers of the liquid into each glass.

"Here you go." He handed one of the glasses to Max.

Max took them and sniffed at the liquid. It had no smell, it was transparent—"clean" was the word that came to mind. It seemed just a little thicker than water, somehow oilier.

"To your little sister!" grinned Quentin.

"To Betty." Max clinked his glass against Quentin's, put it to his lips, and threw his head back. The wonderfully dry liquid ran icily down his throat. It was as if he didn't even need to swallow. The vodka spread warmly across his chest and exploded deep in his stomach. Max puffed out a breath of air and felt the alcohol fumes streaming out of his mouth. At the same time, a tingle spread through his body; it was like being given a shot of extra life.

Quentin held his glass high. "One more?"

Max licked his lips. No doubt the brand Quentin had dug out of the walk-in at his parents' restaurant was one of the best. Still, he shook his head.

"I'd prefer an espresso."

One glass was just right. Max felt the alcohol carrying him—but he also knew it was a fragile balance. One shot too many and it would be difficult for him to stay in control.

Quentin nodded and screwed the cap on. "Good idea."

TODAY

"I'm switching my phone off now, Konstantin. I'll try to be at the apartment tomorrow morning."

Claire is standing on the sidewalk, her head tilted back, phone at her ear.

"Wait!" She hears the insistence in Butz's voice. "Don't you get it? You're in danger."

She is looking up at the facade of the old apartment building, lit up by the streetlamps. A window on the fourth floor is open. A man stands inside the window, his hands propped on the sill. But he isn't looking down. His head is turned and he is looking across the facade, toward the window just a few yards to his right.

"Claire, I spoke to Ms. Bastian today." She can't shut him up. He just keeps talking. "The chief's secretary . . ."

Bastian? Didn't she pick up the application for the crime-scene series from her?

"She showed me some pictures from a boxing fight."

Boxing fight. It hits Claire like an electric shock. She realizes Butz has placed a hand over the mouthpiece of his phone. A moment later, she hears, "Are you still there?"

"Yes. Yes, I'm still here."

She realizes that the man in the window is standing in the stairwell—the stairwell next to Frederik's apartment.

"I saw you in the pictures, Claire."

He knows about Frederik . . . But just then, she sees him appear. Frederik. At one of the windows of his fourth-floor apartment, one of the windows the other man up there is looking toward.

Butz's voice suddenly rings as loud as a fire alarm in her ear. "*Micha!*"

"What?" Claire is so shocked that for a moment she looks away from the building.

"Sorry, Claire, no, not you . . . I just called out for Micha. I'm still here . . ."

Claire looks up again and sees Frederik pulling open the window. He sets one foot on the windowsill, pulls himself up with one strong motion—and steps out onto the ledge, which can't be more than eight inches wide and runs across the entire front of the building.

"I have to hang up now, Konstantin."

She lowers her hand and cuts the connection. Tomorrow morning, she's told him. They can talk about it tomorrow morning. She can't explain it all to him now, not on the phone.

Her eyes, unwavering, are on Frederik.

He hasn't seen her yet. He is fixated on the man watching him from the stairwell window. Frederik presses his back against the wall and edges along the ledge, away from the man. A second head appears at the window in the stairwell.

Claire can see the two men at the window talking. A moment later, the one who has just appeared disappears again.

She shields her eyes with one hand from the glare of the streetlights. Frederik inches his way toward the corner of the building.

From her vantage point, Claire can't see his face clearly—only his chest, rising and falling heavily as he makes his way along the ledge.

Suddenly, he stops. He leans his head back and looks up. Claire follows his gaze.

Then everything happens very fast.

The second man has reappeared at a window directly above Frederik. The one at the stairwell window has a gun in his hand and is aiming it at the boxer. And Frederik launches himself off of the wall—and flies. Claire hears the crack and crash as Frederik slams into the limbs of the large tree in front of the building, which reach all the way up to the fourth floor. She sees his body smash through the branches, his head hit the trunk.

She stands there as if anesthetized. Her arms reach out as if to catch him. He's caught up there!

Frederik has managed to get a hand around one branch and is holding on grimly. But it must still be fifteen feet to the ground.

A sharp, dry report splits the air. Glass shatters. A horn starts honking.

Claire quickly looks back to the man in the stairwell. He is taking aim straight into the tree, straight at Frederik's body.

Bam! Bam, bam!

In her peripheral vision, Claire sees Frederik fall. She sees the impact, hears the blunt, metallic crash as he lands on a car. Then he rolls off the roof and hits the street.

The next moment, Claire is running through the parked cars toward the dark pile that is Frederik, slumped in the middle of the lane. Thirty yards away, a traffic light turns green. She kneels next to him. The cars are accelerating toward them, the blur of head-lights bearing down.

Frederik's eyes are open, but his face is frozen. He doesn't seem to be breathing.

A red-orange flash in front of Claire. The car speeding toward them has its indicator on, swerves into the center lane. Honks its horn—and roars past them in a rush of wind, inches from Claire's head.

Claire tugs at Frederik's arm. He's as heavy as a punching bag. "Frederik!"

The drawn out blast of the next car's horn, the shrill squeal of brakes.

FREDERIK!

He collapses into a fetal curl.

Claire hears a crunching sound. She glances up and sees a delivery van sliding toward them sideways. The van must have been hit by the car behind when it tried to swerve. It is being pushed straight at them.

Simultaneously, Claire senses Frederik's muscular body returning to life. He clambers to his feet. The din of the horns, more added now, merges in Claire's head as one single scream. She straightens up with Frederik and pulls him along with her, feeling a sharp pain in her side from the effort. Claire's arm around Frederik's hunched body, they dodge back between the parked cars. The delivery van, still sliding, spins and hits a car in the center lane, bringing traffic to a standstill.

Frederik's eyes above her are dark.

He is not standing straight, but he looks her up and down. The bullets have missed him.

Claire's eyes turn from his, back to the man still standing at the window—his pistol now trained on her. Frederik's hand closes around hers. Then they are racing along the sidewalk.

Behind them, the horns still blare. The drivers caught in the accident shout at each other. Beside them are dark shopfronts. Above them spreads the clear, cloudless Berlin night.

TWO YEARS EARLIER

"Looks like we're relatives now!" Henning was standing with a group of friends at one of the high tables set up in the restaurant garden. He held out his champagne glass toward Max and Quentin, as if in greeting.

Max stepped up to the table and clinked his espresso cup against Henning's glass. "To brothers-in-law, right?"

Wedding guests were still streaming into the garden at the restaurant, where the wedding dinner was due to start in a half hour.

"Absolutely!" said Henning, laughing sociably.

Don't forget, my sister is only seventeen, Max thought. But his new brother-in-law was talking again.

"Now that we're related, there's something I have to ask you, Max."

Max sipped at his coffee cup.

"Last summer . . ." Henning began, looking him up and down.

"Uh-huh?" Max was thinking he'd added too much sugar to the espresso.

"Malte mentioned something . . ."

Max's eyes drifted across the table to Malte, a diminutive young man standing next to Henning. Malte and Quentin were friends, and they both worked for Henning.

Malte raised his hands and laughed. "Me?" He gave Henning a slightly uneasy look. "Hey, I wasn't even there!"

"Come on, Max," said Henning, probing. "Word gets around. That trip to the Baltic states last summer. What was the deal with that? It's true that *something* happened, right?"

Max set his espresso cup on the table. He felt no obligation to answer Henning's questions, whether or not they were relatives.

"*You* were there, though," said Henning, turning his attention to Quentin. "Right, Quenny? On that trip with Max, last summer. Didn't you go along?"

"As far as Riga, but that was it." Quentin glanced at Max. "Then I came back to Berlin."

"And why only as far as Riga?" Henning stared fixedly at Quentin, as if he was going to get to the bottom of this once and for all.

"I didn't want to be away as long as Max," said Quentin, dodging the question.

"You'd be okay with Quentin telling us what went on in Riga, wouldn't you, Max?" asked Henning, suddenly squinting at Max as if a light were shining in his eyes.

Max snorted. "Christ . . . nothing 'went on' there."

Not there, not just then . . .

"Oh, come on!" Henning nodded to Quentin, who had lit a cigarette in the meantime and was already flicking ash into an ashtray on the table. "So, tell us the story. You only made it as far as Riga with Max. Why no farther?"

Max eyed Henning. He wondered whether he should turn his back to them and walk away while they talked about him.

"That evening . . . I don't know . . . I'd had enough, I guess," he heard Quentin answer hesitantly.

"What sort of evening?"

Quentin glanced apprehensively at Max.

"Go ahead. Tell 'em." Max sighed. *Whatever.*

Quentin took a drag on his cigarette.

"Well, it was pretty warm that night," he began, smoke rolling from his mouth. "We were sitting in a café at the edge of a park, close to the harbor. A small group of Latvians walked up to us. Three men, one woman. At first, I took no notice of them. But then they sat right at the next table. Apart from us, the place was empty. That's when I looked at them. As soon as I saw their faces, I got this funny feeling. You know . . ." he said, looking into Henning's face as if to weigh his reaction, "I don't remember ever seeing faces like theirs before." Henning glanced at Max for a moment, then back to Quentin. "Maybe it was because it was so dark. The only light came from the lanterns in the café," he continued. "Or maybe it was because I was tired, or hadn't eaten . . . In any case, one of them had eyes that looked really dull and flat . . . like those of a dead cat . . . and the eyes of the others practically glowed." Quentin frowned and looked at the table. "I automatically scooted my chair back a little, just to put as much space between them and me as I could, but Max . . ."

Max could tell it was difficult for Quentin to tell the story. But Max also realized that he had to answer Henning—at the end of the day, Henning was still Quentin's boss.

"Well, one of the men tried to start up a conversation with us in broken English, and I have no idea why, but Max got sucked in like he was a poster boy for naïveté."

"Is that what happened?" asked Henning, looking at Max. Outwardly amused, Henning couldn't completely hide the fact that he was trying to figure out what kind of person his new brother-in-law really was.

With exaggerated weariness, Max spread his hands out on the table and held Henning's gaze. *I can't stop Quentin from telling the story*, he thought. *And I don't really give a shit either way.*

"I wasn't sure what to do," Quentin continued. "It seemed strange that Max couldn't see that something was up, that we had to watch out. I was so rattled by how they looked. I was trying to figure out if we could escape them by *running* back to our hotel. It was just a short walk from the café to the hotel, but I remembered the receptionist telling us that after sundown, if the night porter was away, they might lock up the iron gate at the main entrance. We would have to ring the bell. So, I was thinking, *Run away from these people* . . . and then what? We're stuck outside the hotel because no one could open up fast enough? Just standing there till they caught up and mugged us? I figured the best thing to do was avoid a confrontation and just get away from them. So, as casually as I could, I started dropping hints to Max about how late it was and that maybe it was time to hit the road."

Max was studying the backs of his hands, still spread in front of him on the table. There was no denying it; that's what had happened. He felt Henning and Malte casting him intermittent glances, but he avoided making eye contact. Instead, he turned aside and watched the wedding guests arriving or standing in groups at the other tables.

"But Max didn't want to hear it!" said Quentin, beside him. "No, he actually got up and sat down at their table! It was like he was under a spell. Couldn't he *see* what kind of people they were? He *had* to see that there was no way their intentions were good. I leaned over and interrupted the conversation he'd struck up with the woman, and I whispered to Max as adamantly as I could that we *really had to go, right now*. But all he did was look me in the eye, smile, and say, 'You go ahead, Quenny.'"

Was he blushing? Max shifted his weight to his other leg.

"But it didn't feel right leaving Max there with them," Quentin went on. "Maybe he'd had too much to drink, I don't know. I was starting to panic, and I stood up and took him by the arm. I told the woman, 'I'm really sorry, but we have to get up early.' I was hoping Max wouldn't resist. All I wanted was to get him out of there. But when I said we were leaving, the woman stood up and reached out for Max, as if to stop him. I was thinking we couldn't just pull him back and forth like that, and that's when I noticed the chair that the woman had been sitting on."

"The chair?" Henning was grinning, half mocking, half skeptical.

"Right there, on the white seat. Okay, it was dark, but you could see it clearly enough in the light from the café—there was a puddle, a dark-red pool of blood."

"Yech!" Max heard Malte blurt, but he didn't turn back from the other guests to look at the men talking.

"I was speechless," Quentin continued. "I nodded at the chair so Max would see it too. The woman turned around to the men— they were sitting a little behind her—and then you could see clearly that the blood had seeped through her skirt, and that she must have been so stoned she hadn't even noticed."

Max wanted to spit. He hadn't seen it. Quentin had only told him about it later. Maybe it was just a stain on the chair, or a leaf? What made Quentin so sure he wasn't mistaken? Christ, she'd sat down on the chair, and her clothes would have . . .

He had to suppress a shudder—he didn't want to think about it.

"I was seriously disgusted. I'd never seen anything like that before," he heard Quentin saying. "Lucky for us, she let Max go, and I finally got him away from the table—"

"Didn't want to chat with the Latvian girl anymore?" asked Henning, interrupting Quentin and addressing Max.

Max turned to face him. "Wait for it," he said, and nodded to Quentin.

"So, we left the café," said Quentin, picking up the thread again. "And we were walking along this avenue with all these stunted trees that led to the hotel when we heard a voice behind us."

"The Latvian woman!" Henning had narrowed his eyes.

Today's your wedding day, Max thought. *Shouldn't you be attending to your bride?*

"No," said Quentin, exhaling smoke and stubbing out the cigarette in the ashtray. "It was one of the men who'd been with her. He caught up with us and started telling us something in his strange English about a restaurant where they gave him leftovers from the kitchen sometimes. If we wanted to eat there that evening, he'd get a little bonus for sending them the business." Quentin looked at Max. "Wasn't that how it was?"

Max looked at Henning, who pursed his lips.

"Quentin wanted to go back to the hotel," said Max, and grinned suddenly, "But I'd hardly seen anything of Riga!"

"So, did you go with the guy?" Malte, a head shorter than Henning, was looking at Max wide-eyed.

"The restaurant was great. Quentin doesn't know what he missed!" Max smiled at his traveling companion. "It was inside this art nouveau place that must've been at its best in the 1920s or 1930s, and the ceiling in the dining room had to be twenty-five feet high. The place was packed." Max looked around at the audience of young men standing around the table. "Some fat Latvians with their extended family, from babies to the white-haired grandfather, eight or ten Russians who'd come to Riga on business and were celebrating a contract, English guys with their wives . . . when I stepped into the place, I realized I was finally getting to see something of Riga. So, I let a waiter take me over to one of the few open tables." Max frowned. "I'd hardly even sat down when the waiter came up and wanted to know if I was still expecting anyone. 'Unfortunately not,' I told him. And he said, 'Would you like to get to know someone, then?'"

"Saw that coming," said Malte, almost squirming.

"Yes." Max stuffed his hands into his pockets. "I hesitated for a moment, naturally. But when I saw the people who were eating in the restaurant and the kind of ambience the place had, the faded glories . . . suddenly, I thought *If the waiter introduces me to a Latvian woman who has the same style, like it's 1930 and the old Europe still exists . . .*"

He didn't finish the sentence. The others looked at him eagerly.

"So I said yes." He folded his arms. "And when she finally came to my table—" Max interrupted himself. "Have any of you ever met an Estonian girl? Not from Latvia, but from *Estonia*? From Tallin, to be precise."

They shook their heads.

"She was . . . a little like I'd imagined, in fact . . . like a silent film actress." Max glanced at Quentin. "The kind of woman where you think, my God, this has to be good fortune, or beauty, or virtue, I don't know what exactly. Where you . . . where words fail you, where you're afraid you'll break something and so you automatically take the utmost care with everything, it's like you're almost . . . reverential."

"You ate dinner together." Henning's voice sounded like it was made of metal.

"Listen, Henning," said Max, feeling the anger rising in him. "Just because we're relatives doesn't mean I have to explain myself to you!"

Henning nodded slowly. He had obviously not expected such a fierce response.

"So, now you know why Quentin didn't stay with me after Riga. It was too much for him, me taking off with that poor bastard who caught up with us on the street, so he went back to Berlin. But I stayed a little longer in that strange city. Is that okay with you?"

Henning straightened up. He was easily the tallest of the men.

"Don't you think you should attend to your wedding guests?" Max said with a rasp. He didn't wait for an answer, turning instead and walking away from the table.

What happened in Riga that evening and the days that followed . . . he would never tell a soul. He owed no one an explanation.

Without looking back, Max walked straight on until he came to a waiter carrying a tray of glasses among the guests.

"Could you take a bottle of something to the gentlemen at the table back there, please?" he asked, jabbing his thumb over his shoulder in Henning's direction. "Champagne."

Then he went to mingle with the other guests.

TWO YEARS EARLIER

"Max?"

Max turned. It was Felix.

After leaving Henning's table, he had first gone to his sister and embraced her, congratulating her on her big day. He stayed in the crowd around her briefly, and then went into the main dining room of the restaurant, trying to figure out where he would be sitting during the reception. When Max finally found the seating plan and was leaning over it, he heard Felix behind him.

"They won't be serving food for another half hour." Felix was wearing glasses with lightly tinted lenses, his eyes almost impossible to make out behind them.

He slowly moved toward Max.

Max smiled. "I wanted to see if I was sitting next to you."

"Have you got a moment?" Felix's glasses caught the light. "There's something I'd like to talk to you about."

Max found himself looking at Felix's mouth, flanked by two deep lines. "Something important?"

Felix's mouth twitched slightly. "Not really."

Max slipped his hands into the pockets of his pants. "What can I do for you, Felix?"

Felix laughed. "Shall we sit a moment?" He pointed to a small door beside the dining room's main entrance. "No doubt we'll find a little peace and quiet in there."

When Max followed Felix through the door, he saw that two young women were already in the room. They wore short, black dresses with spaghetti straps. One of them had her bare feet drawn up on the sofa. The lower edge of her dress had slipped up over her knee, revealing her tanned thigh.

Felix stopped just inside the doorway and looked at Max. For a moment, he seemed to be trying to read something in Max's expression. But then he turned back to the two women and murmured something about a private discussion. Unsurprised, they stood up from the sofa and left the room.

Max watched them go. He had not noticed them at the ceremony and was fairly certain they were not friends of Betty's. Invited by Henning? A vague whiff of perfume still hung in the air, and he saw one of them stop suddenly and look back once more as she exited the room. Max's eyes met hers and lingered, and Max felt something flare up inside him.

"They would have just disturbed us, don't you think?" Felix closed the door, breaking Max's eye contact with the woman.

"You know those two?" Max asked, looking at him.

"In passing," Felix answered, and sat on the sofa. Max sat down in an armchair opposite him.

"I wanted to talk to you about your father's books," said Felix directly. "The last manuscripts, the ones that were still incomplete when he . . . you know."

Max, who had just settled back in his armchair, straightened up again. Did they really have to talk about *that* at Betty's wedding?

"Your mother told me that she had rearranged the things a little, ahead of Betty's wedding."

"The things?"

Felix leaned back and scrutinized Max for a moment before answering. "The rights, Max. Don't make it harder for me than it already is."

"To tell the truth, I don't really want to talk about that just now," said Max.

"Why not, if I may ask?" Felix laid one arm across the back of the sofa.

"It's just that I haven't really come to grips with it all. It's only been two or three weeks since Mom told us about splitting the inheritance."

"In which *you* were handed the rights to Xavier's last books, right? The ones I'm still missing."

"Lisa and I." Not an unimportant point.

"Lisa and you, exactly. Look, Max," Felix sat forward on the sofa, "I understand it's a sensitive matter for you, so I'll keep it short. As you can probably imagine, the question of who holds the rights to Xavier's last books is of some importance to me. I've invested a lot in publishing the Bentheim oeuvre. But the more I've dug into your father's work, the clearer it has become that most of his books were just groundwork. Groundwork for what he tried to do in his final manuscripts."

"Groundwork for *Berlin Gothic*."

"That's right, for *Berlin Gothic*. So, you can imagine," Felix went on, "how crucial it is for me to be able to publish these final manuscripts. Do you follow me?"

Max nodded.

"It may surprise you that I'm being so open about this. It would have been far cleverer if I had claimed that I was only interested in getting the rights from you for . . . I don't know . . . for the sake of completeness."

But you're not that stupid, thought Max.

"But I want to be completely open with you. Since your father . . . well, let's say, disappeared . . . I've always felt a little responsible for all of you. I have no interest in trying to fleece either you or your sister."

"Lucky us," said Max, still not sure where Felix was going with this. Was he actually planning to make him a concrete offer *now*, between the champagne reception and the meal?

"Just so we're on the same page, Max," said Felix, apparently not yet finished, "publishing *Berlin Gothic* is a project that will keep me busy for at least the next few years, if not decades. Do you have the slightest idea what your father was taking on?"

Max didn't. Once, he'd taken a look in the boxes where the pages were stored, but the texts were encoded and he had no clue how to decipher them.

"Listen," Felix seemed to want to wind this up. "I know you need some time to think things over. On the other hand, I'd like you to appreciate that I have to know as soon as possible what price you are prepared to accept to hand over the rights to me." His steely eyes settled on Max's face.

Had he misheard? Had Felix actually said, *What price you are prepared to accept to hand over the rights*? Did that mean he was not even asking *if* Max would sell him the rights, but only *at what price*?

"Excuse me for saying this so bluntly, Felix," said Max, supporting his elbows on his knees and holding his hands open in front of him, "but I'm not sure I want to sell you the rights at all."

"Why wouldn't you want to sell me the rights, my boy?" A vein by Felix's right eye pulsed.

"Because I don't believe in the things that preoccupied my father . . . and still preoccupy you. Is that so hard to imagine, Felix?"

Felix looked at him in silence. "If that's why you're having misgivings about selling," he finally said, "then I would, of course, like to be able to have the opportunity to tell you about our ideas."

No, thought Max. *That isn't necessary. How would I benefit from that? I wouldn't. The best you could do would be to confuse me, deceive me, and make me believe that I've misunderstood everything all along. But I haven't! When it comes down to it, it's not that complicated, even if it appears to be at first glance.*

Max looked significantly at his watch. "Isn't the meal supposed to begin at half past? We only have ten minutes. I don't think you'd get very far in that time."

Max sensed that he was gaining the upper hand. And why not? Felix wanted something from him—from Lisa and him—but there was nothing Felix could do to get his hands on the rights without their assent.

"Maybe you'd like to stop by and visit me at the office sometime?" Felix said. "I can introduce you to a few of the women who work there, or . . ." He was sitting forward in exactly the same position as Max, his elbows propped on his knees and his hands open in front of him. "Or if you prefer, we can go to lunch, just you and me—and talk it over again . . ."

Forget it.

"Or I'll come to your place, Max. No problem."

"Yeah, sure," said Max. He smacked his lips, unintentionally. For many years, Felix had been something like an advocate for him, for his mother, for the whole family. He had helped them, advised them, supported them . . . but despite all his generosity, they had always been a little afraid of him. Afraid that Felix's benevolence might suddenly dry up, that the kindness he treated them with might suddenly turn into something else, that one day he would want them to pay him back for everything he had done. Was that why Felix had been so friendly toward them all these years, because he wanted the rights to Xavier's last books?

Felix stood up.

"How does that sound?" Felix looked down at him. "I'll give you a call next week?" Again, that mocking smile played across his lips, as if he was trying to hide behind it. *Sure,* thought Max. *Give me a call. Call all you like, but I won't sell you the rights!*

"Okay, let's do that," he replied airily. But simultaneously, to his surprise, he thought *But what if I still need what Felix is convinced of, what my father was convinced of, after all? After what happened in Riga? After what happened down in the tunnels ten years ago? After I drove Till to kill my father?*

TODAY

"Can we run through the likely course of events?" The chief of police is standing next to Butz.

"Of course, but it probably won't get us anywhere," says Butz, turning his attention to his phone.

"Ansgar?"

"Chief?" Ansgar, a forensics tech, has his laptop set up on a sideboard in the living room.

"Got that up and running?"

"Just about. Half a minute."

"Send it straight to the laptop," says the chief to Butz.

"Which address?"

"Forensics."

Butz stabs at the keys on his cell phone, sending on the photo that Micha had sent him. "Should be there any second . . ."

The display on Butz's cell phone reflects the bare lightbulb on the ceiling. Butz tilts the phone so that the reflection isn't so blinding. After discovering that Fehrenberg's body had disappeared, he went through the entire apartment. But there was no one there anymore, so Butz had called in his colleagues.

"Okay . . . got it." Ansgar nods to the screen.

"Jesus . . ." The chief steps up behind the technician and looks over his shoulder at the monitor.

Butz already knows the image from his cell, but on the larger screen of the laptop, it hits him as if he's seeing it for the first time. It's Fehrenberg, still recognizable, stretched out on his bed. Depending on his fitness level, Volker Fehrenberg had always been considered either burly or obese. But what Butz was looking at on the screen had very little in common with the officer he knew. In the final three weeks before his death, Fehrenberg must have physically changed at breathtaking speed.

Chips, Doritos, marshmallows, chocolate bars, Coke, Pepsi. The leftovers from the junk-food binge cover the living room floor, with packaging stacked high in one corner. But it isn't just the body itself—no longer the shape of a body—that makes the image so nightmarish. It's the way the body is curled up on the bed. Every sinew seems to be pulled tight—as if each strand of the network of muscles and tendons pervading the mass of fat and flesh knotted together at the same moment.

"What do you think, Jens?"

The pathologist with the goatee and glasses has joined them. Fehrenberg's abused corpse and the four bodies in the apartment are weighing on them like lead.

"Any other images?" The pathologist looks at the technician over the rim of his glasses.

The technician shakes his head.

"Well . . ." says Jens, leaning forward to look at the picture more closely.

"What?" The chief is growing impatient.

"No idea. I mean . . . it could be practically anything."

"Practically anything."

"Uh-huh."

"Fine. But he wasn't shot, was he?" asks Butz.

The pathologist glances up sharply. Is Butz making fun of him?

Butz answers his own question. "No, because Micha . . ." He stops, rubs his forehead. Micha was shot. *How is this all connected?*

The others turn to Butz.

"Micha was shot." Butz's voice is muted. "I just want to find out what happened here."

The chief momentarily runs his tongue over his lips.

Butz looks at the monitor. "Fehrenberg basically holes up in his apartment, right?" He leans forward and points to the remains of the junk food in the photo. "The way things look, he only left the place to stock up on cartons of crap . . . but . . ." Butz straightens up again. "Why? Why would he say he was going on vacation, then crawl away to his apartment? How did someone manage to get the drop on Micha and the other officers? How did Fehrenberg get so . . . twisted . . . like that?"

He looks to the pathologist, who tips his head slightly.

"It isn't clear what killed him," says Butz, following his train of thought. "But . . . I don't know . . . maybe he was sick, maybe he had some sort of infection, something like that?"

"It's possible." Jens looks to the chief. "It's something we need to investigate, but all we have is one photo."

"Whatever it is," Butz continues, "Fehrenberg didn't die because he was *shot*, at least not just now. The photo makes that clear. When Micha got here, Fehrenberg was already dead."

Jens nods cautiously.

"Good," says Butz. "So, while Fehrenberg's rotting here in his apartment, we take over the investigation into the dead women, Nadja and the woman on the construction site. But we're missing the information that Fehrenberg had collected in the course of *his* investigation. His computer's wiped clean, his desk cleared out. We try to reach him . . ."

"You try to," says Jens.

"And I finally send Micha to check on Fehrenberg's apartment because we can't find the man anywhere. And Micha and the others stumble onto this." Butz indicates the laptop screen. "Micha sends me a photograph"—he holds up his cell phone—"and I talk to him on the phone, then head off for Fehrenberg's place myself . . ." He swallows hard, then pulls himself together. "But when I get here"—he continues, lifting his head and looking over at the others now leaning over Micha's body in the front room—"everybody's already dead. Shot. Micha and the forensics guy and the two guys in uniform . . ."

He breathes out heavily.

"And Fehrenberg's body is gone," adds the forensics technician.

Butz nods. "It seems the officers were taken by surprise when they were already here. They were shot, and nobody in the building noticed anything. Meaning they must have used silencers . . . but one shooter would have had trouble taking out four officers . . ."

The technician at the computer looks up. "Ballistics is assuming three shooters."

"Three shooters," says Butz, picking up on the remark. "With three of them, it would have been relatively easy to get Fehrenberg's body down the stairwell and out of the building." He glances at the police chief, who is looking past Butz to the window.

"So far, so good," says Butz, winding up his summary. "In broad strokes, that's how it could have played out. But what I don't understand is *why*? Why would someone want to carry away Fehrenberg's body?"

TODAY

"What's wrong with her?"

"I . . . I don't know. Merle?"

"Merle! Why is she panting like that?"

"Like I said . . ."

"Maybe . . . she thinks she can't get any air."

"Should I call a doctor?"

"An ambulance?"

"Or I'll just drive her to the hospital."

"And just lay her down in front of the entrance?"

"I mean, how do you see that working? Look at her . . ."

"Merle? What about drinking a little water? Your lips are all dried out, it would . . . I really think you should drink something."

"What did she . . . oh, fuck!"

The man wipes his hand across his face. Merle couldn't keep down the bit of water she drank from the glass. The water practically exploded from between her lips and hit the man in the face.

"Go and clean up."

"Shit."

The woman who gave Merle the water strokes her head gently. She looks into Merle's dilated eyes and can see it inside her: Merle doesn't know what's happening to her. And she knows that she doesn't know.

The woman looks around discreetly. The man has left the room. She turns back to Merle, bends down to her, and whispers in her ear.

"I'm taking you to hospital, Merle . . . I'm not going to leave you here alone."

Merle pants. Blinks. Jerks her head to and fro. Her lips, bone dry, are drawn back, exposing the teeth behind.

TODAY

Butz presses himself against the wall. The wardrobe he is standing behind casts a hard-edged shadow on the floor. The bare lightbulb on the ceiling buzzes softly, and the sound of running water can be heard through the narrow doorway in the long wall. Someone is in the bathroom. Butz hears the person spit into the sink and snort.

"We're taking this back to the station," one of the forensics guys had said, holding a plastic bag containing the trash from Fehrenberg's kitchen.

So you can go through it at leisure in the lab? Butz felt his impatience growing. "That'll take far too long!"

He extricated himself from the crush of officers gathered around the laptop, begged a sheet of plastic from the technicians, and spread it out on the floor. Then he dumped the contents of the trash bag onto the plastic sheet, pulled on a pair of rubber gloves, and started rummaging through Fehrenberg's trash. Empty tomato cans, old tissues, coffee grounds, plastic bottles . . .

That was two hours ago.

Butz leans carefully against the side of the wardrobe and pulls a long-handled flashlight out of his coat pocket.

The bathroom door swings open. The man steps out, hair cropped to stubble, thickset head and neck, big hands. He is wearing an undershirt that doesn't completely cover his stomach, and worn-out white underwear. He switches off the ceiling light and shuffles across the room to a narrow cot pushed along the wall opposite the wardrobe. He lies down, pulls the blanket over him, and rolls over to the wall.

Butz doesn't take his eyes off him.

Lubajew versus Barkar.

That's what he'd found in Fehrenberg's trash: a ticket for the boxing match where Claire had gone to take photographs. Butz had seen her in the pictures Ms. Bastian had taken. Among all of Fehrenberg's other rubbish, the ticket practically glowed.

Barkar. Wherever he starts poking around, he runs into Frederik Barkar.

Butz stares at the lump under the blanket on the cot. The man's breathing starts to slow and become even.

His name is Baumann. Willi Baumann. Barkar's trainer.

It wasn't difficult getting into Baumann's room at the gym where Barkar trains. A boxing hall in one of the arches under the railway line, a wooden door with a lock that was easy to pick.

The room is dark gray. Butz can hear the soft thrum of city traffic through the window.

"HEY!"

He steps resolutely from behind the wardrobe. He vaguely sees the body of the man under the blanket flinch—then he is standing beside the trainer's bed. He holds the flashlight high in one hand, the beam directed straight into Baumann's wide eyes. In his other hand, he has his service pistol, holding it at the edge of the beam of light so that the trainer can't miss the black reflective metal.

"Willi Baumann?"

The trainer's sharply drawn, tanned face seems to have collapsed. He is having trouble breathing. But he nods.

"Claire Bentheim—heard the name?"

Baumann has one hand up, trying to shield his eyes from the beam of light. His lips move, but no more than a whisper comes out.

"What was Barkar doing at my place?" Butz can hear how desperate his voice sounds.

Baumann's face suddenly looks pale and unhealthy.

What if he checks out now?

The trainer's eyes are not completely open.

"HEY!"

His eyelids jolt open again.

"Your boxer buddy shows up and starts fooling around with my girlfriend. You know anything about that?"

"I . . . I dunno what Barkar gets up to . . ."

Butz leans down. "My name's Butz. Do you know what I do?"

If Baumann reports what's going on here, Butz will be up to his neck in shit. But he can practically smell it: it's no accident that Barkar showed up at his place *now*.

"I've been asking around, Baumann," Butz whispers. "Lubajew did his best—but he should never have been allowed to step into the ring opposite Barkar. He never had a chance. The fight would never even have happened if you hadn't been pulling strings in the background."

He reaches down with the hand holding the gun and pushes Baumann's right hand aside. The beam of light falls directly onto the trainer's face. "I sink my teeth in, Baumann, and I don't let go. I turn every stone and shine a light into every corner."

Baumann's face grows slack. His breath is ragged, and his cheeks puff out. But he doesn't seem to be looking for words. It looks like he's trying to get the beating of his heart under control.

Butz kneels on the bed with one leg. He feels sorry for the man. The face staring up at him from the glare of the flashlight is the face of an old boxer. But Baumann is in the middle of this mess.

Butz touches the end of the barrel to Baumann's lips. Then he twists the weapon carefully but relentlessly down and in, and Baumann's lower jaw opens. He pushes the pistol between the man's teeth, into his mouth. Baumann's eyes grow large. Butz tips the gun upward, feels the metal meet the roof of Baumann's mouth.

"Mmmhhhmm . . ."

"Why would Barkar have any interest in Claire?"

Baumann has both hands around Butz's fist, the one pressing the gun into his mouth, and he's pushing against Butz's weight.

"Mmhhhmmmmmmm!!"

Slowly, the need to breathe overcomes Baumann's fear that Butz might pull the trigger.

Butz jerks the gun back out of the trainer's mouth and presses the barrel against his cheek, pushing Baumann's face sideways into his pillow.

"He called me . . ." says the trainer, gasping and trying to speak at the same time. "He said I could do something for Frederik . . ."

"Who called?"

The barrel traces a line across the man's cheek to his ear. Butz sees Baumann close his eyes.

"Who?"

"Fahlenkamp, he said his name is Fahlenkamp."

Fahlenkamp? He knows only one man with that name.

Henning. Claire's sister's husband.

Henning Fahlenkamp.

13

TWO YEARS EARLIER

Henning turned away from his bride and looked straight at Lisa.

Lisa faltered. Had she said they were arrogant? Or had she said that they *seemed* arrogant to her? For a fraction of a second, time seemed to stand still. Henning's gaze made it hard for her to keep talking.

"The estate was built when, Henning?" she asked, her eyes scanning the wedding guests. "In the eighteenth century?"

He laughed, nodded. "Yes. The cornerstone was laid in 1781."

"So much character, simply breathtaking," Lisa continued. "There's even a grotto. They redirected the little creek that flows by the house into it."

Henning's house. Or rather, his family's house. They had been there not so long ago: Lisa, Malte, Quentin, Henning, a few others, and . . . Felix. Lisa had decided to make that the subject of her speech at her sister's wedding: the weekend they had all spent recently at the Fahlenkamp ancestral home.

"An estate, it has to be said, that has a real charm. It perfectly suited the mood we were all in from the start of the weekend."

Everything had gone flawlessly. Lisa had started her speech fluently, had felt her mouth forming the sounds, had heard them pouring forth brightly and well articulated, had seen the way her audience hung on her words, how they smiled and laughed at her carefully placed witticisms, and how happy they were to be able to follow her train of thought so well.

Until she faltered, because she suddenly saw the suspicious look on Henning's face when he realized she was talking about the weekend they'd spent together. Lisa found herself wondering if she had said that Henning and his friends were *arrogant* or if they had just *seemed* arrogant. That was a pretty big difference, and she had wanted to say that they *seemed* arrogant *at first*, but that once she had got to know them better she realized just how kind and decent they *really* were.

Lisa gazed out at the faces of the guests and realized that she had started to go on with her speech again. Relief flowed through her. She didn't have to worry after all! She would get through this without causing Betty any headaches. But even as she went on with her speech, the frightening question remained: *How long could she continue to rely on the flow of her words?* Because her thoughts were already going in a completely different direction than the words she was only outwardly formulating with her mouth.

Even as she went on spinning the threads of her speech on the outside, she couldn't stop wondering whether the main point of her address was really good enough. Didn't the main point need to be far more sophisticated than what she was working toward? Wasn't it just unspeakably *crude* to start her speech with something that sounded like she was complaining about Henning's circle of friends, only to end it with a kind of *April fool*, just kidding, these guys aren't nearly as bad as I thought they were, they're a pretty decent crowd, really, and you can be glad one of them is marrying my seventeen-year-old sister?

But what would be a better payoff? Was she supposed to build in a couple more twists? Instead of starting with the positive, should she turn the screws a few more times, so to speak? Make her audience think *Jesus, what I thought was* bad *is actually* good. The arrogance of these people is not what's bad at all: Henning's friends might be conceited and self-important, but they are also educated, funny, and they have good taste, and that's *good*. The bad is yet to come!

But was that what Lisa really wanted? Did she really want to frighten her audience? Did she want to force this gathering of wedding guests—so carefree, so high-spirited—to force them, just for a moment, to peer into an abyss that none of them had counted on this sunny afternoon? Did she really want them to think she had the power to send them hurtling into that abyss, only to spring one more surprise on them: that the boys, one of whom was marrying her sister that very day, do indeed have their dark side! But even *that* is just superficial, even *that* is not the true core of the matter. The *real* truth is that they *really are* the good guys in the story. Sure, they have their base, evil side—but in the end, that doesn't matter, because *at heart* they're good . . . and her audience could then lean back and breathe a sigh of serious relief, both shaken by the fear of God that Lisa has put into them, and exhilarated to know the kind of sophisticated—and yes, even dangerous—people they were rubbing elbows with. They would stand up and come to her in droves, shaking her hand, embracing her, telling her how wonderful her speech was, what an experience, what a joy to listen to her speak!

"But then I realized that what I had determined to do at first— to talk about this circle of friends—really wouldn't be the right thing on my sister Betty's wedding day. So, rather than talk about Henning, Malte, or Quentin, I decided to talk about *Betty* instead, who—and Betty, I hope you'll forgive me for saying this—I think I probably know better than anyone else in this room does."

Lisa's eyes shifted over the heads of the audience. They were smiling again. The terrible fear—which, for a moment, had seemed to engulf everyone in the room—was gone: the fear of not knowing whether she was up to the task of making this speech. Lisa had found her way back to solid ground. She would talk about Betty. Then nothing could go wrong.

"I have no other words for what I feel for you," Lisa heard herself saying, "no other words but to say I love you—and not just because you're my kid sister, but because I don't know anybody with such an enchanting . . . essence . . . as you!"

She raised her glass. The audience applauded.

Lisa saw Betty stand up next to Henning and, in her wedding dress, push her way between the guests until she had reached Lisa. For a moment, the two sisters embraced.

And in the same moment, it was suddenly clear to Lisa that, earlier, the reason she had faltered was not because she suddenly wondered if the point of her speech was *sophisticated* enough or not. No, she had hesitated because it *wasn't true* that she had come to know Henning and his cohorts as a group of kind and decent human beings.

In fact, they seemed to her much more like a lawless pack of greedy young men. And that was attributable to one thing: Felix had goaded them, incited them, spurred them on. He had given them shotguns and they'd gone out hunting in the bordering woods. And when, muddy and stained and high on bloodlust, they returned to the estate, half a busload of scantily dressed women were there waiting for them.

For two hours, Felix kept the young men in the living room, laughing and joking and drinking with the women. He had the women caress them and pamper them until they were ready to explode from craving, desire, and sheer lust. But then Felix made the women disappear. Unannounced, they left the house. And as much as the young men tried to stop the giggling, glittering women from leaving, it was impossible. All of a sudden, she—*Lisa*—was the only woman in the midst of a frenzied pack of young men. The atmosphere seemed charged with electricity, as if all she had to do was reach out her hand, and everyone she touched would explode on the spot. It was a situation in which Lisa felt more powerful perhaps than she had ever felt before, where the naked desire of the six men swarming around her was practically palpable. But she'd ultimately lost control over what happened, and was pulled down in a whirlpool, the details of which she still balked at remembering. And yet she knew she had drunk her own intoxicated fill of pleasure that night. Because despite the wildness of that weekend, nothing happened that she hadn't wanted to happen.

Lisa, mid-embrace, was looking over Betty's shoulder when one of the doors that led into the dining room caught her eye.

Someone had opened it and stepped into the room.

It went through her like an electric shock.

He had managed to make it to the wedding after all.

Till.

．．．

"I've never done this before . . . I . . . I mean, is it just me *who speaks the whole time?"*

"That depends. You came in here, so I take it you have something to say to me."

"I'm not . . . well, I'm not Catholic, you see . . . I haven't got a clue . . . it's just . . . I really shouldn't talk to anyone about it."

"I don't want you to feel you are under any pressure."

"Perhaps I should call a counseling service if I feel I have to talk, right? There are hotlines for that, aren't there? . . . Aren't there?"

"I don't know anything about that."

"I should just go. I shouldn't be taking up your time. . . . Do you know how long it took me to find a Catholic church? And to find out when you could do it . . ."

"Do what?"

"Well, what we're doing. . . . Do you know how long?"

"Listen . . . I have the time if you need me, if you have something to say to me. But if you don't . . . please don't misunderstand me; I'm not trying to get rid of you. But I'm not sure what you want . . ."

"I broke her arm. Or dislocated it. I don't know. . . . Did you hear me?"

"Yes, I heard you."

"I lured her into my car, I pulled off her panties, and she was ready for me to . . . for us to have sex . . . maybe you don't know about that, but . . . it's . . . it screams *inside you, you know? Maybe not so*

loud at the start, but once you . . . once you've begun, it's like a storm that's triggered inside you . . . you have *to go with it. It's like some kind of all-powerful force is tearing at you. You can't even think straight anymore. It's like every thought you have is getting sucked down in a whirlpool, like they're bubbling out of your head through a drain, and going . . . going to what that woman was offering. Do you understand what I'm saying? . . . I didn't want to let myself be distracted by that whirlpool. I broke her arm."*

"Really?"

"Really what?"

"You broke a woman's arm?"

"Yes."

"Why?"

"Why not?"

"You don't know?"

"No. It seemed clear, but then I started to think about it and now I don't know anymore."

"So, why are you here?"

"Because I want to talk to someone about it. . . . Don't you have anything to say about it?"

"Do you regret doing it?"

"No."

"Then why are you here?"

"Because I want to hear what you have to say about it. . . . Because it isn't over yet."

"Because what isn't over yet?"

"I broke her arm. But that isn't the end of it."

"Did breaking her arm give you pleasure?"

"That's not what it's about."

"Then what . . ."

"It's about being able to do it."

"Being able to break her arm?"

"Yes . . . Maybe it was a mistake to come here."

"I can't help you if you are not penitent. Go to the police, don't come to confession."

"You can listen to me . . . I said, 'It isn't over yet. I'll keep going.'"

"You want me to hear that? Is that why you're here?"

"I'm not going to break the next one's arm. I'm going to rip her soul out of her body . . . Do you hear me? I'll shove my arm down her throat and rip her soul out!"

"Pater noster, qui es in caelis . . . sanctificetur nomen tuum . . . adveniat regnum tuum . . ."

14

TWO YEARS EARLIER

Till.

How long had it been since he'd seen him?

Max stood up from his table. The wedding dinner was drawing to a close and he had spotted Till leaving the dining room and heading to the hall where the dessert buffet was set up.

It had to be well over a year. Till had last come to visit them at Christmas the year before last. There had been phone calls after that and they'd corresponded various ways, but they hadn't seen each other in person.

Till was no longer in the hall, so Max went out onto the terrace, where he could look out over the garden all the way to the shore of the lake.

There! Till had taken Lisa by the arm and they were heading straight for one of the high tables set up on the grass. At the table were some of Lisa's friends, already raising their glasses to Till and Lisa in greeting.

Max smiled. He was happy that Till had decided to come for Betty's wedding. He was just about to trot down the steps that led to the garden when a young woman exited the hall and started down the stairs in front of him. She was an exceptionally pretty girl, some years younger than he was. He'd met her several times with Henning or Quentin, and she had always given him the impression of being a particularly carefree and pleasant person. Nina . . . Nina something . . . her last name eluded him.

Max followed her down the stairs and considered saying something to her, but then he decided that he'd rather greet Till first. So, he passed her by without a word when she stopped at the bottom of the steps to talk to another young man.

"Max!"

He turned his head. Nina was looking at him.

"Nina."

He smiled. She looked fantastic; her dark-brown hair was piled high, and she wore a modest dark-green dress, the material hugging the slim curves of her body.

"Do you still remember me?" she asked.

Max couldn't help glancing over to the table where Till and Lisa had just arrived.

"Oh, look . . ." he heard Nina say. "I don't want to hold you up. I'm sure we'll see each other again."

Max realized that Till must have seen him, because he waved to him from the table. But then he twirled his index fingers around each other like a treadmill, a signal to Max that they should get together properly later, as soon as Till found a chance to get away from the group he had just joined.

Max turned back to Nina. "So? Enjoying the wedding?" He ignored the quizzical glance of her friend, who clearly had not counted on Max being part of their conversation.

"Oh, yes!" Nina beamed. "I just said so to Betty. No kidding, this is the best wedding I've ever been to!" And why not? Max couldn't remember a more lavish or elegant wedding than this one.

"Weren't you going to get us some dessert?" Nina cast her friend a coquettish look. "There was something on the menu with strawberries," she said, now looking back at Max. "That's what I want." She smiled.

Max pushed his hands into his pants pockets. And waited. But the moment passed and the young man was still standing with them, his head up, looking toward the lake, as if he was wondering what he was supposed to do.

"Should *I* bring you the dessert?" Max suggested with a grin.

"Come on!" said Nina. Without another glance at her acquaintance, she turned and ran up the steps. Max followed her.

"So, who was that? The guy at the bottom of the steps?" Each of them was armed with a plate of various desserts, as they made their way somewhat uncertainly through the hall.

"A friend of Quentin's." Nina kept her eyes on her plate.

"Did you come here together?"

She looked up. "No!"

So you're here by yourself? But Max didn't ask it aloud. Instead, he watched Nina move in the direction of a sitting area furnished with white rattan chairs. With a sigh of relief, she sank into one of the armchairs.

He sat opposite her and set his plate on the low table between them. "Do you know many people here?"

Nina dipped a small silver spoon into the ice cream already melting on her strawberry tart. "Some."

She lifted the spoon and held it in her mouth for a fraction of a second while she looked at Max—and pulled it out again, clean as a whistle. "But we know each other, don't we? A little, at least."

Max laughed. "A little. But I don't even know what your last name is."

Nina rolled her eyes. "Is that all you want to know?"

If it were up to me, we could go for it right there in that armchair, Max thought, but he quickly managed to put the thought out of his head again. "What might I want to know?" he said, dedicating himself to a dessert.

"For every question a counterquestion . . . did you notice?"

"She asked," said Max, biting into a marzipan cookie.

Nina leaned back. "You could ask me what I do when I'm not going to weddings."

Max chewed the cookie. *Yes, I could,* he thought, swallowing. "I've discovered that's not such a convenient question for some people."

"Ah, so that's how you see me." Her eyes sparkled.

Man, you are cute! Max felt a tingle in his fingertips. He looked back at his plate. If he wasn't careful, he'd swallow her with his eyes. Resting against the edge of the table, her knee invaded the top of his peripheral vision.

"So, what do *you* do?" she asked.

He looked up. Not an easy question to answer. "I don't know if I really want to talk about that just now." He saw how her expression changed. But it wasn't disappointment he read there, nor a sudden blaze of attentiveness, as he'd seen on the faces of other people he'd given that answer to.

"And of course that makes me extra curious." The tip of her nose crinkled a little. "But okay . . . so, what else shall we talk about?"

"Do we have to talk at all?" *I could just lean over and try to kiss you.*

"What did you have in mind?"

"Well . . ." It was clear to Max that what he was on the verge of saying could spell the end of their conversation, but he decided to say it anyway, although he didn't actually want to interrupt their tête-à-tête. "We don't *have* to sit here and do something. Out there," he said, with a nod toward the park, where more and more wedding guests had begun to gather, "are a few good friends of mine, waiting for me." It was his sister's wedding, after all.

Nina thought about this for a moment, but doing so caused no hardness to come into her face. Instead, Max thought it lent her expression an alertness that suited her. "And why don't you go out to your friends, then?" she asked.

Because you're so pretty.

"Because you're so pretty." It was out before he could change his mind.

Nina looked at him, and it seemed to him that the compliment gave her face an extra glow. The tingling in his fingers spread up his arms and went as far as the pit of his stomach, where it seemed almost to hum in his ears and fill the room.

"Thank you," said Nina, and lowered her head, turning her attention back to her dessert.

Max swallowed. *It doesn't matter; I just said what I thought.* Which meant, of course, that he couldn't just get up and leave. Right? *If she goes on sitting here,* he thought, *even though I've just told her that I think she's pretty, well . . . what's supposed to happen next?*

And suddenly he thought he could already feel what it would be like to embrace her naked body in a freshly rumpled bed.

TODAY

Clattering and screeching, the subway train trundles to a stop in the station. It is still early in the morning and the cars are nearly empty.

A booming, crashing, pounding sound fills the tunnellike passage that opens up to become the subway station—an underlying rumble that mixes with the screeching brakes of the stopping train.

For a moment, everything is quiet. No passengers on the platform, none alighting.

A warning signal and then, with a jolt, the train is moving again, rolling out of the station.

There it is again. That booming and pounding. Stronger and louder than it had been just moments before.

There is no one there to hear it. But it vibrates the walls of the station even so.

16

TWO YEARS EARLIER

"Why didn't you call me?!" Max nearly screamed. "Did it occur to you that I might want to know you were coming? And don't try to tell me you decided at the last minute. When did you book your ticket?" He stared at Till, but didn't wait for an answer, instead answering for him with a distorted imitation of Till's voice. "*When did I book my ticket?* When was I supposed to book? Sunday? Wednesday? Tuesday? How should I know when I booked it? Maybe last month? What do you care?"

Max crashed his fist onto the table. "Like I give a shit, right? Like I give a *shit* if you come to my sister's wedding or not. But I don't. I just would have liked to know. Isn't that perhaps enough of a reason to let me know in advance?" Now he paused and looked wide-eyed at Till, who laid his hands on the tabletop, his fingers intertwined, and said nothing.

Max turned around to Nina, who had come out to the table with him. "Would you look at that? He won't even answer me!"

Nina looked past Max to Till, who was reaching out his hand to her. "Till Anschütz. I don't believe we've met."

Max didn't take his eyes off Nina, but all of her attention was on Till.

"Nina Lowith," she said, and glanced quickly at Max. "Ha! Now you know my name."

Max shrugged. "She didn't want to tell me her last name," he said, looking back at Till. "We finally got to talk to each other today, really, for the first time."

Till smiled. "I wanted to let you know, Max, but . . . you know, I thought it might be nice to surprise you."

Max puffed out his cheeks. He and Nina had visited the walk-in again, just before they'd found Till. He'd wanted another shot of the vodka, but when he was standing in the refrigerator with the bottle in his hand, she suddenly touched him on the arm. "Are you sure you don't want something else?" she asked, her cheeks bright red from the cold air in the room.

Something else?

She took out a flat, silver case from her handbag, set it on a cooler, and flipped it open. Inside was something Max had heard a lot about but had never actually seen. He knew immediately what it was, but had always kept well away from the stuff. His experiences with drugs had never been good. But at that moment, he had thought what Nina was offering might be just the thing to give the day that special kick—and he sniffed a line.

"Come off it," said Max, taking Till by the arm. "Cut the crap! I don't want to hear it anymore. You're working on an investigation into *what*? What *exactly*, Till? You can explain it to me, you know, and I mean in detail!" He was shouting again, but he didn't care. And he was sure that it made no difference to Till or Nina either. He could see it for himself: they were both laughing. He was simply in top form! A little liveliness wouldn't do anyone any harm.

"Max, I'd be happy to explain it all to you in minute detail— but not here, not now. Nina might get bored," Till replied.

"Again with the excuses!" Max blurted, and turned abruptly to Nina. "Tell him, *tell him*, that you want to hear it too!"

She smiled. "Yes, really . . ." But then she cut herself short and said, "Will you excuse me a moment?" And before Max could stop her, she was moving away from their table.

"Something the matter with her?" Till watched Nina walking away.

"No idea. She'll come back soon." The words were bubbling out of Max, but he couldn't completely suppress the idea that she may have distanced herself because he was simply too exuberant, too loud, too unruly. "Now that she's gone, you've lost your excuse for *not* telling me about your work, Till."

But he saw that Till—now really rather confused—was shaking his head. "Another time, Max. Today I'm not really up for listening to you tell me what I'm doing is stupid and won't get me anywhere."

There was a jarring note in Till's words that did not escape Max's attention. What was that? Was Till pissed?

"You two seem to get along pretty well . . . ?" Till asked, apparently wanting to change the subject.

"Nina's great . . ." Max turned his back to the table and propped his elbows on the tabletop, looking out at the garden and the other guests. "I'm glad you're here, Till," he said, overcome by his awareness that that was true, regardless of how strangely exhilarated Till might think he was.

Till nodded. "Me too." But then he added something that hit Max like a bucket of icy water.

"Max . . . I . . . I wish I didn't have to start with this, but . . . you know, since I heard about it, I haven't been able to think of anything else."

Max felt himself flinch. Word gets around. First Henning, now Till. For a moment, it was like a wave of hate welling up in him. "What do you mean? Riga?"

Everything had been perfect. The wedding, Nina, Till being back . . . why did he have to go and wreck it all?

And in a fit of pique, defiance, arrogance, and pride, he turned and leaned across to Till, filled his voice with all the coldness and composure he was capable of, and said, "Don't fret, Till. It's only rumors."

TODAY

The headlights of the approaching cars joggle up and down as the cars shudder across the cobblestones. A wind has sprung up, and Claire sees clouds scudding across the sky.

She runs. Frederik in front of her. He stumbles, his steps look uncertain. He turns around again and again, checking that she's behind him.

There's hardly anyone on the streets. They reach an open square, and Frederik stops and waits for her. Her arms find his, and she rests her weight against him, his head above her tilted like that of a powerful bird.

Claire closes her eyes and leans her head back, feels his unshaved cheek graze her lips before they kiss.

The square around her fades.

A pocket of protection.

"Excuse me. Were you . . . didn't you come from back there?"

Claire's vision is still a little misty when she opens her eyes. She doesn't let go of Frederik. An elderly man has stopped next to them and is pointing in the direction they have come from. "What . . . what is going on back there?"

Claire looks up to Frederik. He wants to get away. "Sorry, buddy. No idea."

Claire's arm is around Frederik's waist when they set off again.

"Did he hear the shots?" Claire looks uncertainly at Frederik.

He squeezes her to him tightly but doesn't reply. Claire slows her steps and turns so he's forced to stop with her.

"Then what did he mean?"

They look back across the square and on the far side, the elderly man is disappearing between two buildings. Only a few lights still burn in the facades and gables that tower into the night sky and in the angular streetlamps rising from the sidewalk.

Claire feels Frederik's chest rise and fall. A gust of wind whips up dust and sand, swirling them across the asphalt. Claire pinches her eyes closed to keep the grit out.

They can't go back to her place. They can't go to his. She presses herself close to the man wrapped in her arms. A calmness emanates from him, and Claire drinks it in greedily.

She exhales.

A brightly lit train rattles into the elevated railway station on their right. Behind it, two or three rundown skyscrapers rise against the blue-black sky. It is a familiar silhouette, the Berlin TV tower with its bulb rising beyond the buildings, perched like a crown.

Claire feels her mouth go dry.

It's as if her retinas begin to register what happens before her brain is able to take it in.

A cloud. A pale-gray cloud rises between the outlines of the tall buildings.

The pressure from Frederik's arm around her increases. Claire hears a dull rumbling sound getting louder, and a siren, which must be on the far side of the tracks, whines to life.

She breathes out . . .

. . . and in again.

The warning beep that announces the departure of the train reaches them weakly. The train starts to roll. And the dust cloud rises higher, lit by the lamps that also light the street below.

Claire watches the lights on the back of the train as it passes by, its wheels squealing.

One of the buildings on the other side of the tracks—it seems to be moving, and Claire can't understand how that is possible. Then the building begins to collapse in on itself.

Claire ducks her head. Frederik's arms close around her. Through the dull rumble of the collapsing building come sharp sounds, like something drumming, like hail pelting onto a roof. Two more sirens start to wail.

There is a loud crack, as if something has burst. A hissing sound like spray from an enormous hose. At the same time, the cloud of dust billows out from under the elevated tracks and moves across the square, heading straight for Frederik and Claire.

She raises her eyes to the skyscraper.

It isn't there anymore.

The other buildings are still there, rising sheer, clear, and hard against the night sky, as the cloud of dust rises and envelops them floor by floor.

TWO YEARS EARLIER

"Come on, it's not so bad. Everything was great at the wedding, and Max took care of the reception, didn't he?" Till sipped from the foam cup he held.

"Okay, but I hardly understood a word he was saying. He was either shouting or mumbling . . ." Lisa leaned back in her chair pensively and watched the people walk by.

They were sitting on metal chairs in front of a coffee shop on Hackescher Markt. Pedestrians passed by on the narrow sidewalk. Most of them had their raincoats unbuttoned, and some were only wearing sweaters. For March, the weather was astonishingly good, with just a few scattered clouds skimming over a deep-blue sky.

"He'd had a few to drink, and who knows what else," said Till, "but when I spoke to him, he seemed to be in a good mood, and pretty levelheaded." Till propped his left elbow on the table. "Really—or I wouldn't say it. I think he was doing well. He had a kind of . . . How can I put it? . . . A kind of resolve? As if he'd come to a decision about things and knew which way he was headed."

"Did he say that?" asked Lisa, glancing up from her coffee. "I mean, did you talk about it?"

"Lisa, I just saw him yesterday for the first time in over a year. It wouldn't have made sense if I'd jumped on him and started peppering him with questions about his plans . . ."

Who'd said anything about peppering him with questions? thought Till. He took his elbow off the table and crossed his arms. "When I meet him later, I'll try to talk to him again, okay?" he suggested. "Do you know this Irina that he wants to take me to meet?"

Lisa seemed to have barely heard him.

"Lisa?"

She jumped slightly. "Irina? Yes. Yes, I've met her a few times. She's nice. She's with Quentin." She sighed.

Till's eyes stayed on Lisa for a moment. He noticed how carefree and casual her makeup and hair looked. That same mixture of freshness, intelligence, and willfulness that he had always found attractive. In his eyes, it was what set her apart from someone like Max's friend Nina. Nina, with her long brown hair, supple body, and velvet eyes. With a woman like Nina, Till's thoughts automatically turned to sex. But with Lisa, he always felt compelled to consider whether he could measure up to her *intellectually* first.

"So, what are you doing next?" he asked, after they had sat in silence for a while. "Are you going to start at the newspaper?" Lisa had told him that her internship at the newspaper had ended. "Working as a real reporter? Sounds exciting."

Lisa set her cup of coffee on the table. "Yes . . . yes, I also thought it might be good . . ."

"But?"

"I don't know." She shook her head and straightened up. "Maybe I'll start there. They've made me an offer, and I've got four weeks to think it over." Her eyes settled on his face. "Do you know how long you'll be staying in Berlin?"

Till swirled his cup around, making a little whirlpool in the cappuccino. "A few days, I was thinking."

"Any plans?" She was still looking at him.

Till smiled. "Meet up with you guys?" Pause. "Meet up with you."

She nodded. "Anything else?"

"Not much. Nothing, really."

"Don't you have anything to do for your thesis?"

Thinking about the pile of work he'd left behind in his office made Till feel a little dizzy. "I'm sure I can grant myself a few days off . . ."

Lisa swept a strand of hair behind her ear. "So, what does your thesis actually involve? Can you tell me anything about it?"

Till glanced at the clock on its column on the other side of the square. Just before four. Max wanted to pick him up here at four, but he was always a little late. Till looked at Lisa. "You really want to know?"

He noticed something like derision flicker in her eyes. "I don't need the uncut version. One sentence!"

"In one sentence . . ." Till thought it over. "Ever heard about the question of whether mathematical objects exist in reality?"

"What?"

It seemed to Till that her pupils contracted slightly.

"Mathematical propositions . . . when a mathematician proves a new theorem, then what has he done? Has he *extrapolated* from existing propositions, meaning a new construction based on the old? Or has he *discovered* part of a mathematical world that exists independently of him, and all he has done is found a path that leads there?"

Lisa moved her head back a little. "Are you getting into mathematics now?"

"No." Till rubbed his eyes with his right hand. "But the analogy is the easiest way to explain it . . ."

"Sorry, it's all Greek to me," she interrupted him.

"Look," he said, shaking his head. "It's really quite simple. Think about what your father did."

"Wrote novels."

"Exactly. And think of the question like this: Did your father come up with the events in his books as something new, meaning he *invented* them? Or did he, in fact, *discover* them, like something that already existed before him and separate from him?"

Lisa had lost a little of her stiffness again. She seemed more intent on following him now—or at least less interested in giving him her skeptical look.

"You know," Till continued, "it's not like a writer can just put together a text any way he wants. When you read stories about writers, a lot of it is about how they have to wait for inspiration, how they have to wait for their muse to come along and whisper in their ear, how the characters don't always want what the writer wants, and so on . . ."

Lisa pursed her lips.

"So, this raises the question: What do authors really do when they write stories? Do they stumble across them? Like they are already in existence somewhere, complete? Revising or fine-tuning a text would support this; the first draft doesn't yet match the independently existing story and has to be gradually adapted to fit."

"This is pure speculation, of course."

"Okay, it's not something you can *prove*. Not yet, at least. I mean, you can't show that, at some level, the stories already exist *before* they are written down. But there are a few indications that there could perhaps be more to this concept than what you see at first glance. What interests me right now is how we might imagine this world of stories and fiction . . . which could exist autonomously, independent of all writers. How we could—or how we have to— imagine it."

Lisa was looking at him with a mixture of attentiveness and a little despair.

"And in my thesis, I'm trying—"

"To find a way into this world. No, to drill a way into it!" She laughed.

"No." Till raised his hand, smiling. "I'm trying to bring some order to the clues that suggest there really could be something to the notion that so-called fictional sentences may correspond to some independent reality."

"What you're saying is that novels and stories, the whole range of fictional texts . . . in some sense, it is all *true?*

Till grinned. She got it. "It's not what I'm saying. I know as little about it as anyone else. All I'm doing is looking at the pointers that support the concept."

Lisa seemed to mull the idea over.

Till continued. "Of course, when it comes to fiction, it could be that it's more about similarity than correspondence or agreement. Stories are better or worse, not right or wrong. This separates them from mathematical propositions, for example. So, you could also come to the conclusion, I think, that things that—somewhere, somehow, in a certain way—*exist* are, in fact, *perfect* dramaturgy, *perfect* story arcs, *perfect* concepts or stories. And what the authors write are texts that correspond either well or badly to these *perfect* ideals. Do you see what I mean?"

Lisa was looking past him to the square beyond, but he sensed she was still with him.

"And what I'm trying to do now is to draw a map of this ideal world that the fictional texts coincide with either well or badly. Okay, that's putting it all extremely simply, but that's basically it."

"Then it's what you'd call poetics . . . or aesthetics? Something like that?"

"Well, if you take it back to its roots, it's probably more like ontology. But the entire thing is close to the field of mathematics in which the so-called Platonists argue that there is a plane of existence of mathematical objects . . ."

"Till!?"

Till jumped. He'd been completely engrossed in explaining his ideas, and now a car had pulled up at the curb directly in front of where they were sitting. Max was sitting behind the wheel.

"Time to hit the road, man!" Max looked over to Lisa. "What about you, Lissi? Do you want to come along?"

Till glanced at Lisa. He could see in her look just how much she loved her brother.

"Another time, Max. I can't go today."

"Meeting Felix?"

Till stood up, as if making a point of how little that actually interested him, although he, too, had been wondering all along *Was she with Felix?*

Could it really be true? With a friend—a former colleague—of her father? A man more than twice her age?

Instead of answering Max, Lisa also stood up and turned to Till. "Call me again before you leave?"

Till opened his arms and embraced her. And in that brief moment, with their arms around each other, he felt that leaving again would not be such a simple thing to do. That Lisa was the real reason he had come to Berlin. That he had to talk to her . . . and not just in passing in a café, but properly.

"Can I see you tomorrow, maybe in the evening?" He released her from his embrace and saw that she had turned her face to him. What he saw there, though, was no smile, but something more like dismay . . . or vulnerability?

"I'll call you, okay?" She turned away and reached out her hand to Max over the low door of the convertible he was driving. "Look after him, Max." Then Lisa turned away quickly and walked away down the street.

Why did she turn away so fast? Till wondered. It was almost as if she were trying to hide her face . . .

The heavy car door swung open. Max had leaned across and lifted the inside handle. Till sank into the passenger seat and pulled the door closed behind him. Simultaneously, he felt himself being pushed back into the upholstery. Max had hit the gas, and now he whacked the CD player behind the gear stick with his right hand.

"He left no time to regret" streamed from the speakers. And the hard tone of the piano prevailed over the sounds of the city around them.

TODAY

"Merle? Merle? Can you hear me?"

The car door clicks open—Merle's gaze swings skyward and the sun shines directly into her eyes. She feels her pupils contract but also feels that she doesn't need to blink. She is looking straight up and out of the car, between the windshield and the open door, past the building at the side of the road, up to the glowing fireball burning at the top corner of the house, staring into radiant, blazing gold.

Someone tugs at her arm and she senses herself being hauled to her feet. The golden sun sinks out of her line of sight, replaced by the blue shadows of the newly built building where they have stopped. Merle staggers across the sidewalk. Nele, who has driven her here, is at her side.

A glass door hisses open and the building swallows them up. Merle looks down at the floor, the tiles . . .

"Wait here. No . . . no!"

Merle's gaze wanders across the floor, and she feels the pressure of Nele's hand on her arm.

"We'll take care of her. It won't be long. Please take a seat!"

"She's not well"—Nele's voice—"she can't wait."

Merle hears running steps drawing closer.

"There!"

"Yeah . . . yeah, okay."

She sees the white pants of a paramedic, and Nele's loose grip disappears. Two male hands take hold of her, push . . .

"No!"

Merle loses her balance and falls. She can already see herself slamming into the floor face first. Then something cracks in the back of her knees, her legs fold under her, she collapses into a seat, and feels ice-cold fury wash over her.

"What . . . is hooking her jaw?"

Her lips pull back from her teeth.

"Aaaaarrrrrr." That's what comes out, but all she wanted to say was . . .

"Rrrrraaagg . . ."

The hands of men—is it four, six, eight?—shove Merle into the wheelchair as though they want to bolt or nail her into the thing.

Something tears in her lungs. Her tongue comes out between her teeth, protruding farther and farther, as if it wants to get out of her.

"Neeeellleeee . . ." Nele has to help her. What are they doing to her!?

A wide leather band closes around her wrist. Her eyes roll back in their sockets and all she can see is darkness.

"Neeeellleeee . . ."

She jerks the arm that they've tied down. Merle sees it lying on the arm rest of the wheelchair, trapped under the leather band. But she doesn't need it . . . all she has to do . . .

is simply . . .

tear it . . .

off.

Merle throws her body around, hears the clattering of the wheelchair, the voices of the men swarming around her, trying to get hold of her, to hold her.

Neeeellleeee . . .

The band cuts into her skin. She throws herself in the other direction, her eyes turned up inside her skull, lost in the darkness in there. Her tongue has practically twisted itself out of her mouth.

And then the chaos, the insanity, the deafening noise raging inside her . . . caves in.

Merle feels something soft settling on top of her, forming to her form—holding her!

Her eyes slowly roll down again, looking ahead . . .

It is Nele holding her.

Merle's head sinks against her friend's breast.

"Aaaaarrrrrr . . ."

Nele gently strokes her head. Her eyes are full of tears. "Take care, Merle," she whispers. "Take care."

TWO YEARS EARLIER

Max propped his left elbow on the door while he steered with his right hand. His eyes were hidden behind teardrop Ray-Bans.

Till looked out the window, watching Alexanderplatz pass by. On the right was the tower with the dilapidated fountain, and on the left were the asymmetrical apartment blocks, some of them both architecturally adventurous and ugly. Max gunned the motor, shot through a yellow light, and turned right onto the impressive expanse of Karl-Marx-Allee.

"She moved in just a few days ago," he said, not taking his eyes off the road. "Today's the housewarming."

Irina. The woman they were driving to meet.

"She's Quentin's girlfriend, right? Where do you know him from?" Till turned up the collar of his dark-blue jacket, shielding himself from the wind.

"From boarding school," Max said, glancing sideways at Till. "You knew that."

True. Max had mentioned it at some point. "But Felix and Quentin already knew each other before, right?"

Max laughed. "That's right. The first time I heard that, it took me by surprise too."

He shifted down a gear, and then accelerated. "Everyone's connected somehow. Quentin also got to know Henning at boarding school."

"The guy your sister married yesterday."

Max nodded. "Henning's a few years older than the rest of us. I think he's already thirty. Quentin told me that Henning more or less took him under his wing when Quentin started at Dornstedt. And Quentin met Felix through Henning."

"So, when you were sent off to your boarding school, Felix was the one who recommended Dornstedt to your mother . . ."

"It wasn't that bad." With a quick jab at the horn, Max scared off an Opel driver who was signaling to move into his lane, and sped past.

"Quentin was there for me when I went to Dornstedt." He tilted his head down a little, so he could look at Till over the rim of his glasses. "He's . . . a bit complicated sometimes. But I was happy I had him there."

"What does he do now?"

"After school, he started travel writing. He's into what he calls 'modern urbanity' or something like that, he says. Ask him yourself. He was in Lagos, Nigeria, two or three years ago. He says that in cities like Lagos you can already see how we'll all be living in a few years. He's working for Felix now."

"And Henning?"

"He also works for Felix's company."

"Doing what?"

Max exhaled, making his lips vibrate like a child imitating an engine, before answering. "Content manager?"

Till leaned back a little and, like Max, propped one elbow on the door. Stalinesque buildings flew past on both sides, lining Strasse des 17. Juni.

"Irina also works for Felix. Just don't ask me what she does."

"And the little guy who was there yesterday?"

"Malte . . ." Max gazed ahead through the windshield, as if he suddenly had to concentrate on the traffic.

"What's the deal with him?"

"I don't think he knows that himself. Not really." Max glanced in the rearview mirror, clicked on the turn signal, and moved into the right-turn lane. "I once told him he was just waiting to inherit his parents' house." Max turned the wheel and accelerated out of the curve. "Man, you should have heard what he had to say about that. But Malte's all right. He wouldn't hurt a fly."

For a while, they sped along the street. "So, all of them know Felix one way or another," Till finally said.

Max nodded, his bottom lip pouting slightly.

"And—" Till stopped short. Was there anything to it? They lived in Berlin, people know each other. So what?

"And?" Max, grinning, looked over at him.

Till shook his head. "Nothing. I don't know."

"What? Out with it!"

"Well . . . Felix was always the kind of guy to run the show from the background. He always had some deal going, right?" Till ran both hands through his hair. "Is it all just coincidence? That of all the boarding schools in Germany, he recommended the one where he already knew Henning and Quentin?"

"No coincidence at all. They're friends. He's a few years older, but they're still friends. And both had praised Dornstedt, the school is really pretty good . . ."

"Wait, hold on, maybe that's what I'm getting at. How old is Felix?"

"Early fifties. Why?"

"Exactly. But Henning, Quentin, Malte . . . you. You're all much younger. I mean, don't you think that's strange?"

Max burst out laughing, but just for a moment. "Where's this going? Are you saying something's not legit? Older man with his boys, something like that?" He looked quickly at Till, his mouth twisted scornfully. "Felix likes women." For a moment, Till saw a shadow sweep across his friend's face. "Take my word for it."

"Fine. But what keeps you all together? You say you're friends . . ."

Max shook his head and concentrated on the street again.

"Me? With Felix? No, I'm no friend of Felix's. With Quentin, yes. With Malte, maybe. With Felix, no way."

"But he's friends with them. Quentin, Henning, Malte, you said."

"Yes, sure." Max turned off again and left the broad thorough-fare they had been following as it swept past a belt of industrial buildings. They drove along a smaller, cobbled street. "And you're right, Felix is pulling some strings in the background."

"But why? I mean, what does he want?"

Max slowed to a standstill. "Ask him yourself. He said he'd be coming today." He pointed to a huge brick building rising in front of them. "The Flaschenturm. We're here."

Till turned in his seat to face Max, who was reversing into a parking space. "Seriously, tell me," he insisted. "Do you have any idea what Felix is up to?!"

Max stopped the car, and still wearing his dark-green sun-glasses, turned to Till. "Are you afraid of asking him yourself? Is that it?"

"I'm asking you."

"Well . . . Felix is convinced that . . ." he paused, laughed. "You wouldn't believe me." With that, he pulled the hand brake and turned off the ignition.

Till leaned back, looking up at the impressive mass of the old factory building they had pulled up in front of. It must have been built in the built in the 1920s or 1930s. High up, on the seventh or eighth floor, he could make out the rail of a terrace or balcony with several people leaning on it.

"End of the line. Everybody out," he heard Max say, obviously in a good mood. He shoved the door open and climbed out. Only when they started walking toward the Flaschenturm did Till realize that it stood directly beside the Spree River. A cool breeze wafted over from the water.

"Nice, isn't it?" Max smiled. "Felix bought it for her."

"What?"

"The apartment."

"He bought Quentin's girlfriend an apartment?"

Max's grin stretched a little wider. "I know. Freaky, isn't it?"

TWO YEARS EARLIER

"*No*, not what he *says* . . . or believes, or means or wants! No. I want it tangible, factual, plain, and simple: What he *does*. Not what he *thinks*."

"Who?" Malte seemed to have lost the thread.

"Felix, of course!" Max, glass in hand, pushed himself away from the wall he'd been leaning on. "Who else!?"

Malte shrugged. "That's not something you can explain in one or two sentences." A little unsettled, he looked to Henning, who was standing beside him.

Max tilted his glass in the direction of Till, who was also with them. "Malte, look, it's really quite simple. On the way over, Till asked me what you guys are working on. I started to tell him, but then I realized I don't actually know myself. So I think, *No problem, we'll be there in a minute, we can ask you.*"

"So, what exactly do you want to know?" asked Henning, joining the conversation.

"We're going around in circles!" exclaimed Max, a touch too loud, too aggressive, Till thought, but at the same time in a way that made it impossible not to give a straight answer—unless you wanted to stand there like an idiot. "What is Felix working on with you in the company? Is that so hard?"

Henning set his glass on a sideboard behind him. They were standing in the spacious living room of Irina's apartment. One wall, nearly fifty feet across, was a glass facade looking out onto a terrace. There were more guests out there, some leaning on the railing—the ones Till had seen from below.

"I don't want to drag this out," Henning said, looking briefly at Till before turning his attention back to Max. "But I think it's very important to avoid any major misconceptions. And the most widespread misconception is that we've all had some sort of predetermined set of rules branded into our brains . . . or something along those lines." He laughed, then, and it was so infectious that even Till found himself grinning. "But in reality, it's more that Felix has gathered a group of people around him, each of whom—in his or her own individual way—is focused on a very specific question. And not just theoretically, but in very concrete, practical ways."

"With the question of freedom," Max blurted, and looked at Till.

"With the question of . . . freedom. That's right," Henning continued. "A question that's been tossed back and forth for God knows how long."

The question of freedom. Till's mind flashed back to that hot summer afternoon ten years earlier, when he had wandered through the tunnels under the city with Max's father. When Bentheim, as if out of his mind, had talked and talked to him . . . just before he . . .

Till lifted his glass and drank. *Not now!* It was the same pattern. Sometimes nothing for months, then suddenly, ten, twenty, five hundred times a day he would think of Bentheim, remembering the man's screams following him as he ran through the tunnels and back to the surface.

"Which is why I say that each of us is connected with this question in very different ways." Henning was speaking again. "If you spend some time on this question, with what I've just called the question of freedom, you'll see that it is something that basically lies at the heart of how we understand the world. At the heart of our self-image, our understanding of society, of good and evil, of responsibility and guilt. And therefore also our conception of law, and so on and so on. And how we answer this question can have extremely far-reaching implications for our worldview—basically, for *all* important perceptions and opinions. Implications and consequences that are anything but simple or transparent."

"Aaaaaaah," said Max, drawing it out.

"You want me to keep going, or have you had enough?" Henning was looking at him with a mixture of friendliness and reserve.

"No, keep going, man! Keep going." Max reached down for the wine bottle that was on the floor between his feet and refilled his glass.

Henning looked at Till. "Perhaps we could spend an afternoon with Felix, if you're interested."

"Yeah, uh, sure, an afternoon would be fine. But tell me . . . I mean, you were talking about the question of freedom. The question? Why is it a *question*? The question of freedom . . . that's a pretty enormous field, isn't it? And that's what keeps you busy?" Till smiled. "I mean, don't get me wrong, but I don't really understand."

Henning looked at him calmly. "The crucial point has to be how the question is *answered*. Of course, this has already been discussed to death, but . . . well, simply adding to the discussion doesn't interest us. No, the point for us is rather that many things will become much clearer if you answer the question for yourself in a *very specific way*—and then *act* on that answer. Which means to act once you're convinced that the question *must* be answered in a very specific way."

"Which would be?"

"In a nutshell, that it's an illusion, and we have to see it for what it really is."

"Freedom."

"Yes."

"Is the illusion."

"Yes."

"I *believe* I'm free, but it isn't actually the case."

"Yes."

"That's it?"

"Yes."

For a moment, it seemed to Till that the entire apartment had fallen silent. But then he heard the music playing again and the buzz of voices in the other rooms. He realized that Max was still standing beside him and that he was waiting for what Till would say to Henning in response.

Of course, Till had heard about the theory before—free will, brain research—and it was true that an immense amount had been written and said on the subject. But he had never looked into it or thought about it very deeply.

"Isn't it irrelevant, though? Does it really matter how you answer the question? It doesn't change anything. Everything stays how it is."

Henning tilted his head to one side. "I wouldn't say that."

"Why? What can change?"

"Like I just said, our social system, how we see the world, all of that is built on one particular answer to the question. If the answer changes—meaning the answer that most people are convinced is right—then society changes."

Till thought this over for a moment. Finally, he said, "Until today, people have believed they are *free* to make the decisions they make. But you, or all of you, are saying that's a deception, an illusion . . . but so what? Is it necessary to change society?"

"No . . . no." Henning took a breath. He seemed to really want to win Till over, but at the same time he gave the impression he'd been through exactly this discussion many times. "The change that takes place doesn't have to be specified."

"Specifying it would be a prerequisite of a free will, of course."

"Right. It's more about freeing yourself from the illusion. Once you've thrown that away like . . . like cheap sunglasses . . . you can suddenly see things far more clearly. You see things as they really are. It's like you become a different person. Then life in society changes *automatically*."

You become a different person—Till was not comfortable with that. He kept his eyes on Henning: tall and slim with smooth hair hanging a little over his eyes.

"If I've understood it right, I can decide for myself whether I think freedom is an illusion or not?"

Henning laughed. "Uhhh . . . yes! Right? I can decide that for myself, but is that the *only* thing I can decide?" He stopped for a moment. "Of course *not!* Like I said, let's meet up one afternoon in the city and talk it all through. You'll see. Once you've started thinking in a certain direction, many things will suddenly seem obvious to you. Think of the earth as a ball. All you see is the flatness around you, but as soon as know it's a ball, you don't believe in the flatness anymore. It no longer matters what you actually see."

"Fine. But when it comes to making the switch to the ball version, it certainly helps to see photos of the earth taken from space, right? But if we're talking freedom, or free will . . ." Till raised his arm. "It's crystal clear to me that I can choose freely to lift my arm or not, as long as it's not . . . I don't know . . . tied down or something."

"Don't start with the arm and whether you can lift it up or not," said Malte, suddenly joining the discussion. He'd been standing in silence next to Henning the entire time, listening. "We can kick arguments around forever, but it won't get us anywhere."

"Really?" Till crossed his arms across his chest. "Arguments get us nowhere? Let's assume for a moment that I believe I'm free. Call me old school. I can freely decide to do anything I want. I'm fundamentally convinced that's the case, okay? And now I'm supposed to switch to your concept that I'm deceiving myself. That it *seems* to me that I'm free, but, in reality, I'm *not*, and I can't actually decide freely at all. Then what, apart from arguments, could sway me to change my conviction?"

"Sure, fine," Malte argued, his lean face growing animated. "But I think you have to watch out, you have to make sure you don't get lost in the arguments. In the end, it comes down to the fact that subjectively you think you're free—but objectively there's no reasonable way to describe a world in which we would actually be free. It's easy if you imagine nerve cells, for example, they spark and those sparks determine how we act . . . Okay, let's assume we're free, and let's assume we're faced with a certain decision: get married or not, for example . . ." He grinned. "Well, how are we supposed to imagine that? All of our nerves just stand around silently, waiting for the decision to be made? And where exactly would it be made? Or to put it a better way: How do we imagine the process of *weighing up* that takes place? Either the cells spark—but then there's no room for that weird free-will thing—or they don't. And then there's no way to *weigh up* anything."

"Then why does it *appear* to me that I'm making a decision based on my free will?"

Malte smiled. "Ever think it might be a myth they feed us, just to hamstring us with guilt?"

Till swallowed. Malte's words echoed in his mind. "Who's 'they'?"

"Hard to say . . ." Malte replied. "Maybe the clever ones—to keep the strong in check?"

Till tried to follow his argument, but what Malte was saying just didn't sound right.

Malte was already going on. "Like I said, arguments for or against. It's all old hat, as they say in England." He glanced up at Henning. "But what's interesting—like Henning already pointed out—is what the consequences are when you've seen through the illusion and then *act*. Then the whole system starts to fall apart."

"The system of our beliefs and opinions, you mean."

Malte nodded. "And whatever new system comes out of that, well, that's not clear at all. Take"—he raised his voice to preempt any interruption from Till—"take, for example, good and evil. This is my personal favorite: I can't decide freely—so there's no more good or evil, right?"

Till thought it over.

"All there is is personal advantage and disadvantage," Malte continued.

"Sounds like we'll have to brace ourselves if that's what it comes to," Till said.

Malte opened his hands in a question. "You think it's more moral to go on pigheadedly living a lie?"

Again, Till couldn't escape the feeling that something was wrong with this. He looked at Max for a moment; he had also crossed his arms without putting down his refilled glass and was eyeing Malte with contempt.

"I can't decide that for myself," Till said, looking back at Malte. "So, you can't blame me for sticking with the illusion."

Malte's smile lit up his face, and Till instinctively felt some sympathy for him. "As I said—and I'll never get tired of saying it—as long as you're stuck on the question of whether freedom is a fact or an illusion, you'll never get beyond the pointless discussions that lead nowhere. You only start to get anywhere when you ask yourself how we want to live together when the old sense of good and evil no longer exists."

"I guess that's something I'll need to consider if I notice more people starting to think free will is an illusion."

"Yes. And *don't* you notice that?" Malte was clearly enjoying himself. "Don't you see exactly that happening? First it was the brain researchers, Gerhard Roth and Wolf Singer, all that crowd. Then came the lawyers. Seems to me the upshot of a new answer to the question needs to be looked at sooner rather than later."

"Bullshit. *Bullshit!*"

Quentin, whom Max had introduced to Till at the wedding, had joined them just a few minutes before. Now it seemed he couldn't contain himself any longer and had to speak.

"No doubt you told him Felix bought this apartment for Irina, right?" Quentin, his hands clenched, stared at Max.

"So what?" Max answered, and Till saw him glance at Henning.

"Why do you think he did that?" Quentin was looking at Till.

Like Max, Till found himself involuntarily looking at Henning. Wasn't Irina Quentin's girlfriend? Till almost stammered, "I don't know."

"Shut up, Quentin," Henning said, and Till thought he saw a crack appear in the facilitator facade that Henning had maintained throughout the discussion.

"Why?" Quentin snapped. "You can try to explain it till you're blue in the face and they still won't get it! They won't understand what differentiates *your* drivel from all the *other* drivel already produced on the topic!"

"Do you want me to kick you out?" A cloud had come down over Henning's face.

"I really don't give a damn what the real reason for giving her this place is," Quentin continued, although he must have known how ambiguous that sounded and how dubious the light it cast on Irina was—and on him, too. "All that matters is one thing: Did Felix want to do it? Did he *have* to do it? Did he *have* to buy her the apartment, because obviously he wasn't able do it of his own free will, now was he? So, was it fate?"

Quentin's eyes moved around the circle as he answered his own question. "No!"

"Everything okay in there?" asked a voice from out on the terrace. The guests outside were looking in through the window. Quentin must have been loud enough to draw their attention.

"*That's* what it comes down to," Quentin went on, ignoring the question from the balcony. "What sort of world is it if we can't believe in freedom anymore? It's a world that just happens, destiny unrolling, a stream of events that we can't influence at all!" Although he was now speaking quietly again, his voice had taken on a piercing tone. "And how do people like you, Malte—or you, Henning—how do you react to this knowledge? One says, 'There are advantages and disadvantages.' Another gives in to fate without out a struggle. The only thing that's clear is that the way a person reacts," his eyes fixed on Till as he spoke, "is a matter of *character*. Felix, for example, reacted very differently than I did."

"But it makes no difference how I react. I can't decide that for myself," Till said.

"You may not be able to make that decision, but *how* you react shows exactly what you're made of," Quentin said. "Is it wrong to go on looking for some meaning in life? Yes. Because it isn't in my power to choose this meaning or that meaning. But if you give in to fate and can't trace the meaning in the stream, then all you're really doing is standing by and watching yourself rot."

"The meaning? What *meaning*? The meaning of life?" Till's head was buzzing.

"Yes, *the meaning of life!*" Quentin replied.

"And what is that exactly, Quentin?" Max rejoined the fray. "If you're so sure about it, what is the meaning of life?"

"Well? Has my dear Quentin got you all to where he'd like to get everyone?"

Till wheeled around. A man was walking toward them, crossing through the foyer between the elevator and the living room, where they were standing. He had one hand at Irina's elbow—she was half a head taller than him—and his steel-gray, almost oversized eyes blazed at them from below his closely trimmed hair. Although he hadn't seen him for years, Till recognized him instantly; it was Felix, Felix von Quitzow.

"The meaning of life—how can you say anything sensible about that?" continued Max, apparently not wanting Felix's arrival to distract him from his train of thought. "You're part of it, right? Your thoughts, your words, they're all part of *being*. It's like a pawn in a game of chess trying to figure out the meaning of the game!"

"I don't believe that," Quentin said angrily. "The idea that our lives should have meaning is clear to every human being on the planet. What matters is this: If we have to give up the idea of free will, then what replaces it? What's the . . . call it the basic unit that gives life meaning . . . what is it that takes the place of the individual human life?"

"Takes the place of being?" asked Max.

"Exactly. Of *being*. Because the second we give up our free will and our guilt, a brand new meaning for our lives appears."

"Uh-huh. And that would be . . . ?"

"What is it we always shy away from? Out of fear of guilt, out of fear . . . basically out of fear of our *conscience*, which only exists as long as we believe in our ability to choose freely."

"From . . ." Max's voice suddenly grew husky, "from evil!"

Quentin's eyes shot to Felix, who had stopped in front of him. "From evil, Felix. Like I've always told you."

"The meaning of our lives is evil?" Till couldn't believe what he was hearing.

"The meaning of our lives is evil?" Felix repeated, now that he had joined them. He had pitched his voice high, as if he were about to laugh. "My God, Quentin, how did you reach *that* conclusion? What's come over you?"

Quentin howled. "It's obvious! That's exactly what the illusion of freedom keeps hidden! That's the secret screened off behind the fraud of free will. That's what has to be brought to light!" His voice filled the room.

Even as Quentin shouted, Till heard a loud cracking noise.

It happened almost too fast for Till to comprehend it, but Quentin's face had suddenly gone deathly pale, his pallor only broken high on his forehead, which was flushed red.

Felix stepped back.

In front of everyone, he had slapped Quentin in the middle of the face with the back of his hand, on which he wore two rings.

For a moment, an icy silence hung over the room. Then Max's voice broke through. He was imitating Quentin, and though the voice was different, Quentin's cadence was unmistakable. "We have to reveal the evil—" then he interrupted himself, speaking for a moment in his own voice. "No, what did you say? Oh, right, *bring it to light*. We have to *bring the evil to light*—" Then again like Quentin, "It is the meaning of being—evil is the meaning of life. And if we dare dig deeper, we'll find ourselves, if not at the end of times, then at least probing the mystery perhaps best demonstrated by the question, why does anything exist at all, and not nothing?"

Quentin glared at Max with a look of fear and hate. It was the look of a humiliated fighting dog. Till had instinctively uncrossed his arms and positioned himself protectively between Quentin and Max just in case it entered Quentin's head to attack his friend.

To Till's surprise, Felix joined Max in his mockery. "The things you get yourself mixed up in, Quentin . . . truly ridiculous. What can I say? Shame on you? My God, we know you can't help it, but . . ." Felix paused and considered for a moment. "But maybe it *is* appropriate—at least, until we've worked out all the connections—to hang on to one or two tricks from the good old days. So, shame on you, shame on you for that garbage you never seem to tire of spouting." His voice dripped with derision.

Before Felix finished his sentence, Quentin sank his head and left the circle.

Till watched him go and could feel only sympathy for him. He had heard the sophistication and thoughtfulness with which Henning and even Malte had spoken. But it seemed to Till that of all of them—and regardless of how grotesque the things he said seemed—it was *Quentin* who had looked the deepest into the abyss that opened up when one took part in the debate that preoccupied Felix and his entourage.

TODAY

Lisa stands at the window, looking at the breathtaking view of the city. She is wearing a bathrobe and watching the first silver rays of morning draw across the summer sky.

To her left, the tower on Alexanderplatz dominates the view.

But Lisa isn't looking at the tower.

She is looking at something down below.

A pale-gray cloud of dust that seems to hang in the air.

The distant whine of sirens hangs over the city.

Felix told her that he would have Till brought to her place that morning.

It is the second time that she and Till will meet again after a long time apart. The first time was two years before, when Till flew from Canada to Berlin for Betty's wedding. Every time Lisa thinks back to the spring weeks that followed his return, it makes her shiver.

And now he's back. This time for the funeral—yesterday was the first time she had seen him since that spring. But this time— and she believes she can be certain of this—there will be no more reunions if they lose sight of each other again. This time, she has to decide what she wants to do with her life.

TODAY

"Dierckenstrasse, corner of Münz. How many?" The voice is tinny, distorted.

"Fourteen."

"Okay . . . are emergency services already there?"

"I can't hear you very well . . ."

"How's that?"

"Yeah . . . better."

"What about emergency services?"

"All on-site. We've got technical services providing support."

"I know you can't say much yet. But . . . are there any leads, any indications as to what might—"

"You're asking about the cause?"

"Yes."

"We're still trying to get hold of the plans. Maybe structural failure. It was built in 1971. Prefab construction. Fourteen floors . . ."

"Okay. Structural failure . . . anything else?"

"An attack. We already have officers on location looking into that. No info yet."

"What else?"

"There's been some test drilling in the area. Looking to extend the subway. They dug out some tunnels, and some of them date from the nineteenth century."

"Okay. Any other thoughts?"

"Look, we . . . we're still in the process . . ."

"I know, I know. Even so . . ."

"It might as easily have been a tenant. Or, who knows . . . maybe someone stored a gas bottle in the wrong place. Maybe someone had a workshop, maybe they were building something . . . we can't rule it out, but . . ."

"But?"

"I'm the last to want to spread panic, as you know. But I wonder if it's wise to focus all our manpower on this particular case? Or would it be smarter to factor in—"

"The possibility of similar . . . events?"

"Yes."

"Are there any signs of that?"

"There was one incident yesterday. On Leipziger Strasse, also a prefab high-rise . . . the details haven't been clarified yet. It seems someone invaded the building."

"I see what you mean—"

"And?"

"Absolutely, you're right. Form a workgroup. Have them put together an action plan to respond if anything else happens. Okay?"

"Jesus . . ."

"Sorry?"

"Jesus, *what is going on?*"

24

TODAY

"It's a goddamned mess, I know. But if I don't get my coffee, I can't think straight!" Felix has his back turned to Lisa while he stands at the stove making two café au laits in oversized cups.

"Did you reach Henning?" Lisa asks.

"They were having breakfast, then he was heading in to the office. Betty's fine, don't worry."

Lisa crumbles the bread roll on her plate. She has no appetite.

"I'm sure they'll figure it out today." Felix sets the cups on the table. They are eating breakfast in the kitchen—it's faster.

"I just don't understand why there are no real details on the news."

"An entire building . . . they don't know the reason for it, Lisa. There could be all kinds of causes." Felix sits, slides a cup of coffee across the table to her, and sips his own.

Lisa tastes the coffee. It's warmth glides down her throat, and she feels the caffeine enter her system.

"You know, since the funeral . . ." says Felix, and Lisa lifts her eyes. Felix is looking at her. His face seems strangely open, even sensitive. He sets the coffee cup on the table in front of him.

"Things have changed . . . there's something I want to talk to you about. Something I've wanted to talk about for a long time."

"Now?"

"Yes."

Lisa also puts down her cup. She pulls the soft wool jacket she is wearing a little closer together in front. She doesn't want to discuss anything with him now. Not before she has met with Till. But she can't avoid it.

"About your father . . ."

Lisa can't help herself—the mention of her father hurts. It's like driving a splinter into her finger.

"With Till visiting again . . . I think it's high time to tell you."

"Tell me what?" Lisa pokes at the crumbled bread on her plate.

Felix looks at her, weighing her reaction. "When I got to know your father back then . . . more than fifteen years ago . . . you were still a child, only eight years old."

"Yes?"

"At that time, I was looking for material that I could use as the basis for the project we're still working on today."

Lisa can vaguely picture her father standing in front of her. She has never stopped missing him. The ache is like a clamp in her chest that never lets up the pressure on her heart.

"I met a lot of writers back then," Felix continues. "I read the widest range of writing you could imagine. There was a lot of good work among it—solid ideas, sophisticated structures. But none of it was really able to convince me. Nothing seemed strong enough to . . . to carry the weight of my project. Until I read one of your father's books." Like Lisa, Felix didn't eat his breakfast, and now his elbows rest on either side of his plate. "His words hit me like a bolt of lightning." His eyes gaze into hers. "And do you know why?"

Lisa fights back tears. Her entire face is tingling, almost buzzing, the sensation filling her from the inside and pressing into the corners of her eyes. What's wrong with her? The funeral yesterday, Till in Berlin—she needs a break, a chance to catch her breath without all this baggage weighing her down. But Felix continues.

"It was like a beautiful song. You know? Like when you hear a song and think *Whoever is singing that, a man or woman, doesn't matter . . . that person will die too.* You hear it in the song, in the singing—the voice that is singing is doomed to die."

Lisa lowers her head and rests her cheeks in her hands. She sees her tears falling onto her plate. The tingling, the buzzing has finally overwhelmed her and now it has found a way out. She watches her tears fall.

"I knew immediately that none of the other authors I'd read would ever be able to create anything comparable. I knew your father was the one who would lay the cornerstone of my project, that it would only be a success if I was able to win *him* over."

Felix reaches across the table and lays his hand palm up on the white tablecloth in front of Lisa. She watches her own left hand come down from her face and settle on the hand Felix is offering.

"So, I spoke with your father," he says, "but . . . it wasn't easy to convince him to work for me." His fingers stroke the back of her hand softly.

"Did you ever hear the name Maja?"

Lisa looks up. "Nina's mother?"

"I introduced your father to Maja, Lisa." Felix's voice drops to a whisper. "He always loved your mother, but . . . you didn't know Maja back then. She had something . . . please excuse me if I say it like this, but some women have something that no man can resist. It's like he's tied up and undressed and twenty virgins are running their lips down over his skin and around his . . . around him. It churns him up so much that he *has* to have more of it. Until he finds release."

Lisa sits on her chair; she has withdrawn her hand from Felix's. She feels both hot and cold inside. He repulses her, yet she can't stop listening to him.

"I think Max saw Maja in the guesthouse once, many years ago."

Why is Felix telling her this?

Her thoughts return to what Felix had told her before breakfast. He would have Till brought to her today.

Why? Why is he helping them to meet again?

"Is it because of your project?" she finally asks, looking at Felix. "Is that why you're bringing Till here?"

"I don't want anything else to stand between us, Lisa. No secrets about your father or about how I introduced him to Maja, no Till. Something may still be drawing you to him. Meet with him. Talk to him. Think about whether you could ever forgive yourself if you didn't get together with him. It's only when you have really gotten over Till, Lisa . . . only then can we be happy together."

TWO YEARS EARLIER

Whoomp!

It was like an invisible padded hammer was slamming against the window from outside, making the glass curve inward.

Max instinctively jerked his arm up in front of his eyes to protect them from the shards of glass he was certain would fly at him. With a hiss and roar—muffled, but still breathtaking—the train thundered past on the other side of the glass. The hard, mechanical noise, interrupted every second or so when a gap between two train cars passed, made everyone look toward the window.

Max lowered his arm again when he realized the window wouldn't break. He could make out individual passengers as they shot by inside the cars—sitting, standing, reading newspapers.

Then the train was gone. The music that had been playing the whole time reemerged from the receding noise.

"Wow!"

Max turned to Felix, who was sitting with him and Till on a raised platform above the dance floor, from which they commanded a view over the club's low-ceilinged main room and the guests milling about and dancing below.

Felix grinned. "Did you know it was *my* idea to break through the subway wall?"

Max nodded. Respect.

"So," said Felix, picking up the thread of their conversation again after the shock wave from the passing train had interrupted them, "Irina didn't want to tell me who it was—and I wouldn't have asked her to if she hadn't described to me exactly what her girlfriend had told her."

They had been at the club for nearly an hour after leaving Irina's party.

"What did her girlfriend tell her?"

"She said she'd been asking everywhere, but no one could tell her anything about you."

"Tell who? Irina?"

"No, her girlfriend." Felix put his hands behind his head, laced his fingers, and leaned his head back into his hands. His elbows stuck out left and right like oversized ears. "No idea what she wants to know. Irina didn't want to tell me that, either—"

"What could she want to know?" interrupted Max.

"What, indeed?" asked Felix, raising his eyebrows. "But no, seriously . . . Irina says the girl is out of her mind. It's been going on for three months—she's obsessed with the idea of meeting you."

Max instinctively turned away from the dance floor so no one there could see his reaction. "Is she here?"

Most of the guests who had been at Irina's party had come here with them. It was the club's opening night, a friend of Felix's had done all the interiors, and word had gotten around at the party that the place was definitely worth checking out. Inside, it looked like a James Bond movie set, a kind of underground grotto, an impression that mainly came from the large water-filled basin in the middle of the main room, not to mention the window onto the subway.

"I believe so." Felix scanned the crush of dancers below them. "You want to meet her?" He laughed.

Max sighed.

Felix lowered his arms and leaned toward Max. "What did you do to get her so hot and bothered?"

"I don't even know who you're talking about," said Max.

"But it didn't come out of nowhere," Felix persisted. "Could there be something about you that Irina's friends gossip about . . . something I don't know? Some rumor getting them all excited?" His eyes sparkled. "Or is it the mere sight of you that drives women crazy?"

Max turned away from Felix. He hated talking about himself.

"Oh, it bothers you to talk about it, I see," Felix went on unremittingly. "But what am I supposed to tell the poor girl?"

"Nothing!" Max said, turning back to Felix with a scowl. "You don't have to tell her anything!"

"Irina made me swear to put in a good word with you, for her girlfriend. She's a nice girl, it seems. Irina's starting to worry about her."

"Why, for crying out loud? What the hell is this?" Max felt like someone was choking him.

"A hello, a friendly wave, a kind word," Felix suggested, clearly delighted to have the opportunity to torture Max. "What are you, a monster? Didn't you ever fall head over heels for someone?"

Max leaned back. Felix couldn't be serious.

"Should I do it for you, Max? Tell me what I should do. I'll come up with something myself, if you like . . . or get someone else to."

"Is this really about the girl?" Max said, fixing his gaze on Felix.

"Of course. Of *course!*" Felix clapped his hands together. "Why not? Not everyone can be a monster like you, let's face it."

What was he talking about?

"Really, Max, I'm at your service, in every respect, whatever I can do."

Max was tired, and Felix's words just sounded slimy to him. He gave in to an urge to yawn, just as a man in a garish jacket approached their table. Felix looked up at the new arrival. "Would you look at that, Niklas," he shouted to the man. "The kid's yawning! He's *bored!* Can you imagine? He's bored in *your* club!"

"And you?" asked Niklas, smiling and leaning down close to Felix.

Felix smirked and looked at Till for a moment. "Me? No! This place really is something, isn't it?" He looked at Max. "The window onto the subway? Even you were blown away when the first train went past! Tell him, Max. It makes Niklas happy when his guests are happy."

Max nodded—but Felix cut in before he could say a word. "Fantastic! And the music? What's that playing just now?" Felix went on without waiting for an answer. "And this glass?" He raised the rather unconventionally formed glass he was holding. "What is this? Grotto design?"

Niklas narrowed his eyes, unsure how to react to Felix.

"You know, Niklas"—Felix looked him straight in the eye—"if someone loved shit, then this place would be"—he leaned forward, convulsing like he was choking on something, as if he had to throw up, and Max saw tears of glee in Felix's eyes! He had his hand over his mouth, but to stop himself from *laughing*—"their El-do-ra-do! That's what you'd call it, right? They'd be in their *El Dorado!*"

Max gazed at Niklas, who seemed to be paralyzed in front of Felix's armchair.

"Am I not making myself clear, Niklas?"

Before Niklas could react, Felix jerked his glass to one side and the drink spilled out, splashing at Niklas's feet, spattering his pants.

Max swallowed. Felix's sudden change in mood had hit them with no warning.

"Hold on a second, Niklas! Wait!" said Felix, rising a little and leaning over the armrest of his chair even as Niklas was moving away. "It isn't just the club," he screamed after him. *"It's your whole life that's shit!"* He was so loud that Max clearly heard every word in spite of the music filling the room.

Felix sank back in his armchair.

In the same moment, Max noticed an attractive, well-dressed woman approaching their table. He guessed she was in her mid-thirties, and he saw her eyes meet Niklas's where he had halted, numb, a few steps away from their table.

"Sonja! Lovely to see you!" Felix stretched out both hands to her in greeting.

It was clear that she hadn't heard a word of what Felix had yelled at Niklas. When she reached their table, she was completely relaxed and her hands closed around Felix's. With a rapturous expression on her face, she leaned down to him, and for a moment, Max thought they were going to kiss and that she'd slide onto his lap. But then she just touched her cheek to his, first right, then left.

She straightened up again. "Everything okay, honey?" she said to Niklas, who just stood there, stone-faced.

"Let's go, Sonja," he started. But Felix had already laid the back of his hand against Sonja's thigh, next to the armrest of his chair.

She automatically turned away from Niklas and looked down at Felix again.

He smiled at her. "Have you got it with you, Sonja?"

"Of course!" She glanced up at Till and Max, as if to gauge the situation. Obviously, the stunned expression on Niklas's face had not completely escaped her.

"Here you go!" She reached into a small bag draped over one shoulder and took out a phone.

Felix beamed. "Do me a favor, Sonja?"

She tilted her head slightly, coquettish and playful, but at the same time leaving no doubt that she belonged with Niklas. A flirtatious glance was the most she had to offer Felix—even if his hand was still on her thigh.

"Call this number for me? Now?" Felix handed her a note with a number and signaled to her to lean down a little closer. As soon as she bent lower, he put one hand behind her neck and pulled her gently down to him. Max saw his lips part and his mouth close onto Sonja's. For a moment she closed her eyes, and the arm she had propped against the armrest buckled. Her stockinged thigh leaned against the armchair, and Max saw Felix's hand slide up her leg and under her skirt.

"Sonja!"

Niklas was back at the table in a flash, his eyes wide and his face distorted. But Felix had already released Sonja—she seemed almost sleepy, confused, not exactly herself. Felix's assault had evidently taken her completely by surprise.

Felix looked past her to Niklas. "You've got such a wonderful wife, Niklas," he smiled. "You'll *have* to forgive me . . . it was . . . uh . . . it was stronger than me."

Sonja looked at Niklas, her face now showing how shaken she was, and she took his hand.

"Niklas?" asked Felix.

But Niklas didn't turn back again. With Sonja's hand in his, he moved back down the ramp that led to the dance floor.

TWO YEARS EARLIER

Just then, the music cut out and the elaborate, indirect lighting was washed out by the glare of several floodlights. The guests on the dance floor turned around in bewilderment, and voices started to rise.

Max saw Felix stand up and step over to the railing at the edge of the platform, a few feet above the level of the dance floor. His powerful voice cut into the relative quiet. "Ladies and gentlemen, have you met the man we have to thank for this evening's entertainment?"

The faces of the people standing around below now turned to Felix. Smiling, benevolent faces.

"Isn't he one of a kind?" Felix called. "Niklas! Come back here, let me embrace you!"

In the meantime, Niklas had reached the dance floor and kept moving away from Felix. But Sonja had stopped on the ramp, cell phone at her ear.

"Oh, come on, Niklas. What's the matter? Afraid of little old me?" Felix spread his arms wide, beaming.

"Niklas! Niklas!" a number of the guests began to chant. They seemed almost infected by the wish to see Felix embrace Niklas.

Never, thought Max. *Never!*

Even as he thought it, he heard Sonja's voice. She still had the phone pressed to her ear as she turned back to Felix. "He's on the line," she called to him. "A Mr. Rittlinger."

"Rittlinger?" Felix raised his eyebrows and looked at Sonja in disbelief. "What does he want?"

She covered the mouthpiece and tottered back up the ramp. "He's from the bank."

"But what does he *want?*"

Sonja lifted the phone again. "Mr. Rittlinger? Yes, do you want to speak to Mr. von Quitzow?" With a look of alarm, she turned to Felix, her hand over the mouthpiece again. "He wants to speak to Niklas!"

Felix pulled a face. "Ouch," he winced. "Then you'd better put Niklas on."

Sonja suddenly sounded like a little girl. "Niklas!" She was back up on the platform now, and turned and gesticulated to Niklas down below on the dance floor. "Come here!" She held up the phone and pointed to it. "It's Mr. Rittlinger. From the bank." Then she spoke into the phone again. "He's coming, Mr. Rittlinger. He'll just be a moment."

As she spoke, she glanced repeatedly back to Niklas who, probably because he thought he had no other choice, had also turned and was now grimly ascending the ramp again.

He reached Sonja, and she handed him the phone. He looked at Felix and whispered, "Fuck you," before putting the phone to his ear. It was loud enough for Max to hear but low enough that neither Rittlinger on the phone nor the guests below on the dance floor caught it.

"Mr. Rittlinger?" Niklas asked into the phone.

Max kept his eyes on Felix, who stepped back from the railing and sank back into his armchair. Sonja stood beside the chair, her high spirits now completely evaporated. She too had heard clearly what Niklas had said to Felix.

"Are you Max Bentheim?"

Max jumped to his feet. Niklas was looking right at him.

"Yes?" What does he have to do with this?

"Yes, he's here," said Niklas into the phone. He listened, then turned to Felix. "What the hell is this?" he asked flatly, no longer angry, but as if something freezing cold had touched him.

"It's about the loan for the club, dear boy," Felix smiled. "I've taken it over . . ."

"Niklas?" Sonja was looking at her husband.

"And transferred ownership to Max," said Felix, finishing his sentence.

What?

Max threw his hands in the air. "What the hell? That's nonsense. I don't want it."

The words ran through Max like electricity. *I don't want it!*

"You don't want it?" Felix said, gazing at Max in surprise. He was the only one still calm.

Max shook his head. *No!*

"He doesn't want it." Felix looked back at Niklas. "Then you can keep it—for goodness sake."

He leaned forward and took the phone out of Niklas's hand.

"Rittlinger? Yes . . . great, thank you, no . . . forget Bentheim, Niklas is staying on. Yes." He ended the conversation and—still sitting, the phone still in his hand—spread his arms wide. "So, what about it, Niklas? Do I get my kiss now?" he said, loud enough for everyone to hear.

Max felt his own mouth open slightly. Niklas awkwardly approached Felix's armchair, leaned down, and put his arms around him.

But Felix locked eyes with Max over Niklas's shoulder. "See?" he said. "That works."

Just then, the lights dimmed again, and the music abruptly restarted, drowning out for everyone except Max and Niklas what Felix said over Niklas's shoulder. "What should I do, Max? Should I have Niklas's legs hacked off? Or have someone ram Niklas's own finger so far into his ear that it smashes his eardrum?"

TWO YEARS EARLIER

The words coming out of Felix's mouth hit Max like a kick in the stomach. For a moment, he had the feeling that a high-pitched whistle was blowing in his ear, as if his whole consciousness was crumbling. Before Max could react, Niklas jerked himself away from Felix, turned his back to the table, and, his legs strangely stiff, made his way back down the ramp. Till had left the platform when Sonja called Rittlinger.

"Max, wait!" Felix laid a hand on Max's arm to keep him in his seat. "What do you think? I was just joking around!"

Joking around? What kind of sick joke was that?

"I'll apologize in a minute, but . . ." Felix seemed to be hunting for the right words. "All I wanted to do was show you . . . all of this was just so that you could see that I could make him dance." He looked at Sonja walking away, Niklas hurrying after her. "I can make him dance," he repeated, and looked back at Max. "But you, Max—you can do it even better!"

"Bullshit!" He wanted to get away from Felix . . . but he remained seated.

"Your father always said that, Max."

"What?"

"That you were special. That you were capable of doing what few could. That you were able to achieve goals that others couldn't even *set*. That you understood connections, that you could make the important decisions—"

"Important for *what*? It's all just empty words!"

"No, it's not! It was his opinion that you could continue what he had begun!"

"Oh, really?"

Felix released his grip on Max's arm. "He was working on a book, Max, you know that. But it wasn't just any book . . . it was more like an invented *world*—" He looked Max in the eye, as if sizing him up. "He was working on a fictional universe. That's the expression we—your father and I—always used. And that universe isn't complete yet."

A fictional universe.

"You think this thing with Irina's girlfriend is just a coincidence?" Felix went on.

"What does *she* have to do with this?" Max looked around for a waiter to bring him a drink.

"She feels it too."

"That I'm something special?" Max nearly laughed out loud—and spotted a waiter at the same time. "Vodka, thanks." He made a sign. "A double." He nodded to the waiter, and let his gaze sweep through the club for a moment to avoid having to return his attention to Felix immediately. Could there be something to what Felix was saying? Max's thoughts turned involuntarily to Nina. At the wedding. Had she sensed it too?

"You can't let yourself fear it," he heard Felix say. "You have to let it happen, Max. I don't know exactly how hard that is; no doubt I lack your talents. But I know it's something you can fear. Some people are strong enough to let themselves be themselves. Others aren't. I imagine it's a task that could drive you to the limits of your endurance. But you can't give up! You can't rest until you are where you want to be. You can't simply accept what others want from you or recommend for you. You have to listen inside yourself, Max, go deep inside and find out if it's also what *you* want. Only then will you find the path to the goal."

Max exhaled audibly. "Find the path to the goal, let yourself be yourself—you should listen to what you're saying!" He leaned forward and shook Felix by the shoulders. "Man, that's such bullshit! It sounds like you've been on some New Age management training course!"

Felix laughed, but the sound he made when he laughed left no doubt that he was serious. "Maybe you're right. But I don't think so. I believe what your father told me about you."

Dad.

It was like someone taking an ice pick and smashing the point through the barrier that Max had allowed to form around himself.

"What?!" he shouted. "You think I don't know what you're up to? You're just messing with my head with all this crap because you want me to sell you the rights to my father's last books!"

Max knew he wanted no part of what Felix was trying to convince him of. He had no desire to be played for a fool.

Felix eyed him calmly. "Have you ever wondered what I need the rights for, Max? To make as much money as I can? Is that what you think?"

Max waved it off. "I can imagine what you're planning, and I have no interest at all in finding out if I'm right."

His answer didn't satisfy Felix. "Really, Max, come visit me and let me explain my plans to you—at least the start. But keep one thing in mind: I'm not trying to somehow scam the rights from you. If you let me have them, great. But I don't just want the rights. I want you too."

Me.

Felix nodded as he continued. "I'm not looking for a workhorse to help me do what I want to do. I don't need bean counters or yes-men, whose best quality is delivering exactly what I tell them to. I don't need people with mediocre ideas, old-school hacks, or flakes. What I need are *minds*. Minds that have perhaps only had one idea in their entire lives, but it was one hell of an idea. I need you, Max. Everything else is just empty words, empty promises, and claptrap."

Max looked at him. Felix's steel-gray eyes shone flatly. The skin was pulled tight over his cheekbones. He'd stopped blabbing, he'd stopped joking; he was finally being direct. His entire attention seemed to be focused on planting the thought in Max's head that he, Max, was something special, and that was *exactly why* Felix needed him for what he had started with Xavier.

"Well, then. I think I'll leave you boys to party on for a while." Felix stood up without waiting for a response from Max. "Staying up all night at my age . . ."

He extended his hand, and Max shook it. "See you later, Max."

"Later."

Max watched Felix descend the ramp to the dance floor and disappear among the guests.

Then Max sank back into his armchair. He was supposed to complete his father's work? Wasn't that what he had spent his whole life dreaming of—that he would finish what Xavier had begun?

TODAY

The electric motor that raises the door starts with a hum. The garage door jerks and rises slowly.

Henning steps back from the switch and climbs back into his car through the already-open door. He turns the key.

The motor of his Italian convertible purrs to life. He slips it into reverse and turns to look back over his shoulder, stretching his right arm along the backrest of the passenger seat. He eases back on the clutch until it starts to grab.

Then he sees them.

The garage door is still opening. The bottom of the door is less than three feet from the floor.

But . . .

The left corner of his mouth pulls up.

Through the half-open door Henning can see two legs standing in front of the garage. He presses the clutch to the floor again, and stomps on the gas at the same time. The motor howls.

What kind of idiot would stand right in front of his garage door?

"Hey!"

Loud.

Get out of the way, asshole, he thinks. *I'm in a hurry.*

Just then, the figure ducks under the rising garage door. But the body is still a silhouette against the bright morning light.

"Can't you see I'm leaving—" but Henning interrupts himself. "Konstantin!"

What's he doing here?

"Henning." Butz straightens up to his full height now that he's inside the garage. "Have you heard what's going on? On Alexanderplatz?"

Henning puffs out a breath. "I . . . sure, of course . . . I'm headed to the office." He turns to the other side to keep his eyes on Butz, who is now moving along the driver's side of the car. "Sorry, Konstantin, if I . . . but . . . what are you *doing* here? Is something wrong with Claire?"

Butz looks down at Henning. "Got a minute?" His left eye squints a little.

"Now?" Henning looks out through the windshield at the garage wall in front. "No . . . let's, uh . . . let's talk on the phone." He draws a breath. "But what's up? You coming here—is something the matter with Claire?"

"Why?" Butz's eyes are fixed on him.

"Listen, Konstantin, I don't want to sound unfriendly, but I'm really in a hurry. Today of all days." Henning's mouth is twisted as he shakes his head.

Butz leans his hands on the car door. "I've just come from Baumann."

"Who?" Henning looks up in surprise. "Baumann?"

"Baumann?" Henning laughs. "Baumann *what*, Butz? Baumann—Bowman, Baumann—Plowman, Baumann—Bauhaus?" He turns around again, checks behind. "Betty's here. I'm sure she'd be happy to talk to you about Claire." Without looking at Butz, he points to a door at the side of the garage and revs the motor. The garage door is now all the way up. "Call me, okay?" The car starts to roll.

"Willi Baumann, Henning. Frederik Barkar's trainer." Butz keeps his eyes on Henning. The car stops and Henning turns to face him again. "He says you told him what Barkar had to do."

Now he has Henning's full attention. The man looks suddenly pale. His long fingers drum nervously on the steering wheel. "*That* Baumann," Henning mumbles. "Sure." His eyes dart here and there. "Look, Butz . . . Konstantin . . . I—"

Henning takes one hand off the wheel.

"Why don't you climb in?" Henning's words are indistinct, like his mind is on something else. "I'll drive you into the city, and we'll talk on the way. Okay?"

Butz has moved back to the wall of the garage.

"My car's outside, Henning. I don't need a lift."

"Ha!" Henning's face twists. "Of course not." For a moment, he sits indecisively behind the wheel. The motor idles, a low throb. "Should we go inside?" Henning raises his eyebrows. "Or you can jump in and we'll do a lap around the block?" He lowers his voice a little. "I'd rather not go inside—because of Betty, you know . . ."

Butz feels something warm on his bottom lip. He reaches up and dabs at the spot, coming away with a little blood on his finger. He has chewed so hard on his lip that he opened a small wound.

"Okay," he says. "Let's drive around the block, Henning." He walks in front of the car to get to the passenger door.

Suddenly it's like a jet engine firing up in the garage.

Butz automatically turns his head toward the sound and locks his gaze on Henning's face—the man's mouth, the ruddy cheekbones, the strangely clouded eyes. Henning's arms are straight on the wheel, pressing his upper body back.

He must have slipped it into first.

Butz sees the car *leap* at him.

A rolled-up garden hose is on the wall, a wheelbarrow leans against the wall below it. In what is more a reflex than a conscious movement, Butz snatches down the hose with one hand and tips the wheelbarrow with the other. The sheet metal screams as the convertible's hood slams into the wheelbarrow.

RrroaaARRRR

Butz can see Henning's face, the rigid jaw. The motor still screams, the wheelbarrow jumps and screeches. Butz leans forward and his hands slap down on the red hood. The sheet metal is vibrating—the wheelbarrow's handles have dug into the radiator. Butz is pinned against the wall. The hose is in front of his knees, but the wheelbarrow is the only thing stopping the car from tearing into Butz's legs, smashing his bones.

He jerks his head up. The motor roars.

Henning's face seems to have elongated. His entire upper body is now leaning forward, and he is pressing the gas pedal to the floor. The squeal of the tires on the smooth concrete floor pierces Butz's ears but the tires can't get a grip. The exhaust fumes swirling in the air almost take Butz's breath away. The room around him seems to be shimmering.

Ssshhrriieeeeeek—the hood of the car buckles and the radiator jumps four inches closer, crushing the garden hose against Butz's legs.

Butz feels his kneecap being driven upward by the pressure and how his torso, arched forward over the hood, is forced upright, twisting strangely. His left arm shoots up of its own accord, his right hangs slackly. In his knee, something pops and splits.

He can see what's coming, how the bumper will cut his legs off at the knee, how he'll collapse on the stumps he has left.

He feels the butt of his gun in his hand. He whips it out and aims the black barrel through the windscreen, straight at Henning.

"TURN OFF THE FUCKING CAR!"

The wheelbarrow buckling, the clattering roar of the motor. Butz feels his eyes bulging, then one eye squinting.

BLAAAAM!

The shot momentarily drowns out the sound of the motor. The bullet shatters the windscreen and slams into the upholstery next to Henning's chest.

"The next one goes in your head!" The words come out of his mouth like popcorn from a pot.

Their eyes meet through the shattered windscreen. Henning's eyes are burning, his teeth bared. Butz sights along the barrel of his pistol but his eyes won't focus properly. He can't feel his knee anymore. His left leg is crushed against the hot radiator.

I'll shoot you dead, he thinks, training the gun now away from Henning's chest to a point right between his eyes.

For a second, he thinks that his hearing has gone—then he feels the pressure slacken, the car sag, and understands that the roar of the motor has stopped. Henning has eased off the accelerator.

Butz has the impression that the car is a chained-up dog that has suddenly lost interest in him. But he keeps the gun raised. Henning's face is dripping sweat.

"Why did you tell Baumann to set Barkar onto Claire?"

Butz's legs are trembling. Henning stares at him, speechless, as if drained dry by the attempt to crush Butz against the garage wall.

"I don't have to kill you anymore, Henning. I can just shoot you in the shoulder."

"Felix wanted it."

Butz feels the pistol swing back to Henning's face, as though it has a will of its own.

Felix?

"What's Felix got to do with this?"

"BUTZ!"

It is a high-pitched shriek, over the idling motor. Butz glances to the right, to the door leading from the garage directly into the house. Someone has opened it and is standing at the threshold. One hand now flat over her mouth, the other reaching in his direction, as if pointing at him.

Claire's sister.

Betty.

But she isn't pointing at him. She is aiming a small revolver at him. Butz swings back to face Henning. He sees Henning's mouth deform into a smile. But it can't completely erase the creases that have engraved his face in the last two minutes.

TWO YEARS EARLIER

"He ridicules me! He crucifies me in front of everyone!" Quentin blurted. "He enjoys it. He likes to see someone go down when he attacks them!" Droplets of spit flew in Max's direction as Quentin spoke.

Max took an instinctive step back, but Quentin just moved closer. He was worried Quentin might grab him by the lapels of his jacket and push him back against the wall.

"Don't let Felix fool you," Quentin screamed. "He's schmoozing you and humiliating me!"

Till stepped up beside them, and Quentin turned to face him for a moment, then turned back to Max again. "Do you believe what he says? Do you think I don't know what he's planning?"

Max and Till had just reached street level, having climbed up the cement stairs exiting the club. The sky was already growing light. Quentin must have spent the entire night waiting for them there. Max could see—almost feel—that Quentin was torn apart by the thoughts popping in his mind. Max felt sorry for Quentin, but this onslaught had taken Max utterly by surprise. He had no idea how to respond.

"Look," said Till, "it's Quentin, right? I know we hardly know each other—"

"Keep your bullshit away from me!" Quentin yelled at Till. He was shivering from head to toe. Quentin turned back to Max. "Tell this half-wit to keep his mouth shut. I'm not finished!"

Max nodded to Till and closed his eyes for a second. "Okay, Quenny, sure."

Quentin's fingers, which had been sticking out like spikes, suddenly closed into fists. His arms were stretched down his sides at full length, as if cramped in that position. "Nothing's *okay*, man. FUCK!"

Quentin had been screaming at him before, but now the distortion that entered his voice made Max wince. He reached out cautiously with one hand and touched Quentin on the shoulder. Max felt his body recoil, as if he had rammed a knife into him. "Quentin, take it easy," Max whispered, "I know what it's like. Let Felix talk, it . . . it's not important."

Quentin's head, which had been tilted down, slowly came up again. His eyes were smoldering coals, and he seemed to be battling his way back to the surface—the present moment—from the depths he'd lost himself in. As if some dark power was pressing down on him, Quentin didn't raise his head completely. Instead, he turned his gaze obliquely up at Max. "Ask him, Max. Ask him what the deal is with Nina. Ask Felix about Nina!" he said.

Who? What? Max didn't understand.

"Nina. The girl with the brown hair. At the wedding. Didn't she sleep with you? Ask Felix what he knows about that!"

TWO YEARS EARLIER

Almost an entire day passed, then Till couldn't hold Max back any longer.

"It's not like we have to force our way in," Max had said. "We say you want to take a look at the company, that's all. And it's true, right?"

Till had nodded. *Sure . . .*

"Then we ask if it's okay to drop in and see Felix for a minute. I'm certain he'll meet us. Then I casually drop Nina's name into the conversation. And we see how he reacts."

They'd been sitting and waiting to see Felix for nearly an hour. They were in a huge hall on the first floor of the publisher's building. It was an opulent ballroom containing just three or four tables, where some of the publishing house's more extravagant productions were on display. Till made a cursory inspection of the various editions. A glossy volume about Persian carpets, another on maps, a third covering construction plans from the seventeenth and eighteenth centuries. They were high-gloss coffee-table tomes. Open, the largest of them took up a good square yard.

Max had no interest in the books. He'd found a place to sit on an upholstered bench by a window and was studying the fresco on the ceiling.

"Mr. Bentheim, Mr. Anschütz?"

A secretary appeared at the double door leading out of the hall. She was blonde with perfect skin and freshly applied lipstick. "Would you follow me, please?" Her smile was at once friendly and a little mischievous, as if to hint that she already knew what you were thinking when you looked at her.

Max and Till followed her along a corridor that led to the office area, and which—like the hall they had just left—was decorated with a ceiling fresco of a picturesque, clouded sky above a wintry boulevard.

"Here we are." The secretary stepped aside to let them enter an office. Felix's office.

"Max!" Felix threw his arms wide. He wore a crisp blue-and-white striped shirt. His sleeves were rolled up and he seemed to be in a good mood. "Till . . ." He shook their hands. "Shall I close the window?" The enormous double windows stood open, and the noise of the traffic reached them even at this height. The hustle and bustle and beeping of horns from a side street off Unter den Linden sounded like a mix of delivery vans, busy waiters, and hungry cats.

"Sure, why not?" Max flopped into an armchair in front of the enormous but tidy desk. "It's okay if I sit, isn't it?"

The two panes of the window slammed together loudly, and Felix turned around. "Coffee, water, tea? Something stronger? Whatever you like."

Till glanced at Max and noticed that the secretary was still standing in the doorway, no doubt to take their orders. He raised his hands. "Nothing for me, thanks."

"What? Not even coffee?" Max smiled at Till.

Felix looked to the secretary. "Bring us a bottle of champagne, Merle. The 1956. That should please Mr. Bentheim."

The young woman disappeared. Felix came back around the desk and half sat on the edge, one foot dangling, the other flat on the floor. "So, what's up?" He was looking at Max. It didn't seem to bother him that Till was still standing.

"Till wanted to take a look at your place here," said Max, drumming his fingers on the armrest.

Felix turned his attention to Till. "Really? Are you in the industry? Max didn't tell me that."

Till propped his hands against the back of the second armchair in front of the desk. "No, I'm still working on my thesis. But it's true. I would like to look around the place. The books in the hall were certainly remarkable."

Felix looked at him for a moment in silence. Then he turned back to Max. "Right now? Should we start right away or wait for Merle to return with the champagne?" He slipped a finger over the knot in his Bordeaux-red tie and loosened it a little. The top button of his shirt appeared, already undone.

Max glanced at Till. "Shall we wait?"

Till nodded. What a stupid cat-and-mouse game. Why didn't Max just come out and say it? They were here to ask Felix about Nina.

For a moment, no one said anything. Max looked past Felix and out the window, Felix didn't take his eyes off Max, and Till got the impression that of the three of them, he was the one least responsible for breaking the silence.

Merle reentered the room pushing a small, silver cart with three wide-rim glasses and a large champagne bucket containing a green and gold champagne bottle buried in a mountain of crushed ice. "Should I open it, or will you?" she asked Felix.

"I'll do it," said Felix, moving toward her. "Thank you." The glasses tinkled softly as he took over the cart from her and steered it back to the desk. "Sooo . . ." He took his place on the desk again and began peeling back the foil on the bottle.

"So, is it true you asked her, or encouraged her, to take care of me?"

Till looked across at Max, who clearly couldn't hold himself in check any longer, his piercing eyes fixed on Felix.

"Her *who*?" Without looking at Max, Felix continued working on the champagne bottle.

"Doesn't matter who." Max's voice had grown husky. "Did you ask anyone to do that?"

Felix puffed out his cheeks, clearly amused. "What makes you think I'd do something like *that*."

"Also doesn't matter. Tell me!"

BANG! The cork flew out of the bottle and hit the window opposite Felix. Felix now leaned forward quickly, pouring the frothing liquid into the glasses.

He smiled. Till could see Max winding up at the lack of a straight answer from Felix. But what else could he do? Stand and grab Felix by the collar? Instead, Max took the glass that Felix had poured for him and raised it in the air. "Right. Cheers!" And without waiting for a response, he downed its contents.

Felix glanced at Till, now also holding a glass. "Cheers." Like Max, Felix drank it down in one draft. Till sipped his.

"Good, isn't it?" Felix leaned back and looked at Max.

Max set his glass back on the cart. "Excellent."

Felix reached for the bottle. "A little more, Till?"

"I'm okay." The champagne was very good, dry as sandpaper and fresh as a field of mint, but Till wasn't in a champagne mood.

A tinkle of glasses; Felix refilled his and Max's glasses and clinked his against Max's, which still sat on the cart. "The last time

I saw you, I said you should come and visit me," he said. "It's nice to see you here."

Max didn't touch his glass. He inhaled sharply. "That's not an answer," he said.

"Answers, answers," Felix laughed. "What kind of answers do you want, my boy? What I did or didn't do, or could have, or want, or can—what does it matter? What do you want? What do you want to know? What do you want to do, to achieve? Are you angry with me? Do you want to take a swing at me? How do you see that happening? What's the point? Are you sure you're not at least a little muddled? That you simply know far too little? That you have to understand what's even at stake before you start puffing yourself up, asking questions, spitting out demands? What's next? 'If you don't answer me before the bottle's empty, I'll . . .' You'll what? Stand up and leave? Then go! I can't stop you!"

Felix looked at Till. "Or maybe we can both try to keep him here?" Then he turned back to Max, who was listening to him with a frown. "What's the matter? Are Till and I in cahoots? Did he bring you here, even though you think it was your decision? Why don't you finally wake up, Max. At the rate you're going, you'll never get anywhere!"

He raised the glass to his lips and again drained it. He looked at his two guests, his expression now frank.

"Did you or didn't you?" Max's hands were clenched over the ends of the armrests. He clearly had not let Felix's blather break his concentration.

Felix set his glass on the desk.

"You remember what we spoke about the last time we met?"

"You want the rights to Dad's last books."

"And what for?"

"To make money, I'd say."

Felix leaned back, still on the edge of his desk. "There, you see? You've got completely the wrong idea of what this is all about. It might be true that I could generate a little profit from your father's books. But what difference does that really make? When it comes down to it, this publishing house costs me a lot of money. Money I only have at my disposal because my wife remains a partner in her family's businesses and finances this whim of mine."

"That doesn't mean you don't want to finally clear your debts," said Max. "Maybe you're hoping *that's* what you'll get out of my father's last books."

Felix shook his head. "I have so much money I can paper the walls with it, Max."

"Then why do you want the rights?"

Felix looked Max up and down. "So that no one else can spirit them away from me? Hmm? How would that be? After all, I own the rights to all your father's other work already."

Max glared at him.

"No, you're right," Felix relented. "There is another reason."

Till swallowed the last of his champagne and placed his glass next to Max's on the cart.

"Xavier told me about his final manuscripts," Felix said. "He was very proud of them. He believed that in his final works he had managed to achieve what he had only hinted at in his earlier books.

"Oh, really?"

"He believed there were things he had only touched on tentatively before, and that he had been able to push these to an extreme."

"Like what, for example?"

Again, Felix fixed Max with his gaze but did not immediately answer.

"Come on, Felix," Max insisted.

"Do you know that feeling? When a story takes over and you can't stop thinking about it?" Felix asked. "When you can't stop reading, even though you should have been asleep hours earlier because you've got an important meeting the next day? When finishing a chapter's like leaving an open wound because the next installment isn't coming out for another week?"

Max pursed his lips.

"There are many techniques in use that aim to have just this effect on the reader. You may have heard of them. And your father, Max, more or less catapulted these into a new dimension."

"What techniques, Felix?"

"The techniques you use to make a reader addicted to a story."

"Addicted."

Felix now seemed more serious than before. The laugh that had been lurking underneath now seemed completely forgotten. "He didn't want to betray any details to me. But these techniques—the laws of suspense, you might say—well, it's still uncharted territory. And I believe that once Xavier had thrown himself and all his energy into this field, he quickly stumbled onto some extremely interesting results."

"So, you're looking for . . . *what?* To maximize your customers' addiction? Is that it, Felix? Despite what you said a moment ago, it really *is* about selling as many books as possible? Right?" Now it was Max's turn to laugh in derision. "You sound like a dealer who wants to get his greedy fingers on some particularly good junk because he knows he can sell it for a profit."

"It's not about the money, Max. I already said that."

"Then what is it about?"

Felix looked down at Max thoughtfully. Then he pushed himself up from his perch on the desk, walked to the window, and looked out. The street noise still reached them faintly.

Beyond the glass, Till could see a Gründerzeit office building across the street. "Did you notice that in the last weeks before he disappeared, your father changed?" Felix asked without turning around to them.

"Yes, I did." Max straightened perceptibly in his armchair.

"That's what it's about, Max. You're absolutely right. It's not directly about the addiction. That's just the form, you could say. The means to an end. The end is something else."

TWO YEARS EARLIER

"It was one particular concept that changed your father, Max—an idea that he took very seriously indeed."

They had left the office and gone to another room where a buffet was set up with cold dishes, fruit, bread, and cut vegetables.

"It was an idea that convinced him that he was doing the right thing by working for me."

"Well, then," said Max, looking at Felix over the buffet, "tell us what the idea was." His eyes gleaming, he glanced at Till.

Pointing with his thumb, Felix indicated a flip chart on a stand, set up across the room from the buffet. "Then I'll need that."

"Go for it." Max grinned, and helped himself to a plate for the buffet.

"Okay." Felix set his own plate down on the sideboard and stepped over to the flip chart. "The basic concept is very simple." He picked up one of the heavy markers sitting in the holder below the chart and with firm strokes drew a forked line on the paper and drew arrows at the end of each line.

"The idea assumes that I am able to choose between two notions. I can either believe that I can choose freely, that I have free will, and I am my own master. Or I can believe that this sense of freedom is an illusion, that I can't freely decide at all, and everything I do is predetermined by factors outside my control."

He scratched a couple of words at the point of each arrow, and then stepped aside.

"Like this, okay? At any given time, I can choose whether I act as a free man, so to speak, or as an unfree man. That is, I can look at what I do either as an expression of my will or as an expression of . . . what? . . . of something like nature or some higher power, which I'm also part of."

"Okay," said Max.

"Good then . . ."

Felix turned back to the flip chart and added two curves to his sketch.

"Let's say that at one particular moment, I decide I'm 'free,' but in the very next moment I can once again choose between the two options. Right?"

"Right."

"Okay," Felix took a step toward them. "But let's think about this for a moment." He looked at his sketch. "Isn't there a problem here? If I've chosen the 'not free' option and the very next moment can again choose between 'free' and 'not free,' then what does it mean that I chose 'not free'?"

He looked at them again.

"Isn't it rather the case that I'm really only able to choose 'not free' if I continue to be 'not free' afterward? So, I no longer have the choice between the two options!"

He crossed out one of the curves.

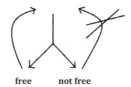

free   not free

"This is the only way it makes sense, right? Only if the way back is cut off to me after I've chosen 'not free'—that is, if I'm really 'not free' afterward—only then can the choice between 'free' and 'not free' even exist, right?"

Felix paused. Till's thoughts wavered a little. He wasn't sure if he was ready to admit that Felix was right, but he had to admit that the way he explained it made sense so far.

"But in reality—and this is the key point—in reality, the way back is NOT cut off at all. At any given moment, we can make a new choice between 'free' and 'not free.'"

Till nodded. Clearly.

"So, we have to draw our diagram like this," said Felix, turning over to a fresh page of the flip chart and quickly producing a new sketch.

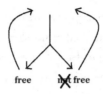

"Or like . . ." Again, a new page, a new sketch.

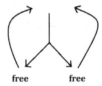

"This."

He stepped aside. "But this quickly reveals that the idea is nonsense. If I can only choose between two identical options, then I have no choice at all, and am therefore *not* free to choose at all. To put it another way . . ."

Felix turned back to his sketch and modified it.

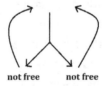

"We have to look at it like this, or . . ." He flipped the sheet back and with a powerful stroke of the marker drew a simple straight line on the clean white paper.

"Like this." He tossed the marker back into the tray he'd taken it from. "Right?"

Obviously satisfied with his brief presentation, he returned to Till and Max at the buffet. Max, in the meantime, had set his plate down. "That was the idea that changed my father?"

Felix smiled. "It convinced him that it was right to give up what we call—in short—the illusion of freedom." Felix picked up his plate and helped himself to the different berries sorted in bowls on the table. "But that's not all. He was also convinced that it was time to open other people's eyes to this."

"To the idea that they were caught in an illusion of freedom, as you put it," said Max.

Felix nodded.

"That's why you want his books." Max seemed to have forgotten about Till completely. He was fixated on Felix, but Till could not shake a sense that Felix was only playing with Max.

"That's it, my boy. That's why I want to have the rights from you. At the same time, though, seeing through the illusion of freedom is just the first step." With obvious relish, Felix tipped a spoonful of berries into his mouth and chewed.

Till narrowed his eyes. The first step? And then? What came after that?

. . .

When did they start lighting the fires . . . see how the flames are blown around as I drive past . . .

Whooooooooooooossssssssssshhhhhh . . .

But it's not even dark yet. How late is it? Just before ten . . . and warm . . .

Whooooooooooooossssssssssshhhhhh . . .

There's one by each little fire . . .

And who's keeping an eye on them?

No one in sight. Perhaps sitting back there in the field?

Or in one of the other cars cruising around here . . .

Those are old fuel drums, aren't they?

Why doesn't anyone clear them away? The drums stand around the whole day, and no one bothers . . .

Or now?! Why doesn't anyone clean up around here?

Come in with a few patrol cars, load it up with girls . . . same thing tomorrow . . .

I'd like to see how long they'd stand around here if the cops did that. No, they don't want *to get rid of them. They want them here.*

No one has a problem with it.

It hasn't been this way for long . . . but it's growing.

There. Another one.

See the flames, the way they twist and flicker? The way the orange tips flare up out of the drums, the glow lighting up one side of the girls . . .

What do I look like to them?
A big, black car . . .
Whooooooooooooossssssssssshhhhhh . . .
Zooming past.
Fine.
I can turn ahead.
I'm in the right place.

TWO YEARS EARLIER

"The first step . . . what's that supposed to mean?" Till asked.

Max had also picked up on it.

"Quid pro quo." Felix turned to the door, where Merle had appeared with a message about a telephone call that needed his urgent attention. "Quid pro quo. Let's talk about whether you're going to give me the rights, and then I can show you what your father's books really contain. But I can tell you this much already, Max: if we unleash *that*, then nothing will ever be the same again—not just here but around the world." With that, he turned and left the room with Merle.

Till sat on one of the chairs scattered around the room, balancing a plate of cold roast beef on his knee. "So, what does the one have to do with the other?" He was looking at Max, who was still loading his plate at the buffet. "People get excessively addicted to a particular story, and because of that they're supposed to come to the conclusion that their belief that they can choose freely is an illusion? How is that supposed to work? Or have I got it all wrong."

Max, chewing, looked sidelong at Till. "If you can't stop reading . . . that's exactly it, isn't it? A phenomenon of weak will, or something like that. You want to stop, but you *can't*. Or better yet, you don't really *want* to stop at all, because if you did . . . I haven't got the slightest idea. Gambling addicts, sex addicts, workaholics, it all has to be related . . ."

"Yes, but *how* exactly?" asked Till, raising his voice.

"How would I know?" Max said, annoyed now, his voice rising. "Ask Felix, not me!"

He turned back to the buffet.

"Did you already know what Felix had in mind?" Till carved a slice of beef from the chunk on his plate. "Not in detail, but the broad strokes?"

"That it had something to do with what he calls the 'illusion of freedom'?"

"Yeah." Till tried to read the look on his friend's face. Then suddenly, it occurred to him. "*That's* the reason you won't sell him the rights, isn't it? Because you don't want him to destroy the illusion?"

Max's eyes wandered beyond Till to the window.

But Till wasn't finished. "Is that it? Is it that you think you can find a way to cope with the guilt for your father's death *without* accepting Felix's ideas about not being free?"

The words came out of Till's mouth softly and rapidly, almost without him realizing what he'd said. But he sensed he was heading in the right direction. If Max had been unable to make a free choice, then he wasn't guilty. At the same time, Till was well aware that he himself was inseparably bound to Bentheim's death, that the guilt weighing on Max was a fraction of the guilt that he himself had had to live with since that afternoon. He was the one who had slammed the door behind Bentheim after all. He was the one who had left the man in that underground dungeon. He was the one who caused him, in his desperation, to throw himself against the door until his head was bloody and his skull staved in.

"*My* guilt?" Max eyes were again sharp and fixed on Till's face. "Are you sure *I'm* guilty for what *you* did?"

"You said you'd seen that ward in the hospital. You said he was part of it all—that he'd kill you if you didn't defend yourself." Till hissed the words, but he knew that Max was speaking the truth, that everything Till was constantly trying to drive out of his head would never have happened without Till himself being part of it. Max may well have said—and lied about—too much, but Max was also the kind of person who talked and talked and talked; it was he, Till, who had *acted*.

"I thought I had to help you, Max," Till whispered, distraught, turning his eyes to the floor. "But maybe you're right."

Max touched his arm. "No, Till," he had lowered his voice again. "It's not that simple. Your guilt, my guilt. It happened, that's a fact. But not because anyone forced us to do it. It happened because that's how we *wanted* it!"

Was that true? Had Till truly wanted it that way? Or wasn't it rather Max's *will* that he had carried out?

"It's true," he heard Max say. "I'm guilty of the death of my father. But I will never accept that I acted involuntarily, that I'm not responsible for it—"

He turned around. They could hear voices approaching in the hallway. The next moment, the door flew open. It was Felix, with Henning at his side.

"Henning Fahlenkamp . . . you know Till," said Felix, in a good mood. "Henning's going to show you around."

Henning bowed very slightly toward Max, then shook Till's hand.

"Oh, by the way, Till," Felix said. "You said you were interested in working for us, didn't you? Are we still on the lookout for editors, Henning?"

"Oh, yes. Definitely," Henning murmured, glancing at Till.

"Creating the fictional universe that we generate from Bentheim's work . . ." said Felix, turning nimbly toward Till, "sequels, prequels, spin-offs, translations into new media and different genres—it all demands an exceptionally sensitive feel for the huge range of settings, narrative structures, characters, histories, and backstories. No doubt Henning can explain all of it far better than I can. But what do you think? Wouldn't that grab you?"

Henning had moved aside, and Till was now face-to-face with Felix. The offer had come so suddenly, so out of the blue, that for a moment he was left speechless.

"Well certainly, uh, of course, no doubt it could be interesting," he stammered, and looked to Max, who seemed a little taken aback. Evidently, he had not reckoned with Felix suddenly approaching Till like this.

"We would have to think about precisely where you can be of most use to us," said Henning, sounding more formal than he had at their first meeting. "We're developing this side of the business even as we speak. But there are certainly openings among the outliners and what we call the exporters, and there's the opportunity to take part in the think tank, definitely." He glanced at Felix, who nodded encouragingly. "That's where we collect ideas about how the Bentheim universe can be further expanded and developed. Or with the narratologists, who focus on maximizing the addiction factor—"

"Take your time, think it over," said Felix, interrupting Henning suddenly, "and let me know when you've come to a decision."

"Really, it sounds very exciting—"

"I know you're in the middle of your thesis," said Felix, cutting him off, a touch impatient now, apparently because Till should have just held his tongue after he'd told him to think it over. "But if I were you, I wouldn't let this opportunity slip by. You can pick up where you left off with your thesis in a year or two. If you're still interested."

He raised his eyebrows challengingly and looked at Till.

"Yes. Maybe that wouldn't be such a bad idea," Till said, with another glance at Max.

"You see!" Felix almost shouted, also turning to Max. "Your friend isn't against the opportunity at all! Don't be such a spoilsport, Max. We're working on exciting stuff here. You should really consider selling us the rights! And I can tell you this: only when we have all the rights in one place will we be able to turn this fictional universe into what your father had in mind!"

Is he making me this offer just to get to Max? Till wondered.

Max waved it off. "Let's drop it for today, Felix."

But Felix took a step toward Max and hooked one arm under his. "Look, that thing with Nina, that I'm supposed to have put her up to something. You could only have heard that from her, am I right?"

Till, confused, looked to Henning, and realized that Betty's husband, otherwise deliberately indifferent and blasé, suddenly seemed tense.

"So, what did she say, exactly?" Felix asked. Till looked uneasily at Max.

Max's eyes met Till's, and Till could see alarm in them. Max had told Till about how Felix had abused Niklas the night before, after Till left the platform. And it was obvious that Max only now understood the danger he had put Nina in by confronting Felix like this. Max knew that Felix had induced her to come on to him at the wedding. But if Felix went looking for whoever had revealed that to Max, he would turn to Nina—and no one else.

. . .

Whoooooooooooooossssssssssshhhhhh . . .

There she is . . .

Stupid headlights, blinding . . .

See how the flames in the drums make the shadows dance? See the light illuminate the girl's face and make her seem to flicker? See the reflection of the fire glittering in her eyes . . .

She has to . . . be standing out on the street, or . . . or I won't be able to swing the car around again before I hit the drum . . .

Whoooooooooooooossssssssssshhhhhh . . .

Did you see her? As I drove past, she turned her head and looked at the car.

She said something!

Her lips moved.

Did you see the flames dancing behind her?

She had her arms extended . . . she was waving you over . . .

Isn't she freezing in those clothes?

But no . . . it's warm today . . . only in here . . . this damn air conditioner . . . it's only cold in here. Out there, they're sweating; out there, the sweat is running down between their thighs . . .

It's dark and a warm wind is blowing.

And the clothes cling to their bodies.

They want you to pull up next to them.

Did you see her face, the one who waved to you?

Where did they find one like that?

What was that in her face? Innocence?

How can she look so innocent and still be standing here?

Where in the world can things be so dire that they send girls like that here, to stand on the streets?

It's a hot wind stirring the leaves on the trees . . . making the flames flicker and the girls' hair swirl.

Up ahead, another one.

Uhhhhhhh . . .

Her!

She's the one!

You can turn up ahead . . .

Okay . . . good . . . slow now . . .

There she is . . . exactly where you need her to be, out on the street, a few steps from the drum. You don't need to go so fast . . . fifty is plenty . . . all you have to do is drive straight ahead . . . see? She's looking at you . . .

Oh man oh man oh man . . .

What . . .

She's looking you in the eye.

Now!

The steering wheel.

This is what you have to do! Jerk the wheel around!

You have to swerve out of the lane!

Don't you get it?!

She's standing just right!

Ram her with the car! Ram the bumper into her body!

You don't want to?

That's just it, asshole!

That's why you have to do it!

BECAUSE YOU DON'T WANT TO!

If you wanted to do it, you wouldn't have to!

Her eyes—she throws up her hands—the headlights blind her—
she stumbles back . . .
The drum . . .
The sparks . . .
Aaahh!

TODAY

Frederik spins around. Claire holds onto him tightly.

Behind them, several vehicles—police cars, ambulances—speed one after the other out of one of the side streets leading to the public square. They race straight across the pavement, heading toward the railway line, the tower, the dust.

Four vehicles, six . . .

The lights on top of the cars spin and flash, breaking against the dim facades of the surrounding buildings. The sirens blend into a shrill din. Claire sees an officer waving and shouting something from the passenger window of a patrol car. The patrol car careens past, and the next and the next. They stumble back, making room.

The cloud swallows the vehicles, their brake lights glowing as if through fog. Then there is only the sound of the sirens fading, muffled, invisible, mechanical . . . nearly dead.

Claire leans against Frederik. She can't think straight. She feels the cloud of dust envelop them, the fine particles covering her skin, her hair, her eyes. The cloud of dust is warm and something metallic-tasting coats her lips.

She automatically wipes one hand across her eyelids. She holds her hand in front of her, looking at her fingers, but can only see them blurred and hazy through the fine fog of dust. Then she feels Frederik start to move again.

They run toward the street from where the emergency vehicles have just come and reach the corner just as more arrive, racing toward them. This time, the string doesn't let up. The air shimmers with alarms, sirens, the noise of engines. Claire can make out the men's helmets and tense faces as they roar past. In the distance, a tinny voice can be heard, electronically amplified, urgent, unintelligible.

They run, holding tightly to each other. Claire's lungs are burning from the dust, which now fills the entire street between the buildings. High above them, unseen through the cloud, the sky is graying toward dawn.

"Here!"

Frederik pulls her into a building entryway.

The air in there is better. The dust hasn't yet completely filled the entrance. She reaches for Frederik's other hand, wraps her arms around him, presses close. She realizes he is trying to protect her body with his.

For a moment, they stand like that in a tight embrace, and the pandemonium just a few steps away seems very distant, unable to hurt them.

Claire's cell phone starts to ring—once, twice, a third time. She slips her hand into her jacket pocket to retrieve it and stares at the display.

Has the dust damaged her eyes?

Columns of numbers stream down over the display.

What is that?

It rings.

She presses the button, presses the phone to her ear.

"Hello!"

Simultaneously, she hears a cracking sound behind her and sees Frederik, his head above hers, turn toward the street . . .

. . . and she knows they have found them.

They have used Claire's phone to track them.

She tries desperately to hold Frederik to her; now she's the one protecting *him*.

"FREDERIK BARKAR!"

How can it be that she has only gotten to know him now, now that it's too late?

Claire spins around. It's the men from Frederik's building.

She hardly hears the shot. But she feels the bullet slam into the plaster in the wall beside her. Then Frederik has pushed her through the open door that leads into the building, along a hallway and down a set of stairs.

Claire hears their pursuers breaking through the door. Her heart seems to be fluttering more than beating. She dashes along the basement corridor as fast as she can, side by side with Frederik. Suddenly, over their own rapid steps and the shouts of the men chasing them, she hears it . . . squeaking.

Still distant, but a squeaking as if entire mountains of cockroaches are being bulldozed.

A squeaking far down the corridor they are charging along.

Coming toward them.

TODAY

"I'll call Felix and tell him you brought Till, okay?"

Lisa looks past Till to the man who has brought him to her. He's still standing at the open front door. The man squints at her, and wraps his arms around his chest.

"You can go. It's okay."

The man snuffles, lowers his eyes, and then shuffles sideways out into the hallway.

Till watches Lisa as she closes the door behind the man. Apart from the funeral yesterday morning, he hasn't seen her in two years. She is more mature, clearly, but she's still only twenty-three.

"Why am I here?" he demands. "Why the rats, why the rat man—or his voice—behind the wall . . . ?"

"Felix wants to know whose side you're on, Till." Lisa returns his gaze unflinchingly.

Suddenly, Till hears himself screaming in the basement again, where he had woken up the night before.

"But he's dying—he's dying!"

There they are again, the rat man's screams behind the wall, sounding like a single, endless noise bubbling out of his mouth. It was as if the rat man no longer had to draw breath. As if the terror simply poured out of him—even as the animals were burrowing into him.

"He told me what happened," said Lisa. "That you listened to him, down in the basement . . ."

"Isn't now the last chance to save him?!" Till had screamed.

"What's it going to be, Till?" Felix had answered. "Listen to your head—or your gut?"

"That you thought about it, that you vacillated, hesitated, wavered . . ." Lisa says, looking at Till.

"It was a test! Felix said so himself. I just didn't understand it . . ."

Till hasn't eaten for twenty-four hours, and the torn stitches in his sides and legs are burning. He feels filthy and sweaty. "I always said I didn't know, I couldn't commit . . ."

"Wasn't it *obvious* that the right thing to do was to set the rat man free? To set a man free when he screams like that?" The sound of Lisa's voice is something Till has never been able to resist.

"And the rats? The rats that really came?" He can feel the exhaustion on his face.

"Don't you know? Felix believes you can only talk compellingly about things you have personally experienced."

Felix is toying with him.

"Is he coming here? Felix?"

She nods.

When? Till wonders. *In twenty minutes, in ten? Is that long enough to throw my arms around you, carry you through the door back there, lay you down on a bed in one of the rooms? One last time? It may never be possible again.*

Her eyes are on his.

Is she thinking the same thing?

. . .

"Come on out . . . I won't bite."

She had to drive. *In* my *car. The goddamned drum . . . I should have had my seat belt on. The car skidded sideways and my head hit the side window. She thought I'd lost control of it.*

But I told her straight away that I didn't want to go to hospital— even if I wrecked my car three times over. That all I wanted to do was lie down for a minute, rest—on my back—on a bed.

She smiled.

She's much too . . . sweet . . . for what she does.

"Why do you do this?" I asked her.

"Don't you want me to do it with you?" she replied.

And now I'm sitting on the lid of a motel toilet, staring at the bathroom door. I got her to drive us to a motel. I told her I was just a little dizzy.

"Are you coming? I'm already lying on the bed. But I'm still wearing something. I want you to take it off for me."

What is she still wearing?

I'm not finished yet. I still have something to do!

She drove us here.

Does she come here often?

"Do you want me to join you in the bathroom?"

Yes.

NO!

The door's locked; I'll be out in a minute, I . . . I have to just pull myself together a little. Then it can . . .

"Should I get started . . . with me? What do you think?"

No. Don't get started, don't . . .

You don't have to wait much longer . . . you'll be surprised what happens . . . I just need a moment . . .

"Hello?"

What . . .

Whoa! She's at the door! She's standing right outside! I can see her figure through the frosted glass . . .

And she does have something on . . . but not much . . .

"Can you see me?"

What has she done to her voice to make it get under my skin like that . . . ?

Her hands, sliding over her own body . . .

. . . if you don't stop I'll smash the glass to pieces!

I . . . I have to get my head together . . .

"Hey? You like what you see?"

Yes, yes . . .

Yes, I like it!

"Should I stop?

"Hmmm? I can't hear you."

No. "No!" *No, don't stop . . .*

"Ah. You can speak . . ."

"Open the door for me?"

Yes. I'll open it, I'll come out—to you—to finish what has to be finished.

"Hmmm?"

Doesn't matter where you've got your hands . . .

I am master of myself. Not you!

I say what we do.

"Coming out?"

Yes. I'm already turning the latch. But not to throw you onto the bed, not to feel you . . . I won't let you mess with my mind like this!

"There you are. Finally . . ."

I . . .

"Come here. Here, feel that?"

Ahhh . . .

"Here . . . oh, yesss . . . do you feel it?"

Yes.

TWO YEARS EARLIER

"What do you think?"

Lisa laughed. "It's not me who has to like it."

The apartment was small, no more than four hundred square feet, Till guessed. The living room faced a side street; the kitchen looked out onto a courtyard. There were wood floors throughout and decorative plaster ceilings twelve feet high. A typical old Berlin apartment, simply but thoughtfully renovated, including a relatively modern bathroom with the basics: shower, toilet, sink.

Till turned to the small kitchen and looked out at the courtyard. He didn't have to think it over long. The place was exactly what he was looking for now that he had accepted Felix's offer of work and decided, at least for now, to stay in Berlin.

He gave a thumbs-up to the rental agent, who was leaning on the stove in the kitchen. "Okay. I'll take it."

Fifteen minutes later, Lisa and Till were sitting at a table in a café on the first floor of Till's new apartment building.

"You didn't know?" Lisa slouched in her chair, her chin tilted almost down to her collarbone, her brow creased.

Of course she's got a boyfriend, Till thought. *I never expected her to be single. But why* him?

"How could I know?" he said. "*You* never said a word!"

"From Max?" Lisa shook her head. "You seem to spend all your time together."

"Max didn't tell me anything about it."

Her eyes flashed. "So, you didn't even ask him about me!" Her tongue darted over her bottom lip.

All Max told me was that I should ask you, not him, Till thought, and murmured, "I thought I'd better find out for myself."

"What about you?" Lisa looked at him keenly. "Did you live alone over in Canada? Or . . . okay, none of my business!" She looked around, trying to spot someone to take their order.

Till shrugged. "There were a few . . . nothing you'd call serious."

That was true. The year before, he'd dated a girl in the same major as him. But that fell apart when she transferred to a different university. Since then, he'd had two or three flings. But it was like he'd said: nothing serious. With Lisa, though, things looked a little different; if she was with Felix von Quitzow . . .

"So, what does 'with' mean, exactly? Do you *live* together?" When Till's eyes met hers, it was clear to him that it made her uncomfortable to talk about it.

"Well . . ." She hesitated.

"How long now?"

"What's with the third degree?"

Till raised his hands in an 'I give up' gesture. "How long have you been together?" He laid his hands on the table again. "I'll be working for the man starting Monday—of course I'm interested in this!"

"Well, I'd have to work it out exactly . . ." Her eyes swept the café, caught those of a waiter just delivering a cappuccino to another table. "Can I get one of those too?" she asked loudly, indicating the cup in his hand.

Till was about to say something, then checked himself. She slept in Felix's bed? That was hard to imagine. She made love to him? He pressed her onto the mattress while she wrapped her legs around him and pulled him into her?

Till's hand was shaking slightly as he wiped his eyes.

"Me too." He nodded to the waiter.

Lisa had turned away from him and was gazing out the window.

Outside the rain had stopped. Rays of sunlight broke through the gray, overcast sky and were reflected in the puddles. A strand of Lisa's hair had freed itself from the knot on the back of her head and fluttered gently in the café's heated air. Till noted the curve of her cheek, her eyes as she looked out the window, the taper of her eyebrow.

And suddenly it was as if his desire for Lisa, something he'd been struggling with his whole life, transformed into something else, a gnawing pain that made his arms feel paralyzed.

Till heard himself exhale painfully. He stood up.

She turned back to face him, her eyes large and her face like chiseled marble. "You're leaving?"

He reached out and touched the loose strand of her hair before he could stop himself. Lisa tilted her face a little to one side so that her lips were touching the palm of his hand. He felt her kiss him, felt his fingertips brush across her cheek.

Lisa's eyes were closed.

Till turned away.

What was she doing? What was the point? What did she want to show him by doing that? Something in his chest was burning, and for a moment he was unable to breathe. The next second, the bell on the glass door of the café tinkled, and he was out on the street.

It was still cold in Berlin—but the air was already filled with the harbingers of spring, coming late to the city as it always did, in the last days of March.

Till removed his scarf and stuffed it into his coat pocket.

The palm of his hand smoldered where Lisa had kissed him. He lifted his hand to his face and pressed it to his mouth. Lisa's scent was still there, as faint as a sigh.

TODAY

Frederik twists his torso a little to one side without slowing down. Claire hears the wood splinter as his shoulder slams into the rickety door. The latch breaks and the door swings back on its hinges and cracks against the unplastered wall of the basement corridor then bounces straight back at Claire.

She jerks her hands up protectively and the door hits her, bounces off again. Claire races through the doorway and into the basement of the neighboring building. The two apartment blocks are connected by the wooden door, which must date from the war, when Berliners joined their basements into a huge network for protection during air raids.

"Here!" Frederik grasps her hand and turns sharply into a side corridor. Even narrower than the first one, it is low and unlit.

This time, she runs in front of him. She can feel his breath on her neck. She lunges almost blindly down the corridor, past partitioned storage units with half-rotted shelves, the stuff hoarded down there collected over the last fifty years: canned food, jars and bottles, but also old strollers, sleds, lamps, and piles of stale-smelling newspapers.

The shimmer of light still penetrating the side tunnel is growing more feeble with every step Claire and Frederik take. Claire has both arms stretched out in front to protect herself from any sudden impact. The air is saturated with the odors of musty clothing, sprouting potatoes, spilled beer. Then the crunch of Frederik's steps behind her stops.

Claire gasps for air, stops running, turns around. Frederik's eyes, barely visible through the gray-brown gloom of the corridor, gleam flatly in her direction.

She can faintly hear the shouts of the men after them. They must have stopped where the narrow passage branched off.

Claire sees Frederik take a step toward her. The shadow of his body falls across her, and he seems to be shielding her from the men pursuing them.

The voices recede.

Frederik leans forward. His fingers touch her chin. Claire turns her face to his.

Then she feels his other hand fumbling its way under her top, slipping her pullover up. As if out of her control, her lips part, the palms of her hands slide across the roughly plastered wall at her back.

Frederik works open the heavy buckle of her belt, carefully slides her jeans and panties over her hips in one motion. The wall feels sandy against her naked bottom.

Claire freezes.

The squeaking sound. It sounds almost like something rustling, squealing.

Frederik seems not to have heard it. His face is buried in her neck, his right hand clasped around her ass, pulling her to him, at once strong and gentle—

"Wait!"

Claire presses both hands against his chest, pushing him back, and his face emerges in front of her from the darkness, his eyes glazed as if enraptured. His arm tenses and he slides his own T-shirt up, her already exposed breasts pressing softly against his chest, skin tautening at the contact—

"Wait," Claire says, more a gasp than a whisper. She wants to have him for herself, but at the same time she wants to listen—*has to* listen—to whatever it is rustling and squeaking back there in the darkness of the corridor.

With determination, she tugs her pullover down again, pushes his body away from hers, separating them. She tries to break free from his embrace, but feels his hand move across her hips, around to the front, feels it glide across the stubble of her pubic hair, slip down . . . she hears how heavy his breathing has become.

Then she is lying on her back, Frederik's jacket spread beneath her on the gritty floor of the corridor. Above her, his powerful body, moving down over hers. Her eyes are only half open, but her senses are at their limit, fervent, filled to overflowing by the sheer desire he triggers in her. She feels the sweat covering her body, feels how her every movement is matched by his. It's like they're climbing a mountain, climbing to a summit, a pinnacle that seems to rise higher than any cloud, its height making her dizzy, taking her breath away, promising a fall she has never known. A fall for which she can hardly wait, but fears at the same time, afraid it might be the end of her . . .

"AaaahhhhHHH!"

The scream forces its way out of her. She could not have stopped it if she'd wanted to. Her thighs close around Frederik's head—but it's not the release her body has craved, not the fall triggered by her arousal. It is a scream of horror, dismay, and fear.

In the darkness of the passageway beyond Frederik's back, a figure has appeared. A figure with dark-green, glittering eyes, gazing at Claire. At her nakedness, her body, her lust—her passion at its peak, her hands closed over her own breasts.

TWO YEARS EARLIER

"Hey!"

Max had to smile. He'd thought it was the mailman.

"Bad time?" Nina raised one eyebrow.

"No, not at all." He threw open the front door of his apartment. "Come in!"

Max hadn't seen Nina since Betty's wedding. She was wearing a light-colored raincoat over a gray silk blouse and a tight skirt that ended just above her knee.

"D'you always run around like that?" She looked like a model from the pages of a fashion magazine. Max closed the door behind her.

"I've just come from work."

He helped her out of her raincoat. "Is your office near here, then?"

"We had an appointment—a viewing—a couple of streets away."

"A viewing?"

"A property."

Max narrowed his eyes. "What was it you said you did, again?" She hadn't mentioned it at the wedding.

"It's just an internship." Nina smiled and folded her hands behind her back, as if to make herself look particularly well-behaved.

"An internship . . . with an architect?"

He saw that it troubled her to correct him. "I wish. Much more boring—a real-estate company."

Max smiled. "Okay." They were still standing in the hallway of his apartment. Her silk blouse pulled tight across her chest.

What does she want? Max wondered.

Nina looked past him, along the hallway. "I heard you had a nice place."

Max took a step back. "Oh, sure, come on in." He followed her along the hallway. "Can I offer you anything? A glass of wine or something?"

"Oh, gladly!" Nina turned through the first doorway leading off the hallway, which opened into a large living room. "Wow!" She stopped in her tracks.

Max stepped up beside her. "Like it?"

"How did you manage *that*?" She turned to face him, and he could see that she was genuinely impressed.

"I had it done," Max admitted. "I thought . . . I just thought it might look nice."

Nina swept her gaze around the room. It was the kind of huge loft found in old Berlin buildings, connected to another large room through a sliding door twenty feet wide. Together, the two rooms made up almost the entire front of the building. But it wasn't just the size of the rooms that had impressed Nina. It was the floor. Max had had the old one replaced with a massive sheet of Plexiglas six inches thick. Looking down through this glass floor, she could see into the rooms below, where the remains of the construction work were still visible: tools, building materials, tarpaulins.

"It must have cost a fortune!" Nina stepped cautiously onto the clear floor.

"Well, of course, it was kind of crazy." Max strolled over to a sofa and two armchairs he'd picked up cheap at a flea market. "If you want to sit, I'll get us a bottle of wine."

She's wearing makeup, he thought, as he watched her teetering cautiously toward the sofa—not entirely trusting of the floor.

"Okay," she said, pleasantly enough. "Why not?"

Was she just some treacherous hustler who used her pretty brown eyes to work on anyone Felix told her to?

In the kitchen, Max reached impatiently for a cold bottle of white wine and slammed the refrigerator door again.

He liked Nina. He'd liked her since they met again at Betty's wedding. Maybe she was in some kind of trouble? Maybe Felix had something on her and was using her? Max didn't think that Quentin had made up what he'd said with such vitriol outside the club: Felix had told Nina to come onto to him.

With the bottle and two glasses in his hands, he turned back to where she was sitting. He had to decide. If he didn't want anything to do with her, he had to get her out of his apartment as soon as possible.

"There you are!" said Nina brightly, when he reappeared in the living room. But she had hardly seen his face when her own expression clouded over. "Oh. Should I leave?"

"No!" The word was out before Max could think twice. "Don't go."

He set the bottle and glasses carefully on the arm of the sofa and looked at her, sitting on the edge of the cushion, watching him. The next moment, he had his hand behind her head. Leaning down, he pulled her gently toward him, and kissed her lightly on the lips. They were cool and firm. Something inside him melted. Max felt her slim, curvaceous body pressing against his. *She's only doing it for him*, flashed through his mind, even as she lay in his arms as if she had been created for just this reason. Instinctively, he laid her back on the sofa until they were side by side. Nina opened her eyes, as if waking from a dream.

Then he saw it. Her eyes were not glazed over, not mocking, not teasing. No, she was looking at him as if to say, *Don't hurt me; I'm very, very fragile.*

Did Felix send you?

But instead of actually asking the question, Max buried his mouth at her ear, felt her hair falling over his face—and felt himself driven by the urge to undress her. Her body tensed beneath his hands. Then he was kneeling in front of her, opening the button on her skirt.

TWO YEARS EARLIER

When Nina awoke, she was lying on the floor next to Max. He was still asleep and, like her, naked. Her clothes and his were strewn around the room. Outside the window, it was dark. Nina pushed aside the wool blanket Max had laid over her earlier in the evening and, as quietly as possible, stood up.

It took her a little while to get her bearings in the apartment. Max owned not only the side wing, which was accessible from the living room, but also the side wing on the *other* side of the building. She found his bedroom there, as well as a large bathroom covered in a mosaic of tiny tiles of every conceivable color. Without hesitation, Nina turned on the shower and stood under the hot stream of water, rinsing herself clean. Then she took a large, pale-gray towel hanging from a hook on the door, wrapped it around her body, and looked around Max's room.

The first thing that caught her eye was a walk-in closet, its mirrored doors standing open. Inside hung endless rows of shirts, jeans, suits, ties, and T-shirts. Nina slipped one of the white shirts from its hanger, let the towel fall to the floor, and pulled on the shirt. It was much too big for her; the sleeves, which needed cuff links, dangled below the tips of her fingers. But the white cloth was wonderfully flattering to her complexion and her dark hair.

She wandered thoughtfully back into the bedroom. She noticed that Max had suspended his bed from the ceiling on cables, and it swung from side to side a little when she sat on it. The bedding was gray cotton, rough to the touch, and matched the gray tones in the rest of the room well. The nightstand, like the bed, hung from cables; a simple, square steel plate that felt icy under Nina's fingers.

Her eyes fell on the objects on the nightstand. On top was a paperback with a gaudy cover—apparently an Italian thriller from the seventies. Beneath that were a few sheets of paper covered in small, determined handwriting, which Nina thought might have been Max describing her. For a moment, she was tempted to read what he had written, but then she decided to leave them where they were and stretched out on the bed instead.

She had slept with him. Not because *Felix* had wanted her to, but because *she* had wanted to. She'd liked him since they talked at Betty's wedding.

"He's got a lot of money, you know," Felix had said to her before the wedding. "But basically, he's still just a little boy. Make friends with him! He'll be useful to you—and to me too."

Her memory of that conversation with Felix made Nina feel almost physically unwell.

"Be Max's girlfriend. That's all I'm asking you to do, Nina . . . make sure he wants to see you, that he calls you and wants to be near you. I'll take care of the rest myself." She knew what Felix was capable of if someone refused him. She knew what he had done to her mother, Maja. And to herself, as well.

As long as Nina could remember, Felix had shown up at their home. Not every day, not every week, but at least once a month. Nina knew how afraid of Felix her mother was, even though Maja had never spoken openly to her daughter about it. Nina would never be able to forget the noises she had heard when Felix stayed at their home. Just as she would never forget the words he had whispered in her own ear when she was younger.

She tossed in the bed, disgusted. She did not want to think about Felix. It felt as if her thoughts of the man coated everything she had just experienced with Max with a layer of filth.

But she could not drive out her memory of Felix. Hesitantly, she opened the shirt that she had thrown on and looked down at her own body.

When she slept with Max, it was obvious he was infatuated with her. But how long would that last?

Max was crazy, there was no doubt about that. But maybe that was what she liked so much about him. There was no bitterness in his obsession with her; it seemed more like a game.

So, why should she do it for Felix? Why should she master Max for Felix? Why shouldn't she keep him *for herself*?

She started to feel cold. She closed the shirt again and pulled the blanket over her.

Didn't she have to tell Max that Felix had asked her to get close to him? But wouldn't that automatically mean the end of their . . . what? Their friendship? Their relationship? Their love affair? Whatever you wanted to call it. Wouldn't Max turn away from her, justifiably furious at the secret she had kept from him?

Drowsy—exhausted—she rolled onto her side and fell asleep.

The day was growing light when Nina heard Max enter the bedroom. She blinked awake and saw he was wearing no more than a pair of boxer shorts, which looked baggy on his thin frame. He squatted beside the bed and smiled at her.

Nina threw the blanket back. She could see in his eyes how the sight of her affected him; he seemed almost in pain. As if he had longed for this moment for such a long time—and now that it was here, he suddenly understood that the moment was also past, never to return.

With care, he laid his lean body beside her on the mattress, and Nina let the blanket drop over both of them again. Max's eyes seemed huge as he gazed at her, as he touched her sides with his hands. Nina arched her back a little to feel his bony form against hers. She felt his arms slide around her, draw her close, hold her tight.

TWO YEARS EARLIER

"I hope I haven't kept you waiting, Mr. Anschütz."

Till stood up from the low armchair as Henning hurried toward him. "Nothing worth mentioning." He reached out his hand. "But weren't we on a first-name basis?"

They shook hands.

"Sure, of course, you're absolutely right." Henning's slightly watery eyes glinted. "Felix asked me to welcome you on his behalf."

"No doubt he has a lot going on today."

Henning smiled mildly as if to say *you have no idea*. "Shall we take a look at your office?"

"Love to."

"This way." Henning hurried ahead of Till, out of the lobby where Till had been waiting and into the hallway that led to the rear rooms of the publishing house. He glanced at his wristwatch as he walked.

"I can take a look around the place by myself later on," Till said; he had not missed Henning's gesture.

"Really?" Henning turned a little and gave Till a sidelong glance. "Okay, here's what we'll do: I'll show you your office, we'll chat a little, and then I have to leave at eight thirty for another appointment."

And this is why I had to come by specially this evening, Till couldn't help thinking, even as he nodded.

His first day at the publishing house had been postponed several times already, apparently because Felix wanted Henning, and no one else, to explain a few things to him—but Henning had been far too busy the last few days.

"Here." Henning stopped and indicated a door that opened into a room with three large windows looking out onto the same street that fronted Felix's office.

"Nice!" Till said, entering the office with curiosity. Empty white shelves lined every wall, and in the middle was an antique desk big enough to lie down on. A keyboard, a phone, a monitor— and that was all. Till felt instinctively that he would able to work well in the space.

"Want to try the chair?" Henning gave him a skewed smile and pointed to the expensive office chair behind the desk.

Till didn't need to be asked twice. He sank into the swivel chair, which looked like it had more than two hundred moving parts. "Fantastic!" His own office in the middle of the city. It was like a dream.

Henning sat down opposite Till in a comfortable club chair. "So, Felix already told you what he needs you for?"

"Not really." Till leaned forward a little and laid his hands flat on the desktop. "I'm supposed to get to know the material. That's actually all I've been told so far. Then we'll see where things go from there." It suddenly occurred to him how intensely Henning was scrutinizing him. "Have you got a . . . a what would you call it? A bible or something?"

"A bible?"

"Isn't that what it's called? Where the entire mythology—"

"Mythology? Bible?" Henning pulled a face. "No. Look, Till, it'd probably be best if you spent some time getting an overview first, see where we're at, before . . ." Henning thought for a moment. "Please don't take this the wrong way—before you open your mouth. Okay?"

Sure, no problem, whatever, thought Till, making an effort not to get angry. The fact was, he really wasn't very well informed. *Don't always think you know better*, he told himself. *Listen to what Henning has to say first.*

Henning jabbed his thumb toward a door that connected Till's office to the one next door. "Malte's in the next office. You know him already, don't you?"

"From the wedding."

"That's it. He can give you all the material you need to find your way in."

"Find my way in *where*?" Till was growing impatient. Henning would be gone in a few minutes. If he didn't want to screw things up completely, Till needed to have at least a rough idea of what he was supposed to be doing before Henning left.

"Into what we call the fictional universe. Felix already mentioned that, didn't he?" Again Henning looked at him sharply.

"Yes, but . . . what does he mean by—"

"Listen, Till," Henning interrupted him. "This ain't rocket science. We call it the fictional universe. It's simply the fictional world in which the stories are set. It encompasses the locations, the characters, what they do—"

"How many characters are we talking about?"

Henning thought for a moment. "That changes from day to day. I don't know the exact number. Somewhere between three and four hundred."

Till nodded. Three to four hundred characters? How long would he need to find his feet in a story like that?

"At the moment, we're still primarily caught up in the planning," Henning went on. "For the actual work, we're going to need a lot more people . . ."

"So, a publication date hasn't been announced yet, right?"

"Felix is calculating on starting publication in two years, three at the outside. He wants to use the time before then to put together a precise vision of this fictional world."

Till leaned back in his chair. "Four hundred characters. If I'm understanding it right, there's never been a 'fictional universe'—as you call it—like that before."

"No. Definitely not," Henning said, his eyes gleaming. "Or Felix wouldn't be bankrolling the whole project. For him, that's exactly what makes the thing so exciting—it's something completely new. There are a few TV series that headed in the same direction. Think back to *Dallas*, for example. That show went through several hundred episodes telling one continuous story. And there are soaps and telenovelas that have been around much longer, but those projects are not even close to being in the same league as ours."

"Why not?"

"The field we're playing on is simply far, far bigger. And that's apart from the fact that we're not planning on three hundred or so episodes, but ten or fifteen *thousand* . . ."

Till interlaced his fingers behind his head. This could be very interesting indeed.

"You'll really have to get Malte to show you what it's all about," Henning continued. "Since we started, all sorts of different regions of this fictional world have opened up. There's a huge region for children and teenagers, where we tell the stories of the characters in their younger years. Then there's an entire partial universe aimed at a female readership, and another that is off-limits to anyone under eighteen. There are story strands that are deliberately being kept

very plain and simple, and others that are . . . challenging, to say
the least—"

"Hold on," Till's head was spinning. "What do *region* and *story
strand* mean?"

Henning sat upright in his chair. He was obviously feeling
stressed. "Like I said, Till," he said, again glancing at his watch, "I
can be maybe five or ten minutes late, but I definitely don't have the
time to explain everything in detail now."

"Not in *detail*." Till let a degree of sharpness enter his own
voice. Felix had given Henning the task of inducting him into the
place. He couldn't just leave him in the dark. "How am I supposed
to conceive of all this? There are different kinds of spin-offs? Or
what?"

"Yes, in principle, that's exactly what it's about. There's a core
region, narratively speaking, with the main characters, who Xavier
Bentheim developed in his later manuscripts. We've built on those
original characters to create what we now call the main strand or
the central core of the universe."

"So, is this main strand complete, at least in the planning?"

"Hell no!" Henning said in a tone that implied Till was rather
dense. "Of course not. That's impossible. The secondary strands are
not entirely independent of the main strand. We'll only be able to
see how the main strand can end when we've finished planning all
the secondary strands. Everything's dependent on everything else."

Okay, that's clear, thought Till.

"To put it another way," Henning continued, "the main strand
is something like a novel, just a lot longer—"

"How long?"

Henning smiled. "We've spent a lot of time trying to guess that
one. Maybe eight hundred, nine hundred—"

"Eight or nine hundred pages?" *So few?*

"Eight or nine hundred *thousand* pages."

Till stared at Henning. Was he insane?

"Like I said, hard to say. We haven't even worked out whether the main focus of the story should be published as *text*, or whether it would make more sense to try to set up a partnership with a film or TV production house. Really, that's just one of thousands of details that are still up in the air. Right now, the actual form of the thing—as text or film or whatever—isn't so important to Felix. What matters most to him is the story. And not just in broad strokes, but with a certain degree of detail, even at this stage."

"Okay." Till was gradually getting the feeling that even if they sat there for the next two weeks, Henning would not be able to tell him definitively what they did.

"Good. The heart of this story, or rather of this story system is the main strand," Henning said. "Some characters who are secondary figures in the main strand have now become the main characters in what we call the secondary strands. This way we come up with all kinds of variations, and our aim is to get the widest possible range of people to connect with us . . . I mean, with our stories, with our fictional universe. It's like I said: there are secondary strands for children and teens, for women. There are different genres—and all of these strands and genres are part of one and the same universe!"

Till nodded. *Let him talk, he's on a roll*, he thought.

"You can see it, can't you? There are parts of it for teenagers, but at the same time there are also horror strands, where we dig into the dark side of the fictional universe. If someone is so inclined, he can spend two or three years wallowing in the murky visions of a practically endless nightmare. At least, that's the plan." Henning looked at Till. "Or there's the erotic strand, for people who are into that kind of thing. We're planning on several episodes that pose various theoretical questions of the universe, and another region that's more fragmented, for people who just want to take a quick bite of the universe while they're on the bus or train."

Till pulled on a spring lever on his chair. "Nice." With a hiss, the chair sank a few inches lower.

Henning wasn't distracted. "In essence," he continued, "it makes no difference what kind of person you are. If you want to, you'll find a way into the universe. And a way to stay inside it. Whatever your mood, your need, your taste, we have corresponding levels and strands. The key, though, is that all of these levels and strands are part of the *same* universe. Which means that from every one of them, there is a network of relationships to as many other strands and levels as possible. Which means that as you grow older, as your tastes change—for whatever reason—you can always find ways to satisfy your new interests and cravings *within* the same fictional universe!"

Henning stopped talking and caught his breath.

The thought came to Till unbidden. *It's like a prison. It's like a prison built by someone who's invested a hell of a lot into making sure no one ever finds a way out.*

TWO YEARS EARLIER

"To earn money?" Henning stood up.

Till had asked Henning whether Felix was planning this enormous universe to make as much money as he could, but the question seemed to confuse him. "Well, yes, that too." It was clear he really wanted to leave.

"But not just that?" Till pushed. "I mean, it makes perfect sense. The harder it is for someone to extract themselves from the world of a story, the more money it means for the publisher."

"True." Henning hesitated in the middle of Till's office, and then turned back to the desk and picked up the receiver on Till's phone. "Okay?" He looked at Till for a second as if asking him for permission to use his phone.

Till laughed. "Does it belong to me now?"

Henning smiled and pressed three buttons. "Merle? Could you run across to the conference room and let them know I'll be a little late? They can start without me. I need fifteen minutes." He hung up, sat down on the arm of the club chair, and looked at Till. "You know what Felix is planning with the project, don't you?" Henning frowned. "You knew Bentheim—you probably know more about it than I do!"

Till sat in his new chair awkwardly. "All I've heard about Bentheim's work in recent years is bits and pieces, hints, little details. But how does it all fit together, Henning? Sorry to keep you from your meeting—"

"It's okay," Henning cut him off, not particularly pleasantly.

"But . . . you know . . . I'm not sure I'm really clear what Bentheim's work is about. The illusion of freedom?" An involuntary grin crept across Till's face.

"You know that's important to Felix, of course," said Henning, a little stiffly.

"What exactly is important to him, for Christ's sake?" Till suddenly burst out.

"Nothing more than what you're already thinking, Till." Henning ran his hand through his hair. "The entire project is supposed to communicate Felix's ideas."

"His ideas about our conception of our own freedom, whether we can freely decide or if we're just imagining it all? Is that it?"

Henning nodded.

"So, how *are* the two things connected?" Till wouldn't let up. "The illusion of freedom and the work on the fictional universe."

"What exactly *is* a reader when he reads a text?" Henning pinched the bridge of his nose as if in pain. "Imagine someone reading a story. Imagine the thoughts in his head. Got it?"

Just roll with it, thought Till.

"Okay. So, in a way, the *movement* of the reader's thoughts when he's reading is different from the movement of his thoughts when he's not reading. When he reads, his thoughts are on the same track as the author's. The author has laid the tracks—it's a metaphor, of course, but a surprisingly useful one—the author has laid the tracks and the reader's mind, like a train, follows those tracks."

"So, the reader isn't free."

Henning nodded. "That's what it comes down to. But that's not all. For us, what matters is not just that the reader isn't free, *but author isn't free either.*"

"Really? How do you figure that? The writer can write whatever he wants, aside from the fact that he wants to sell his work."

"But can he really?" Henning sighed. "I don't think so. And it has nothing to do with speculation about sales. No, the author is not free, because the book he's writing has to make sense. Say, for example, he starts a story with a character named Tom. Then he can't turn around and start calling Tom Tim on page two. If Tom lives in Berlin, then he can't live in London on the next page. If Tom meets Dick, he can't suddenly *not* know Dick afterward. Basically, the author is forced to tell his story coherently. And this limits his choices."

"Okay, fine, but . . ."

"This is one way the fictional universe helps us dispel the illusion of freedom," Henning continued. "We draw the reader into our story, and we make him aware that his mind is being led by the story, like a train on rails . . . and then we show that the one who laid those rails was anything but free when he or she did so."

"And instead was . . ."

"Compelled."

He's gotta be kidding, Till thought.

"A writer," Till said, "is someone who breathes air into a character's lungs and brings that character to life."

Henning nodded. "Like the reader. If you're following the story of that living-and-breathing character, then you're dependent on the writer's vision."

"But the writer was free!" Till persisted. "Okay, I admit, once a writer decides to bring a particular character to life, he has to go with that until he comes up with a reason for stopping that life again. But the decision to *bring the character to life* was a *free* choice. The author could have . . . What? . . . Made the character able to run incredibly fast. Just one example. There was nothing limiting his choices!"

"That's how it appears to him, true."

Till snorted. "Why just *appears*? What makes you so sure that's not the way it *is*? People have been busting their heads about this for hundreds of years, and suddenly *Felix*, of all people, is lucky enough to get his hands on the gospel truth? Once and for all? Where did he find this knowledge?!" Till felt exasperated. The people here were behaving like members of a cult, and he felt as if he were being indoctrinated. Maybe he should have listened to Max and kept his distance.

Henning just looked at him, a picture of calm. "Ever wonder why so many people like crime stories?"

"What difference does that make?"

Henning glanced at his watch as he continued. "Think of the kind of whodunit, where you know the murderer is one of several suspects. The thrill of this kind of story lies in what's called the bluff."

"Which I'm guessing is the suspect we all think is the killer because everything points in his direction. But in the end, it always turns out to be someone else, right?" Till said. "But it doesn't always work. When too many clues point to this one suspect, then the reader—the *experienced* reader—pretty quickly realizes the writer wants him to think that this suspect is the killer. So, it definitely *can't* be him! Because the writer has to surprise me."

"That's exactly it." Henning smiled. "And this formula works because as human beings, we are, as we say here, sense-seekers."

"Ah."

"And that may be a little too much to take in at the start, but since you absolutely had to know."

"So, what does that mean, *sense-seeker*?"

Henning sighed. "It works in a film exactly the same as in a book." He laid his hands on his knees. "When we follow a crime story, the smallest details are enough to make us suspicious. A suspect's frown, for example, or a mysterious gesture. We put on our shrewd-detective hats and we interpret the details. And we interpret them in a way that makes *sense*. We can't stop ourselves from doing it! We follow all of the elements of the story, every step of the way, and we use these to construct our theory of what's happened. In doing so, as many details as possible have to be considered. If the writer wants to lead us down a blind alley, then he feeds us more details that would make sense if the *wrong suspect* were the perpetrator, and fewer details that would make sense if the one we *should* suspect were the *real* perpetrator. So, we think the wrong person's the killer—basically, we fall for the bluff. Get it?

"It's a process of constructing a theory as a reader or a viewer, and we can't do much about it; it simply happens in our heads without any conscious decision making on our part. And this automatic search for sense, well, that's what a good whodunit writer toys with. But as you said, once you've read a few of them, you get sensitized to the genre and wary when too many things point to a particular suspect as the perp. So, a clever writer could ensure that many of the clues point to the *real* criminal, just to make us think, like you said, that the author *wants* us to think he's the one, so it *can't* be him. But in reality, it's exactly *this* character who turns out to be the killer. And the writer's set up an opportunity to surprise us when he reveals that the one character we'd ruled out turns out to be the culprit after all! Of course, you could fine-tune all this as much as you like, that was just one example. What matters to me, though"—Henning continued, raising his voice to prevent Till from interrupting his train of thought—"is that this interpretation of the clues, this attempt to put together a meaning from what we've already found out in the story is something that, as human beings and readers—as I said a minute ago—we are practically damned to do. We can't *not* do it."

"We can't not do it," Till repeated.

"Exactly. Which is the same as saying we are not free."

"Okay, but . . ."

"Hold on, hear me out. I'm not just talking about whodunits. Humans are hardwired into this search for sense, for meaningful structures. In every part of our lives, in every situation, and at every moment. Take how we see the world we live in. What do we know about the creation and development of our universe? It's really no more than a *sensible story*, and we've built it up—or scientists have built it up—over the last hundreds and thousands of years. There was a beginning—the big bang. And there's a story that has grown based on the big bang as the starting point. And what you find at the other end of the spectrum—religion—is no different. Anyone with a bit of knowledge on the subject will tell you that religions are primarily stories. Take the Bible, God the Creator, the stories about his son . . . you can talk about those things forever.

"But only one thing is relevant for what we're talking about: we are bound by the need to find *sense* in things—whether we want to or not. And once you've understood that, it's like a veil being lifted. Not only are we *not* free when it comes to deciding whether or not we want to construct meaning but also we're not free to decide *which* meaning we want to construct!"

Henning seemed vaguely relieved to have reached this point in his argument.

Till, on the other hand, felt a deep need to argue against it. "Seriously? We're not free to decide which meaning we want to construct? Why not? I can freely decide if I want to believe in this or that scientific theory, or this or that religion!"

"Are you really so sure about that, Till? Isn't it rather that you are convinced of one religion or theory, but then, at some point, you let yourself be convinced of one of the alternatives, and then switch to that alternative and stick to it? Wouldn't it just be arbitrary if you said you believe in one of them—but that you could just as easily believe in something else?"

"Sure, that is arbitrary. But when I form my opinion, I'm free. I can choose this, or I can choose something else."

"That's how it seems to you, but it's not really true."

"How can you know that?" Till was far from convinced. "Sense-seeking or looking for meaning—fine!—maybe you're right. I'd even say *probably* right. But that doesn't change the fact that I *feel* free, as long as I'm not lying in chains somewhere! Free to leave this room if I want. Or free to choose if I want to let myself be convinced by you or not!"

"You *feel* free, I'm not denying that. But at the moment you make a decision—for example, to *not* let yourself be convinced by me—then there's a reason for that. And it's this reason that lies behind your decision. If we're talking about my arguments and your convictions, for example, I'd say it's pretty clear that you're *not* about to let yourself be won over. You can't do anything but remain *un*convinced, at least for now. Or in other words, you can't do anything unless there's a particular reason for it—unless you expressly did something *without* a reason. But in that case, *that* would be your reason for doing it: you wanted to do something *without* a reason."

"So, it's the search for meaning itself that makes me think I'm free." It was as if the thought welled up spontaneously inside Till.

Henning nodded slowly. "Exactly. And this belief is the wrong response to the search for meaning."

"Then what would be the right one?"

Henning stood up. He reached across the desk and gave Till a light thump on the shoulder; it came so unexpectedly that Till actually flinched. "I really have to go, Till." He strode quickly to the door but turned at the threshold. "You asked me what the connection was between the fictional universe and being able to see beyond the illusion of freedom . . ."

Till nodded.

"With the fictional universe, we'll be giving people the right answer to their search for meaning!" He smiled. "We'll get them to trace the meaning of the story, and by doing that, we'll show them the meaning of their lives, the meaning of their existence. By following the tracks laid down by the writers, if you see what I mean."

Till felt his heart pounding in his chest.

The thought suddenly flashed in Till like something branding itself on his brain: *what Henning, Felix, and the others are doing is dangerous.*

TODAY

The man just stands there, cringing, pressed against the wall. His arms are above his head, his elbows sticking out, and his face is turned to the floor. He is trembling from head to toe.

Frederik is on his feet instantly, tight as a coiled spring, leaving Claire fully exposed for a second. His back hunched, arms like two huge pincers poised to strike in front of him, he confronts the man who has suddenly appeared in the tunnel.

"WHAT . . ." Frederik's voice thunders in the narrow passage, "DO YOU WANT?"

Claire sees a shudder run through the man, as if Frederik's anger has physically slammed him against the wall. She wraps herself in Frederik's jacket and curls up against the opposite wall.

Then Frederik hits the man for real; his fist shoots out, and the other man's body doubles up in a hopeless gesture of defense. Protective, submissive. He slides down the wall, sinks to the floor, his arms desperately shielding his body. And Claire realizes that the stranger is not someone they need to fear, but someone who needs their help. She quickly pulls on her jeans.

"What's the matter? What's wrong with you?" Cautiously, she stands and reaches past Frederik, touches the man's arm.

"Hmmmhnnnn." The man's arms open a little and Claire can see the pitiful face beneath—how battered his features are, how pale, how sunken. A thin layer of sweat coats his face.

"Can you understand me?" she asks.

"Yea . . . yeeeaaggh." He is practically curled up at her feet.

"Do you need help?"

He shivers.

Claire looks up at Frederik. He is under control again, but she can tell he is still agitated.

"We all need help," Frederik says. "Remember the building up there? On Alexanderplatz? What the hell's happening, Claire? The whole fucking city's gone crazy!"

She leans down to the man on the floor and takes him by the arm. He seems to pull himself together a little; his eyes are wide and locked on hers.

The squeaking!

The squeaking they had first heard when they were racing down the passage. The squeaking as if a mountain of roaches were being steamrollered!

The sound is close now, and loud, as if swarms of the creatures are closing in around them.

Claire feels Frederik's hand on her back and she turns around.

Frederik is staring into the depths of the tunnel, where two dull points of light return his gaze. They are the eyes of another figure, a woman.

"Hey!" he shouts at her.

Claire takes a step toward the woman, who slowly moves toward them. She is as pale as the man cowering at the wall behind Claire. Her cheeks are slightly flushed, her forehead wet with sweat.

TWO YEARS EARLIER

"Again and again they heard the trampling, the scrabbling above the ceiling of the low room. It was as if mice were running across the boards, but mice the size of grown men."

Malte looked up from the monitor and eyed Till, who had taken a seat on the sofa between the two large windows in Malte's office.

Shortly after Henning had left, Till knocked on the door that linked his office with Malte's. Despite the late hour, Malte was at his desk, tapping away at the keyboard.

They had spent some time just chatting and then Till had asked Malte directly about what he was working on. After some hesitation, Malte revealed that it was his job to edit "the somewhat grimmer nooks and crannies"—as Felix put it—of the fictional universe.

"Cora looked over toward the pallet where Jakob was sleeping, in the back part of the room." Malte was reading aloud from the file he had just opened. "She stood and went to him, and laid another wool blanket over the boy.

"*Triddeldriddeldiddeltrapp*—the feet scrabbled overhead. It was a sound she put up with constantly, and it always gave her goose bumps."

Malte glanced toward Till, but when Till said nothing, he turned back to the monitor and kept reading. "The shack that Cora and Jakob were staying in lay beneath the plank floor of a passageway connecting two subway stations that were being rebuilt.

"Cora moved back to her chair. It had been three weeks since the outbreak of the infection. Of the food and provisions they'd brought with them, there was only a little water left. Her eyes swept across her son's drawn profile and came to rest on a white bag that lay on a shelf beside her. When they had taken off, she'd hurriedly packed a few medical supplies in the bag. Bandages, disinfectant, creams. Cora reached out, took the bag from the shelf, and slid open the zipper."

Malte looked up again at Till. "It goes on like that for pages and pages. But I just wanted to give you the idea of what's in there, just a taste, really . . ."

"Read a little more," Till suggested.

Malte looked at the screen and hesitated.

"What is it?" Till realized that Malte was anxious. He was pushing the mouse back and forth indecisively on his desk.

"The things in here, at least partly . . ." Malte's voice trailed off.

"Are you sensitive to that kind of thing?" Till's brow furrowed.

"Actually, no. I mean, I can understand that certain things have to be described in a story, but when someone is just being indulgent, like, *reveling* in the descriptions of certain things . . ."

"So, tell Felix you'd prefer to work in a different section. I'd think there would be something for everyone on a project like this."

Malte didn't answer, just ran his fingers over his forehead. Till stood up, moved behind Malte's chair, and looked over his shoulder at the monitor.

"Cora knew what she needed to do," Till read. "Carefully, she withdrew anesthetic and a scalpel. Then she kneeled in front of the chair and pulled a transparent plastic sheet from under it. Everything happened quickly. She spread the sheet over the armchair, took off her clothes, and began to inspect the various parts of her body.

"*Triddeldriddeldiddeltrapp* . . . the feet of the creatures above her rattled on the boards of the ceiling.

"The forearm was out of the question; she needed the arm to operate. Her side? Toes? It wouldn't be enough. Her bottom? She would never be able to sit down—and in that room, that was all they ever did . . . in the end, she settled on her left calf. With well-oiled movements, she injected herself, and then waited for the numbness to spread. She had to hurry; Jakob could wake at any moment.

"*Triddeldriddeldiddeltrapp* . . .

"When Cora placed the blade against her skin, when she cut into her numb flesh, it seemed to her that she . . . grew. Actually grew. *Don't cut too deep,* she admonished herself. Her leg lay before her like a lump of someone else's meat. The piece she cut from her calf was half as big as the palm of her hand. And although she dabbed at the blood the whole time, a disconcertingly large pool rapidly formed on the plastic sheet. Cora had to fight to keep her rising nausea under control.

"*It doesn't hurt, it doesn't hurt,* she told herself again and again—and that much was true. She felt the movements of the knife in her hand, but not in her leg.

"When Jakob awoke, she had bandaged herself and hidden the plastic sheet. She felt tiny droplets of sweat beading her forehead, and the pain starting to prickle through the anesthetic. But she managed to force her thoughts away from her leg, concentrating instead on the plate she had set beside her boy's bed. The piece of flesh looked like a bloody steak.

"*Triddeldriddeldiddeltrapp* . . .

"'There are more and more of them,' Jakob whispered, and looked at her with eyes like moons. 'Aren't there?'

"Cora nodded. The trample of feet seemed to be increasing by the day. By the hour, even. 'Don't be afraid, they won't get us.' She prodded at the chunk of flesh with a fork. 'Don't you at least want to try it?'

"The boy looked down apprehensively at the plate in front of him on the floor. He poked the plastic fork she had given him into the meat and cut off a small piece.

"'Raw?'

"'It's fresh. You don't have to worry.'

"'Where did you get it, Mom?'

"'I'll tell you that when we're out of here.'

"Jakob lifted the fork to his mouth, but he only sniffed at the morsel and didn't put it in his mouth. Cora watched him. Finally, he pushed the fork between his teeth.

"'So?' she asked. 'Is it okay?'"

Till glanced at Malte. Malte shook his head.

Only now—seeing him this close for the first time—did Till notice how weary Malte looked.

"I'm supposed to coordinate the different parts," he said.

Till nodded.

"Sometimes, the images get into my dreams," Malte murmured.

"So, why don't you tell Felix—"

"Maybe I will!" Malte blurted, but immediately looked up at Till. "I don't know exactly . . . I only showed you a little bit of it . . . you're not going tell anyone I've been complaining, are you?"

Till waved it off.

"It's pretty much impossible to meet with Felix, and if I say anything to Henning, who knows what he passes on to Felix," Malte stammered.

"The woman was hiding down there with her son, right?" In his head, Till was still in the text. "Or maybe it's something else?"

"How do you mean?"

"Maybe she kidnapped the boy and only talked him into believing that monsters were waiting for them outside?"

Malte looked at Till with a look on his face close to revulsion. "Why would she do *that*?"

"Because she enjoys getting eaten by her son?"

Malte looked like his stomach was turning. "And why would her son let himself be talked into hiding there like that?"

"Couldn't a mother talk a son into it? How old is he? She could tell him someone was after them, that their lives were in danger. But the truth is that the footsteps on the ceiling overhead are nothing more than the noise made by people walking from one subway platform to the other!" Till bent down to the screen again, reached over Malte's shoulder for the mouse, and scrolled down.

"'What's that?' Jakob yelped, his voice cracking." Till's eyes latched onto the words and he read on. "'That bandage . . . you're bleeding!'

"Cora could no longer get out of bed. Her leg felt like it was burning. As if the part of her brain that was connected to her calf was literally on fire. As if the pain, like an endless, giant wave, was crashing against the fragile wall of boards that still protected her ego . . . a wall that kept her ego divided from the madness it would fall into, the instant the wave smashed through.

"'Did you . . .' the shine in Jakob's eyes seemed suddenly to cloud over, 'did you cut it off yourself?'" Till had to cough, then, and punched at his chest with a fist to settle the itch there. "'What will they do to us, Mom? If we go out there—what will they do to us?'

"'You know what they'll do, Jakob. I've told you a hundred times.'

"'They'll bite us, won't they?'

"*Triddeldriddeldiddeltrapp-triddeldriddeldiddeltrapptriddeldri ddeldiddeltrapptriddeldriddeldiddeltrapp . . .*

"'Yes. They'll bite us. They'll rip chunks out of us with their bare teeth . . .' Cora sank back on the bed. She would find a way to explain it to Jakob better. He would understand. All he needed was a little time. She had to get him through this.

"'But isn't that just what *you're* doing, Mom? Tearing meat off a living body? Are *you* the one who's infected?!'

"A sudden metallic taste in her mouth prevented Cora from answering him. She leaned to one side and spat. The blood that spewed from her mouth hung in strands from her lips. When she looked up again, she saw Jakob lifting the beam she had laid across the door.

"*Triddeldriddeldiddeltrapptriddeldriddeldiddeltrapp!*

"'Here,' Jakob screamed. 'HERE! She's here. *We're* here.' The trample of footsteps overhead suddenly ceased.

"Cora tried to get up. She tried to stop him, to keep him by her. But Jakob took no notice of her shouts. He was already picking up the beam he'd removed, and he rammed it with all his strength against the door . . . but the door, in that instant, was smashed from outside, brute force shattering it to matchwood.

"Cora's eyes widened in stunned horror. A mass of deformed bodies poured into the den they'd managed to hold out in for three weeks."

Till stared at the monitor. Malte stood up and opened a window.

The sounds of Berlin at night came through the window. When Malte turned back to Till, Malte's eyes seemed to have sunk even deeper into their sockets.

"The story . . . it never lets go of you," he whispered. "The deeper you go into the universe, the more it sinks its claws into you."

"Do you believe what Felix says?" Till cautiously asked. "That we only imagine that we're free? That you can't decide to not read this stuff?"

Malte's jaw tensed. "Yeah. Yeah, I believe it."

"You think the Cora story is as valuable as any other story, because nothing has *any* value? Because there's really no such thing as values? Because everything that *is* has to be the way it is, because there can be no doubt, no hesitation, no changing your mind?"

Malte didn't react. He just stood there and looked at Till.

Can you really stand up for that? Till wanted to ask, but he didn't get that far. Because instead of that question, another—rather different—question reared its head: *What about you, Till? How can you accept being here? Being part of this?*

* * *

Mmmmmmm . . . that . . . I mean, that's what you expect from a truly first-class meat!

She seems to like it too . . .

Delicious . . . as tender as it gets—how long did they cook it? Two seconds? It practically dissolves on the tongue . . .

"Let's order another drink, shall we?"

She smiles. Sweet!

"Waiter!"

But a half hour before . . . MOVE the CAR!

I had to move the car . . . just when I'd stepped from the bathroom into the motel bedroom. The manager came to the door and knocked. Get in the bathroom, quick, I told her. No one should see you like that . . . oh, sure, the motel guy would've loved that . . . but I didn't want it!

And then when I came back from moving the car—stupid, I'd parked in a no-parking zone—the magic was all gone. She'd put her clothes back on! And she asked if we could go and grab a bite to eat before . . . before she gave me all her attention.

"Another bottle of white, please? Thanks."

I know I shouldn't have let it happen like this . . . but after everything, I just didn't have the strength to go through with it—at least I had to eat something first!

And the fillet here is outstanding . . .

I'm wondering . . .

I'm wondering how long . . .

Why's she got that look on her face?

"Everything okay? Really? Good."

I'm wondering how long it's been since the last time I ate a decent meal . . . perhaps I should have taken it a little slower with the meat . . .

"What is it? Smiling like that?"

Meat . . .

Meat . . .

That's it!

Exactly!

That's what was bugging me!

I started writing something . . . before I had to do the dog. Something about a father and his daughter.

"Oh, thanks, no, we can take care of that. No need to fill the glasses, really."

But the idea, that the father persuades his daughter to eat him . . .

That didn't come from me!

MALTE told me about that!

I only thought of it now . . . the meat . . . that's what made me think of it.

But with Malte it was the other way round. It was a mother and her son—not a father and his daughter . . . Malte got a lot of stories like that at Felix's company.

"No, everything's fine. I just thought of something . . . I . . . are you getting bored? No? Everything's okay?"

I'd completely forgotten about it! Why did I think I came up with that idea by myself?

The meat here, on my plate . . . I . . . I think I need to get a little air . . .

Oh, come on, man! Get your act together!

I can't put it off anymore. I can't just sit here with her, stuffing myself . . . and putting it off.

I have to get this behind me!

"No. I was just lost in thought . . . don't worry—"

Killing her . . . is not the end.

"Okay, you're right, I've lost my appetite . . . the second bottle? A little more? No? Should we just get going then?"

Whisper something in the girl's ear!

"I can't wait to have you all to myself again . . ."

What does she have in her hand . . . she's reaching toward me . . .

"I should take it? What do you have in your hand?"

Just take it!

What . . . what is that?

Oh!

She took it off! It's just a scrap of cloth.

"No, wait . . ."

She's standing up. The whole place is looking at her. No wonder! I'd turn too. Just look at the way she walks.

She crosses the restaurant, passing every table . . . looking around, looking back at me . . . in that short skirt—and nothing on underneath. She handed me her panties.

Where is she going?

This place is expensive! The ladies room—I'm sure it's clean.

She's going into one of the cubicles!

All I have to do is follow her!

That's where I can . . . where I can put this behind me.

That's where I can . . . in one of the cubicles . . . I'll lock it . . . that's where I can . . .

You know what you have to do!

It's not what you want. It's what you must do.

43

TWO YEARS EARLIER

"We can do whatever we like!" Max laughed.

Morning light flooded the bedroom making the gray tones of the floor, the steel nightstands, and the mirrors on the wardrobe doors sparkle. Using both hands, he picked up the blue-spotted mug from the tray beside him on the bed, raised it to his lips, and sipped the hot, milky coffee.

Nina had put on the white shirt again and threw a blanket around her shoulders. She loosened it a bit to reach what Max had brought in on the tray; she suspected he'd emptied his fridge to put together this breakfast.

"An exhibition? The zoo? Go for a walk? What do you feel like?" The heat was on, but the room was still a little chilly. Nina shivered.

"Do you have the whole day off?" Max was wearing a red T-shirt and had pulled on a fresh pair of boxers.

Tell him. Tell him now, thought Nina.

But Max was so excited, and she had no interest in ruining that with such a serious, sad discussion. Why should she let Felix destroy everything? She was a free agent. She could be with Max when she wanted. She could sleep with him or not. It was entirely up to her! She was not dependent on Felix; she would stand up to him, she would defy him. *And Max will help me*, she whispered to herself. *Won't he?*

She smiled at him, trying to dispel her gnawing doubt. It was as if she had some kind of power over him; the instant he saw her smile, his face lit up.

"So, what do you say?" He set the coffee back on the tray.

"Yes," she laughed. "I'm free the whole day. I'd love to spend it together!"

"Terrific!" Max looked at the small digital alarm clock on his nightstand. "Just after eight. If we're quick, we can still jump on a plane—any city you like."

A plane? That startled her.

"Rome, London, Moscow—where do you feel like going?"

Paris! She'd never been there.

Max reached for the cordless phone lying beside his bed on a pile of newspapers and pressed a speed-dial key. "Aventur Travel, please," he said after a moment.

"Paris." Nina leaned against his back, and threw one arm around his neck. "Let's fly to Paris!"

"But no bags, okay?" She could hear how keen he was to get going. "We'll just take off. And we'll come back tonight. Okay?"

The excitement pulsed in her veins.

"Two tickets to . . ." Max laughed into the handset. "No, it's me, Max." He glanced back at Nina. "To Paris. The next flight." He looked at the clock again. "And the one after?" He grinned at her. "Nine twenty-five. We can make that, can't we?"

She jumped up so fast that she nearly fell off the bed when it swung away. "Yes!" Nina laughed, and hopped down to the floor. "Of course we'll make it!"

She ran to the bathroom. *Who's paying for my ticket?* she suddenly thought. But Max had booked it and tossed the phone back onto the pile of newspapers. She heard him jump off the bed and run into the bathroom behind her.

"Lunch in the Latin quarter!" he shouted as he came in. "I know just the place!"

Nina lifted her head from the sink and looked at him. Max's face was still youthful looking, but there were already two deep folds framing his mouth. He grinned at her. And she suddenly realized that not only was he infatuated with her but that she had fallen for him too. At the same time, it also became clear to her that Max was doomed—and she with him. She would never be able to let him go again.

TODAY

Butz's arm is slammed back by the recoil. For a second he thinks he's dislocated his shoulder. His fingers instinctively tighten around the butt of his pistol.

Henning's forehead splits. His head is thrown back against the headrest, but his hands continue to grip the steering wheel.

Butz ducks and lies on the floor.

The bullet from Betty's little pistol hits the garage wall above his head. Butz holds his pistol firmly and stretches out with one arm, aiming the gun out between the wheels. From below the car, he can see Betty's slippers. She is still standing in the doorway connecting the garage and the house. She doesn't move. She doesn't shoot.

The engine idles. Henning is no longer pressing on the accelerator.

Butz's mind replays the way Henning's chin tipped up as the bullet hit him in the forehead.

I had to do it, Butz thinks. His mind is racing.

"I had to do it before he skewered me against the wall with his car." He whispers it to himself so that Betty can't hear him. He sees her feet descend the two steps from the door down into the garage. He slides his gun hand across the floor, keeping the weapon trained on her feet. He could shoot her. *Isn't she afraid?*

Betty's slippers draw closer to the car and come to a stop at the driver's door. Apart from the idling motor, there is nothing to hear.

Butz carefully draws his legs up and starts to stand. He can't lie there on the floor forever. He knows that if Betty is aiming at him, she can shoot him the instant his head appears over the hood.

Butz's scalp burns as he slowly stands upright. The red steel of the hood, the smell of fuel and oil.

Betty's is staring straight at him but her arms are hanging slackly at her sides. The gun falls and clatters when it hits the cement floor.

Henning's head has sunk to one side. The blood streams over his face. His eyes are open and staring at a point between his seat and the hand brake.

I had to shoot him, Betty . . . you . . . you forced me to do it.

But Butz doesn't say that. He lays his own gun on the hood of the car.

How long has he known her? She must have been just six or seven years old when he saw her for the first time. It was twelve years ago, when he was involved in the case of the missing Xavier Bentheim.

That's when he first met her sister too.

Claire.

Butz feels numb—dull and hard inside. He knows the hardness he feels inside will make many things impossible from now on. In a single stroke, everything lighthearted that might still have lain dormant inside him has been driven out.

He shot Henning dead.

Betty sits on the edge of an oversized terra-cotta pot in the front garden, alongside the driveway that leads to the garage. Her hair hangs loose. She's still in her pajamas and slippers. She looks at Butz, her gaze candid and totally helpless. With a tiny movement of one finger, he has snatched Henning from her side. Butz sees in her eyes that until the day she dies she will never really come to terms with what has happened.

Her elbows are propped on her knees and her face is now buried in her hands. She seems overwhelmed. She cannot put her thoughts in order.

Butz looks at the garage, its door standing open like a mouth. Above the trunk of the convertible, he can see the driver's seat. And Henning's head, tipped to the side.

You should have shot the gun out of her hand, he tells himself. *Then you might not have had to shoot Henning.*

But shoot Betty's hand? Claire's sister's hands seem too delicate, too finely formed for that to have been an option.

"Henning told me about the killings," Betty says. "That you were looking at a series of murders."

Butz stares at her. *It's true, I did mention that to Henning at some point . . .*

"But it's everywhere, Butz. It's not just one." She turns her face up again and looks at him. "You shouldn't have killed him."

He squats in front of her and reaches for her hands. He looks into her eyes—they are perhaps a little less beautiful, less feline, less seductive than Claire's, but they still remind him of her sister's. "You have to tell me what you know, Betty."

She shakes her head in silence. But she is not refusing to tell him anything. It is more a gesture of helplessness. Nothing makes sense anymore.

"Everywhere—where, Betty? What's everywhere? What do you mean by everywhere?"

Her voice is no more than a whisper. "Haven't you heard about it? The building on Alexanderplatz . . ."

Of course he's heard about it.

"It isn't just two or three women, Butz. It's everywhere."

His hands close firmly around her thin wrists.

"But what does that mean, Betty. Help me out here! I don't understand what you're saying!"

She flinches. Butz knows that his grip is hurting her. But not much, just a little. A tiny fraction of the pain that Henning must have experienced when the bullet went through his head.

"All I know is that you're chasing someone who doesn't exist," she whispers. "It isn't just one killer, Butz. It's everywhere. And it's spreading. No one, Butz—*no one* will be able to stop it. It'll break over us, and over the city, like a tidal wave."

She speaks as if she's in a trance.

"They hunted down those women," she says. "The women whose deaths you're investigating. They hunted them down. Henning told me about it himself. They tried to get away. They crawled on their hands and knees across the ground, but there was no escape for them." Her eyes seem to transform as she speaks, moving from the clear blue that she shares with her sisters to a dark-violet shade.

"Betty . . . what . . . what are you talking about? How do you know this?" He can't let her get lost in her muddled thoughts. He can't let her sink into the confusion that must be caused by Henning's death, by that one bullet.

"You can't do anything about it, Butz! You're looking for a phantom. Don't you see? Don't you get it? The man you're looking for doesn't exist! This isn't just some crazy loner with those girls on his conscience!"

TWO YEARS EARLIER

"Incredible, isn't she?" Max raised his eyebrows ironically.

Till saw her dark eyes settle on him. For a moment he forgot the other people in the low chairs and at the small tables dotting the theater. It had something to do with her form—or with the lines of her body, from her thighs to her breasts and up to her throat. Or perhaps it was the shape of her ass, forced into that pose by her high-heeled shoes, or the way her hair was piled high on her head, or the look in her eyes, or the movement of her lips. Till could not put his finger on exactly where it came from, but it radiated from her, some force that held not only Till but all the other onlookers in the theater spellbound and helpless. He sensed it in the breathless atmosphere around him.

Max had picked him up at the publishing house late that evening after he'd met with Malte and brought him here. With its ornate plaster ceiling, ascending rows of box seats, and tattered velvet chairs, the red-and-black theater hall reminded him of a miniature version of one of the great nineteenth-century opera houses. But instead of arias, the guests here were treated to drinks and snacks at their tables. There were no singers on stage; the dark-eyed young woman—dressed in feathers and sticks to look like some sort of oversized bird—had taken their place.

"D'you want to stay in front, or should we head back?" A dozen more girls in various animal costumes appeared on stage.

"Out back?" Till turned to face Max. Backstage?

Max laughed, took him by the arm, and led the way.

The bouncer standing guard at the small passage beside the stage appeared to know Max. He merely nodded and let them pass without another word. From the passage they entered a foyer, which, like the theater, was decorated entirely in red velvet.

"You can get to know the dancers back here," said Max with a lewd grin. But he laughed when he saw the look of surprise on Till's face. "No, I'm just messing with you." He strolled over to a tall double door that led off the foyer and pushed it open. "Much better."

A cloud of cigarette smoke greeted them. A few faces looked up as they entered, inspecting the new arrivals, but when they saw it was Max their focus returned to the large table in the middle of the room. Twenty or thirty men and women were grouped around the table, some sitting on the array of different chairs in there, others standing—all intent on the action on the table. For a moment, Till thought he'd see some beautiful young woman lying naked on the table, her perfect body a plate for those gathered around, sampling remarkable delicacies from her bare skin. Instead, he saw something far less remarkable; a grid with red and black numbers on a green background and a kind of black bowl. They were playing roulette. But not at a professional table—it was a homemade layout. The numbers and fields had been painstakingly painted on green felt, and the layout itself then stretched and nailed over a huge, antique table. But what was most remarkable was that the guests—unlike in a real casino—were not playing with chips. They were playing with real cash. Coins and bills were piled in front of each guest.

"What do you think—should we try our luck?" asked Max, biting his bottom lip and glancing inquiringly at Till.

I don't have money to waste on something like this, thought Till. "Maybe in a while," he said. "You go ahead." He spotted a bar in the back of the long room. "I'll get us something to drink."

He returned with two glasses just as Max was gathering a few coins from the felt. The croupier, in jeans and a sweater, had pushed them across with a rake that looked like a fly swatter.

"Come on, see if lady luck's on your side." Max threw a twenty on red, and then reached one hand out to Till; it held a few more bills and the coins he'd just won.

Till hesitated for a second, then took a twenty from Max's hand and laid it on "even."

"No more bets."

The croupier had already flicked the white wooden ball in its track on the spinning wheel. It clattered, jumped, and settled into a pocket. Everything else might have been homemade, but the wheel was the real thing.

"Eighteen, red."

Hey! Max jabbed Till in the ribs and chuckled. The croupier pushed a second twenty across the felt to Till. Because Max left his money on the table, Till let his ride as well.

"You want to sit down?" Max pointed to a seat that had just opened up in front of them. But before Till could react, a woman had already slipped past him and sat on the empty chair. She was wearing a heavy leather jacket over a thin dress.

"Thirty, red."

Now there were four twenties in front of him on the table. He decided to let Max take over the decision making; it was Max's money, after all. "I'm going to get another drink." Till had no interest in playing roulette at Max's expense, and not enough money to play on his own.

Max took no notice of him. He'd let his bet ride on red again, and the ball was already spinning.

"You should have seen her," said Max half an hour later when he rejoined Till. "She just let my hundred ride. Totally cold-blooded. Let it ride, let it ride, and kept on winning."

Till looked at him. "*Your* hundred?"

Max dropped into an armchair across from Till. "Yeah, my hundred. In three spins she racked up $2,700!" He ran his hand through his hair. "If I hadn't insisted on splitting the winnings, she'd have let it ride till it all vanished again!" Till realized Max was talking about the woman in the leather jacket. He'd already struck up a conversation with her when Till returned with the second round of drinks. He'd left them to it.

Till looked at him. "You should just try to break whatever hold Felix has on Nina," he finally said. Max had told him about his trip to Paris with Nina. Why didn't he just call her instead of flirting with total strangers playing roulette?

"I should have talked to her about Felix," Max replied. He suddenly looked as if something was weighing heavily on him.

"Then do it now. Call her, meet up somewhere—clear the air once and for all!"

"Tonight, you mean?" Max thought it over for a moment. "Do you think I can still trust Nina? After she let herself get mixed up in Felix's business . . ."

"You know her a bit better now," Till said. "You were in Paris. What was your impression? All a lie? It sounds like you two get along well."

"Yeah. Of course you're right." Max looked at him. "That's not what I mean. Sure, the trip was . . . nice. And I really think she felt the same way. But still, it was Felix who got her to, well, I don't know exactly what Quentin meant—"

"Maybe he just . . . just said it, you know? Was just messing with you. Have you asked him about it since?"

Max shook his head. "I don't believe that Quentin just made it up. And when I confronted Felix about it the other day, at his office, he didn't deny it. Not directly . . ."

"But he doesn't seem to have talked to Nina about it yet."

"Quentin?"

"Felix."

"No . . ." Max, pensive, sank back in the armchair. After a while, he said, "At least, Nina didn't say anything to me if he had."

"You didn't say anything to her, right? About what Quentin said . . ."

"I just don't know if I can trust her." Max looked at Till. "What do you think?"

Till shrugged. Hard to say. He didn't want to recommend that Max give himself over heart and soul to Nina, only to discover a few months later that it was *bad* advice. "You've got to have it out with her. Or do you want to play cat and mouse forever?"

Max had brought a glass of vodka with him from the roulette table and was rotating it absentmindedly in front of him. "Sometimes I wonder what Felix actually had in mind when he got her to come on to me. I mean, how much can it matter to him to get some pull over me? And if he's even leaning on Maja to do it—"

"Maja?"

"Nina's mom. She's been in Felix's corner for a long time," said Max, and wiped his mouth. "I don't know what their relationship is exactly. But he could get Nina to do just about anything if he went through Maja."

Till turned and let his head rest on the back of the sofa. That could be why Nina did it, of course. "He asked you to sell him the rights to your father's final manuscripts. And you turned him down. So, maybe he wants to change your mind somehow."

"Nina's probably supposed to make herself indispensable," said Max, his eyes scanning the room thoughtfully.

"And once you've started really wanting to be with her, then he'll go to work on you," said Till, finishing Max's sentence.

Max crossed his arms across his chest. "Stands to reason." He seemed to ponder this.

"Do you have any idea what the manuscripts he wants are about?"

Max looked up. "Do you remember those handwritten notes about Haiti? The ones I found down in the basement and showed you when we went on that bike ride?"

Of course Till remembered. He'd talked to Bentheim about them not long before his death.

They were silent for a moment.

"I poked around in my father's papers again, a while later. Before Felix had everything picked up," said Max, picking up the thread again. "I read some of it . . ."

"Uh-huh?" Till sipped at his beer.

"My father was planning three books. One story split over three volumes. It was never finished, but in the first book—as far as I could make out—it seems it was about a boy who stumbles across a family that seems odd to him from the start. But he isn't able to put his finger on exactly why, until he realizes that some of the family members are progressively . . . changing . . . until he can't tell if they're even human anymore."

"If they're not human, then what are they?"

"Infected. Monsters. I don't know exactly. I think my father imagined creatures that *were* human once. But an infection transforms them, slowly turning them into something else."

"What happens to the boy?"

Max clicked his tongue. "Well, he manages to beat the creatures in the family before they're able to infect him. But what looks like a victory at first turns out to be a double-edged sword, because it doesn't go undetected. From then on, the monsters come after him in the hundreds, trying to make him one of them. In this part of the story, it seems, he was going to be using typical apocalyptic images, disturbing scenes with masses of mindless automatons overwhelming everything with their sheer numbers. But the main point was that the kid manages to disguise himself as one of them, so that—in the third part—he's able to get to what my father envisioned from the start as the goal or the climax of the whole thing."

"Which was?"

"Well, not so easy to say." Max took his hands from the armrests and leaned forward. "My father apparently planned to title the three volumes *Access, Zone, Core. Access* is about the family where the boy . . . where he first comes in contact with the creatures. In *Zone*, he makes his way through their world as a kind of undercover agent, making his way to the 'core'—which is what the third book is all about."

"Hmm."

"The core is supposed to be what everything comes down to."

Till laid his hands on his calf, his ankle resting on his other knee. "So, what's in this core? What's the kid supposed to discover there?"

Max's jaw muscles flexed. "I wish I knew."

"It wasn't in the notes?" Till sighed, disappointed.

But then he realized Max was just getting up to speed. "Till, look, you're working for Felix now . . ."

"Yeah?"

"I mean, these creatures . . . they're not vampires, or were-wolves . . . my father always worked with classical material, the classical fantastic beings."

Till was finding it hard to follow his friend. "So, what you're trying to say—"

"What kind of creatures did he mean, Till? You remember what we read in the diary back then? Haiti. An infection. Transformation . . . those are very clear signs pointing to the kind of things he had in mind."

"Zombies?" Till instinctively grinned.

"Bingo, zombies! But not like the stupid staggering things in Hollywood movies. We're talking about old-school zombies, the originals, from Haiti. Beings that wander around the island like marionettes under a magic spell. You understand? Ethnologists investigated the phenomenon in the early eighties. To find out if zombies really existed. And they came across all kinds of clues! It was the movie guys in California who ruined it all."

In his mind, Till saw a field at night, leaden with Caribbean heat and a spindly figure pushing its way through the plants, its torso naked, long-limbed, gaunt. A strange, dull glimmer in its eyes.

"No will of their own," Max said. "Zombies act like they're . . . like they're remote controlled. What does that remind you of?"

"Felix's ideas. About free will . . . that it's just an illusion?"

Max pressed his hands together. "In Haiti, zombies are seen as people who have lost their own will and are subjugated to the will of a magician in everything they do. It's an ancient image. For the Creoles in the Caribbean, it was the most terrifying thing they could think of."

"Okay, but—"

Max wouldn't let Till interrupt. "I don't know exactly how it's all connected, but if Felix denies the existence of free will, then he has to think about the *difference* between humans and zombies, right? So, it's *no wonder* that my father's work interests him!"

"You think he wants us to see that we're really *zombies*?"

Max stared at Till. "You remember what he said when we saw him at his office? That getting past the illusion of freedom is just the first step?" His eyes glowed in the low light. "That's what has to be lurking in what my father called the core: the sorcerer who controls the entire legion of zombies! That's what the second step has to be, then—to spot the sorcerer!"

46

TODAY

"By *itself*?" Butz is close to hurling his phone onto the driveway when it rings yet again. "Don't try to shit me, Betty!"

Claire's sister is still sitting on the planter in front of the garage. Her face is wet with tears. He should give her some time alone, he knows. He should call an ambulance. He should get her into the house, or at least away from *him* . . .

"What do you know about it, Betty? An infection? Henning knew about it? *How?*"

She is sobbing, both hands pressed to her ears. Because he has shot Henning—but also because she *knows* something. Butz is sure of it. She knows that, through Henning, she's up to her neck in something she can't handle. "An infection, Betty—no one knows how to control something like that! And the longer we wait, the harder it's going to be to do anything about it! You have to start talking!" Butz's voice sounds as hard and sharp as a scythe. She wipes both hands over her eyes, clamps her teeth together, and tries to calm the quaking that racks her body.

Butz won't stop. "It's already everywhere. You just said so your-self, Betty!"

Suddenly, she stands up from the planter and steps toward him. "You always were an asshole, Butz!" she says furiously. The top of her head barely comes up to his shoulder. "Who do you think you are, yelling at me? What do you want from me? You think you've got a right to demand *anything* from me? After what you did?"

Butz's scalp begins to crawl.

"It was several years ago, Butz," Betty says with a hiss. "I was maybe fourteen, but I remember it like it was yesterday. I would hear you down in the living room, just by the hallway. I felt safe when I heard your voice down there, Butz. I could see how relieved Mom was when you were with her—in the months and years after Dad vanished. Until it all came crashing down. Because you're an asshole, Butz. You were an asshole then and you are now—the way you stand there yelling, acting like I owe you anything at all!"

He hears Betty whisper angrily, "You should never have let it happen." He knows only too well what she's talking about. He should not have let it happen: Claire and himself.

He had never loved Julia Bentheim. But *her*—he had loved her more than anyone else, ever.

Claire Bentheim, Julia's daughter.

It was a few years after he'd first entered the Bentheim house as an officer investigating Xavier's disappearance.

Julia wanted Butz close to her, and he obliged. He'd had every-thing under control. Until Claire started playing her games with him.

She started talking to him, inviting him into her room to show him her things. She smiled at him, brushed his hand in passing, came out of the bathroom wrapped in just a towel when he was walking down the corridor. She sought him out with her eyes, grazed his cheek with her lips when he left. She was vulnerable, tender, at his mercy. Confused. Alone. Even then, years after her father had disappeared. The entire family had never really recovered from the shock.

Claire. She was much too young.

Butz knew it then. He knows it now. And he will always know it: he should never have let it happen.

What had gotten into him? Why did he let her lure him into her room?

Hadn't he heard the buzzing, the humming, the droning in his ears when she reached out and touched him? Hadn't he known she was off-limits?

Yes, he had heard it. But he was too weak to withstand the storm she had unleashed inside him.

"Felix," he says, his voice shaking. "Henning mentioned Felix—how is he mixed up in this, Betty? How is he connected to the dead women, to everything hanging over this city?"

But Betty just stares at him. She seems to still be in the past—still back in the days when she first realized that the man now standing in front of her had slowly moved away from the mother and toward the daughter. Her sister Claire, just two years older than Betty herself.

"Have you seen him in the last few days, Betty? Have you seen Felix?" Butz knows he should be begging for Betty's forgiveness for what he did to her mother.

She looks beyond him, her eyes glazed. "Leave me alone, Butz," she whispers. "Just leave me alone. Whenever you show up, shit follows."

47

TWO YEARS EARLIER

Max was sure that Nina would welcome him with open arms. He knew she would want to know why he hadn't called her since their return from Paris.

There was only one way to free himself from the hold that Felix already had over him: wash Nina out of his system completely. At first he'd planned to do that with the woman he'd met at the roulette table, but after Till—wanting to be well-rested for his first day on the job—had left him there alone, Max had lost interest. He left shortly after Till.

The traffic light turned green. He eased the car forward. *You can't do this! You can't confuse her like that. She didn't do anything to hurt you.* He could already hear Till's objections, but he pushed the thought aside and floored it.

"Fuck it!" he said under his breath. "That's exactly what I'm going to do!"

He jerked the steering wheel left and raced through the intersection, leaning sideways to counter the centrifugal force. Not toward Nina, but toward the Flaschenturm! Toward Irina.

Let Henning, Malte, Quentin, and all the others believe they couldn't decide for themselves.

He could—and he would!

He would cut out his desire for Nina like a diseased organ. He'd sleep with so many women that the mere thought of seeing Nina would nauseate him.

And Irina would be the first.

48

TWO YEARS EARLIER

"Is that mint?" Max pointed through the expansive window to a pot out on the terrace.

"Yes." Irina seemed pleased that he was able to recognize the plant.

"Why don't we make ourselves a mojito? Got any rum?"

She hesitated. "Good idea," she said, but she seemed a little confused. "Quentin isn't here . . ."

Max smiled. He knew that already. Till had told him what he'd heard from Malte: Felix and Quentin were away for two days on a business trip.

Max went to the glass door and slid it open. "I know." He looked back at her for a moment. "Let's make some mojitos, then we can talk, okay?"

It was already well past midnight when Max got to the Flaschenturm. Irina had buzzed him in downstairs when she heard his voice. But her expression when she opened her front door clearly showed her bewilderment at his surprise visit.

She slipped past Max, through the glass door, and out onto the terrace, where she plucked two thick bundles of mint. When she came back into the living room, she pushed one of the bundles into Max's nose playfully.

Max grasped her hand lightly and held the mint to his nose for a moment, breathing in the fragrance. "I ran into Quentin the other day," he said. "That's why I wanted to talk to you."

She lowered her arm. "Oh, yeah?" She sounded slightly uneasy. "This way. The glasses are in the kitchen."

"He was pretty wound up," Max said when they were standing at the sink and Irina was rinsing the mint. She was wearing fleecy cotton pants that flapped loosely around her legs. The waistband sat low and sexy on her hips.

"I really didn't understand a word he was saying. Has Felix completely screwed up his head? Do the two of you talk about this stuff?"

Irina shut off the water and turned to face Max. It was clear that she wasn't expecting these questions. "It's true," she said slowly. "Quentin's been . . . nervous lately. No, not nervous, more . . . *drained* or something." She looked thoughtfully at Max. "I've tried talking to him a few times, but it wasn't easy."

"No?"

Irina smiled bashfully. "I don't know, Max. Maybe you don't want to know all the details."

"Yeah, sure." Max was thrown a little by her answer. "But I mean, you live together after all. Quentin changes and you simply let it happen?"

A look of guilt crossed her face. She suddenly seemed much younger, like a teenager, but Max knew she was in her early twenties, about the same age as himself.

"You're right . . ." she said, relenting.

"You should have seen him," Max said, dropping onto one of the kitchen chairs. "He started screaming! It started here, at your party. You saw what happened. But when Till and I left the club that night, he was waiting for us. I had no idea what he wanted from me! He'd lost all self-control, you know? He was out of his mind." Max paused and looked at Irina.

Irina said nothing. She seemed to have forgotten all about the mojitos.

"Does he get like that with you sometimes?"

She looked down at the floor in silence, but she'd definitely heard the question.

"I don't want to step on anyone's toes," Max went on. "But when I saw Quentin like that, right there in front of me, I was worried. What if you're here alone and he suddenly loses it like that?" Irina still hadn't raised her eyes. "Has anything like that happened?"

Now she turned away from him completely.

Max stood up cautiously and went to her. He stood very close behind her, but did not touch her. The scent from her hair mixed with the fragrance of the mint that filled the kitchen. "I know you love him," Max whispered. "How long have you been together? A year?"

"Ten months," Irina murmured. She had her hands clasped together and was leaning on the kitchen counter.

Max felt like he was being carried along by a wave. He couldn't resist.

"Is that what you like about him?" His voice was calm, but it betrayed his effort to control himself. "Do you like that it nearly drives him crazy with desire when you're weak?"

"What do you mean by weak?" She turned around abruptly. Her pretty eyes were glaring at him. "Because I allowed Felix to buy me this apartment? Is that it? Where do you get off, saying something like that to me?"

"Should I leave?"

"Yes!" She started breathing faster. "Do what you want." He was still standing very close to her. If she leaned her head forward, it would rest on his shoulder. "What the hell is going on, Max? You're right, I don't know how to handle Quentin anymore. Aren't you his friend? Can't you—"

"Friend is too strong a word," Max interrupted her. "We've known each other for a long time." He reached out one hand and touched her chin lightly. "Or . . . why not? Sure, Quentin's my friend. That's why I'm worried about him." He tilted her chin back a little and her face turned up toward his like a small bird's.

"Should I have a word with Felix? Tell him he should go easier on Quentin?" He let his hand drop. Her eyes remained on his.

"Would you do that?" Irina's face lit up—but just for a moment. Because in the next moment, Max leaned down closer to her. Being this close nearly took his breath away. The sensation overlapped with his memories of the days he'd spent with Nina; the impressions of the two women blended into an intoxicating mélange.

"I want to sleep with you," he whispered, and he sensed more than saw that she was on the verge of pushing him away from her. "Or I'll tell Felix that he should just let poor little Quenny fall flat on his face."

The words were out of his mouth before he could think about it. So quiet that he almost thought he hadn't said them aloud. He kept his gaze on Irina's face. Her eyes flicked from one of his eyes to the other—then came to rest on his lips. Max saw that what he'd said repulsed her, but at the same time made her think that he felt nothing but disdain for her boyfriend. And he knew she found his lack of regard for Quentin seductive because it meant the only thing making Max act this way was how close and desirable she was. And then his lips touched hers and his hand slid carefully under the waistband of her pants. She was naked underneath, her ass smooth and cool.

TODAY

"He hasn't been in today, Chief."

"Really?"

"Not yet."

"Did you call him?"

"First thing. He said he had to take care of something, said he'd call later. But he hasn't."

The chief's eyes drift back to the monitor on the wall beside him. On it is the image of a room painted completely white. It's a low-quality, grainy image. The camera is obviously high in one corner of the room.

"You want me to call him again?" he hears the voice beside him ask.

The police chief doesn't take his eyes off the monitor. "Who, Butz?"

"Yeah."

He leans forward a little. This close, the pixels making up the image flicker. Should they call Butz again?

The thoughts in the chief's head mingle sluggishly, like passengers alighting onto a platform that is already too full. There are just too many new things, too many things to keep in mind, too many imponderables, too many *risks* . . .

"What's wrong with her?" he asks, not answering the question. He turns in the opposite direction, looks at the other officers standing there with him, all eyes on the screen mounted halfway up the wall. He's talking about the woman they are watching on the screen. She is covered by a blanket, lying on a bed in the room.

"There are conflicting reports," a young officer on his right reports hurriedly. "Her name is Merle Heidt, twenty-four years old. She was brought in yesterday at midday—"

"Hey!" The police chief suddenly recoils. His heart is pounding.

A murmur goes through the gathering of officers.

Without warning the woman on the screen has leapt to her feet, as if pulled up by cables. She is now standing on the bed, her fists directed at the camera, her head thrown back. Slowly, the blanket that was covering her slides down the bed and lands on the floor.

The police chief stares at the woman's mouth. It is twitching so violently that the pixels are blurred. Her eyes are practically vibrating.

But there is no sound at all.

Just then the image is replaced by black-and-white static. There's a crackling noise, then a man in a white coat appears on the screen, sitting at a desk.

"Can you hear me?" The man is looking into the camera, his expression serious.

"Loud and clear, Doctor."

"You've seen the footage? Of Ms. Heidt?"

"Yes."

"Good." The doctor lays his forearms on the desk. "The security camera recorded that about two hours ago. Since then Ms. Heidt has been sedated. The seizure was particularly strong—"

The chief interrupts him. "I'm sure you know how to handle cases like this."

We'd better call Butz again, the chief thinks. *The whole city is going crazy.*

He casts a glance at the young man on his right and lowers his voice. "Do we have a time for the conference call about the building on Alexanderplatz?"

"One forty. Does that work?"

The chief nods. At least he has one man who does what he's told! He turns back to the doctor on the monitor.

". . . don't match with the symptoms we would have expected in a case like this," the doctor says. Apparently, he's been talking the whole time.

"Okay," says the chief, nodding slowly. "Keep us posted." He is about to turn away when the strangely pained voice of the doctor causes him to stop.

"Don't you get it!?"

"What?" Confused, the police chief looks back at the screen.

"Ms. Heidt is not just an isolated case!" The doctor has risen to his feet and is propping himself with his fists on the desktop, his upper body leaning toward the camera. "Since yesterday evening, they've been bringing them in by the dozens . . ."

By the dozens . . .

"It is *imperative* . . . do you understand what I'm saying . . . *IMPERATIVE* that we get support! And I don't mean just sending us a handful of doctors from another hospital. I . . ." the doctor's head flicks back in small, jerky movements, as if he's trying to catch his breath. "I . . . I don't know if it's advisable to send anyone here at all. Do you understand what I'm saying?"

No, I don't understand, the chief thinks.

"I've considered whether we should quarantine everyone in the building—"

"Look," says the chief—he almost adds "buddy," but stifles the urge in time—"it doesn't help anyone if we go losing our heads . . ."

The chief feels his lips continue to move—but suddenly there is no sound. He just gapes at the monitor.

The doctor has abruptly turned away and, as if mesmerized, stares past the camera he's been focused on, then at the same time, the officers hear a rapid gurgling sound, a cracking, a broken-off shout.

The police chief's hand rises instinctively—but stops halfway.

A figure has entered the frame. Only the back of it can be seen. The doctor's wide-open eyes are still visible over the shoulder of the hulking figure as it lumbers slowly toward him.

The chief feels the muscles in his face go numb . . .

The doctor's glasses slide crookedly up his forehead as the figure wipes them from his face.

In the same moment, it's as if the screen in front of them bursts open.

The police chief's half-raised hand flies to his forehead, palm out.

The man . . .

The man who wiped the doctor's glasses aside . . . has turned.

He's staring at them.

The skin of his cheekbones . . . it's as if someone has burned it off with acid.

Something liquid splatters onto the camera lens . . .

Droplets ooze down . . .

Through the streaks, the officers can make out torsos, arms, legs, hair, all forcing their way, pushing, cramming, crushing their way into the doctor's office . . .

. . . almost as if a new creature is trying to assemble itself from parts.

TWO YEARS EARLIER

"Are you sleeping?"

Felix's voice sounded so soft, so friendly, that Lisa heard herself answering without thinking. "No, not yet."

She had already put out the light before she heard him opening the front door. It was not unusual for Felix to come home after she had gone to bed. Normally, he just stopped for a moment at her bedroom door and checked to see if she were already asleep—which she rarely was, although she often pretended to be—and then continued down the corridor two doors to his own bedroom.

Lisa blinked. She lay on her side and saw his dark outline entering her room. The only light came from the hallway behind him. He walked over to her bed and sat on the edge of the mattress. Felix felt in the dark for her hand where it lay on the blanket.

Lisa rolled onto her back without pulling her hand from under his.

"Everything okay?"

She could make out his face dimly through the darkness.

"Yes," she answered, although it wasn't true.

Lisa had spent the whole day struggling, and failing, to come to a decision. Of course, there was no pressing reason that she had to reach this decision today or tomorrow. But she'd been putting it off for weeks, even months; the question of what she actually wanted to do with her life was bothering her more and more.

Several weeks had passed since the internship at the paper had ended. But Lisa could not bring herself to seriously entertain the idea of taking the editorial position they'd offered her. She could not put her finger on *why*, exactly. Because the traditional business of newspapers would not exist much longer? Because she felt that she could do something else just as well? Shouldn't whatever she was supposed to do with her life seem inevitable, necessary, urgent? Something that she *had* to do? She felt none of that about the position she'd been offered.

She'd spent the entire day brooding over how she might set a new course for the future. But—like every other time she had racked her brain on the subject—she had come up empty-handed. Deep down, she knew the reason for this was that, as fixated on what to do with her life as she may have been, her head was somewhere else entirely.

Since Till had returned to Berlin for Betty's wedding, Lisa's thoughts had focused more and more on him. It wasn't as if she and Till had spent much time together. They had met just a few times. But since his arrival, Lisa had been increasingly haunted by a hazy feeling, a kind of distress that had its roots in the fact that she was living with Felix—but thinking about Till.

"Henning just told me that your brother is throwing some kind of party. Tomorrow night at his apartment," Felix said.

Lisa's thoughts returned to the bedroom she was lying in. "Didn't you know that already?" She looked at Felix in confusion; she'd assumed Max had invited him.

"No. I didn't get an invitation."

"Max must have forgotten—"

"Nonsense. That's not something your brother would forget."

Lisa said nothing. Felix was right, of course; it was no oversight. Felix had not received an invitation because Max didn't *want* to invite him, and when she thought about it, it didn't really surprise her.

"It's not that I . . . that I would have liked to have been invited," said Felix, and Lisa felt the pressure of his hand on hers increase slightly. "But I'm concerned about Max, you know? I saw him at the office yesterday when he came to pick up Till, and I got the impression . . . how can I put it . . . that he was up to something."

"Yes?"

"And now this invitation. Sure, why not? It's just . . . no, I really don't want to get involved, it's just . . . you know Max better than I do. You know how he tends to get carried away by certain things . . ."

"What do you think he's getting carried away by?"

"I don't know, Lisa." Felix's voice carried a whiff of impatience. "Maybe I'm blowing it all out of proportion. All I'm trying to say is that maybe you should have a word with him. Or at least keep an eye on him. It might be best to do that before his party. And if it turns out that he's . . . not really up to it, then try to talk him out of it."

"You think he's not up to throwing a *party*?"

Felix sighed. "Yes, well, that's true . . . maybe you're right."

Lisa extricated her hand from his. "What is it you're thinking?" She leaned over and snapped on the light on her bedside table. Felix's distinctive profile appeared in the sudden light. His large eyes were on Lisa's. She lay her head back on her pillow, and felt how her hair fanned out around her on the soft fabric.

For a moment they just looked at each other.

"You look troubled," Felix finally said softly, almost cautiously.

Lisa knew he was right. "Are you concerned about me now too?"

He smiled and reached for her hand again. She let him take it. "That's different."

She looked at their two hands, their interlaced fingers.

"Max can go to hell for all I care," said Felix. "I only worry about him because I know you love him, Lisa."

Was that really the only reason he was worried? Lisa was not entirely convinced.

"Have you thought about what we talked about?" Felix continued. "Should I make a few calls? See what I can do for you . . . for your . . . well, career? Maybe you could look at a few different companies?" He reached across and propped his other hand on the other side of her, so that he was leaning over her.

Lisa felt her expression instinctively harden. Couldn't he give her a little time? She knew she couldn't put it off indefinitely. But when he constantly raised the subject like this, she'd never make up her mind.

"Lisa, I don't want to put any pressure on you or offend you. I . . . I just want to help you."

"Yes," she managed to squeeze out, wishing he wouldn't lean over her like that, wishing he would just leave her alone . . .

"Do you need a change? A little space, some fresh air? Is that it?" As if he were reading her thoughts, he sat up straight again and put his hands in his lap. "Could it be that you're still afraid of me?" His voice now sounded jittery, almost shy.

Lisa felt as though she were wrapped like a mummy in her blankets. How was she supposed to answer a question like that? Some years before, after a great deal of hesitation, she had admitted to him that despite their intimacy, she could never really shake the feeling that he might lose control one day, that he might hurt her, even if he didn't mean to. That he could do her serious harm, even though it might be during a moment of ecstasy, of passion, in a moment when he yielded to the power of his own lust. And although she knew that, since then, he had made an effort to keep himself in check, he was still the same man he'd been before she spoke to him. There were still nights they spent together when it came back again—crystal clear, radiant, glittering—the fear of this man who pushed her into things she dreaded even to think about when she was alone. Things she had never read about in any book, nor seen in any film. Things that picked her up and swept her along, things she barely experienced as herself. She knew that her vague memories of them kept working inside her, infiltrating her personality.

"I love you, Lisa," she heard him say. "You know that."

She nodded.

"I know I've messed up a lot of things."

Her eyes moved up to his face. He looked haggard and drawn. It was rare for her to see him this way.

"When your mother asked me to take care of you, I tried to do the best I could," Felix said. "It never worked with Max. But with you, Lisa, it did. You turned me into a different person. Can you believe that?"

No.

"You know, I've had tenants in your old house since your mother moved out." Felix locked his eyes on hers again. "I've been thinking about this for a long time. I'd like us to move there, Lisa. I want to give you the house. You always wanted me to hold onto it and not sell it. Maybe that's what you need: your father's house, where you grew up. Then you'll be better able to see which way the road ahead lies."

The house . . . the garden . . . the shed where Till spent his first night . . . the guesthouse—her father's study beyond the hedge . . . It all came back to her. Her parents' house had always seemed like a castle to her, and to move into it again would be a kind of coming of age for her. Felix had bought it from her mother years before—and now he wanted to give it to Lisa?

He leaned down toward her once more. He was so close she felt his breath on her cheek. "I want to have a child with you, Lisa. A baby. Can you make this dream come true?" he whispered in her ear.

TODAY

Frederik takes a step in the woman's direction. Claire moves to stop him, or at least hold him back. But then she looks again at the woman's face, at the lips pulled back from her teeth, at the dark rings surrounding her eyes, at her hair, lank and sticky with sweat—and realizes that they can't just turn away. Just like the man crouching against the wall behind them, the woman needs their help.

"We have to get them out of here," she whispers to Frederik as he touches the woman's arm. "They need water—their lips are completely parched."

Frederik leans forward. "Can you hear me? Can you understand what I'm saying?"

The woman nods. Claire sees her lay one hand on Frederik's arm. Her fingers close around his wrist. Very slowly the woman's eyelids lower over her eyes and then lift again. Claire hears the woman's breath whistling slightly as it streams from her mouth.

"Come with me. I'll help you." Frederik looks around at Claire. "Can you take care of him?"

"Yeah . . . yeah, sure." Claire turns—the man is staring at her. He is back on his feet, leaning against the wall. His neck is long and thin, and it juts crookedly from the too-large collar of his shirt. "We'll take you up," Claire says, gently. "Don't worry; everything'll be okay."

She goes to take him by the arm, but the drops of sweat covering his forehead catch her eye. What is it that's making them sweat so much? What is he doing down here? And the woman?

She shudders; instead of her taking his arm, *he* has suddenly laid one hand on her shoulder. Lean and pale, almost unnaturally long, his face rises above Claire's. An unhealthy odor escapes his mouth, penetrating her nose.

"Craaaarrrgrouugh," she hears a guttural sound in the man's throat. Or was it, "Can you—"

"Sorry?"

"Craahrrrgrouprrr—"

"I . . ."

"Craahrrllagrrr . . ."

Claire shifts her weight to her other leg to stop herself from being pulled over by the man. "Come on, Claire. They're not well," Frederik says to her over his shoulder as he pushes past with the woman. He makes his way along the passage, heading back the way they'd come. Claire tries to turn the man around in front of her and follow Frederik.

"CRAAHRRllagrrr . . ."

"Please, come with us. Frederik is helping us."

Yellow. The whites of the man's eyes are not white. They're *yellow.*

His other hand comes up and grasps her other shoulder and suddenly he is standing in front of her, his legs apart.

"Frederik!" Claire's own voice sounds thin in her ears.

"What is it?" Frederik is already ten yards down the passage.

"Can you wait . . . here—"

Past the man's shoulder, she sees Frederik almost swallowed in the darkness of the corridor. He stops and turns back.

"Rrrrrlllllgrrrrll . . ." The sound bubbles out of the man's mouth, his lips now pulled so far back from his teeth that she can see his receding gums, his teeth so long and thin she can almost see the roots.

"Wait for us . . ." *No sudden moves now, girl,* Claire thinks. *He'll turn any moment . . .* "Just so you don't get too far ahead," she calls to Frederik.

"Claire? Everything okay?" she hears him reply. He seems not to have understood her.

And suddenly it's like she can see it all in front of her, as clear as can be.

"Frederik?"

"Are you coming?"

"They're everywhere, Frederik . . ." Claire feels the tears streaming over her cheeks. "It's everywhere. It's started. We won't be able to stop it anymore." In front of her, the man's pupils flicker, following every movement she makes. As thin and spidery as his hands are, they are digging into her shoulders like pincers.

They are everywhere—*they* are what brought that building down.

And then she hears it again. The squeaking. This time like the wave leading an unstoppable flood. The floodgates are open. The masses once kept in check are now surging through these passages with unimaginable force.

Through the passages. Toward them.

They are everywhere—and they will sweep everything along with them.

Claire sees the man's face closing on hers. In horror, she throws up her hands to protect herself, presses them against the man's face.

The dead stench that exudes from his mouth, his throat . . . it oozes through her fingers, creeps into her nose, her eyes, her mouth, as if he has forced his tongue between her lips, inside her.

TWO YEARS EARLIER

"Max?" The front door of Max's apartment was wide open. Lisa walked in the door and wandered down the hallway that was painted black. "Max!"

It was the afternoon after she had talked to Felix in her room.

"Down here! We're downstairs!" Max's voice was muffled and distant.

Lisa walked through a corner room that connected the front of the building with the side wing, and then down the steps to the floor below, which was also part of Max's apartment. Reaching the bottom of the stairs, she saw Till and her brother, both in white sweat-soaked shirts, clearing up the large front room.

"Just a table," Max was saying to Till when she entered the room. "There's only supposed to be a table here, and chairs. I've already got those. The less there is down here, the better!"

Lisa strolled over to them and cast a quick glance at Till. He nodded his acknowledgment.

"Come on, Till, the sofa's next!" Max ordered, bending down to get a grip on the heavy, dark-red couch.

"The taxi's waiting for me," said Lisa, and looked at Max. "I've brought something with me."

Max straightened up. "Oh, yeah? What?"

"A surprise!"

"Need a hand bringing it up?" Till straightened up too.

"Good idea."

It turned out to be two boxes of champagne. Till hauled them out of the trunk of the taxi while Lisa paid the driver, and then they strolled back to the main entrance of the building together. Before going in, Lisa stopped and touched Till's arm. "I spoke to Felix."

Till turned to face her. He was still holding the boxes.

Lisa hesitated. After talking to Felix the previous night, she had not been able to sleep. She had convinced him to leave her alone in the room without causing too much offense, but she could not imagine where things would go from there. She wouldn't be able to stall him much longer.

"Can we sit for a minute?" Till nodded toward a bench on the bank of the Spree, where it slid past in front of the apartment building. From there, they could look out over the Gotzkowsky Bridge and the converted factory buildings on the other side of the river.

"So, what did he say?" Till asked when they were sitting down and he had set the boxes on the grass beside him.

That he wants me to have his child, Lisa thought. "It was about Max," she said. "He said he was worried about him."

Till's brow creased.

"How do you like it, working for . . . for Felix?" Lisa asked.

She noticed that Till paused for a moment before answering. "It's interesting, what they're trying to do there. As far as I can tell, no one in the world is doing anything like it."

"And you want to work there?"

Till shrugged. "Yes, maybe . . . why not?"

Lisa looked him in the eye. She had known Till so long, and looking at his sincere, strong, honest face had always calmed her.

"Because of us," she replied slowly. *Do I really have to tell him that?* she thought. *And if I do, isn't everything all wrong anyway?*

And even as she thought it, something happened that she had wished for without consciously thinking about it. Till reached for her hand and held it tightly. Her head grew heavy, and she let it lean to the side. Till lay his arm around her shoulder and she felt the warmth that his body radiated mingle with the warmth of the air. "Is that really the right thing for you?" she asked, not moving her head from his shoulder. "Working for Felix? Do you really want him telling you what to do?"

"I'm still learning," Till's voice was soft, and she could almost believe they were kids again, on an outing to the city. "Felix knows about things I know nothing about."

It's important to him, Lisa thought. *That's why he decided to stay in Berlin after Betty's wedding—because of work. But he can't work for Felix if I leave Felix for him.*

Reluctantly, she raised her head. "Are you sure you want to work for Felix?" If he was certain, then her way forward was clear.

Till's eyes were shining. Was Felix stronger than him? But then Lisa thought of her brother. Wasn't Max's own pride holding him back? It meant no one was able to tell him anything. So, wasn't it *right* that Till was not as arrogant, as egotistical as Max? That he had his feet firmly planted on the ground? Wasn't that, perhaps, his *strength*? Unlike Max, he didn't lose himself in his latest go-nowhere folly but realized when he could learn from someone. Wasn't it a strength that he didn't let such an opportunity slip by?

She stretched forward a little and her lips brushed his chin. She felt his arms enfold her, felt how his movement caused her face to move toward his. She closed her eyes and sank into his kiss. She had imagined this moment so many times, but in all the years, it had never come.

TWO YEARS EARLIER

"Hey . . ."

Nina turned. "Irina! What are you doing here?" Nina had just left the real-estate office and stepped out onto the sidewalk.

"Quentin told me you worked here."

Nina hadn't seen her since Betty's wedding. "Were you looking for me?"

"Have you got a minute?" Irina was the picture of innocence, but at the same time, she gave the impression that whoever was responsible for creating girls like her had anything but innocence in mind.

Nina shook herself slightly to clear the thought. "I'm heading home. But I was just going to grab something to eat on the way."

"Can I join you?" Relief was etched on Irina's face; it was as if she had feared Nina turning her down flat.

"Sure! I could use some company."

They set off down the street and walked in silence for a while.

"You're going to be at Max's tonight, aren't you?" Irina finally said.

Nina nodded. Max had invited her when they were in Paris. *So what?*

"You're . . . together, right? You and Max?" Irina stopped and looked at her. There was no mistaking that something was on her mind.

"Hard to say." Nina gathered herself. Suddenly, she thought she knew why Irina had stopped her.

"Nina, I don't know how to tell you this—"

"Is it about Max?"

Was Irina's face turning red?

"What's going on?"

Irina's lips moved, but no sound emerged. She looked past Nina, back up the street.

Nina had only spoken to Irina a few times, when they'd attended the same dinner or birthday party with Henning or Quentin. But they had never really been friends. Perhaps because Nina had always found Irina a bit tedious. She would never have said so openly, but sometimes she found her views a little . . . pedestrian.

"Is it what I think?" Nina felt her blood rising.

Irina nodded.

"When?"

"The night before last."

Shit! Is that why Max hadn't called her since Paris? Nina took a deep breath.

She felt Irina touch her arm. "I didn't want to. He . . ." Her voice faltered.

"I'm not sure I want to hear the details," Nina snapped at her. She was angry, but worse was the feeling that so many things she'd been looking forward to, things she would have enjoyed, were now sinking in quicksand.

"It's not just about Max," Irina said, looking Nina in the eye. "It's about Quentin too."

"What do I care about Quentin?" Nina nearly shouted. Quentin was not her problem!

"He found out this morning. I . . . I couldn't stand it any longer. I . . . I don't want to lose Quentin. I don't know what . . . it's like Max was toying with me—"

"And you weren't able to stop him!"

"I . . ."

Nina pushed Irina's hand away from her arm in disgust.

"Quentin went ballistic," Irina whispered. "I think he would have hit me if I hadn't run away."

Nina said nothing.

"And he wants to go to Max's tonight," Irina said softly. Another blow for Nina—she would have no time to think about how to deal with the news. There probably wouldn't be any way to keep Quentin away from Max's apartment, and he'd confront Max without a second thought.

"Can't you stop Quentin from showing up at Max's? That can only go badly!" said Nina, glaring at Irina, who stood in front of her looking like a lost dog. Nina was clearly going to have to take control of the situation herself. "You don't want to lose Quentin?" she said, grasping Irina by the shoulder to make her look at her. "Then tell him! Tell him it was an accident or something . . . a mistake . . . a *mistake*. That Max . . . that you couldn't defend yourself." She tried to look Irina in the eye. "Did he . . . did he rape you?"

"No!" Irina seemed close to tears. "No, I . . . Max and I . . ." Again she broke off.

"Whatever! You have to talk to Quentin! You have to convince him that you don't care about Max, that *he* is your future!" Angry, she looked Irina up and down. She had everything she should need for a task like that, goddamnit!

"He won't even let me explain. But it's not really about me," Irina stammered. "He and Max—they've been circling each other for years."

"He doesn't want to admit that Max is better than him."

"Maybe that's it."

"And tonight he wants to find out once and for all."

Irina nodded.

She wouldn't be able to keep him away. Nothing would stop Quentin from showing up at Max's place tonight.

"I wanted to let you know, at least," Irina looked at her wide-eyed. "Maybe you can warn Max. Maybe he can put off the party—"

"Because he's afraid of Quentin?" Irina didn't believe that herself. No, that wasn't the answer. "Look, if you're afraid, you'd better not go home. Can you stay with friends? At least until everything has settled down a bit?"

"He said I wouldn't dare *not* to go to Max's. He screamed at me. When I was running down the stairs."

"Makes no difference. Don't go. What do you think will happen?"

"And you?" Suddenly, something like defiance flared in Irina's pretty eyes. "You're not afraid of being there tonight! Why should I be the one to run away and hide? What's he going to do? Slap me in the face in front of everyone?"

Perhaps. Quentin was unpredictable.

"I can't just abandon Quentin . . . certainly not on a night when he could fall apart completely."

"Suit yourself," said Nina. She checked the time: just after 3:30. She had to get to Max. There was no time to lose.

TWO YEARS EARLIER

In the euphoria of their first night together, Max had given Nina a key to his apartment before they left for Paris. A half hour after leaving Irina, she used it to unlock his front door. At first she thought no one was home. It was only when she had taken off her coat and prowled around a little that she heard noises from below. She walked over to the stairs and went down.

Max was so caught up in what he was doing that he hadn't heard her come in. He'd brought plates and glasses from the kitchen and was laying them out on a long board he'd set up on sawhorses in the large living room. He only noticed her when she was already standing in the doorway.

His eyes flashed.

"How long have you been here?"

Nina leaned against the doorframe and crossed her arms. His hair stood up crazily on his head, and his white shirt was soiled from all of the preparation he'd been doing. "Got no one to help?"

"Sure. Till's here. He just ducked out with Lisa . . ." Max walked over to her, leaned down, and kissed her fleetingly on the lips.

But when he went to straighten up again, she held onto him. "We have to talk."

"Really?" He grinned, but with an expression that said *Have to? Why would* I *have to do anything?*

Nina was well aware of Max's resistance to anyone telling him what he could or could not do, and she wished there were something that might temper it. But maybe that was exactly what she liked about him: his autonomy. Liked so much about him, in fact, that she threw caution to the wind. "There's something I have to tell you."

He stood in front of her, his hands open, waiting.

"Things have changed since Betty's wedding."

Max narrowed his eyes. "Really?"

Of course they had. Since then, they had spent a lot of time in bed together. But that wasn't what Nina was talking about. "I like you," she said. Not *I love you.*

Max's head tilted up again. His expression had something stony in it.

"Mmm." His voice was pitched almost mockingly high—but it didn't make any difference. She'd started, and now she had to finish.

"I don't want you to misunderstand me." Nina lowered her eyes and saw only the deck shoes he always wore. Max said nothing, so she continued. "Felix asked me to . . . take care of you. He wanted . . . I don't know, actually, what he wanted. But that's why I spoke to you at the wedding. Because Felix asked me to get to know you better." She raised her eyes again and scanned Max's face. It looked strangely tense, as if someone was forcibly tugging at his features.

"But I've fallen for you since then, Max. I . . . everything that's happened between us . . . none of it happened because of Felix. It happened because I wanted it to happen."

"Have you told him that?" Max said, his voice raw.

"No, I haven't. You don't know Felix—"

"I don't know Felix? I've known him since I was twelve years old."

"You don't know him like I know him."

"So, how *do* you know him?"

You don't want to know that!

She spun away from him and started to walk away. She wanted to get away, she had waited too long, she had done everything wrong—but he was behind her in two steps. She felt his hands reach for her and turn her gently. He wrapped his arms around her. He held her tightly and spoke to her in a breathless voice.

"I already knew, Nina. I'm sorry, I should have told you, I . . . I don't know why I didn't tell you before—"

He knew about Felix?

"Quentin told me. That night when we all went to the club, the opening . . ."

Quentin. Like a slap in the face, Nina was suddenly struck by something else—what Irina had just told her. But she didn't want to betray what she knew. Max's embrace was too soothing, too much of a relief after all the agonizing she had done since first speaking to him at the wedding.

Nina nestled in his arms, but she found no peace. Should she really conceal something else from him now? Shouldn't she tell him that she knew what happened between him and Irina?

With a fierce twist, she freed herself from his embrace and shoved him away. She fixed her gaze on his face and noted again the furrows already there despite his young years. "Quentin's going to come tonight. Irina just told me." She practically spat the words.

That mocking look in Max's eyes.

"Why did you sleep with her?" she suddenly screamed. And even as she said it, she knew the answer: *because you knew Felix sent me to you.*

"What did you expect?" Max yelled back at her, equally vehement—but it was liberating too. As if yelling at Nina suddenly shredded the web they were caught in, tore through all the entangling plots. "Yes, I slept with Irina!" he said. "Yes, it was wrong to do it. But not because of you, Nina. It wasn't wrong because of you; it was wrong because of *her*. Irina!" Distress distorted his face. "I shouldn't have done that to her! She won't be able to keep it from Quentin—and he won't be able to deal with it. I've put her at his mercy, and she did nothing to deserve it!"

TODAY

The rails had to be three meters apart! *Three-meter gauge?*

Malte stumbles along the track bed.

Three-meter gauge . . . he has an impression of giants or Cyclopes from long, long ago laying a train track down here . . .

But it's just a train track! They didn't build a megalithic tomb or pile rocks into a wall. No, they built a railway line, something more from a steampunk dream than a fairy tale . . .

Land of the steampunk giants, he thinks. In the middle of Berlin . . . or more accurately, under the middle of Berlin, in the tunnels beneath the city.

"Hey. Got a smoke?"

Malte looks up. He isn't the only one walking along these tracks. He's part of a crowd, thirty or forty people walking together. They had all spent the night in the huge room and had left just an hour ago.

A young man's pale face blinks at him out of the tunnel gloom.

Malte shakes his head. "I don't smoke."

They stumble on.

How much longer? Just after they'd woken up, the guy in charge claimed they had a long march ahead of them.

Malte glances at his neighbor for a second. "You got any idea what's waiting for us at the other end?"

The young man beside him twists his face into a grim smile. "Nothing good."

Yeah, that much was clear.

"Anyone know if any more buildings have collapsed?" Malte has turned his gaze back to the track in front of him to avoid falling.

"Pfff . . ." he hears his companion mutter.

No one knows anything.

Out of hand . . . it's out of hand . . . wasn't that what they'd said when they notified him?

Out of hand.

But what?

And how seriously?

Malte is aware of the way his arms dangle at his sides. What is *he* supposed to do about it? He's been a desk jockey the last three years. He's completely out of shape.

Malte reaches into the pocket of his jacket and takes out his cell phone. He has only a weak signal.

Henning was the one who told him he was needed.

Malte touches the screen and scrolls down to Henning's number. Makes the call.

"Please leave a message after the beep."

No ringing, no dial tone. Just voice mail. Just like the last time.

Malte cuts the connection and drops the phone back in his pocket. It's not like Henning to be unreachable. And Quentin? Does he know anything?

Out of hand . . .

Malte sighs and walks on, following the gigantic train tracks through the tunnel. In the dim light, his neighbor has all but disappeared.

Calling Quentin . . . no, that's something he'd rather not do, Malte decides.

It's been two years . . . he hasn't spoken to Quentin at all since then.

Not since what happened to Irina.

56

TWO YEARS EARLIER

Irina handed the glass to Quentin. "Would you like some?"

He took it from her, drank it down in long swallows. The ice cubes clinked.

After talking to Nina, Irina had gone straight back to her apartment. The sliding glass door to the terrace stood wide open, and the pleasant scent of the first warm days of the year filled the living room. Quentin had been sitting out on the terrace on a deck chair with his back to her—one foot propped on the chair, one on the floor, leaning back. He was looking absently over the waist-high balustrade, out toward Rummelsburger Lake.

Irina had slipped into the kitchen, filled a glass with mineral water, tossed in a slice of lemon, and approached the deck chair cautiously. When she had laid a hand on Quentin's shoulder from behind, he nearly jumped out of the chair in surprise.

He set the glass down, wiped his mouth, and looked at her with disarming openness. And she knew, just then, that coming home again was the right thing to do. "It was a mistake. What happened, Quentin. I know I love you; I don't want to lose you." The words practically bubbled out of her. She squatted next to him on the terrace, wrapped her arms around his legs, and laid her head on his lap. She felt his hand stroke her hair gently.

"Promise me you'll do me a favor?" he said.

"Whatever you want, Quentin, whatever you want."

He went on stroking her hair. Irina turned her head a little and looked up into his face. "What is it? Tell me what I can do for you—I'll do it."

His eyes settled on hers. She saw that he was still wound up but that he had begun to regain his self-control. The desperation and panic that had filled him when she fled the apartment . . . those things had disappeared from his eyes.

"I'll let you know when the time is right."

She nodded. Waited a moment. Was it really a good idea to go to Max's?

"Why don't we go off by ourselves? Somewhere out in the country? To Potsdam, away from the city!" she suggested. "Spring is starting, and it's so lovely. We could go walking in the fields. I could pack a picnic for us!"

He looked at her. "I want to go to Max's party tonight."

"But why? What's the point? It'll be horrible!"

He pursed his lips, but he didn't stop stroking her hair.

"What are you going to do, Quenny? Try to beat him up? In his own apartment?"

Quentin frowned and turned away, gazed back out over the railing.

Irina propped her arms on his legs, climbed into his lap, threw her arms around his neck, and straddled his hips, his face almost touching her breasts. She tilted her head down to bring her eyes to the same level as his, the tips of their noses touching—as they had done so many times in the past. "What do you want to do there? Isn't what already happened enough?"

"Do you know what it's actually all about?" he whispered.

She grew cold. "It's about us, baby, about us not losing each other."

"And about what Felix does, about what concerns all of us. Malte, Henning . . . and Max too."

Irina didn't want him to start on that again. This all-consuming idea, this fixation that Quentin—just the day before, like some kind of crazed apostle—had tried again to talk her into believing. She knew there was nothing she could do to stop him if he set off down that road again. She knew he wouldn't listen to her. On that particular topic, he was a man obsessed. All he would do was to shout—*scream*—his version of the subject. As if the louder he shouted it, the more convinced he became of how important it was, how deeply all of their lives would be changed if they would only *get it*!

"It's not your fault, what happened," he whispered. "It's not Max's fault. It doesn't matter—"

"Then why do you want me to promise to be there for you when you need me?"

"I want you to do a favor for me when I ask you to, Irina— that's what you just promised me."

"That's fine—but why? Why do you want me to promise you that—if what happened doesn't matter . . ."

"You didn't *have to* promise me. But you did. Did I force you to promise? No. You did it because you *wanted to*."

She shuddered. Was he starting to drift off to that dreaded place again—where she would no longer be able to get through to him?

"You and Max, you're not to blame, I'm not to blame; no one is even the slightest bit guilty of anything." When she had climbed onto his lap, Quentin had tilted his head forward to meet hers. Now he leaned back and rested his head against the back of the chair. Irina was suddenly aware of how she was sitting on his lap.

There was something ridiculous about it now. But she didn't want to lose the feeling of nearness that climbing onto him had created.

"Do you know what that means?" he went on, lost in thought. "When none of us bear any responsibility for anything? It means we can act very differently than we have in the past." His eyes were fixed on her, but she had the impression that he wasn't really seeing her anymore. "People have always let themselves be held in check by the fear of doing something bad—by the idea that they can choose what they want to do and should do what's right. But that's a mistake, a delusion! All well and good, but what does that *mean*?" His hands closed over her elbows. "It means that we are finally able to—finally *have to*—shine a light into the dark corners that human beings have always shied away from!"

What he was saying was crazy. But the thoughts in his head seemed to light him up from the inside. Despite Irina's fear of Quentin's rapturous proclamations, she couldn't miss the way his face tightened as he spoke, how his normally striking features grew even sharper. His face seemed almost gaunt, his cheekbones stood out sharply, his eyes were a brilliant blue—a blue that awakened in Irina a longing to cover his face with kisses. The desire was even stronger than her fear that he might lose himself forever in what he was saying. But she did not give in to the desire. Instead, she swung one leg over his lap so that both feet dangled on one side of the deck chair, and she lay down in his arms.

"Human beings have spent so long living in fear of doing things that are supposed to be forbidden! It's never even occurred to them that it might be fantastic, exciting—even *noble*—to light up the dark corners! But that was a mistake," Quentin said. "If there is no guilt, no freedom, no crime, Irina, then those are the depths we *need* to plumb. How far can one go into that place called evil—but which, in truth, is no more evil than any other place? The fact is, Irina, there is no evil! Or maybe there is a region that people call evil, but you can't judge it. Every region—*every single one*—is equally good or equally bad. Do you understand what I'm saying?"

Irina shrugged. Reality couldn't be that bad. What he was saying sounded horrible, but he held her tightly as he said it. It was just a theory, just words, just crazy ideas. Nothing more.

"How far down can someone go? How far down into what used to be off-limits? It's so much more interesting than the region of so-called good. More interesting . . . but why? Maybe because it has been *shunned* for so long! How far down can you go? What would it even involve? Killing? Torturing?" He sighed, but then began speaking again immediately. "How does torture work? Do I crush a man's head in a vise? Do I pump his guts full of filth? Do I sleep with his wife?"

Irina jerked away from him. Upright now, she propped her hands against his chest. His eyes were blazing, his face distorted.

"It's not your fault," he said. "Believe me, Irina, these are not just loose words. No . . . in fact, maybe I should be thankful to Max for taking a step in this direction! But we haven't gone nearly far enough!"

TWO YEARS EARLIER

Leaving his office, Till pulled the door closed behind him. It slammed with a loud bang, but there was no one there to hear it. The corridors were empty. Besides, his coworkers didn't go around on tiptoe. The opposite was true, in fact. During the day, loud talk, laughter, and heated discussions were the norm. Doors slammed, receivers banged onto their cradles, people shouted from one office to another. Till liked that. His new colleagues were mainly young, cheerful, and one hundred percent committed to their work. It was always dynamic and there was always something to laugh at.

"Mr. Anschütz?"

Felix's secretary saw him pass by her office and called to him in the corridor. Till stopped and looked through her door.

"Mr. von Quitzow would like to talk to you for a moment."

Since Till's first visit to the firm with Max, he hadn't exchanged another word with the man who ran the place.

"Sure thing."

Merle nodded to one side, where—as Till knew—a door led to Felix's office. He smiled and walked past her desk toward the already open door.

Felix stood with his face to the window but turned around as soon as he heard him enter. Self-composed, he walked over to Till.

"Till, Till, Till! Nice of you to find a few minutes for me!" He took Till's hand in his and actually placed his left hand over the top, enclosing Till's. "So, are you enjoying it here?"

Today, on a park bench, I kissed Lisa—that was the thought running through Till's head.

"Yes"—*oh, yes!*—"very much! I mean, really!" Till smiled. it was all so absurd. "It's fantastic."

Felix smirked and looked at him with satisfaction. "Henning explained things, I take it?"

"He did."

"And? Have you been assigned a region to focus on?"

Till raised his eyebrows. "Right now I'm still trying to get an overview of the material you already have . . ."

"Ah. Well, that could take a while."

"Absolutely. But it's fascinating."

"No doubt." Felix looked around his office a little distractedly. "Can I get Merle to bring us a little something? Coffee? Something to drink?"

I was actually on my way to see Max, Till thought. But he finally had an opportunity to talk to Felix, and he didn't want to waste it. He had time. He knew Max's party would go late.

"A glass of water would be fine."

"Two waters, please, Merle," Felix called through the open door before returning his attention to Till. "Which section do you think you'd like to be part of, Till? Have you thought about it?"

"Oh, well, there are plenty of sections that seem exciting . . ." *Come on*, Till thought, even as he went on speaking. *Take it! You know what you want!* "Maybe the 'essentials' section?" He looked a little doubtfully at Felix. Was he maybe being too audacious trying for *this* section so soon? He was sure it was one of the company's centerpieces.

"And where exactly?" Felix looked at him pleasantly.

"Experimental narratology," Till said. That was not only the unit he'd had his eye on since first hearing of it, but it was also the unit that held out the most promise as a place where he could find out more about Felix's true intentions. "If you ask me, it's the most exciting section. As far as I know, there's nothing like it anywhere else."

Felix laughed. "Experimental narratology! I might have guessed that you'd be drawn to that. Of course, it's also the juiciest plum I have to offer anyone just now . . ."

"If that doesn't work, then . . ."

"No, no, no. Don't be so quick to give up," said Felix, and for a moment his tongue flicked across his lower lip. "Ah, there you are, Merle," he looked toward the door. "Thank you very much. Just put the tray on my desk."

Till and Felix watched as the young woman set out a bottle and glasses and exited the room without closing the door behind her.

"So, have you already come up with something—for experimental narratology, I mean?" Without looking at Till, Felix filled two glasses from the bottle of water.

"Complementary points of view," Till quickly replied. "Okay, it's not a new idea. But as far as I can tell, in the plan of the universe, you haven't gone very far in that direction. Not yet, at least."

"Complementary points of view—how do you see that, exactly?" Felix lifted the glasses from the tray and approached Till.

"The main storyline," Till answered, "has already been worked out pretty thoroughly, and it's great. The twists and turns in there . . . I have to admit, I've never seen anything like it."

"Well, thank you." Felix handed him a glass.

Till accepted the water, drank a deep swallow, then went on quickly. "What happens is so suspenseful that I want to find out more about it. Basically, what I want is to be able to take any character from the main strand and experience what happens from his or her perspective!"

Felix smiled. "We've already thought of that."

"Have you? Of course, up to now the story's been set up in a particular way because the main character's point of view seems to be the best one. From that perspective, everything can be shown in its most dramatic, most moving, most exciting manner. But the other characters' perspectives are a gold mine! To me, that material is more interesting than some of the spin-offs. They're interesting enough, but they aren't able to develop the incredible force that the main storyline does."

"Why not?"

"Because the main story simply manages to get the most out of the basic premise underlying this world: the infection. So, I'd build the fictional playing field wider. I'd take the same events and look at them again, but this time through the eyes of the other characters you've already introduced, instead of constantly having to come up with new material. And I'd be very rigorous about it. Not just one or two secondary figures, no. I'd do it on the same scale in which it's already been laid out. With three or four hundred characters . . ."

Felix sipped at his water and then dangled his glass casually in one hand. Still standing, he angled one leg across the other and propped the toe of his shoe on the floor. He looked at Till. "Yes. Yes, you may be right . . ." said Felix, turning and setting his glass on his desk. "Do you want to start with the narratologists next week?"

"You bet!"

"Great!" He turned back and smiled at Till. "And tonight you'll be at Max's, I imagine."

Till nearly choked at the suddenness of the change. "Yes, sure. He's invited a few people over. It'll be a good night."

"You know, Till," said Felix, forming his mouth into a rather strained smile that disappeared a moment later, "in the last ten years, I've been following what Max has been doing pretty closely." He seemed to be offering Till the opportunity to respond, but Till decided to wait. "And I have to say that lately," Felix continued, "I have the feeling he's losing the plot somewhat."

"The plot?" Till came within a hair's breadth of adding "sir" but managed to stop himself in time.

"Yes . . . I mean, Max rarely talks to me anymore." And then Felix's voice changed, as if to say, hey, let's tell it like it is. "But what I've been hearing leaves a very bad taste in my mouth." He crossed his arms. "Max is no fool. On the contrary, he demonstrates considerable talent. I'd go so far as to call him brilliant—perhaps . . ." Felix fixed his eyes on Till as he said the word *perhaps*. "The problem is that Max doesn't know how brilliant he really is. He's proud—you know that probably better than I do. Obsessive too, and crazy, if you will. And I'd wager that he's prepared to go a very long way to find out just how much talent he really has!"

"You may be right." Till had to admit it was likely.

Felix nodded. "You see? And that's what's troubling me. Is Lisa going to be there tonight?"

The sudden mention of her name cut Till like a knife. Not only because Felix spoke her name as if she belonged to him, but also because Till suddenly realized that Felix was a man who would not simply lie down and accept that he was beaten—he was not the kind of man to willingly forgo *anything*. Nor was he accustomed to doing so.

"Yes, I think so," Till blurted out. And even as he did, he wondered how suspicious it looked that *he* knew that Lisa was going, whereas *Felix* had to ask him about it . . .

"That's exactly it," said Felix. "That's exactly what I find so exasperating. Tonight—God only knows why—Max throws a party, and of course, his sister is going to be there. But Max is growing more and more erratic. And Lisa, quite naturally, jumps in front of her brother whenever things start to get out of hand. She's always had it in her head that she has to protect Max." Till knew this to be true.

"I'm very happy we've had this opportunity to chat, Till," said Felix, and leaned against his desk. "Do you think you could keep an eye on Max this evening for me? Just so nothing goes wrong?"

"Of course," Till heard himself saying—cursing himself even as he did. What was this? Was he suddenly Felix's errand boy? This had nothing to do with his work at the company. Had Felix *really* handed him the task so that he could spy on Lisa for him—on *Lisa*?

"And keep an eye on Lisa too, will you? You've known both of them for so long, Till. If you only knew how much you mean to them!" Felix's eyes almost seemed to soften a little. "Knowing you're there to make sure things don't get out of hand would take a tremendous weight off my shoulders."

Just like Bentheim, thought Till. *He asked me to keep an eye on Max too.*

"I can't really pin it down, Till," said Felix, "but I get the feeling that your levelheadedness is exactly what Max needs to stop him from going out of his mind completely."

Till exhaled. What could he say to that?

"Okay then!" Felix pushed himself away from the desk and approached Till. "So, I can rely on you?" he said. "Of course, of course. After all, I've known you since you were this big!" Felix held one hand at the level of his chest.

Till felt like he needed to swallow, but he couldn't.

Felix shook his hand. "Have fun tonight, Till. Say hi to Lisa for me." With that, Felix turned and went back to his desk, and Till got himself out of there.

58

TWO YEARS EARLIER

"True? Truth? What is that, exactly?" Max's voice rang sharp and clear from the kitchen.

By the time Till arrived at Max's apartment, a good two dozen guests were already there. Till threw his raincoat onto the mound of coats piled in the entry area and strolled toward the kitchen. Several guests turned and eyed him briefly as he passed, but he only recognized Henning and Betty. They and a few friends had taken over some floor cushions in the corner room.

"When a sentence or image expresses something that corresponds with the real world." The voice that was responding to Max's questions was somewhat quieter and more measured than that of the host, as if the speaker were trying to substantiate a claim.

"So, you'd say a Superman comic wasn't true?"

Till poked his head into the kitchen. Max was leaning on the refrigerator, a beer clamped between his crossed arms. In front of him was Malte—slighter and thinner than Max—his face positively glowing. They were surrounded by five or six guests, all of whom were engrossed in the exchange. Some were already holding plates of food from the buffet.

"There are all kinds of modes or ways of existence that you can illustrate or represent," Malte defended himself. "It doesn't always have to be a picture of a factory. It could be a description of the state of someone's soul, or a poem about a dream—all of that can be true too. But," he said excitedly, "I don't want to contradict you at all. To say that . . . that a painting, for example, has to be *true* to be good, well, that doesn't go far enough. A Mondrian or a Pollock, those are not true."

"What are they supposed to be if they're not true?" Max took a swig from his bottle.

Till nodded at a guest sitting on some crates of beer and helped himself to a bottle when the guy moved.

"People can paint whatever they want, I don't care," said Malte, who'd had to search for words for a moment. "I'm not going to be small-minded about it. To me, what really matters is whether the artist's stuff sells. Whether it's in demand. That's what separates good pictures from bad ones—even if that's too shallow for you."

Max tilted his head to one side. "Bullshit, Malte. And you don't believe it either. As far as I remember, Van Gogh never sold a single picture. But his work is great art, isn't it? Success when you're still alive, or in the first two hundred years? Where do you draw the line?" His voice grew louder, and it seemed to Till to waver a little. "No! The one who tries something *new*, that's who paints good pictures. *That's* the truth!"

"Okay, then," Malte shot back, "why don't I take this refrigerator here, which no one has ever called a sculpture, and I say, as a sculpture, it's my work—"

"Except *that* is not new," Max, surprisingly vehement, interrupted him. "Duchamp was already producing his ready-mades—you *know* about them—at the start of the twentieth century."

"Then let's talk about what I dreamed last night," Malte tossed back. "Okay, it was just subjective, but at some level, it existed.

Then I declare this dream to be a work of art. No one's done that yet, have they?"

Max stared at him.

"Okay, you're right, that's crap," said Malte. "All I'm trying to say is, by my definition, people can decide for themselves what they think is art. But you're looking for some sort of objective criteria . . ."

For a moment, Max made as if he was going to hurl his beer bottle into the sink, but he turned the motion into a joke. "I'm not interested in defining how the word *art* should be used," he said loudly. "What interests me is what's going to be done next. Don't you get that?"

Till narrowed his eyes. Max had clearly already had quite a bit to drink, and he was handling it pretty well. But things could easily flip.

"In your fucked-up fictional universe, for example!" Max shouted at Malte. "What decisions, what creative decisions, I mean, are you going to be making next—"

"But that's not art," Malte threw back at him.

"Then what is it? Propaganda? A cash cow? *What?*"

"You know what it is. The project serves a very specific purpose."

"Which would be . . . ?"

"To open people's eyes."

"To the fact that we're all just imagining that we're free!"

"Exactly!"

"You really don't see how much of a dope you are!" The irony in Max's voice was gone in a stroke. "You want to open people's eyes to the fact that they're deceiving themselves. So, really, what you want to do is nothing less than reveal a *truth*. But that's precisely what you were rejecting just now."

"I . . . I—" Malte was trying hard to rally. But Max wouldn't let him get a word in.

"Yes, rejecting! You said what matters about a painting is that it sells. But *I* say, what matters about a *picture* is that it's *true* and *new*, meaning it's an image that's right, and that has never existed before in that particular way! Everything else is bullshit!"

Max stepped very close to Malte and his voice turned razor sharp. "But what you're doing with Felix—"

"But that's not pictures . . ."

"Really? I thought the final form hadn't been decided yet! Maybe it'll turn out to be a photonovel or something like that!"

"Yeah, okay . . ." Malte was back on the defensive.

"Okay, then! And anyway, it doesn't matter what form it finally takes. What you're doing with Felix is the exact opposite of truth. You're not trying to open people's eyes—you're trying to *mess* with their *heads*! You're building a machine for screwing with their thoughts! Correct me if I'm wrong . . ."

The kitchen had been filling with guests throughout their exchange, drawn by Max's shouting. Max's shoulders were tense, and he was glaring at Malte. And even though Till wasn't about to let himself be Felix's pawn, he felt he had to step in and help Max a little before he lost control completely.

"Hey, hey," he said quietly, reaching out and touching Max's arm. "It's still early. Most of your guests are still arriving." He glanced at Malte, who was breathing heavily, as if the vehemence of Max's reaction had pushed him to the limits of his strength.

"Hi, Till," said Max, his voice suddenly back at a normal level. He looked at Till uncertainly. His thoughts still seemed to be somewhere else entirely.

"Want to check out the buffet?" Till clinked his beer bottle against Max's.

"It's downstairs. You know where to go. I'll be down in a minute."

"Aren't you coming?" Till asked with a frown. A thought flashed in his head: *you're talking to him like you're his nurse.*

"Just. Go. Down!" Max snarled. His tone was repellent and Till recoiled from it. Max had not spoken to him like that since he'd returned to Berlin. The excitement of the party and the booze weren't doing Max any favors, which increased Till's concern. Perhaps leaving him to his own devices now would not be the best move. He glanced at Nina leaning on the window a few steps beyond Max.

"Everything okay?" he said, and looked back at Max, leaving no doubt that the question was meant for him.

"*Everything's fine*—isn't it, Till?" Max's anger shifted from Malte to Till in a split second.

"Forget it, Max. I'm going to the buffet." He turned away before Max could get off a clear shot.

"Just come from Felix, have we?" Till heard Max hiss behind him, but he didn't turn.

"Hey, Till! I'm talking to you!"

Till turned. The other guests were looking at him with shocked faces as they edged away from Max.

"I've just come from work, yes."

"And? Did he ask you to keep an eye on me?"

Till took a breath.

"Of course he did!" Max barked. "I knew it. What the hell is up with you, Till? How long have we known each other? What are you doing? Turning into that asshole's stooge?"

Till was fuming inside. *That wasn't true!* Within seconds, Max had managed to push him to the brink.

"You know what?" Max spat, disappointment etched on his face. "I've been waiting for the day you did something like this. It's just like you!"

Max shoved himself away from the refrigerator, swayed for a moment, and then stalked out of the kitchen, passing Till without touching him.

Till's face was burning. He felt the eyes of everyone in the kitchen turned in his direction. But that wasn't what was upsetting him so much. It was the contempt he heard in Max's words.

"Don't listen to him." Nina laid a hand on his shoulder. "He doesn't mean it like that. He was telling me just this afternoon how happy he is to have you in Berlin. Hey . . . okay?"

59

TODAY

"God, what a view."

The windows are floor to ceiling and give a clear view over the rooftops of the city. The sky has taken on a leaden tone, against which the pale-gray cloud of dust still shrouding the foot of the Fernsehturm on Alexanderplatz is barely visible.

Till turns his gaze into the distance. He sees the skyscrapers over on Leipziger Strasse, the red clock tower of the town hall, and, almost on the horizon, the old listening station on the Teufelsberg. Berlin. It lies at his feet like a sacrifice. As a boy, he thought he knew every nook and cranny of it. He's been away for years, but he has never felt as at home in any other city.

"Till?"

He turns around. Lisa is standing there. She has gathered her dark-blonde hair into a knot at the back of her head, and her pale face looks pensive. It pains him to see her here—here in Felix's apartment, a place that Till has always reviled, and where she has been living for so long now.

"Didn't you want to come back?" she asks softly. "After Betty's wedding . . . after everything that happened?"

Till turns back to the windows. He'd thought about Lisa every day. But to come back here again? What would be the point? To visit her at Felix's place?

"But I did come back," he murmurs, although he knows only too well that that's not what she's talking about.

"For the funeral," she says.

His eyes follow the oddly fluffy billows of dust. Looking closely now, he can see the clouds slowly moving apart.

"What is going on in the city?" Lisa steps forward and stands beside him at the window. He can *feel* her presence, standing there. It is as if the air around them is electrically charged. "I hoped . . . I hoped you'd get in touch." Her voice still sounds to him like it did the first time he heard her speak in the kitchen of the Bentheim house, where Julia drove him after the accident.

"Don't you understand?" She has turned to face him, and he sees her hand reach out to him, take his arm, how her tender lips part, the tiniest of gaps remaining open for a moment before her lips close again. Then, she continues. "Don't you understand that we should have talked, Till? Nothing is fixed. We've wasted two years, and I haven't moved even the smallest step forward."

He looks down at the torment in her face and forces himself to fight back the urge to stroke her cheek. "It would have been unbearable, Lisa. It wouldn't have worked, nothing would have worked . . . we couldn't . . . I couldn't . . . I couldn't see you anymore."

It isn't because of Felix that I didn't get in touch . . .

"*Why*, Till? Why couldn't you see me anymore?"

She still doesn't know . . .

"Do you think you know what's going on in my head? What I think, what I feel, what I *want*? How can you make decisions that matter to us more than anybody else without talking to me about it? Don't you see how wrong that is? How wrong it is that we haven't seen each other for two years?"

Yes, he sees it.

"Nothing's simple. Nothing's *ever* simple! But now that you're here . . ." She trails off, leaving the sentence unfinished.

"Yes?" His voice is tentative, but he can't let it go. He wants— he *must*—know what she wanted to say.

"At last, you're here."

He is standing with one arm held crooked across his body, and she slides her hand between his forearm and his stomach.

Till eyes wander from the part in her hair down to her ear, her throat, the top of her shoulder where it disappears under her blouse. He has the impression that she can actually feel his gaze on her skin, like the cool tip of a knife tracing across it.

"Do you see that cloud—over there, beside the tower?"

Till presses her hand closer to his stomach. It has become like a law for him—every thought of Lisa must be suppressed, banished, beaten down like a dog . . .

"We don't have much time left, Till," she says. And he knows she is right.

Gingerly, he reaches out and places his left hand on her neck. Hesitantly, she turns her face toward his and she leans her head back. Her eyes are now only slightly open. He can hear her breath escaping past her soft, familiar lips. Then he has both arms around her, feels how she gives herself over to his embrace, drawing her body to his, a little higher . . . as his face moves down over hers, and he is a captive to the touch of her skin and the pressure of her body, which he feels everywhere. Her eyes close and her mouth is ready to accept . . .

"HELLO-O!"

. . . to accept . . .

"LISA!?"

Her eyes flash.

"HEY!"

Her hand pushes against Till's chest.

His head comes up, but slowly—as if he is struggling through quicksand.

It is Felix. Just entering the room.

He had called out to them from the foyer.

His eyes blaze as they meet Till's—but Lisa has freed herself from his arms.

"Till! Nice to see you're already here!" says Felix, his voice raspy as he approaches them.

Did he see their embrace?

"Haven't you offered him anything to drink?" Felix looks to Lisa, who Till now only sees in profile.

"I was just about to," she says, then looks back to Till, her eyes perhaps more beautiful than he has ever seen them before. "What would you like?"

TWO YEARS EARLIER

The anger was stuck fast in Max's throat. Till should die, slowly and painfully. Working for *Felix*! Of all the places he could find a job! On a project that disemboweled his father's books!

But at the same time, he knew that he and Till got along so well because they shared the same interests. So, wasn't it *obvious* that Till would go to work for Felix? If he were Till, wouldn't he have done the same thing?

He crossed through the connecting room downstairs and entered the living room, where the buffet was set up. From the corner of his eye, he noticed someone staring at him, but didn't bother to see who it was. Instead, he went over to the table and reached for an open wine bottle—an expensive red he'd been looking forward to all day. Max poured himself a full glass and turned to see who else was in the room. As he did, he realized who had been staring at him. The person had turned away again in the meantime. So, he had come after all.

"Quentin." With open arms—glass in one hand, bottle in the other—he walked over to him. "And Irina." They were standing in a group that also included Henning and Betty. Why not? He would simply act as if nothing had happened. Quentin could fret all he liked about how to deal with it! "Glad you could make it!"

Quentin wheeled around. His eyes were icy. "It's the last time I come here, Max."

Max stood in front of him with a grin on his face. "Do you think that makes me sad, Quenny?" He noticed his sister Betty give Henning an uneasy glance.

"Why do you think I showed up, asshole?" Quentin had planted himself with his feet wide apart, as if to make himself as stable as possible.

Max took a slug from his glass. The wine was truly outstanding. "I don't really give a shit one way or the other. Or, no . . ." he said, holding the bottle and glass in his outstretched arms, "now that I think about it, it might be best if you left."

"Let's go . . ." Irina, not daring to look at Max, tugged cautiously at Quentin's arm.

"What's the matter?" asked Betty, looking with incomprehension at her brother. "Max, what's going on?"

Max set the bottle on a small table beside him, but kept his eyes on Quentin. "What are you waiting for?" Facing Quentin, Max felt absolutely calm. Nothing like the agitation and anger he felt with Till. "Or am I supposed to physically kick you out?" Even as he said it, it was painful. Less because of Quentin than Irina. He'd always liked her, and now here she was, an innocent bystander. But he was like a different person. It was as if some kind of subterranean fury was at work inside him, something that would literally tear him apart if he didn't use it to hurt someone else.

"You can't push me around." Quentin's voice was low, bitter.

"So, what are you still *doing* here?" Irritated, impatient, as if dealing with a dog that had run up and refused to be chased off, Max was on the attack. At the same time, he was plagued by images of what had occurred two nights earlier with Irina.

Then, to his surprise, Quentin suddenly looked to Henning. "He won't be the one who'll suffer," Quentin said to Henning, "but it'll get him just the same."

"What?" Max grabbed Quentin's sleeve angrily. "Are you talking about me?"

Quentin turned back to face him. "You'll never get rid of this one, Max. And your pride will disintegrate like shit in rain."

Without thinking, Max let go of Quentin's arm. "Hey, fine with me. If you don't want to go, then stay!" He grinned then. Derisive and aloof . . . but all of it just show. Something seemed to be stuck in his chest, something felt downright *jammed* in there.

For a moment, Max's face flushed warm. One of the guests standing farther back had taken a flash photo of the group standing there. It was a photo Max would never get to see. But he knew that in it he looked skinny and ugly, with deep-set, drooping eyes, his mouth frozen in a sucking motion.

TWO YEARS EARLIER

"Quentin's seriously upset." Nina had closed her eyes for a moment, then opened them and looked at Till again as they made their way from the upstairs kitchen to the living room below. "And that mostly comes back to Max."

Till looked down to the other end of the living room, where Max seemed deep in conversation with Henning and Quentin.

Henning had turned to face Max. "You want to know *my* theory?" Till heard him ask.

Max leaned back as if to say, *Well gosh, that's just what I was missing.* At the same time, a look of amusement crossed his face, and everyone standing around breathed a collective sigh of relief. Clearly, the current discussion had been preceded by a bitter exchange.

"My theory is that you're just jealous of Quentin," said Henning, "because he gets to work for Felix on your father's universe. But you're too self-important for that!"

"Ah, that's what it is." Max turned to the small table where he'd set down the bottle of red—and his eyes met Till's. "Have you heard?" He nodded encouragingly to Till. "My old man's to blame for everything." Then he looked back at Henning. "But by saying that, you're not accusing me of anything, are you? Of course not—there are no accusations in your world."

"Don't go changing the subject," Henning replied. "Admit it, that's the monkey on your back. Your father wrote a few significant books, which is not something anyone could say of you. And you can't deal with that, so you take it out on someone like Quentin."

Till stepped over to the small table with the bottle, picked it up, poured himself a glass, and joined the group standing around Max.

"Monkey or no monkey," Max was saying to Henning, "I mean, not everyone can be the kind of guy you are, Henning. It doesn't seem to matter to you if you work for Felix, shine his shoes, jack him off, or anything else—"

"See?" Henning interrupted him, and then said to Betty, who apparently wanted to hold him back, "No, it's fine, your brother can say what he wants." Then he turned his attention back to Max.

"You can be as offensive as you want, Max. You simply can't stand the fact that other people are continuing your father's work. What's the matter? Are you pissed because you think that should have been *your* job? Pissed you had to hand over the privilege to us? If that were true, then wouldn't your father have taken steps to make sure that as his eldest child you, and only you, would be allowed to work on his material?"

"Zombie stories?" Till could hear in Max's voice that Henning was completely off the mark—that really was not what was troubling Max. "You can tinker with those until you're blue in the face, Henning," Max shot at him. "But I'll tell you this: if I were you, I wouldn't do it. One day, you'll wake up and realize you could have done something different with your life than pick up the crumbs that fell from my father's table." He glanced at Till, but then immediately turned back to Henning. "So, what exactly do you do at

Felix's? Oh yeah, that's right, you're not allowed to say. Imagine that, not even being able to tell someone what you're working on! And not because you might put someone in danger if you *did* actually talk about it, oh no. You can't do it simply because Felix doesn't want to show anyone his hand! Don't you see how you're subordinating yourself to someone else?"

Till noticed that Quentin, whom Max seemed to be ignoring now, had said something to Irina and slowly began distancing himself from their group. But Quentin was not headed toward the corner room where the stairway led to the floor above. He went in the other direction, moving from the living room into an adjoining room that connected the front of the building to the wing on the other side.

"Man, you've got a chip on your shoulder," Till heard Henning say. "Felix is an outstanding businessman. *Of course,* I subordinate myself to him when it comes to business. Why not? He pays me!" But Till had more or less stopped listening to them. Where was Quentin going? Till knew he was upset because of Max . . . so what was he doing wandering off to the back rooms of Max's apartment?

He nodded at Nina, who had come up behind him and joined the throng. "Back in a minute."

Then he, too, set off toward the side wing where Quentin had just disappeared.

62

TWO YEARS EARLIER

"Come on, Malte, what's the big deal? It'll be fun. I promise!" That was Quentin's voice.

"No!" said Malte. "Forget it! Find someone else."

Till stayed out of sight behind the door that led to the room where Quentin and Malte were talking. He'd followed Quentin through an entire suite of rooms that he didn't know were part of Max's apartment.

"But I'm asking *you*," came Quentin's voice again.

"Great, but the answer's no."

"Why not?"

"Leave me alone, Quentin. That's . . . it's . . . no, never!"

"But why not? Come on, man! You have to at least be able to tell me that. It isn't easy for me to ask you for this favor. Take my word for it. I'd be grateful to you. I'd *owe* you!"

Silence.

Till took a step closer to the door, which was ajar. The door itself hid him from their line of sight.

"I figured you'd resist at first," he heard Quentin again, working on Malte. "You probably don't even want to think about it."

"And you'd be right."

"But that's the old way of looking at it. That's not supportable anymore."

Silence.

"You're ashamed just thinking about it. You're probably overcome by the idea that . . . well, that people simply don't do stuff like this. But that's crap, Malte. Those are yesterday's rules. That's not what it's about. Just look at this."

Till hears a rustling noise.

"Take that away, man. I don't want to see it!"

"Oh, yes, you do. Take a good look . . . you see? Nice, right? Come on, you can't deny that!"

"Sure, but—"

"Come on, it doesn't get any better than this!"

"But—"

"Take a closer look! Just imagine I'm not here!"

"Quentin, it's crazy—"

"No, look, just stop with that, you've gotta stay on track here!" Quentin's voice was energetic now, insistent. "I can see it in you! I know you like what you're seeing—I mean *really* like it! And you know what that means? It means let it happen. Okay? You just go into the room like we talked about. You don't say a word. We've been through all this. And then we see what happens. If you can't do it, fine. But I don't believe it. It'll just happen. It'll be something that just takes place. It's got nothing to do with shame or conscience or . . . or whatever. With any of that shit! The only thing that counts is that you're doing me a favor. That you let things run their course."

"I . . ."

"Malte, don't try to tell me anything. Your only possible objection is that you feel like what you're doing is wrong. But there's no wrong, no right. All there is is what happens and what doesn't. If you shy away from this, even though your body wants it, then . . . I'm sorry, but I'll have to tell Felix that you don't have what it takes to act according to what we believe. Is that it? Do you just pay lip service to what the others say, but when push comes to shove, you can't follow through? You fall back on the same old habits, and you're too chickenshit to break out of them?"

Malte seemed to be looking for something to say.

"Get going, Malte! And don't worry, it'll be great! Come on!"

63

TWO YEARS EARLIER

"I'm not sure what they're planning, but maybe we should tell Max?" Till looked at Nina intently. He had returned quickly to the living room, where many of the guests remained. In the time he was gone, however, Max, Irina, Henning, and Betty had left the room. Till assumed they'd gone upstairs.

"Didn't you ask Malte and Quentin what they were up to?" Nina's expression was skeptical.

"I didn't think it had anything to do with me. But Max . . . this is his place . . ."

Nina looked at him as if to say *So what do you want from me?*

Till lowered his voice. "I know I should have a word with Max, but earlier . . . he was pretty, well, not drunk but somehow . . . tense. It might be better if you spoke to him?" He hadn't forgotten how Max had turned on him in the kitchen.

"And what am I supposed to tell him?"

Till sighed. Was he blowing things out of proportion? He really was turning into Felix's flunky! Quentin and Malte could do whatever they wanted.

Nina smiled when she saw his hesitation. "Sorry, Till, but maybe it's really best if you talk to him yourself."

He swallowed hard. She was right, of course. It was all crazy anyway! He smiled too. "Yeah, naturally. Where is he?"

She nodded toward the corner room. "Upstairs again, with the others."

Till headed for the stairs, pushing his way through the crowd still buzzing around the buffet. It wouldn't be easy to find Max in the huge apartment, he thought.

And he was right; when he finally tracked him down, it was already too late.

TWO YEARS EARLIER

She had tried to talk to him. She knew it wasn't right. But Quentin wouldn't listen. He just kept repeating: *You promised to do me a favor. And this is it. This is the favor I'm asking you to do!*

As he tied her up and blindfolded her, Irina thought about refusing. But she had no idea what he was planning to do, and he had insisted that that was part of it. It wouldn't take long—ten, fifteen minutes at the most. He had wrapped her eyes with the black cloth and laid her gently, face down, on the bed in the room he led her into. The last room in the side wing of Max's apartment. Then Quentin had left her alone and locked the door. A little later, Irina heard it being unlocked again.

Steps. A man's breathing. She felt a hand touch her, and for a moment she thought it must be Quentin. But the hand was too small and frail to be Quentin's. She heard a belt unbuckling.

"Quentin?"

"I'm here, don't be afraid," whispered a voice in her ear. Quentin. But the other hand was still on her back. There were two of them!

"Please. Untie me."

"It'll be over soon."

Just then, Irina felt Quentin's grip on her tighten, while the other man, whoever it was, suddenly pressed himself against her from behind.

Irina yelped.

"You said you would do me a favor. Have you forgotten?" She nearly passed out with revulsion, with indignation. Who was it behind her? What was he doing to her?

"Let me go, Quentin . . ."

She felt the other man back off. Had Quentin given him a sign?

"Are you sure? You're breaking your promise!"

Tears were pouring down her face. "Just stop, Quentin. This can't save us. We wouldn't get through it . . . I can't . . . you can't—"

"I know how hard it is, Irina." His voice was low, so terribly soft and tender. He held her firmly in his arms. "It'll be over soon. Then we'll leave here and never come back."

She cried. Her mind was racing, but she knew only one thing: what Quentin was asking of her was repugnant, inhuman. He'd gone mad. He'd lost all sense of right and wrong. She couldn't be part of this insanity!

"Quentin, this is senseless. We'll never be able to look each other in the eye again!"

"That's why I'm asking you, Irina. You promised me. And I promise you I'll never mention what happens here ever again. Have you already forgotten what *you* did to me? I'm prepared to forget that. We can finally start our life together after all the terrible things that have happened. We can put the past behind us. Do you really think I can bear what went on in our own apartment if you break your promise now? You made me this promise when you asked my forgiveness."

"This is wrong, Quentin. Listen to me, this is wrong . . ."

"I know it's wrong. I know it's horrible. But it is how it is. And you have to do it. For me."

She buried her face in his arms.

And then it happened. She wanted to twist around, but Quentin held her fast. She didn't dare to scream. But even as she was enduring it, she knew that something was breaking apart—something that could never be mended.

TODAY

"Claire!"

She swings her fists and knocks the man out of the way. Frederik looks back toward her through the dark corridor. "Come on!"

Claire runs. She can run fast when she wants to. She is strong and focused.

She runs after Frederik, who is hurrying along the passageway. He is hauling the woman along with him, past the individual storage units partitioned with wooden slats.

Claire's own breathing hisses in her ears. She has clenched her eyes together a little, and every muscle in her body is taut.

The steps. At the end of the passage. The steps leading up again, back to daylight.

Claire can already hear the sirens from the emergency vehicles that continue to race along the street toward the fallen building. The rubble and debris must have spread far up the side street by now.

"*Wha . . . ?*"

It is an arm. Claire sees it suddenly in front of her, even before she registers the sound of smashing wood.

She feels the blow from the fist as it hits her in the abdomen. She hears the shattering of the slats that separate the storage unit from the passage. A fist . . . how is that possible? Rammed straight though the slats?

Claire's thoughts muddle. She doubles over, and Frederik's back disappears from her field of view. She sees her shoes. A grip of iron closes around her arm, and she is thrown down by a power far beyond anything she could resist.

Splintered wood tears the skin of her cheek open as she falls—and is held, and then pushed up again.

She is jerked out of the passage, hurled into a room. One of the storage units . . .

It is a sea of limbs.

Deformed. Fused. Swollen.

Claire gasps for air.

The tiny room is like the mouth of a shaft that opens straight into hell.

And pain. A sharp, clear pain.

She is standing and she lowers her head, her line of sight moving down over her body.

And she sees what is causing the pain. It is a torso. An upper body with a neck and a head on top. The head seems to Claire to be as big as a horse's, but it is just a human head. The hair plastered onto the scalp, skin fish-belly pale, lips pulled back from teeth.

From teeth that are buried in Claire's ankle.

Claire looks down at the creature lurching at her feet. It is holding her foot tightly in both arms, the better to chew at her. A torso with no legs. Just two arms and a head.

She opens her hands, halfway between her eyes and the thing, and between them she sees how the head at her feet turns slightly, and the creature—without loosening its teeth from her flesh—rolls its eyes into the corners of its eye sockets to meet her stare.

She looks at it—it looks at her.

Below, the head gnawing noisily. Above, Claire lost in a buzz that slowly and with frightening speed is overwhelming every sense she has.

TODAY

At the other end of the city in another branch of the same system of tunnels, Malte cowers against the wall of the shaft that he and the others have been marching through. He is just as weedy and small as he was two years earlier. He has pulled up his legs and wrapped his arms around his knees. He presses his forehead against his arms.

But he remembers. He remembers her movements, the sounds she made. He remembers the guilt he felt, but that he still did it, forced himself between her thighs, too turned on by the contact with her body, by her nakedness.

It wasn't my fault, he tells himself. *It was Quentin, Max, Felix. Not me! At that moment, I loved her. I've never loved a girl again as much as I loved her.*

And yet, again, a shudder runs through him as he remembers Irina. He should never have let Quentin push him around like that. The catastrophe waiting for them at the end of the tunnel . . . hadn't that started because he couldn't restrain himself? When he saw Irina—the blindfold over her eyes, her skirt pushed up—lying before him on the bed?

"Okay, listen up!" The voice penetrated beyond the jutting piece of wall that Malte was leaning against. "No one knows exactly what the situation is in the subway tunnel. We'll pass out the masks now, then we move on!"

Malte feels something hit him. He raises his head. Someone has tossed a protective rubber mask against his legs.

He stretches the rubber strap and pulls it over the back of his head, adjusts the mask on his face. His own breathing hisses in his ears, and the smell of rubber assaults his nose. Someone grabs him and hauls him to his feet. Through the eye protection, past the yellowish plastic, he can see that one of his fellow marchers has pulled him up. "Get it together, man! We're doin' it!" comes the voice, distorted behind the other man's mask.

Sluggish, Malte starts to move.

Irina. When he did what he did to her, he had loved her. He would give anything to be able to tell her that.

. . .

"So, close the door already!"

Okay, okay. Hold your horses.

"Come on, over here . . ."

What's she doing there . . . in the women's restroom in this bar. That it would be squeaky clean was obvious, this place is expensive enough. But, man . . . it's like being on a luxury yacht . . . are those orchids in that vase?

My hands are shaking—but it doesn't matter! Make sure it's closed. Good that the cubicle's so big . . .

"I'll sit up here, okay?"

Do that . . . close the lid . . . good . . .

She sits on the tank of the toilet. I've got room on the lid.

Ah!

Her garters. They cut into her thighs. But she's not wearing panties . . . there's just . . . just . . .

"What's that?" she whispers.

Someone has come into the restroom. Something clacks. A woman's heels. Well, of course. It's the women's restroom.

Can you hear how she's breathing, panting? Not the one outside, this one here, in the cubicle, her breathing . . .

She takes my hands, strokes them along her thighs and under her skirt . . .

The heels clack. She moves my hands up her thighs, above the garters to her bare skin. She presses her finger against my mouth . . .

The one out there enters the cubicle next to ours!

Silence . . .

Only my hands wandering, gliding . . .

She flushes! The one next door . . . the heels clack. The one in here, she's running her hands through my hair, she pulls my head forward to hers—

"Hold on . . ."

What does she want?

"You haven't told me your name."

My name . . . you don't need to know that now . . . I can't stand it any longer . . . then I'll show you what my name is.

"Your name! I want to know . . . before we do it."

Every heartbeat in my chest is like a slipknot, pulling tighter . . .

"Yes?" *Her hand slides across my neck, into the collar of my shirt. She slides down from the tank, sits on my lap, her hand on the buckle of my . . .*

Okay okay okay . . . you're right . . . I'm not here to fall in love with you. I'm here to tear your soul from your body.

The catch—open.

Buttons—open.

Again, she pauses. She looks at me.

"Max." *Right? Isn't that my name?* "My name is Max." *My mouth at her ear. Come on! Go! Or don't you believe me? Don't I look like someone whose name would be Max?*

"Max," *she whispers.* "Really . . . Max?" *Her hand feels its way past the buttons.*

Yes. Yes, it's Max . . . now come on . . . up a little, let me pull you forward. Or it will drag me down. I'll explode.

TODAY

"Do you think I didn't see how the two of you doted on each other, Till? Do you think I don't know how the thought of you fills her whenever her mind drifts for a moment? When she's eating, Till. Or in the shower . . . or in bed. Her memories of the days you experienced together, of the touches, the words, the looks that passed between you . . . they pervade and inspire her. She is yours, heart and soul; in everything that makes her a woman, she has totally given herself over to you . . . but you *have* to let her go! You can't exploit her love, you have to protect her from herself, Till. It's the only way to prove you love her!"

The wind whistles around Till's ears. The cloud cover has torn apart, and the sun has broken through. Golden rays light up patches of rooftops.

Till and Felix have climbed to the top of the building. Till wears a borrowed jacket; Felix wears a padded cap with earflaps that stand out horizontally from his head.

"You haven't put yourself in debt just *once*, Till. You've done it *twice*." Felix's voice slices the words out of the ice-cold air.

"You're in debt to her, Till! Or have you managed to blot that out?" Felix's eyes seem to leave scorch marks on everything they touch. "It was you who killed her father, you who slammed the door, you who swung the bar into place. You might as well have smashed his head in yourself. I visited Max in Rome. He really . . . wasn't himself. He told me everything. You won't be able to lie to Lisa forever, Till. You will have to tell her! You will have to tell her that the man that she has loved for years is the same man she's spent years looking for—you're the man who drove her father to his death.

"If she finds that out after she's thrown in her lot with you, Till—she won't be able to handle that truth. It will destroy her. *You can't let that happen, Till*. You can't let this cast a shadow over her soul forever. You have to let her go, Till. You have to free her from her devotion to you. You have to turn her away and extinguish the flame that burns in her for you. Only then will she be able to handle the truth . . . Do it. Release her from her love. It's the only way to show you're worthy of your love for her."

An icy blast hits Till with tremendous force, penetrating through the material of his jacket. He wraps his arms around his body for protection, but he can't stop himself from teetering a little as gust after gust slams into him.

It booms inside him: *she really loves me*. But he can't ignore what Felix said. He will never be able to make Lisa happy. Only deeply, deeply miserable.

He has to set her free.

TODAY

"We're looking at *Lyssavirus*, from the *Rhabdoviridae* family. They multiply in the cytoplasm of cells. In the Negri bodies, to be exact. If we can show that they're present, then we can say beyond a doubt that infection has occurred."

Butz peers through a window into a room. Inside, a man is lying on a hospital bed.

"The virus has already reached his brain," the doctor continues. "Administering a vaccine now would be pointless."

"So, there's nothing you can do to help him?"

"At this stage in the process, death is virtually certain. Look now." The doctor nods toward the steel bed. "Classic hydrophobia."

The man in the room strains with all the strength left in his emaciated body against the leather straps wrapped across his chest, pelvis, knees, and ankles. He lifts his head and stares at an orderly entering the room, a plastic bottle in his hand. A rubber tube is attached to a spout on the bottle.

"The symptoms include anxiety, restlessness, and paralysis," says the doctor at Butz's side. "Then sleeplessness and hallucinations.

The man hasn't slept for four or five days, and his nervous system, naturally, is completely overloaded."

The patient's eyes flick around the room, his line of sight passing over the window from where Butz is observing him. For a moment, the man's eyes lock on one corner of the room, then swing back to the orderly. The orderly is unsure how to proceed and looks through the window at the doctor for instructions.

The doctor uses hand signals to indicate that the orderly should give the patient the plastic bottle. "The virus causes an infection of the brain, which leads to the paralysis of certain cranial nerves." The doctor's hands are back in his pockets. "This leads to paralysis of the throat and impedes speaking and swallowing. In some cases, it makes it impossible."

Butz places one forearm high up against the glass, and watches the patient from beneath his forearm. The patient, in the meantime, has managed to twist an arm free from the leather straps, and is jerking it around in the air.

"It hasn't yet been researched fully, but there are many indicators that even the sight of water causes constriction in the throat and larynx. This, in turn, leads to the classic foaming at the mouth."

The orderly looks over at the doctor; it is impossible to give the bottle to the patient. The doctor nods and signs to him to set the bottle on a nightstand and leave the room. Then he knocks gently against the glass. The effect on the patient is instantaneous, as if someone has fired a shot from a pistol next to him. A powerful jolt runs through him. His muscles contract and make his gaunt skull shoot several inches forward and up with such force that it must have damaged the tissues beneath his skin. Butz sees the man's lower jaw wrench downward, sees the skin draw tight at the corners of his mouth, stretch, strain . . . until even Butz, ten or twelve feet away, can see that the tissue is tearing apart. Blood trickles from the wound.

The doctor presses a button on his pager before turning back to Butz. From the shadows ringing the doctor's eyes, it is clear that he too has hardly slept for days. "It won't be much longer. No living thing can endure such violence directed against itself, such a will for self-destruction. Not for long. Even a shift in the light can do it . . . cause fits of extreme rage among those infected . . ."

The patient's mouth is stretching wider and wider. His jaw-bones are pressing against his collarbone. Dizzy, Butz can only stare into the dark hole of the man's mouth. His mouth is so wide open that his nose, eyes, and forehead have disappeared from Butz's view.

"This manifests in screaming, lashing out with the fists, and snapping at anyone nearby. A bite is particularly dangerous. The person bitten will almost certainly be infected."

Butz turns away.

A disease that humans have known about for thousands of years. Its name means *madness, violence*. Once known as mad-dog disease, it is sometimes still called hydrophobia.

But it is nothing more and nothing less than rabies.

TODAY

"It's everywhere." Betty's words. "It's everywhere."

In the sewers and ditches, the pits and wells, the pools and passages of the city.

Rabies.

His colleagues had finally managed to reach him on his cell, and when he heard what was going on at the hospital, he had gone there without delay.

Where did it come from, this virus infesting the city? Spreading like an epidemic, or a curse.

The doctor has left him there, and Butz can see him hurrying along the corridor, one hand in the pocket of his white coat, the other on his pager. He has apparently just received another message.

Where did the infestation start? Some fox that lost its way in a tunnel? A marten foaming at the mouth? A ferret that nipped a kid who'd gone to fetch apples from a crate in the basement? A bat that bit some curious explorer in the city's tunnels? A rat that infected someone poking through the rubble and ruins that have been lying dormant under Berlin ever since the city was buried beneath a hail of bombs?

Butz flinches.

There's a crashing sound behind him. He spins around and looks back through the window at the patient on the other side— and is chilled to the bone at what he sees. The patient has torn free from the straps holding him down. He presses his face against the safety glass, his nose crushed to one side and one eye distorted from the pressure.

Where did it get hold of him, this virus that's consuming him? Was he clambering around underground in the city's old ruins? Foraging between the walls, the concrete bulkheads three feet thick, in the secret bunkers, the stockpiled provisions, the shafts and dungeons down there? Where the perspiration, the bodies, the excrement has all been buried for decades . . . all of it preserved since Berlin was flattened? A reservoir that looks to have broken open, like a scab on a wound, oozing pus at the slightest pressure.

For hours, days, weeks, explosions shook the walls of the city. Bathed in sweat, the people lay awake at night in the hundreds of thousands—millions—all in fear of the bombs, the injustice, the insanity. A city that went under, that was buried by an avalanche of rubble, but that never completely disappeared from the earth.

The patient behind the glass crashes to the floor, as if someone has chopped through whatever was left of his contaminated will-power like it was a string.

Simultaneously, Butz hears the screams, distant but electrify-ing, rolling toward him through the corridors of the hospital. A choir of voices that doesn't break off, but rises higher, as if the other patients in the hospital can sense that one of their kind has left them. But they rage on, more fiercely, more unseeing, more self-destructive than before.

70

TWO YEARS EARLIER

"Malte!" Till jumped to his feet. "Where were you?"

Malte had just stepped into the living room on the top floor of Max's apartment. He looked pale, dazed, tired. His head was hung low, and he looked like he was trying to attract as little attention as possible as he slipped past the others, heading for the stairs, getting out of there.

"Downstairs. I was down . . . but I think I've had too much to drink. I need to go home." He barely raised his head.

Till hesitated. "Is Quentin still down there?"

Malte nodded. "See you at the office in the morning," he mumbled, pushing past Till.

But Max, in a cheerful mood again, had spotted him. "Hey Malte, there you are!" he shouted clear across the room. "Till was getting worried! What were you doing?"

Malte glanced quickly at Max and tried to wave him off. "Nothing. Really nothing." But now the heads of other people at the table and standing around the room were turning in his direction. Malte pressed a hand on his stomach. "I think I'm getting a stomachache."

"Bullshit!" Max stood up and strode over to Malte and Till. "Don't try pinning it on the food! What were you guys up to down there?"

After Till eavesdropped on Quentin and Malte, he'd gone looking for Max. He'd searched everywhere, but when he finally tracked him down and told him what he'd heard, Max just shrugged. As far as he was concerned, Malte, Quentin, Henning, and their cronies could tear each other apart. There was nothing he or Till could do to stop them.

"If Quentin wants anything from me, he'll find me," Max had said, trying to convince Till to join him and the remaining guests around the table upstairs. In the meantime, Lisa had joined the party. She offered Till the empty chair beside her, and he accepted. It was only a few minutes later that Malte had slunk into the room.

"Everything's fine, don't worry about it," said Malte, dodging Max's question. But it seemed to Till that an edge of fear, a tinge of wretchedness had crept into Malte's eyes.

"Out with it!" Max said, not about to let himself be shaken off so easily.

Malte lowered his voice helplessly. "Seriously, Max. I just want to go home . . ."

"Hey, Henning, are you getting this?" Max, positively chirpy now, turned around to Henning, who was still sitting at the table. "Your sidekick here wants to take off!"

"Malte? Everything okay?" Henning put on a well-practiced concerned look.

"Are you trying to keep me here or something?" muttered Malte peevishly to Max, who was blocking his path.

"You mean like this?" Max joked, slinging one arm around Malte's neck in a mock headlock.

"What the hell?" asked Malte, ducking angrily out of Max's grip with unnecessary force. He was clearly uncomfortable with the eyes of everyone in the room suddenly trained on him.

"So, is Irina still downstairs?" Nina had turned in her chair to look at Malte. "Or did she leave already?"

"No . . ." The slight young man suddenly seemed to grow even paler, and tiny beads of sweat broke out on his forehead. Then he couldn't hold it back any longer. "I'm so sorry, I . . . I didn't want . . ."

"What?" Max was beaming at him. "Christ, Malte, you chickenshit! What didn't you want?"

"I . . . I said I didn't want it—"

"But you did it anyway, didn't you?" Max wouldn't stop.

"I . . ."

"What?" Nina's face darkened.

"I told Quentin it wasn't right." Malte suddenly lunged forward, holding Nina by the shoulders with both hands. "I'm sorry, I'm really sorry! Ask her to forgive me . . . please . . . it . . . it shouldn't have happened . . . ever . . ."

Max frowned, half laughing but confused. "What are you going on about? I thought you guys automatically denied responsibility for everything." He threw a sardonic look at Henning. "Haven't you got your team on the same page, Henning? Do you know what he's babbling about?"

Henning had stood up now too, and looked furious as he stalked over to Malte from his place behind the table. "What the hell is going on?"

"It was Quentin. He made me do it. He's still downstairs . . . ask him—"

"Quentin? Oh, sure, I'm all over that one," said Max with a sneer. "But what's that supposed to mean? Quentin can't talk you into doing anything, right? Not if everything's preordained!"

"Yeah . . . yeah," Malte stammered, "but . . ." He turned his eyes pleadingly back to Nina. "Will you tell her I'm sorry?"

"Jesus, Malte," Henning snapped at the much smaller man. "Pull yourself together!"

But Till, unable to stand it anymore, was already pushing past them and disappearing down the stairs.

"Wait, Till," he heard Max shout behind him. "We all want to see!"

TWO YEARS EARLIER

Till practically flew down the stairs.

The rooms below were empty. The guests who'd been there earlier had already found their way upstairs. He ran into the wing where he'd heard Malte and Quentin talking earlier. When he reached the last room, he turned the handle and pushed open the door.

It was a large guestroom with a wardrobe, a desk, and a king-sized bed. And Irina, sitting on the bed. Her legs were pulled up to her chest and her face was buried in her knees. Her arms were wrapped around her shins. She was still in her dress but barefoot.

"Are you okay?" But Till only had to look at her to know that she wasn't.

She didn't move.

He couldn't take his eyes off her long, brown hair, which flowed over her arms and legs. "Should I call you a taxi? Do you want to go home?"

"Is she here?" It was Max's voice.

Till spun around.

From where he stood in the doorway, he saw Max and two or three other guests coming toward him through the series of rooms that made up the wing.

Simultaneously, the sound of a toilet flushing came from the bathroom.

"Yeah, she's here," rang a voice through the bathroom door. "Take a close look, Max!"

Max and the others moved past Till and into the room.

Quentin had emerged from the bathroom and was standing next to the bed. "Don't you want to take her in your arms?" he said to Max, his voice strangely thin. "She loves to cuddle."

Till took a step toward Quentin. "What the hell is this?"

"Keep out of it, Till. It's nothing to do with you," Quentin said with a snarl.

"Irina!" Ignoring Quentin, Max moved across the room to the bed.

But Irina pressed her hands to her ears and jumped to her feet. "Go! Run away!" Quentin yelled. It sounded like something inside him had snapped. "I never want to see you again! Never!"

The other guests, still standing near the door, moved aside to let Irina through.

"It's your fault!" Quentin was suddenly next to Max and grabbed his collar. "You're the one who ruined her!"

Max jerked himself free. "I thought guilt was a thing of the past," he said, his voice furious.

"For me—but not for *you!*" Quentin seemed energized, as if he knew that Max could not take this victory away from him. "Malte was a beast. He couldn't stop himself! And she just spread her legs and let him in—just like she did for you, Max!"

Max glared at him. "You're trying to hurt *me?* You've destroyed your own life, Quentin! You loved her! You should've figured out how to deal with what happened between her and me . . ."

"You mess around in my life, you take whatever you feel like, you play your games—and then tell *me* what I'm supposed to *deal with*?" Quentin spat on the floor. "I'm not the one who ruined Irina. It was you, Max. And it'll destroy you."

TWO YEARS EARLIER

Nina walked out the last of the guests, and then returned to the large room where the table stood.

Not everyone knew what had happened, and the party had not ended at once. Till and Lisa—like Quentin and Irina—left immediately, but when Nina suggested telling the other guests to go home, Max only shook his head bitterly and took his place again at the table upstairs. But as much as he tried to put on a brave face, it was clear that for him the party was over. His grim and gloomy mood poisoned the atmosphere, and soon all the remaining guests were gone too.

Now he sat alone, elbows propped on the big table, and stared out the window into the darkness. Nina took a seat next to him. They sat there for a few minutes, saying nothing.

"We'll take care of Irina," Nina finally said. "She'll bounce back."

Max looked at her for a moment and nodded. Then he stood and left the room.

A few minutes later, loud noises could be heard coming from below. When Nina pulled open the door to the lower floor, Max was standing in the middle of the room, legs apart, slamming a pickaxe into the floor with all his strength. He had used a crowbar to pry out the planks covering a section of the floor, revealing bare concrete beneath. Max raised the pickaxe high over his head, his muscles straining, and swung it hard into the floor. Shards of cement flew like shrapnel in all directions.

Should she leave him alone? Go home? Go to bed upstairs?

"I signed a contract yesterday," she heard Max say between puffs. "For the apartment underneath. Now it's part of this one." With a loud crack, the pickaxe smashed into the cement again.

Max battered relentlessly at the floor while Nina started collecting the empty bottles and dirty dishes in the other rooms. When she was done, she lay down in her clothes on the burgundy sofa and pulled a woolen blanket over herself. But she couldn't sleep. She kept getting up and poking her head into the room where Max was working. It went faster than she'd expected. It couldn't have been more than three hours after he started that he called out to her.

"Coming?"

Along with the pickaxe, he must have had other tools and equipment stored away in a workroom, because he'd laid a heavy wooden plank across the hole in the floor. A rope ladder was tied to the plank. Nina stood at the edge of the hole and could see through to the level below. The hole was big enough to slide past the plank and climb down the rope ladder.

Max sat on the floor beside her, dangled his legs down the hole, and reached out for the rope ladder to find his footing. Then he pushed off. The free-hanging ladder swung across the hole and back, and Max hit the rough edge of the hole quite hard. Unfazed, he began his descent.

When he reached the floor on the lower level, a good twelve feet beneath the hole he'd dug, he put all his weight on the ladder, pulling it tight, and looked up at Nina.

"What are you waiting for?"

Like Max, Nina slipped over the edge of the hole. Down below, Max held the ladder tight, and she had no trouble at all climbing down.

The apartment they found themselves in was completely empty. The layout was the same as the two above that already belonged to Max. A somewhat stale, dusty smell hung in the air. Before Nina could look around, Max had already taken her by the hand. He seemed to know where he wanted to go, and steered her resolutely in one direction. They passed through large rooms with parquet floors, white-painted walls, and huge, elaborately adorned, tiled stoves squatting in the corners.

At the outer wall of the large living room, Max stopped in front of a narrow door that did not exist in the corresponding location on either of the floors above.

"This is why I wanted this apartment," he said, pulling the door open and stepping through.

Nina followed him. After passing through a short corridor, they came out into a long, brick-walled gallery, high on the side of a huge, open hall. It was the church next to the apartment building! The door led straight into one of the raised galleries.

"They connected the apartment to the church. They did it for the priest, back around 1885, when both buildings were built." Max stepped past the wooden pews to the stone balustrade of the gallery.

Nina came up beside him and looked down into the neo-Gothic nave, all white and brick red. She felt Max's hand touch hers.

"I think Quentin's right," she heard him murmur next to her. "It scares me, you know. There are no borders, no limits, no escape. Not anymore."

She slipped one arm around his waist, wanting to say something to cheer him up—she wanted to say something to drive out the fear, the ghosts, the melancholy. But as hard as she tried to find the right words, it was as if her mind had been swept clean—she feared that Max's gloomy foreboding might be justified.

So, she kept her silence, even as the first rays of morning shone through the windows of the immense hall.

TODAY

"From what?"

"A deadly form of encephalitis."

"Which means what?"

"It varies. Headaches, visual impairment, paralysis . . . it's an infection of the brain. Once the virus gets into the body, it travels along the nerve fibers until it reaches the spinal cord. From there, it spreads throughout the central nervous system.

Encephalitis.

"The vector could have been an animal or an insect."

"So, he could have caught it anywhere . . ."

"Anywhere. A cat, a dog, a rat . . . they wouldn't even have to bite him. A bat gets caught in your hair, tries to escape, scratches your cheek with a claw . . ."

Butz stares at the corpse in front of him. Fehrenberg. He must have been infected just over two weeks earlier.

"And the virus can spread from person to person, of course." The pathologist who has come in with him continues his explanation. "Unprotected sex with an infected person could do it."

Rabies.

A deadly infection of the brain, triggered by a viral infection.

Fehrenberg had died of rabies. They found his body in a car parked in a side street out in the suburbs. Dogs kept sniffing around and barking at the car until it finally caught the attention of the locals.

"But the women . . ." Butz glances at the pathologist. Before stopping at Fehrenberg's table, they inspected the bodies of the three female victims again: Nadja, the girl from the parking lot who'd been living in the empty high-rise; the woman from the construction site; and Anni Eisler, whose body Butz's colleagues had fished out of the Spree. All three were still in forensics.

"The women didn't die of rabies. We can rule that out." The pathologist starts pulling a transparent sheet over Fehrenberg's lifeless body. "They tried to escape, but were attacked, killed, and left behind. There is some evidence of animal damage, but the virus wouldn't have been able to spread because the women were already dead."

"And the wounds on their hands?"

"From trying to escape. But having said that . . . exactly how it happened—I can't really help you out there, Konstantin. I just don't know." The pathologist looks at Butz through his glasses. "But the signs are undeniable—they were *hunted*. They tried to escape down on their hands and knees. They literally tried to crawl away. And not just a few yards, but eighty, a hundred yards . . ." He nods toward the door, a signal to Butz that they are done and can leave the room. "Still, I can't help wondering how that was possible, you know? That whoever attacked them let them get so far! Frankly, the only theory that makes any sense is that he . . . or she . . . or maybe it was more than one person . . . that they must have been playing with the victims. Letting them crawl away, then reeling 'em back." The doctor pauses for a moment in the hallway outside the room.

"Have you ever watched a cat do that? Hold a mouse by the tail with one paw?"

Butz shakes his head.

"Is it just a rumor?" Suddenly the doctor looks less like the all-knowing expert in white, and more like someone getting wind of an approaching threat, something that could endanger him as well.

"A rumor? What do you mean?"

"That there are actual tribes down there."

Tribes.

"It's incredible how fast it's spread, Konstantin." The pathologist lowers his voice. "When you consider we've had the virus more or less under control for decades. Have you guys got any info, anything about mobs down there?"

Butz sees them in his mind's eye: the people living down in the tunnels, shafts, and burrows beneath the city. Every cop knows there are more of them than in the official stats.

"Yeah. There are lots of indicators. It's probably more than a rumor . . ." He looks his colleague in the eye. "Would a mob like that fit the clinical picture? Would having rabies make people form packs?"

The pathologist looks away uncertainly. "Hard to say . . . it's true that different people infected with the same virus demonstrate the same deviating behavior. Like avoiding light, for example. Anyone infected with rabies will do that. And the fear of water, of course . . . and any sudden stimulation can trigger an extreme reaction."

An epidemic. An epidemic, forcing them up and out of the holes they've been creeping around and multiplying in.

"Those infected form packs," the doctor says. "It's not so much because they act as a group. It's because the conditions and the situation tend to drive them in the same direction." He rubs one hand over the stubble on his cheek. He hasn't shaved in days.

"And you'd say it's unusual for the virus to spread so fast?"

"When was the first death?"

"Ten days ago. Give or take."

"That *is* surprising. I mean, the speed of propagation." The doctor frowns. "The conditions down there are perfect, of course. That much is clear. There's practically no sanitation. A lot of people crowd around the ventilation shafts because it's warmer there. Open cuts and scrapes, close physical contact—it isn't hard to imagine how the infection might spread . . . but still . . ."

"An attack? Is that what you're thinking?" Butz is afraid of speaking the words, but keeping them to himself will get them nowhere. They have to try to organize and assess every bit of information they have.

The doctor shrugs. He won't rule it out, but he doesn't want to jump to conclusions.

"How many people would you need for an attack like that, if that's what it was?"

"One would do. If he had the virus, just one would be plenty. All he'd have to do would be . . . what? Maybe inject a pack of dogs with the virus and drive them down into the tunnels. Infected dogs can be extremely aggressive. Once they began to spread in the tunnels it could happen very fast. But that's just one scenario. If someone really wanted to start an epidemic, he could spread the virus through a brothel, for example. We'd be looking at explosive propagation within a *single day*. You don't need a big organization for something like that. One person with enough determination. Really, that's all it would take!"

TWO YEARS EARLIER

"Can I take that for you?"

"Certainly. Thank you."

"Everything okay?"

"Outstanding."

Felix leaned back a little to give the waiter some room and looked at the man sitting opposite him.

"That—exactly *that*—is the trick," said the man, and pointed his index finger at Felix's tie. "The hero does it one way, but you, as reader—you see where I'm going?—you keep on reading. And then we say to the reader 'Ha! Now you've done it.' And we say it when he least expects it. Or, to be precise, what we write in the text he's reading is 'Now, you, dear reader, have continued reading. And by doing that, you've done *exactly the opposite* of what the hero in the story did!' The hero stopped, but the reader kept going, right? That's the trick, if you will." The man leaned back in his chair and raised his hands as if to surrender. "And then you've got him. Then you've got the reader."

Felix had to smile.

"Pretty sweet, right?" The man let his hands fall and reached for the glass of water by his plate.

Felix nodded. "Yeah, not bad at all."

His companion drank from his glass. He seemed to be waiting for something.

Felix scanned the restaurant briefly. Most of the tables were occupied. In the reception area, separated from the dining room itself by a heavy curtain, a few guests waited for a table.

"Felix?"

Felix turned his eyes back to his companion. The man raised his eyebrows. "So . . . what? Are you buying or not?"

Felix smiled. He seemed to think it over for a moment longer, then nodded twice, quickly. "I'll call your agent, Larry. Done."

Larry beamed. "Glad to hear it!"

"Don't mention it," said Felix. "What you're offering fits with the concept. I'm not entirely sure that we don't already have something similar—I'll have to clarify that with Henning. But I think we're better off all around if we buy the idea."

He noticed a young woman approaching their table. He glanced up at her for a second before returning his attention to his lunch companion. "Anything else, Larry?"

Felix knew the woman. Very well, in fact.

"No, nothing." Larry stood up, moved around behind his chair, and pushed it in to the table. "Thanks a lot, Felix."

Felix also stood and shook Larry's outstretched hand. "Take care," he said. He turned away slightly, as if to dismiss him.

"See you." Larry didn't want to keep him any longer. He turned around and strode off briskly through the restaurant, obviously thrilled to have sold his idea.

"Bad timing?"

Felix looked at the young woman. She had stopped and was waiting a few steps away but now came up to his table. She wore a black silk blouse and carried a light jacket over her arm. A touch of lipstick and a hint of makeup around her eyes accentuated her femininity.

"I was just about to head back to the office," Felix said, his expression not unfriendly. He was clearly aware how striking Nina must appear to the other diners in the restaurant. Yet when he looked at her, there was nothing particularly sympathetic in his eyes. He seemed more to be sizing her up.

"Do you have a moment to spare?" Nina was making an effort not to let her nervousness show.

"Of course." Felix gave the waiter a sign and sat down again. "How are you? You're looking well."

"Thanks." Nina sat in the chair still warm from Larry, and turned and draped her jacket over the back of her chair.

"Espresso, please," Felix said to the waiter, who had returned to the table. "Would you like anything?"

"Espresso would be great, yes."

"Two, please."

He didn't need to say or do anything. Nina could tell that Felix would give her very little of his time.

"Perhaps this isn't the right place to discuss this," she said, "but I didn't know where else to find you."

Felix's face tensed.

"It's about Max. You probably knew that already."

Felix pursed his lips. A kind of "hmmmm" emerged.

"Listen, Felix," said Nina, the words suddenly pouring out of her. "I'm sure you have some idea . . . no, you already know it. I can't—"

"Can't what?" he interrupted her.

"I can't . . . can't make him . . . what did you call it? Compliant? I can't make Max . . . oh, Christ . . . I can't make him wild about me."

Felix's face reflected something like derision.

"I mean, I like him. And he is—"

"Wild about you?"

Nina sighed, glanced to one side.

"Whatever, Felix," she continued. "I can't do it. I can't deceive him. I can't pretend that he's everything to me and in reality be . . . working . . . for you." Her eyes were firmly fixed on Felix again.

"Have you already told him that?"

"Felix, I like him. And he likes me. There's something special, and I don't want to risk it . . ."

"I want to know if you've already told him what you just told me!"

What did he want to know? Whether she'd told Max that she liked him? Or whether she'd told him what Felix had asked her to do? The answer to both was the same.

"Yes . . . I told him."

Every muscle in Nina's body instinctively tensed. In retrospect, it had been a good idea to catch Felix here, among so many people. He couldn't touch her here. "But he already knew," she added, hastily. "Quentin had said something to him—"

She jumped in shock as Felix's fist slammed down on the table. A few faces turned in their direction. "That idiot," he murmured, and then snorted, more amused than angry. "Quentin's about this close to losing it, don't you think?"

"Don't you get it? I *had* to talk to Max, I had to tell him everything, or else . . . or else things would have gone too far." Nina realized that she was starting to sound like a schoolgirl. The pitch of her voice had automatically risen a little. It was something she didn't switch on deliberately, but she'd often found that it turned things in her favor.

But Felix gave no sign of being impressed. On the contrary, a flash of annoyance crossed his face. "I don't doubt it. But even so,

I'm feeling a little let down, Nina," he said. "I didn't ask you to take care of Max for the fun of it."

She pulled her shoulders a little higher. "What do you want from him?" she whispered.

Felix looked up. The waiter was back, setting the tiny espresso cups in front of them. Neither of them thanked him. He left without a word.

"Max is Bentheim's son," said Felix, tearing open a thin tube of sugar. "He would be the perfect public face." He sprinkled the sugar from the paper tube into his little cup. "Bentheim is dead. Who better to pick up the baton than his son? At least publicly." He looked up at Nina. "For the project I'm working on, I mean."

All that Nina knew about Felix's operations were fragments and hints she'd picked up from Henning, Malte, and Quentin. Still, she thought she understood what he meant. "Why don't you just ask him?" she said, stirring a spoon in her cup. "It sounds like a pretty attractive deal. Maybe he'd be into it."

Felix shook his head. "I've already tried that. Several times, in fact. He flatly refuses any support at all. He's absolutely categorical about it. Maybe he's just not interested in continuing something his father started."

That could be the case, of course.

"If I can be frank, Nina, I had been expecting more from you when I asked you to do me this favor." Something about Felix's voice sounded like a dentist's drill starting to whine. "Your mother—"

"Leave Mom out of it," Nina said, cutting him off. There was no way she wanted Maja dragged into this. "Till Anschütz," she blurted. "Have you talked to him about Max?" Why didn't he try Till? He knew no one had as much influence on Max as Till, didn't he?

Felix tilted his head a little. "Till started working for me a few weeks ago. What about him?"

"I . . . I'm not sure," said Nina, automatically leaning forward. "But Max mentioned that something happened, a long time ago. I think Max's father took Till into the family. Do you know about that?"

Felix looked at her impatiently.

"The first time I saw Max and Till together, I could see straight away that the two of them shared something," said Nina. "I asked Max about it and he told me they were close friends even when they were kids, that there was something that made his connection to Till much stronger than with anyone else."

She had to throw Felix a bone. She couldn't just tell him he wouldn't be able to get to Max through her. He'd never let go. He'd sink his teeth into her mother to get Nina to do what he wanted her to . . .

"Don't stop." Felix narrowed his eyes.

"I tried to find out more about it. I wanted to know what the closeness stemmed from, the understanding between them that Max always talks about."

"And?"

Nina shook her head. "Every time I bring it up, Max changes the subject."

"Hmm." Felix licked his lips.

From the look on Felix's face, Nina could see that she had stirred his curiosity. She could almost physically feel his attention shift from her to Till.

"Till Anschütz," he murmured, and he bent the small espresso spoon between his thumb and index finger. Then his eyes caught hers and he bit down on his lower lip. "Thank you, Nina." His chair scraped on the parquet floor. "Come to the office with me. Just for a minute . . . I want to show you something."

They both stood up. Nina lowered her head to escape his eyes. "I'd love to, Felix. But I can't." She glanced up again. "Is that a problem?"

His elegant hand reached out and touched her arm. "Not at all. Don't worry about it." And then he turned away and she was left alone.

Nina's eyes followed him as he went to the coatrack at the entrance. He nodded casually to a few diners who looked up as he passed.

Nina's silk blouse was sticking to her skin between her shoulder blades. It felt like someone had poured a glass of cold water down her back.

TODAY

The fucking mask wraps around his face like a fist. He can't hear properly, can't see properly, and all he can smell is synthetic rubber, which stinks.

Half dazed, Malte stumbles on. He comes to a heavy steel door that's wide open, and he pushes against it until it closes on its old hinges with a muffled clang. Malte grasps the dinner-plate-sized wheel in the center of the door and tries to turn it. Nothing. He leans on it with all his weight. It grates, and the wheel turns a fraction of an inch. He tries again, his muscles straining. The wheel rotates a little farther. The rust or whatever was blocking it must have crumbled. Malte feels the wheel turn more easily, notes how the turning motion wedges the door into its frame.

He locks the wheel as tightly as he can and takes a step back. He looks down the tunnel. How many of these bulkheads has he sealed now? Twelve? Fourteen?

Through the dust swirling in the air, Malte can see the doors he still has to close disappearing ahead of him in the darkness, a seemingly endless series of them.

This is the task he's been given: check the shaft and seal all the bulkheads. Then they'll flood the place.

He trudges on.

The next door. Malte braces himself against the locking wheel, fighting the rust.

And jumps.

Did something just grab at his foot?

Or suck at it?

He looks down at the bottom of the tunnel, at his shoes. Nonsense. There's nothing there. He's just standing in a shallow puddle and the water has soaked through his shoe.

He grabs the wheel again but he hears a noise. It's soft, but it's definitely a noise that wasn't there before.

He releases the wheel and peers into the darkness. Is something gleaming down there? His eyes shift back to the water underfoot. The puddle seems to have grown. The water is lapping around his foot, sloshing over the top of his shoe.

Splashing? Is that splashing?

"Then we'll flood the place . . ."

Suddenly, he feels it hit the bottom of his jeans. The water.

He can't see his shoes anymore.

What is that? A swish, a hiss, a roar?

He jerks one foot out of the water. It feels as heavy as mud.

His shoes are full of the lukewarm water. The waves are already above his knee, climbing fast, more waves flooding in, now at his hips, his waist.

Malte feels his feet lose touch with the ground.

He pulls his arms up in front of him, instinctively supporting himself in the water even as the next wave hits. It picks him up, washing him along, pushing him upward, driving him at terrifying speed up toward the roof of the tunnel. He reaches above his head to protect himself from the impact and manages to turn around in the water.

What he sees behind him is no longer the tunnel. It's a wall of water that completely fills the shaft. He sees it coming as if in slow motion. Not clear or transparent, but black as night.

He feels the irresistible pressure of the wave push him against the tunnel roof and drag him across the rough cement. The mask is ripped from his face, and half his skin is shredded.

Then the water swallows him.

He hears a scream escape him underwater as his body slams against outcrops in the wall. Swirling water drags him to the bottom—then something touches him, something resilient. It slides past and is gone.

Then Malte is swallowed in a pliable mass, a swell of bodies in the water, and now he's one of them, engulfed—as the last of the air in his lungs gives out, and with it, his life.

TWO YEARS EARLIER

Monday morning.

The traffic in the city always seemed extremely loud on Monday morning. Max noticed it often. The drivers stomp the gas pedal extra hard as they pull away from the traffic lights, as if plagued by a need to make up for time lost on the weekend, and the sooner the better.

He turned up the collar of his jacket and walked faster. It was just before nine, and Max was on his way home. He'd been out with friends in the city, another all-nighter, and now he felt like he'd passed out in a train station toilet. His mouth was an ashtray, and the alcohol he'd poured down his throat had worked its way up to his eyes, and everything looked too bright. But he was not in a bad mood. He was actually looking forward to getting home. All night he'd wanted to get back to his desk; he had a ton of good ideas to write down.

He turned the corner onto the street that led over Gotzkowsky Bridge and saw that the small café on the corner had already opened. A cappuccino, maybe a double, two croissants to go—then he wouldn't have to waste time fixing breakfast when he got home. He could disappear into his study and get to work.

Fired up, he went into the café, stepped up to the counter, and placed his order.

While waiting he gazed out through the large window that made up almost the entire front of the café. Behind him, he heard the girl at the counter preparing the coffee. He watched the traffic as it hurtled up onto the bridge in a steady roar or, from the other direction, flowed down toward Moabit and dispersed into the side streets.

His nose itched and he turned his head. Was the guy sitting back in the corner watching him? Max looked at the man calmly, but he had his head down and was reading a paper on the table in front of him.

Let's go! Max nearly said it out loud as he stepped out onto the sidewalk a minute later, coffee and croissants in his hand. Up to the apartment and straight to his desk, today was the day he'd finally start—

"Excuse me?"

Max turned.

Approaching him was the man who'd looked at him in the café. He must have left just behind Max.

"Yes?" Max pursed his lips.

He didn't know the man. And although he could not have said why, he didn't like the man's face. Was it the shape of the guy's head? It was elongated, almost pointed. Maybe it was his narrow skull?

"Excuse me, but I was observing you back in the café. You were totally lost in thought."

"Yeah," Max smiled, "yeah, true—"

"I'd like to be able to do that. Just forget the world around me and focus on my path."

The guy was maybe five or six years older than Max, maybe in his early thirties but no older. His face looked a little waxy, and Max instinctively thought that his hand would feel clammy.

"Can I ask you that? I've thought about it a lot, you know. About how I could do it. Can I ask how *you* do it? How do you forget everything around you, left and right, and keep so focused?

What the hell's he on about? Max thought. "I don't understand . . ."

"No!" The man spoke quickly. "It's not what you think. I don't want any money, I . . ." He reached into the breast pocket of his anorak and took out a letter. A computer printout, unsigned, covered in numbers and small print.

Max took a step back. "I really don't have the time, sorry, but . . ."

Then he saw it. In the other man's eyes. A mixture of fear, humiliation, and sadness. A gleam that seemed to reflect the fact that no one had ever had time for him. He was dull, perhaps. But not sneaky or evil. Just someone who's misfortune it was to be perpetually passed by.

Max wiped one hand across his forehead and felt the dirt still on his hands from his sleepless night smear in a thin, grimy film.

"I can't do that so fast, not out here . . ." he murmured, but found himself suddenly holding the man's letter in his hands, almost not realizing that he'd reached out for it.

Mr. Lennart Boll was written above the address.

We'll go up to my apartment. Just for a few minutes. We'll look at this quickly, maybe make a call, get him back on his feet again, Max thought. *I can do that much.*

He raised his head, looked at the man, and smiled. "Do you want to go up to my place? I live just across there." He nodded toward the building beside the church that was across the square from where they were standing.

"Could we?" Boll's eyes gleamed.

Isn't he beautiful? thought Max. *Doesn't he look beautiful, a human being like this, when he's happy, no matter how far he's fallen? Isn't that a miracle?*

And he was already turning away again to cross the street at the light.

I can do this, Max said to himself. *I'm free to choose. I shouldn't do it? Bullshit! What's the big deal, lending a helping hand? Isn't that my duty, even? Wouldn't it be unbearable* not *to?*

TWO YEARS EARLIER

It was about his insurance, his health insurance. Boll had canceled it four years earlier to save money. Now he wanted to reverse that decision, but it was too expensive.

"It just isn't right, is it?" He looked at Max like a confused child. "They can't just abandon me like this!" Then, "So, I don't have the money . . . what am I supposed to do?"

Max had been sitting there for a while, listening to him go on like this.

"I called 'em, but they just shuffle me from one person to the next. First no one answers, then it's the wrong one, then one's on vacation and the other's at lunch. I can't do anything!"

Max knew what Boll meant. A vicious circle, a slippery slope, whatever you call it; once one part of your life starts to get beyond your control, things can go off the rails fast. The longer Max spoke with Boll, the clearer it was that Boll wasn't really talking nonsense. On the contrary. If you looked at things from his perspective, it all made sense. You could understand the man . . . or at least Max could. Besides, Boll had experienced things that would have knocked even a more robust person off his feet, not least a stay in what he called "psych"—meaning he'd spent a few months in an institution for mentally ill offenders.

He'd always dreamed of being an actor. And as he told Max about it, he rolled his eyes and his voice rose alarmingly. Max thought the man looked rather strange when he strutted across the room like a rooster with its comb standing high and proud, but he couldn't deny his dramatic energy.

"Oh, sure," he said, his eyes on Max, "you look at me today and it's ridiculous. But back then, six or seven years ago? I was young, I wasn't bad looking!" The man stared at him and yelled, "But it didn't work out. I went into the theater, and they kicked me out, and I crawled back again. I waited outside the director's door. But did they want me? No!" Then, suddenly, he grinned. "But why not? Am I really so bad?"

Max could almost see Boll's life taking place in front of him. He had hoped he could just make a quick call to Boll's insurance company. But the longer he listened to him, and the longer he put off making the call, the clearer it became that he probably couldn't really do anything to help him. Unless . . . unless there was some way to get him back into a low-cost insurance plan.

The sudden jangle of his telephone startled Max out of his thoughts.

It was Felix. "You're home? Marvelous! I was just on my way to the airport. Okay if I stop by for a minute?"

Caught off guard, Max paced the room with the phone at his ear.

"I'm flying to Milan today. They're excited, they want to have everything, the whole Bentheim—" Felix interrupted himself. "But I have to talk to you."

"I'm here. If you want to come by—"

"Got it. Twenty minutes." There was a click on the line. Felix had hung up.

Max turned to Boll and tried to break the news to him gently. Lennart had to understand, he was really sorry about everything, but he was expecting a visitor . . . Max tripped over the words.

Boll's face seemed to fall in on itself. From his odd but strangely evocative posturing of a minute before, he turned into a picture of despair. As if someone had thrown open the door and the wind rushing in had blasted all the strength from his body.

"I'll pay for it." Max stuffed his hands in his pockets. "Okay? You go and reregister, and I'll pay. Whatever it costs." It couldn't be too expensive, after all. And money wasn't an issue, not since his mother had signed his share of his father's estate over to him before Betty's wedding.

Boll looked at him in incomprehension. "You can't do that."

"Says who?"

Boll's face slowly began to light up again. Despair turned back to delight.

"It won't cost that much, right?" It made Max happy to see Boll coming back to life. "But I really, really have to ask you to leave now. Let's meet another day."

Boll was already at the door. "I'll never forget this." And it was clear that he meant it.

Max shook his hand. It was as clammy as he'd feared. "Take care," he said.

Boll twitched left and right uncertainly, then quickly threw his arms around Max, and just as quickly let him go again. A moment later, he was out on the stairs, clanking his way down to the street.

78

TWO YEARS EARLIER

"Can you guess what they're willing to pay?"

Max didn't want to know.

He and Felix were sitting in the upstairs living room. There was ice-cold white wine and caviar that Felix had brought.

"What do you want, Felix? I was just about to get to work . . ."

"Have we ever talked about what you're working on?"

"No. We haven't."

"Why not, Max? You'll need a publisher. Show us your work sometime." Felix dunked a spoon deep into the roe. "Or do you want to work with some other publishing house?"

"Honestly, I'd rather not talk about it at all yet. Least of all with you."

"*Yet*? Did you say *yet*? That's good. Maybe later? When you've got a clearer picture."

Max poured water into his wine glass.

"So, have you thought again about what we talked about at Betty's wedding?"

Max raised the glass to his lips and drank a good mouthful. He might have guessed *that* was on Felix's mind.

"The Milan deal alone is worth a fortune."

"And won't happen without my consent."

Felix licked his lips. "Probably not."

Max's eyebrows twitched up for a second. "I don't much feel like making a decision right now."

The spoon clanked into Felix's plate, but when Max looked him in the eye again, Felix's smile was back in place.

"Meaning?"

Max set his glass back on the table, taking care that it came down softly. "I won't sell the rights today."

"And tomorrow?"

"Nor tomorrow."

"The day after?"

"Nor the day after."

Silence.

"At the end of the year?"

"I don't know when I'll sell them, I don't know *if* I'll sell them at all, and I also don't know—if I sell them at all—if I would sell them to *you*, Felix."

"So, you don't know anything."

"That's what it looks like."

"This could kill the Milan deal."

"There you go."

Silence.

"Shame about the money."

Max shrugged.

Felix stood. "Time I was off, then. My plane leaves in half an hour. Guess we'll see what they say in Milan when they find out." He laughed and reached for the coat and silk scarf he'd thrown carelessly over the chair's arm. "Can you at least show me out?"

Am I supposed to apologize for fucking up your business?

Max remained in his seat. "Sorry to be so costly . . ." he said, mentally adding *asshole*.

"It isn't the money, Max. I don't care about the profit."

"I know. It's about your ideas, the ones you want to contaminate everyone with."

Felix clucked his tongue. Max's words dripped off him like oil. And then he said something that, in the first instant, made Max feel as if he'd somehow misunderstood the words: "So, tell me about this secret Till mentioned . . ."

"What?"

"Till works for me now. You knew that, right? He said he didn't want to talk about it, but that something happened, back when you were both kids—"

"What did Till say?"

"He didn't actually *say* anything . . . except that he couldn't talk about it . . ."

"How did you get on the subject at all?"

Felix sighed. "He's working with the narratologists now. We were talking about different mechanisms to hook a reader on a text, specifically that one should try to create a bond with the reader's unconscious mind, with the subconscious . . . with feelings the reader isn't aware of—"

"And?"

"And I said everyone had a secret, and right *there* was where you had to grab them."

Max crossed his arms.

"Then it went around, a kind of brainstorming session. Everyone was supposed to say something about himself and his secret. Henning said something about stealing something when he was a kid. Quentin—"

"I don't want to hear about Quentin!"

"Okay, okay. Then it was Till's turn. He said he couldn't talk about it. It was a long time ago, back when he was still a kid. In the home? *I don't want to talk about it,* was all he said. Then I told him I'd ask Max, but he just shook his head. You should have seen him. Squirming like he'd sat on a hot stove."

Max's mind was ticking.

"You know what he's talking about?" Felix looked at him.

Don't let anything show! But at the same time, Max felt his face contorting, every muscle drawing tight and turning into a sign, there for anyone to read.

"Okay, Max. I don't want to know," said Felix. "You were kids, right? How bad could it be . . . ?"

"Right." Max turned away.

"Were you mixed up in it? No, wait, I'm not asking that." Felix seemed to Max to be almost dancing on the threshold. "Did you mess up, and Till's covering for you? I know you, kiddo. You've fucked things up often enough."

"He did it! I was the one who covered for him, not him for me! What did that idiot tell you?"

"Hey, no problem," Felix was nearly laughing. "He said that. He said, 'Max kept his mouth shut—'"

"He said that?" Max stared at him in disbelief.

"Didn't you just say the same thing?"

"What the fuck did Till say, Felix? No," said Max. "Just go! Leave me alone. I don't want to talk about it anymore."

"Seems to be your favorite phrase these days, Max. I don't want to talk about it. Not about your work, not about Quentin, not about whatever it was you and Till did back then . . ."

"You got it."

Felix looked like he was contemplating striking Max again with his light—but unbearable—barbs. "Maybe you should have a little chat with Till," he finally said. "Tell him he should be more circumspect, if you don't want us all getting worried."

Max had left his chair and was standing at the window. He had his back to Felix. It annoyed him—it infuriated him—that Felix had managed to get him so worked up. He knew there was no way he'd be able to get his head together if he sat down at his desk now. The entire day was wasted.

He heard the front door click shut. Felix was gone.

Max turned. The huge loft with its Plexiglas floor lay in front of him, empty. The rest of the day stretched away endlessly in front of him. He couldn't work anymore. He felt wiped out by the sleepless night, and demoralized to the core by his encounter with Felix.

It makes no difference! he growled at himself. *I'll just make myself work!*

Legs trembling, he crossed the room, kicking aside a chair that was blocking his path.

TODAY

"What's takin' so long? Claire?"

"Here."

"Claire, what . . . what's the matter?"

She's lying on the floor in a narrow space. Did she stumble? Fall through the boards? She's in one of the storage units lining the passage in the basement.

Claire pushes herself up. She feels Frederik's hand grasp her arm above the elbow and help her to her feet.

"The woman . . ." Her tongue feels stuck to the roof of her mouth, but she forces it free. "The woman, Fred—"

"She's waiting up on the street. Why didn't you follow us?"

"I . . . I . . ."

"Did you fall?" His face is pure concern. He is earnest, waiting.

"What about the man?" Claire glances past Frederik, down the passageway.

"He must have gone in the other direction. He wasn't well, Claire. Come on."

The horse head—no the human *head, it wasn't a horse's, it was just very big . . .*

"Fred, I . . ." She looks back at the storage unit. She must have broken through the planks, must have fallen and hit them, and they were so rotten they simply broke . . .

Her eyes move to the rear wall of the unit, where a cupboard stands. Beside the cupboard is a tunnel that looks like it winds deeper underground. The feeble light in the basement barely reaches the shaft.

"Let's take a look, there . . . the shaft there, can you see it?"

He doesn't let her go. "Now's not the time, Claire." Frederik's voice is gentle, but firm. "Poking round down here's too risky right now. Let's head back up." He leads her cautiously out of the cramped unit.

The boards. They just broke when she hit them. Right? Claire supports herself against Frederik and steps out into the corridor. Her legs suddenly give out.

"What is it?"

She looks down. Her ankle . . . the splinters . . . she must have caught her leg on the wood when she stumbled into the storage unit.

It'll be okay . . . it's not that bad . . . Frederik is right, of course. They've got to get out of there!

He has one arm around her waist, and she leans on Frederik so heavily she barely has any weight on her foot at all.

Suddenly, she feels a wave of relief and well-being wash over her. The building that fell? The men chasing them? What was the big deal? Everything was fine . . . her whole life lay ahead of her. She would finish her photo series for the newspaper, publish her book. She can already see it in front of her: a picture of Frederik gracing the dust wrapper, a shot of him in the ring after the fight with that Russian, Lubajew.

She squeezes against him, almost floating through the corridor to the stairwell, where daylight is already streaming down the steps to the outside world. The sun burns bright in the morning sky.

Claire pinches her eyes closed. There's something almost painful about the brightness, but Claire soaks up the light, the warmth, the radiance.

She is radiant herself. "Isn't it wonderful?"

Frederik turns to face her. She sees his expression brighten when he realizes how good she feels.

"Yeah," he says, almost laughing. "You're right."

She presses close to him.

"Aaaahh!" The sudden pain stabs like a needle. Her arm tightens around Frederik's waist. She manages—just—to hang on to her smile. Then she tilts her head and looks down at her ankle, visible below the leg of her jeans.

It is difficult to see, but unmistakable: the skin around the cuts and scratches has changed color.

Green-black.

And it hurts.

TWO YEARS EARLIER

"That's most important thing. You gotta leave the reader with a question at the end of a chapter, and it has to be a question they care about, that they absolutely have to know the answer to. The hero's hanging from the cliff. Will he fall or does he manage to climb back up? This is at the heart of the narrative stuff we deal with here."

"The point being . . . ?"

"Well, first and foremost, to drag the reader in, as we say." Quentin hesitated and then went on. "There is one particular word you'll hear a lot around here. I personally don't like it much, but since you'll pick it up anyway, I'll go ahead and use it. Probably the fastest way for you to get the gist of what we actually do . . . *Addiction*. That's what we're all about. How to maximize the addiction factor, the *need* to keep on reading."

"Ah."

At first, after what had happened in Max's apartment, Till had stayed out of Quentin's way. But that morning they'd struck up a casual conversation in the kitchen, and Till decided to go along with it because he realized that, when it came to talking about the work they did, Quentin was much less tight-lipped than his colleagues.

"So?" Till asked. "What have you come up with—apart from the classic cliff-hanger, I mean? How do you get the reader hooked?"

Quentin sized him up for a moment, then he settled onto the armrest of a low, orange armchair. They were in a small room connecting the kitchen and the offices. "Has Felix actually told you what you're supposed to be doing here?"

"For now, simply to try to figure out exactly what you all do."

Quentin eyed him mistrustfully.

"So, tell me," Till probed. "Maximizing the hook factor? That really interests me. It's why I asked Felix if I could work in this section. Have you come up with something new? I mean, something out of the ordinary?"

"Well, we're experimenting with the material a bit."

"But you can't talk about it. Right?"

Quentin hesitated. "You're one of the team now, aren't you?"

"Of course! Ask Henning!"

"Okay, okay, but this is for your ears only."

"No sweat."

Quentin slid off the armrest and flopped into the chair. "The first thing, of course, is the length." He seemed to enjoy the role of inducting Till into what they'd discovered. "The longer you can keep the reader in the story, the more you drag him in, the more addicted you make him—as long as you don't bore him. We've had fantastic results with six thousand, ten thousand, fifteen thousand pages—"

"With whom?" Till interrupted him, sitting down in the armchair opposite.

"Internal, the people working here. But also with test readers. They have to sign a nondisclosure agreement."

"Okay . . ."

"But the sheer number of pages isn't the only thing," Quentin continued. "There's also the way the story branches, the number of secondary characters."

"Felix mentioned that too."

"Another thing we've looked at, and which worked very well at the start, is the *twist*," said Quentin. "You tell a story, but leave out certain details. The reader will automatically form an opinion about what's missing. Then as the story continues, you hit him with the twist; you show the reader that what *really* happened in the gap is totally different than what he thought happened. And you also show that what really happened fits in perfectly with the other things the reader already knows. Voilà! A surprise for the reader. This pleases him. And he'll be on the edge of his seat wondering where it goes next. Will you be able to surprise him again? He can't imagine it's possible. It's a bit like watching a magic trick: the more often you surprise him, the more conscious the reader becomes of how mistaken he's been all along, how wrong everything he took for granted really was."

Till creased his brow. Was that really all they'd come up with here?

Quentin leaned forward. "But most of all, we've given a lot of thought to what we call the death of suspense."

"Uh-huh . . ."

"Let's assume you've roughed out a thriller, something really white-knuckle. Anything that threatens the story's suspense is your enemy, in a way."

"Clearly."

"Suspense breeds addiction, and addiction is what we want to maximize. So, what would be the death of suspense? We wanted to know more about that. As it turns out, the answer is simple: the death of suspense is *resolution!*"

Till smiled.

"Think of a puzzle," Quentin continued. "Who was the murderer? Where's the attack going to take place? Or will the guy and the girl get together in the end? If you solve the puzzle and answer the question that's been teasing the reader like some kind of delicious poison, then what? Then the reader will be satisfied, the hunger satisfied, and he'll put the book aside. It's a bit like a striptease. You have to simultaneously *tease* the reader and promise him something: 'You'll find out the secret if you just stick with it.'" Quentin studied Till's face. "You know what I mean; the better the tease, the better the sex. Everyone knows that. But the sex itself, or the climax if you like, that's the death of suspense. So, you draw it out! That's all you can do if you want to ratchet up the addiction. But be careful; the moment the reader starts to feel like the teasing's just marching in place, you lose him. It has to go somewhere!"

"Have you tried out anything else?"

"We've looked at how we can link the time a reader spends reading a book with the content itself, for instance."

"Wow."

"Really. It was hard work. We gave a group some test material and then put them up in a hotel and told them that while they were working for us—for money, of course—all they could talk about was what happened in the book. And apart from reading the book, we made sure there was nothing else for them to do in any case." Quentin grinned. "When you read a book, what you read about and what happens in real life have more or less the same status in your head. With our group experiment, our aim was to do everything possible to make the fictional world feel more real than the real one. So, we started rewarding the people for answering certain questions based on the text. With especially good food . . . and with sex." He laughed. "That was toward the end of the experiment. A few guys actually got laid if they were able to answer the questions correctly. And the woman we brought in for the sex was made up to look like the heroine in the book! You can imagine how enthusiastically they started reading once they found out they'd get to sleep with the heroine just by giving the right answers! If they gave the wrong answer, she simply left!"

Quentin was enjoying himself, no doubt about it.

"And then," he said, looking at Till, his eyes flashing, "once we'd really got them into the material, we did an about-face and started directly addressing the reader. *'Stop reading!'* we wrote, *'If you're free, then stop!'"*

"But the text kept going, right?"

"Absolutely! The text kept going. Any amount of letters, any amount of words, any amount of material still ahead of them. But in the text, the narrator addressed the reader and said: *'Stop reading, although there are still a hundred pages to the end!'* It was right in the middle of the narrative, when there were still a thousand unanswered questions about the characters and what would happen to them." Quentin opened his mouth, held it open for a moment—then abruptly barked *"'Stop reading!'"*

"And?"

"Brilliant! It was like a trap about to snap shut. *'If you're free,'* they read, *'then you can stop reading, can't you?'* But none of them did! Not one! They all kept going!" Quentin's eyes were bright.

"Yeah, okay . . ."

"Yeah, sure, but wait for it! The book wasn't done. In the story the hero had to either overcome a certain dependency—or not."

Till narrowed his eyes a little.

"And he *does* overcome it!" Quentin slapped his thigh. "He overcomes his addiction—the hero in the book! And then the trap snaps shut! Because once the hero overcame his dependency—meaning he stopped seeing the woman, or stopped gambling, whatever he was hooked on—we addressed the reader again: *'The hero beat his addiction, and showed that he was free.'* And then: *'But the hero's fictional, he's just someone we thought up. He doesn't really exist! But you, dear reader, you are not a fictional character. You are real. And you did not break your habit! Or else you wouldn't have read to the end. This shows that you are not free!'"*

Quentin opened his mouth and spread his hands apart, as if to say "You see?"

Till had to laugh. "Not bad at all."

But at the same time, he was thinking *But what's the point? Why does Felix want to show everybody that they're not free—whatever the cost?*

TODAY

Claire sits on the grass in Monbijou Park, ignoring how sparse and rutted it is. They are opposite the Old National Gallery, which rises from the other side of the Spree like a Prussian temple.

"I can almost see it right in front of me." She doesn't shift her gaze from the Museumsinsel across the river. "I'm going to call my photo book *Berlin Now*. And you"—she smiles to imagine it—"will be right on the front cover."

"Ha!" She hears Frederik laugh beside her.

Claire slings her arms around her knees. "One of the pictures I took after you beat Lubajew." She tips her head a little to one side to look at him.

Frederik nods. He looks so happy, almost like a little boy. "Wow," he says. "I'm gonna be on the cover. What's inside? What kind of pictures?"

"*Berlin Now*," says Claire, turning back to look at the temple. "It's about the people and their work. The women working on the assembly line in Tempelhof, the public servants working for the government in Mitte, the doctors in the Charité just before an operation."

She hears Frederik sink onto his back beside her on the grass.

"The all-night DJ walking home in the morning, the old man at the counter of the local bar, the subway conductor saying goodbye to his wife. The reporter looking out the window of the Springer building, the Turkish wholesaler directing his fleet of trucks. The gatekeeper at the prison in Tegel, the road worker on his steam roller, the cultural attaché in the lobby of the French embassy on Pariser Platz. The maid in the Adlon Hotel, the secretary of state's intern, the unemployed guy in his basement apartment in Spandau. The roofer on the high-rise in Marzahn, the carriage driver standing beside his droshky, the girl at the supermarket checkout. The mother picking up her daughter from school, the retiree who never leaves his apartment." She glances down at Frederik, but he has closed his eyes.

"*Berlin Now.* What kind of city is that?" She looks at the river rolling by at their feet. "Is it just the history, the Nazis? Hitler's bunker? It was really here. It's not just an urban legend or anything like that. It wasn't far away from where we're sitting right now. And he lived in there; he died in there. I mean, it always feels like something in a movie, but it wasn't Hollywood. It really happened, here, where we live, in Berlin." She has her eyes closed now too. The light is so blinding.

"Did you ever visit Tresor? The club with the lockers from the old Wertheim department store? When they turn up the techno so loud you feel like you're underwater? That's Berlin, isn't it? The whole world knows about the Berlin aura, or whatever you want to call it. When a guy like Blixa Bargeld sings 'Der morgige Tag ist mein.' Marlene Dietrich, the dividing up of the city, the Russian tanks on Stalinallee. That's all this city." She can almost feel herself already flipping through the pages of her book. "It's all transforming, Frederik. We can already sense it, but we can't give it a name, not yet. The city still looks the same as ever, but we have this foreboding; it's just the outside walls, the facades, and behind them everything is in flux, changing, moving." She stops and takes a breath. "We'll be able to explain it later, looking back: 'And then that happened, and that, and that, and don't forget that. And all of it was no more than the displacement of a long overdue system. First, it started to teeter like a clumsy giant, then it fell down—at a speed no one saw coming.' Looking back, everyone will be able to explain it, Frederik—but we're standing on the threshold!"

A slight throbbing sensation has started to make its way up her leg.

"But we can't see anything!" Suddenly, her eyes are filled with tears, and she looks at Frederik in despair. She sees that he wants to console her, but that he doesn't know what to do.

"WE CAN'T SEE WHAT'S COMING FOR US!" she bursts out, and her body is racked with sobbing.

TWO YEARS EARLIER

When Lisa awoke, the sky—she could see it through the window from the bed—had already turned the steel-blue shade so typical of Berlin in the early morning. It was no longer dark and not yet light, but Lisa could already see that the day would be overcast and that a light rain would start to fall any moment.

She turned to one side. Next to her, under the thick, down cover, lay Till. His mouth was slightly open, and she could hear him breathing deeply. She had known his face since she was eleven years old, but she had never before woken up naked in bed beside him. They had kissed for the first time three weeks earlier. Last night wasn't the first time they'd slept together, but it was the first time Lisa had spent the night.

She wadded the pillow she'd slept on and stuffed it behind her head. Her hair spread around her head on both sides of her face. She pulled the cover up to her chin and folded her arms beneath it. It was the middle of May, but still cold in the Berlin morning.

Felix had flown to Milan the day before, and was spending the night down there. He was hoping to sell some licenses to an Italian business partner, he said. Lisa had struggled for a long time about sleeping over at Till's, but had finally decided yes. And it was the right choice, she now thought, even though she found more and more things to worry about the more she awake she became.

She was not married to Felix. On the contrary; he was still the husband of Sophie von Quitzow, whose name he had taken. As far as Lisa knew, she wasn't even his only girlfriend. Lisa didn't think he'd slept with Nina or Irina for a long time, but she knew that he kept up contact with both of them, as he had with Maja and maybe with other women as well.

And in the years they'd been together, she had never been with another man. But she was constantly aware that what bound her and Felix was far more important to him than all his other liaisons and affairs. She knew it because she was the only woman he had physically lived with in the last ten years, and because he wanted a child with her. But she also knew that it mattered to Felix that she was the daughter of Xavier Bentheim—the only man, as far as she could tell, that Felix had ever admired. Sometimes it seemed that the esteem in which he had held her father had, in some way, transferred to her after his death.

"It's over," she whispered, and listened to Till's breathing.

If she hadn't already known it, then the previous night had made it clear to her that she was in love with Till, had perhaps always been in love with him. Her relationship with Felix had finally become unbearable.

But how was she supposed to leave him? Should she just tell him that she was leaving him and moving in with Till? That would be problematic. Not only was Lisa certain that Felix would not just let her go, but also because Till worked for Felix. Could she ask Till to resign his position at the publishing house, a position that meant a great deal to him?

Lisa sighed. In that particular regard, she did not understand Till. It must have weighed as heavily on him as on her that there was no way to reconcile their love with the work that Till was becoming more and more immersed in from one week to the next. How did he see this working out? Did he think it could go on like this forever? Didn't it bother him that sooner or later he would have to make a choice, that he would have to decide between working for Felix and being with Lisa?

She rolled slightly onto her side and looked out the window at the developing morning. Was it possible that Till would choose the job over her?

The thought shot through her like a red-hot shard in her belly. She drew her legs up with a sharp jerk to try to shake off the stabbing pain. This could not be happening! She could not start being suspicious of the man she'd known and loved for so long—not the morning after the first full night they'd spent together! But what was going on in Till's mind? Was he too weak to work through these things, to bring them to a conclusion? How could he just go along with things like this?

Silently, Lisa pushed back the cover and sat up on the edge of the bed.

It made no sense to lie there and sink deeper and deeper into her thoughts. Either she confronted Till or she banished the questions from her mind and instead concentrated instead on what *she* would do next. Maybe it was best if she gave Till more time to come to a decision on his own.

Her eyes drifted back to the window. The morning light had finally won out over the night's dark blue. The evening before, Lisa had left the window slightly open. Now the birds outside, apparently feeling called upon to announce the end of winter, were twittering away, loud and piercing.

Lisa carefully turned around. All she could see of Till was the back of his head, visible above the bedcover. But she could no longer make out the regular sound of his breathing, which she had heard at her side throughout the night like a quiet confirmation.

Was he awake too?

She glanced at the alarm clock on the bedside table. Just before 6:30. Lisa suddenly stood up and shut the window. A chilly draft was coming in.

It was time for her to get home, before Felix called.

TWO YEARS EARLIER

Till's apartment was in Schöneberg, so Lisa decided to take the subway back to Mitte. As she ran down the steps to the platform, she had already made up her mind; she would not wait any longer to take charge of her life. And she knew how she would do it. The internship *had* been fun; she would start working for a newspaper as soon as she could. And hopefully for a good one, not some dubious rag where interns wrote articles based on third-hand information. No, she'd work at a national newspaper, staffed by well-informed people and publishing well-considered opinions. A paper that exerted a degree of influence on society and public discourse.

As she stepped into the subway train that had just pulled into the station, she felt energized by the prospect. Lost in thought, she let herself be carried northward, below the traffic, noise, and chaos on the surface.

Half an hour later, Lisa unlocked the apartment that she shared with Felix and slipped out of her coat. Eager and ready to make her new goal a reality, she was heading to her room when she heard a voice.

"Lisa?"

She jumped in fright. Was Felix already home? But it wasn't his voice!

Wearing a look of surprise, Henning appeared in the doorway that opened into Felix's study. "I thought you were in your room."

Lisa inhaled sharply.

"Felix asked me to pick up some papers for him. He needs them at the office. He's going there directly from the airport." As if to prove the truth of what he was saying, Henning held up a few sheets of paper. "He said I should let you sleep, that it wouldn't disturb you."

"No, it's fine. No problem, Henning, don't let me hold you up." She tried to move past him as casually as she could.

"Are you just getting home?" An angular smile crossed his face.

None of your business! But Lisa pulled herself together.

"I took a letter to the post office!" *Good!* she thought.

"Ah. I see." The suspicion in his voice was palpable.

"What is it you want, Henning?" She swept a strand of hair behind one ear. "Sniffing around after me for your master?"

One corner of Henning's mouth twitched upward a little, as if the insult had struck him like a fine whip. "Felix will ask me if I saw you. What am I supposed to tell him?"

"I went to mail a letter, Henning. What's the problem? If you must know, it was a job application for a newspaper. I finished writing it last night and wanted to send it off as early as I could today. That's what you can tell Felix."

She had the impression that her brother-in-law was happy to be handed a script.

"So, why wasn't your bed slept in?"

The question left her speechless for a moment.

"You looked in my room?" Her voice was quiet, as if she had suddenly fallen ill.

"I'm sorry, Lisa. He—"

"He asked you to."

The floor under her feet felt like it was moving. He would tell Felix, and Felix would take her to task. What was she supposed to say now? Tell him the truth? Did she really want Felix to find out from Henning?

"Lisa, if you want, I can just as easily tell Felix you—"

"What do you want from me, Henning? Has spying for Felix made you stupid?" She was yelling at him. "Leave me out of your disgusting suspicions! I took a letter to the post office! I slept in Felix's bed because I missed him. Do you want to know if I touched myself? Is that it? You want me to come onto you, want me to get you off in there too? Is that it? In your master's bed? Would that cheer you up? Or would it be too dangerous because I could rat on you?"

Henning had turned pale, and he backed up a few steps into Felix's study.

"Get out of my apartment! I don't care what Felix told you to do. I'm going to talk to him about you. Then we'll see what he has to say!"

She stood in front of the door to the study, her feet firmly planted on the floor. "Get out, Henning! Do you hear me?" She took a step toward him, snatched the papers from his hand, and hurled them to the floor. "Get out of here!"

Taken aback, he reached for the jacket he'd thrown over a chair in the study and pushed his way past her into the corridor.

Lisa was left behind in Felix's study. She felt numb. A moment later, she heard the front door close.

Then silence.

Henning was gone.

JOURNAL ENTRY

It's an expedition!

It can't be left to simply happen. It has to be EXPLORED. What this way conceals . . . it's a voyage into uncertainty, a push into uncharted territory.

Which is why there needs to be a record of what we—what I— find there.

Right?

It makes no sense for me to go down this path if no one finds out about it. No! This is not a stroll, not a Sunday jaunt, not just something to pass the time. It's an ordeal!

But this doesn't mean I'm going to stop. I'm going to forge ahead! And I will report on my progress. Not to broadcast any particular message, not to educate or exert some sort of influence, but simply to document what is down there!

So, I'm writing down how it was when my hands closed around her throat . . .

We were still locked together.

She embraced me.

She lowered herself onto me.

At first, she thought it was part of the act.

She went along with it.

I'm sure she couldn't imagine I'd do anything to a girl who was giving me so much pleasure.

But I knew I wouldn't have the strength to finish it . . . if . . . if I finished the OTHER part first.

So I squeezed.

With so much force that there was no longer any doubt about my intentions.

With so much force that it was impossible for her to scream.

We were alone in the cubicle, in the women's restroom—but anyone could have come in at any moment. So I squeezed with all the strength in me, all the power I could summon from my muscles, from my sinews.

Who can imagine what goes on inside when you're choking the life out of someone else? What it's like inside when you're choking to death the one you're with in the act of love? How desire suddenly switches to the desire to kill?

What did I discover by doing this?

Was lust part of it? Was lust part of going down this evil path?

Was it lust that drove me to crush the life out of her?

It burned, like I was standing in a sea of flames.

Her small hands were clasped around my wrists.

She looked at me; she knew it was time.

She didn't scream.

She couldn't.

She knew immediately there was no going back, no slackening of the pressure, no mercy.

That it was almost as if it wasn't me killing her, but that it was death coming to claim her.

Still, she looked at me. She did not close her eyes to what was happening, she did not turn away . . . no, she looked at me as if she wanted to see how she—as beautiful, as desirable, as delightful as she was—had earned death.

I can almost believe she simply had the bad luck to meet me.

My hands were shaking so much I could hardly release them from her throat, even when her body just hung slackly on my lap.

She slid into the corner beside the toilet bowl, and I was not able to stop her head from banging against the tiles.

I buttoned my pants and stood up. I could barely breathe.

These were the thoughts that kept me from falling down: by choking her I had done what had to be done. I had taken a step in the right direction. There was only one more thing to do: bring the journey that I had begun to an end.

I had *to kill her because I would never have been able to complete my journey any other way.*

I left the cubicle and climbed out a window near the sink. I knew it wouldn't be long before they found me. The waiter, the guests in the restaurant . . . they all saw me, they could all describe me. It wouldn't be long before I would no longer be able to show my face in public.

But it hasn't come to that yet.

And it isn't over; I know what I still have to do.

The final step.

Xavier Bentheim described it. I *will make it a reality.*

Felix is betraying Bentheim's legacy with his plans. I won't make the same mistake. And no one will be able to stop me.

I know the hidden meaning in Xavier's text—it is not what Felix is planning!

TWO YEARS EARLIER

"What you told me about is worse. Much worse! I would never do anything like that!"

Nina sat bolt upright. She pricked up her ears. A murmur of voices. Suddenly:

"NO! I'm . . . look, I might be crazy but what you're talking about . . . I'd never get myself into a situation like that. I'd . . . much earlier, I wouldn't be able to keep focused on what I was actually aiming for . . ." The voice faded again. The man must have gone into another room.

Nina turned over in bed and glanced at the clock. 8:30. The bed swayed slightly. She was alone. Carefully, she sat up and slipped down from the mattress. She knew whose voice she'd heard. It wasn't Max's voice, but Boll's. And Nina couldn't stand Lennart. She found him so odious that she preferred to leave a room rather than share it with him. But Max was bent on spending time with the man. Max never sent him away, no matter when he showed up. On the contrary. More and more often, Max and Boll went out together in the evening, even when Nina was there. Like the previous night. Max had said a fleeting good-bye, and that was the last she'd seen of him. But Nina realized that if she could hear Boll's voice, Max could not be far away.

She threw on the light robe that lay on a chair next to the bed, and pulled open the door, which stood ajar.

"So, now you think it was good? Is that it?" She heard Max's voice now, coming from the kitchen.

"No. I don't know . . ." Boll again. "I mean, I can see how it's got to be tormenting you, that sometimes it really gets to you, and then it comes back again, the feeling like you did something wrong. That it would've been better if you didn't do it in the first place. But on the other hand, what can you do about it now? It happened. Who knows what it's good for?"

"What it's *good* for?"

"Sure. Good. It's sort of got inside you now. Right?"

Boll had stayed overnight in Max's guestroom several times. Each time Nina had tried to talk to Max about it, tell him that she wasn't comfortable with the arrangement. But Max had always dodged the subject. And she was left feeling stupid. After all, it was his apartment; Max could let anyone he liked spend the night.

She stopped in the hallway, a few steps short of the door to the kitchen, undecided as to whether she should join the two men.

"You did it. You went through it, you know what it looked like, how it felt. And obviously it's not something for everyone, but it's . . . intense. Isn't it, Max? Isn't it? It's intense."

What she was hearing sounded creepy. Perhaps it wasn't such a great idea to burst in on the two of them right then.

It was almost half an hour later, after she'd gone back to bed, that she heard someone moving in the hallway. Nina instinctively closed her eyes. The steps sounded unsteady, as if the person walking toward the bedroom had to support himself against the wall. The door was pushed open. Steps approached the bed and someone sat down next to the small curve her body formed under the covers.

Nina heard someone puffing and panting. Then she felt the bed rock and realized that whoever was sitting there had bent forward to untie his shoelaces. Without moving her body at all, she opened her eyes.

Thank Christ it isn't Boll, she thought when she saw Max sitting there. But there was also perplexity mixed with her relief, because even from the side she noticed something different about Max's face. His cheeks hollower? Paler? Older?

"Max." She whispered, but Max jumped—and turned his face to hers.

It was as if the outer layer of his face was stripped away to reveal a different one beneath.

Nina inhaled sharply and involuntarily jerked her forearm up to cover her mouth.

His lips twisted, his mouth stretched in a vague smile. "Oh, babe, what a night."

Nina braced her legs on the mattress and pushed herself up onto her pillow. She fumbled for the lamp on the bedside table and switched it on. But Max had already turned away again by the time the light hit him.

"I gotta sleep," she heard him murmur.

"Did . . . did something happen? You look pretty wrecked."

She stared at his back.

"Everything's okay. Everything's fine."

He started unbuckling his belt, stood up, and pushed his jeans off without turning around.

"Where were you?"

Max laughed. "I'll tell you in the morning . . ."

"It is morning."

He threw his pants over a chair and began to unbutton his shirt.

"Is Lennart sleeping here?"

"Uh-huh."

"Max, you know I . . . I don't like him. I'm sorry, but . . . I don't think he's good for you."

Max eased off his shirt and tossed it over the chair with his jeans. Then he slipped off his boxers and turned around. His body was pale and his bones stood out under his skin. His short hair stood up on his head. But it was his eyes that really got to her, sunk so deep in their sockets. He took a step toward the bed and threw back the blanket. She wanted to get out of bed, but in the condition Max was in, she didn't want to seem cruel.

He lay down beside her, pulled the blanket over himself, and sighed. "Let's talk about it another time, okay?"

But it would always be like this if they didn't start talking. "Max, you look totally . . . changed. Did you guys take something?"

Max closed his eyes.

Nina threw back the blanket angrily and rolled off the other side of the mattress after all. She stood and faced him. "Fine, you want to sleep. But am I supposed to just stand by and watch you go off on more and more all-nighters with Lennart and see you come back looking like a ghost?"

"Come on, don't exaggerate . . ."

"I don't want him sleeping at our place anymore."

Max opened his eyes, looked at her, and smiled—but somewhere behind his gaze, something else was lurking. A strange desperation, insecurity, vulnerability . . . she didn't know what to call it. It was not something new to her, not something she hadn't noticed before. But on this particular morning, this aspect of his personality, normally hidden deep inside, appeared in the foreground for the first time.

"Lennart normally sleeps on the couch in a friend's living room," said Max. He was making an effort to stay calm. "It helps him and his friend get along better when he spends the night here occasionally. At my place—or ours—there's lots of space. How can I tell him we need the whole apartment for us? No, it's nonsense!" Max raised himself up a little and propped himself on one elbow. "I can see what you mean. Any normal person, the first time they see Lennart, they think, *Where did this weirdo escape from?* But Lennart's no idiot, you know? And he hasn't exactly had the luckiest life up to now."

Nina sat down on the chair where her clothes were lying and drew her robe around herself.

"I feel like it's good if I look after him a little," said Max.

"Is that what you call it? Looking after him!? You go out with him at night, you pop pills or smoke God knows what—what kind of looking after him is that?"

Max laughed and lay on his back again. "Don't you ever feel that the way we pass everything by . . . that it isn't okay? Everything that happens in the world, all the beggars, what we do to animals?"

Nina watched him staring at the ceiling. "What does that have to do with Lennart?"

"I thought, why not try it? Why not try *not* just passing by?"

Nina pulled the robe around her a little tighter. "So, tomorrow you're turning vegetarian?" she said sarcastically.

Max didn't answer.

"Max, how far is this going to go?"

"No idea."

"What are you thinking? That you want to be a better person?"

"Fuck being a better person," he said. "I just don't want to throw Lennart out, okay?"

"But if he ends up wrecking you . . . ? I've never seen you look like you look tonight. I'm not trying to upset you, but have you looked at yourself in the mirror? I know we haven't known each other that long, but since you've been mixed up with Boll, it's like you're in some kind of trouble."

Max laid one arm across his eyes, the back of his hand resting on the pillow.

"Max?"

He didn't answer.

JOURNAL ENTRY

Blood will rain.

The bodies of the dead will block the sewers. Pus will ooze from the drains, and screams will fill the streets.

The people will understand that the end has come. They will run, they will be hunted out onto the streets. They will fall to the ground. They will trample each other. Their faces will be pushed into the mud when the ones behind tread on the backs of their heads. They will open their mouths to scream, but their screams will choke in the mud.

Buildings will come tumbling down. The rubble will bury the fleeing families. Emergency vehicles will race through intersections and hit the refugees at full speed. Windshield wipers will be turned on to wipe away the blood. There will be looting, weapons will be stolen—each must protect himself. Cars will be stopped, the drivers hauled out.

Children will be hurt, and they will change.

Dogs will skitter along the sidewalks on shaking legs.

The sick will perish in their beds and ooze their toxic fluids.

Men will take whatever they desire, and their heads will be cut from their torsos the next moment.

Animals will feed on the bodies piling up in the ditches. Birds will fly low over the city, darkening the sky.

Greasy black smoke will rise, while the people, confused, their throats raw and their eyes inflamed, wander through the alleys. Smoke from the pyres where the bodies burn. Smoke from the houses going up in flames, smoke from the wrecks of cars that have been set on fire, smoke from the mountains of rubbish, set alight because no one is left to cart it away. Smoke that brings with it a pitiful stink—the odor of rot that makes a man weak, spreads disease, chafes the senses. Flays, corrodes, eats away.

They will blame each other for the moldering bread and the stinking soup. Doctors will amputate limbs without anesthetic.

They will bleat loudly, and four will kill one to silence him. They will leave him lying there and will not drive away the dogs that bite his face.

They will force a woman into the corner of a cellar. Two will hold her, one will take his turn, one will wait.

They won't be able to look themselves in the eye after what has happened. The lust that had taken hold of them will not make it as far as their brains but stay locked in their groins.

They will creep back from the cellar to the dingy light of day and will once again hear the sirens, the screams, the panic in the streets.

The city will be haunted and will fall to its knees. But it will be no ghost, no devil—nothing mystical or mysterious haunts these people.

It will be ME who haunts them, ME who brings this down on them.

ME, if I am to be true to Bentheim's vision.

I need no zombies—the people themselves are zombie enough—it doesn't matter what Felix is planning.

Forget what he wants to achieve. He has disfigured Bentheim's message. But I will revive its true purpose.

I need just one small thing to do it. One tiny grain, and it can be bought in a city like Berlin.

It won't be zombies that attack the city, but they will act like zombies.

They will be infected like zombies.

But they will not be the living dead—not ghosts, not supernatural beings.

They are the sick. The raging, raving sick.

Foaming-at-the-mouth sick, carrying the infection with them. A contagion like a fizzing fuse, burning up through their spines to their brains.

The sick, reacting to every stimulus as if a pistol has gone off next to their heads.

The sick, with nothing to pit against the fury driving them out of their minds.

The sick, who demonstrate with such wondrous clarity what we have long suspected lies deep inside us but which we have tried to keep buried for so long.

The sick, driven by the rage inside.

The sick that I have infected.

Let the RABIES come.

The time is ripe.

85

TWO YEARS EARLIER

"Behrenstrasse, please." Felix leaned back in his seat and looked at her. He smiled. "I had to spend the whole evening gazing across at you."

Lisa placed her handbag on the backseat, noticing as she did that it stood between them. She left it where it was.

"Have I told you what it does to me to see you looking so beautiful?"

Lisa took a breath, and her dress drew tight across her chest. She knew she looked good.

"Your lipstick, is it new?" He wasn't going to stop.

Lisa laughed. "What's with you?"

With a glance toward the taxi driver, who was taking no notice of them, Felix reached for Lisa's hand. He whispered, "You're my addiction, Lisa."

Lisa let him take her hand. She sensed his desire for her; the air in the car was almost heavy with it. His lust made her uncomfortable, but she didn't know how to tell him that.

"Did you have a good time?" She was looking down, and Felix lowered his head to look into her eyes.

"Yes, of course." She smiled.

"You didn't really eat much, did you? Haberlandt, the man on your left . . . how old is he now?"

"It was fine, really."

"And on your right? The spring chicken? Talk about wanting to be the center of attention!" Felix let go of her hand. "Really, Lisa, let's talk about it. It's fine with me if we turn down invitations like this in the future, stay home more . . ."

God no!

"Or you can tell me what you'd rather do. I know they're my friends, but we don't have to see them all the time. Maybe the opera would be a nice change? The theater? Whatever you want!"

She smiled again. "The opera? Are you sure?"

"Why not? I'll talk to Henning. He knows the assistant director of the city opera. We could go backstage afterward. Have you ever done that? We buy a bouquet and pay the singers a visit—it's marvelous!"

"Yes . . . yes, maybe we could do that sometime." Lisa's lack of enthusiasm was palpable.

But Felix was not about to admit defeat. "Forget the opera, then. I don't care. I can talk to Haberlandt. He called not long ago and wanted to know if we were interested in visiting their house in the Uckermark."

But the more he spoke, the more she had the feeling that she was sinking deeper into the seat of the taxi.

"He has a small landing strip on his property. I know I've mentioned that. He'd love to show us one of his sport planes sometime."

"Yes, certainly." Lisa smiled. Her cheeks were almost hurting from smiling. The taxi turned onto the autobahn on-ramp, which would take them from Wannsee back into the city. Felix had come back from Milan that morning and driven straight to the office. In the evening, he had picked Lisa up from home and they had driven to the dinner party together.

"Is everything okay?" He was still leaning toward her.

"I don't know." She looked forward, out through the windshield. The taillights of the car in front smeared reddish in the rain spattering the front window. Then the wipers swept the rain aside.

Felix finally leaned back in his seat. They rode in silence for a while, and the heavy diesel Mercedes hummed along the AVUS.

"I spoke with Henning," Felix said. "He said you were rather distraught."

The feeling that went through Lisa when she heard his words was not fear or shock. It was more a kind of weariness. She had spent the entire day thinking about the years she had spent with Felix. And she thought, too, of Till's hands caressing her body. Memories and impressions that she could not reconcile, that made her uneasy, confused. She had tried to tell herself that it was not fundamentally about Felix or Till, that it came down to *her* finally getting her life in order. But for that, she thought, she would need a clear head.

"I don't want to know where you were this morning . . ." Felix said. He, too, was peering out through the windshield. "If you went to post a letter or whatever you did. It was humiliating for Henning to harass you like that, and I'm sorry." He looked at her. "I didn't ask him to go sniffing around after you. I merely asked him to collect a few papers from my study, papers I needed in the office today."

Lisa said nothing.

"I love you, Lisa. You know that."

Lisa eyes wandered to the back of the taxi driver's head. The man was sitting upright in his seat, his eyes fixed on the road ahead.

"Could it be that you need some time for yourself?" Felix's voice was low, pillow soft. A pillow she could lie down on, as exhausted as she was. "I can understand that, Lisa. You're young, I . . . I'm sorry about what I said the other day. I can understand that you're not ready yet for a family."

Don't touch me! The thought flashed in Lisa's head.

"Tell me what I can do for you, and I'm happy to make it happen."

Lisa's mind was buzzing. The taxi driver turned on the indicator, and the even click-click coming from the dashboard filled the vehicle. The heavy car swung into the left lane, following the route that led to Mitte.

Lisa propped her right arm against the door panel and placed her hand on her forehead. Her head felt hot.

The time had come to choose.

86

TWO YEARS EARLIER

When the taxi pulled up at the side entrance of the publishing house, which also led to their apartment, Lisa knew she wasn't going up with Felix.

She stood waiting on the sidewalk while Felix paid the driver. It was after midnight, but the air was not nearly as cold as it had been just two weeks earlier. Spring was coming. There seemed to be no holding it back.

The taxi pulled away from the curb, and Felix walked over to her.

"Maybe you're right," she said, and looked at him. She could see how their conversation in the taxi was weighing on him. "Maybe I do need a break."

Felix's face tensed.

"Won't you come up? You can arrange whatever needs to be done in the morning, in peace and quiet."

"I . . . I want to stretch my legs out here a little longer."

Felix nodded in silence. Finally, he said, "It's Till, isn't it?"

She felt like a red-hot iron was pressing on her neck. She shrugged.

"It's because he's come back."

"I don't know."

"You never got over each other."

Lisa shook her head. "I was with you the entire time, Felix." Her voice was little more than a whisper.

He stood in front of her as if all the strength had been sucked out of his body.

"Max and Till, when they were in boarding school, after Papa was gone . . . I was with you, Felix."

"It was too soon!" He wiped his forehead, and she almost believed she saw his hand shaking. "I should have let him have you. Then you would be coming to me now."

But the words rang hollow. Lisa suddenly felt that not only was she able to leave him but also that she could do it without guilt.

"Aren't you going up?" She looked at him.

Felix nodded.

What an absurd situation, she thought. *It can't end like this.*

But without another word, he turned away, entered a security code on the number pad, and pushed open the door. It closed behind him with a click.

TWO YEARS EARLIER

"Can you come down? I'm on the steps at the Konzerthaus."

When she reached Till on his cell, he was still at the office. Not much more than a hundred feet from where she'd just broken up with Felix.

Five minutes later, she saw him emerge onto the square from Charlottenstrasse. Lisa got to her feet and went to meet him. Wouldn't she have been better off not calling, better off looking for a hotel for the night instead? Wasn't she still beset by how close she was to Felix, by the demands he had placed on her?

The next moment, Till's arms closed around her, she felt the way they pressed her to him, to his skinny, almost bony, body, how they held her tight as if that was what she'd been created for.

After Lisa told him what had happened, they walked without saying anything, holding each other close, past the dark shops, in the direction of Friedrichstrasse.

"I don't want to stand in your way, Till," she finally said, releasing him from her arms. But she was not playing the coquette. She briefly considered whether it might be better to keep the thought to herself, but then it slipped out.

Till touched her chin, and when she looked up, he leaned a little lower and kissed her. Lisa closed her eyes and leaned against him. His hand pressed firmly against her back.

When she opened her eyes again, his face was over hers, very close. "There's a pensione on the side street here," he said. "Let's go in there."

Lisa felt relief flood through her. She would have gone back to his apartment, but to spend the night in a pensione, to not fall headlong into a new life . . . it felt like a kind of salvation.

The room was tiny. The window didn't even open onto the street, but onto a light well instead. There was no bathroom, just a tiled corner with a sink. But the bedclothes were freshly laundered and smelled clean, and the plain wooden floor had been scrubbed.

Lisa pulled a chair from under the tiny table against the wall and sat down. Till dropped onto the bed. They had bought a bottle of red wine from the night porter and Till opened it. Without standing, Till reached for the two glasses on the little shelf above the sink and poured the wine.

He handed Lisa a glass and held his in the air. "To this place," he said.

They clinked glasses, and Lisa threw back the wine. When she set the glass down again, she realized that Till was watching her.

"Don't you want any?"

"I do," he said, and drank.

Suddenly, he was standing in front of her. He leaned forward and for a moment, seemed to hover above Lisa before lowering himself onto her. Driven by an unrelenting urge, he first undressed her, and then himself. As he peeled off his clothes, his desire for her felt very close to rapture.

TWO YEARS EARLIER

"Does he know we're together?"

It was the middle of the night. Lisa was on the verge of sleep when she heard Till's low voice beside her.

She turned her head toward him. "He has some idea."

Till lay on his back, his hands folded behind his head.

"Does that worry you?"

He seemed to ponder this.

"It's just . . ." he said after a while, "I mean, it's not so bad, finally earning a bit of money, you know?" He turned his face toward hers. "Your mom paid for my education. I've waited the whole time—no, not waited—but I've always been kind of fixated on earning some money of my own. And I'm doing that now, at Felix's company. It's not a bad feeling . . ." His voice trailed off.

A little light filtered in through the small window above their heads, projecting a skewed rectangle on the wall opposite.

Of course his work matters to him, Lisa told herself. That's why she'd told him she didn't want to stand in his way earlier. But when it came down to it, this was about the two of them—and if that's what really counted, then Till shouldn't give a damn about his job, right?

For a moment, Lisa thought she was going cry. "All I know," she said, "is I'm not going to play hide-and-seek anymore."

"Sure, that's a good thing, of course."

"You should think about what you want. Me or your job."

It came out sounding much harsher than she intended. But isn't that what it came down to?

She heard him laugh beside her. "Yeah, you're right." He pushed himself up a little and stuffed the pillow behind his head. "What could happen?" He grinned at her.

When Lisa saw him smile, all the despondency she'd been feeling was washed away with a wave of trust.

"Tell him in the morning that you're with me now! I don't care if he fires me." Till leaned across to her, looking into her eyes, beaming. "Or call him! Right now!"

She had to laugh with him. "Right now?"

"Of course! He wakes up, answers his cell, thinks maybe you've changed your mind—"

"But it's you on the phone, not me. *If you would like to know where Lisa*—"

"Too formal."

"Want to know where Lisa is . . ."

"That's it."

But she went on lying there. "Sometimes, I feel sorry for him. Felix . . . always took care of me; he was always affectionate." Something inside her said *And I won't have him out of my system so fast.*

"Didn't you ever think he was . . . creepy?" Till had leaned back again, pulled his knees up.

"Oh, yes . . . though I could never put my finger on exactly what made me think so." *Except sometimes, at night*—but she didn't want to think about that. "I'll call him tomorrow morning and tell him."

Till nodded. "Good."

She sat up next to him, so that they were leaning against the wall side by side. Till had opened the window above them a little, and the fresh air, the first breath of the new day, drifted in.

Lisa pulled the blanket up to her neck. Underneath, she was as naked as Till.

Why did Felix let me go so easily? Why, when he had just asked me if I wanted to have a child with him?

The thought stirred inside her, uninvited.

But when Till turned and looked at her, she said nothing. Instead, she pulled him to her and kissed him on the lips, to prevent herself from speaking.

89

TWO YEARS EARLIER

"Come on!" Max gestured brusquely, not wanting to leave Lennart behind. "We have to see Felix!"

The receptionist at the front desk had let them in without incident. Now Max wanted to make it to Felix's office before anyone stopped him.

"Max! What are you doing here?"

Max looked around. Henning, wearing a broad, cheerful smile, was walking along the hallway toward them. "Reception just told me you were paying us a visit."

"I have to see Felix." Max jabbed his thumb at Lennart, who was standing next to him, looking forlorn. "Lennart . . . Henning."

Henning cast a glance at Max's companion, but kept his hands in his pockets. "What's up, Max? Have you been thinking it over?"

"Is Felix even here?" Max asked, ignoring Henning's question. Henning shrugged. "He's—"

"What, not here? Don't lie to me! I want to talk to him—"

"Max, take it easy! Go and look in his office yourself if you want."

The sense of excitement that Max had felt since entering the building was going to his head. Was Felix really not there?

"Then call him and tell him I want to talk to him!" he barked at Henning, then nodded to Lennart. "I want him to work here. Lennart's good. He can help at reception, he can be a driver or work in the warehouse—whatever, I don't care." He slapped Lennart lightly on the stomach with the back of his hand. "Right, Lennart?"

But Lennart couldn't get a word out.

"Felix wants something from me. Fine," said Max, deftly turning his attention back to Henning. "But I want something from him first. I want him to give my buddy here a job." He saw Henning glance down the hallway past him and spun around.

Two men in cheap guard uniforms were walking toward them.

"What the hell? You're going to have me thrown out?" Stunned, Max stared at Henning.

"Listen, Max, I'm sorry, but you're acting totally unreasonable." Henning looked over at the two guards. "It's okay. Mr. Bentheim will exit the building by himself."

"No!" Max suddenly burst out. "I will not! And I don't think Felix is going to be too thrilled if they drag me out of here! Call him. Or go get him out of his office. I'll bet he's in there and just doesn't want to show his face."

Max pointed to an orange sofa standing in the hallway next to a water cooler. "I'm going to sit down there with Lennart. And I'm going to wait till Felix comes to us. Or else"—and as he said it, an honest smile spread across his face, because he was so certain that he had Felix in the palm of his hand—"or else I'll sell what Felix wants from me to someone else!"

90

TWO YEARS EARLIER

"Max is here. He's downstairs. Ms. Heidt just called me."

Till looked up from the monitor on his desk. Felix had come into his office without bothering to knock. Till had spent nearly the entire night talking to Lisa about Felix. Now, with the man suddenly standing in front of him, several thoughts went through his mind simultaneously.

"Uh-huh?" Till shoved his bottom lip a fraction forward.

"Seems he's quite upset."

Has she already called him? Till wondered.

"It might be better if I didn't go see him . . ." Felix began, striding back and forth on the far side of Till's desk. "I don't want to . . . escalate things to a point where Max says something he can't take back."

Till stood up. "Okay," he said, unsure how he was supposed to respond.

"I was wondering if maybe *you* could have a word?"

Felix looked at him.

"Of course."

"Tell him . . . I'm out."

"Lie to Max? That—"

"No, of course, you're absolutely right. Tell him I can talk to him this afternoon."

"Why not now?"

Felix stepped over to the window and gazed out. "I just told you that."

A beat.

Till ran his thumb and index finger over the corners of his mouth.

Felix turned. "It makes no sense at all to talk to him right now. Max is completely wound up. He'll simply lose it if I try to talk to him, and that's not good for him. You talk to him, Till."

For a moment, it seemed to Till that Felix must already know . . . that Lisa had spent the night in bed with him, with Till. Naked.

"Will do," he said, and headed for the door.

"Till?" Felix stopped him before he got there. "I'm glad to have you on board. I don't want that to change anytime soon."

"No worries, Felix. I'm happy to be here."

"Even if you don't exactly make things easy for me," Felix said, and turned away to the wall. "Best if you go see Max now."

"Where's Felix?" Max stood up from the sofa and approached Till when he saw him coming.

Lennart Boll, whom Till had met in passing on one of his last visits to Max's place, remained where he had been sitting on the sofa behind Max.

"He's afraid to see you, Max. What's going on?"

"Nothing. Why?"

"Felix came in to my office and said you were upset. He asked me to come down and talk to you."

"He's afraid of me?"

"Looks that way." Till noticed how sunken Max's face appeared. He looked like he hadn't slept for three weeks.

"What do you say, Lennart?" Max looked back at Boll.

"Really, Max, you don't need to do this for me . . ."

Turning back to Till, Max said, "But I want to. I want them to give you a job here."

Till nodded. "Did you already talk to Henning about that?"

"I did."

"And?"

"You know what Henning's like. *Sure, sure, no problem*, he says—then he turns round and does the exact opposite."

Till had, in fact, gotten the same impression.

"Could *you* put in a word for Lennart, Till?"

Lennart had lowered his eyes and was staring at his hands, which were wrapped together in his lap. There was something about him that set every alarm in Till's head ringing. Drugs? Or had he done time? Till didn't know.

"I can talk to Felix, Max, no problem," he said, but the words somehow rang hollow. "Happy to," he added, hoping to mitigate the discord between his voice and his words.

"Really?" Max leaned his head back slightly.

Till nodded silently.

"Till was taken in by my father," Max said, looking at Lennart again. "We were eleven or twelve years old. And now," he looked back at Till, "you're the one who'll be putting in a good word for me with my father's publisher, is that right?"

There was nothing to say. That's exactly what Max had just asked him to do.

"Doesn't that seem strange to you?"

This is heading in the wrong direction, Till thought. *Where are you going with this, Max?*

"Come on, Max," said Till, rather awkwardly, and took Max by the arm. "Look, let's get out of here. I know a café close by. We can sit and talk there—"

Max shook off Till's hand with a terse movement. "You want to get me out of here, don't you? Did Felix ask you to do that?" His face tightened. "That's why *you* showed up out of the blue. Felix told you, 'You talk to Max. You're friends. He's going crazy down there.' Right?"

Till pressed his hands to his temples.

"Did you come down to throw us out, Till? You've settled in nicely and now you're giving me the boot?"

Max's eyes seemed to have sunk deeper into their sockets. His eyelids were at half-mast, but underneath, his dark-brown, near-black eyes looked to be on fire.

"Is that the only dirty work he's getting you to do, Till? Throw me out? Give me the old heave-ho? Or do you take care of other things for him as well?"

"I don't want to fight with you, Max," Till murmured. "I'm sorry if you're not feeling well. I want to help you, you know?" *Like you helped me, back then.* "Like you helped me back then, with the shed in your garden." Overcome by the sudden recollection, Till dropped his eyes to the floor.

"And you know what he did then, Lennart?" Till heard Max say. "He went down into the sewers with my father."

It was like someone took Till by the hair and jerked his head up. He saw Max blurrily, the laughing mouth, the burning eyes.

"Tell the story, Till. What did you get up to down there, my father and you?"

The next moment, Till grabbed Max by the arm and jerked him close. Fury flared in Till's head. Was Max planning to broadcast what had happened? Using both hands and all his strength,

Max pushed himself free from Till. He laughed as he did so. "Jeez, Till, let go. Take it easy."

Max wiped his forearm across his mouth, and Till saw how the beads of sweat that had formed on his upper lip left a moist track across his skin.

"Lennart." Max made a sign to his friend on the couch, and Lennart stood up. "We're leaving. I've had enough for today. Say hi to Felix for me, Till. But if he doesn't give Lennart a job, he might as well forget the rights to my father's manuscripts."

TODAY

"She was the first. We thought we had it under control when she was brought in. We were wrong."

The woman lies on her back in the hospital bed, more panting than breathing. Her hair sticks to her forehead, and one of her hands lies on the blanket, looking emaciated.

The orderly who brought Butz into the room leaves him alone with the woman. *She's no longer dangerous . . . she's too weak*, the man had told Butz in the hallway before they entered the room.

Butz pulls a chair up to the bed and sits down.

Her eyes bore into him. "I'm going to die," she whispers.

Yes, she's going to die. The infection reached her brain long ago.

"I know," he says, gently. "I'm sorry, Ms. Heidt."

Merle Heidt.

She worked for Felix von Quitzow at the same firm where Henning, Betty's husband, worked.

"You're from the police."

Butz nods silently.

She looks at him, seems thoughtful.

"You were one of the first to be infected, Ms. Heidt. That's why I wanted to talk to you. Could you perhaps tell me how it happened? How you were infected?

Her eyes widen a little. "How should I know? It could have been anywhere."

"Did your boss have anything to do with it, Ms. Heidt? Felix von Quitzow?"

When Merle hears the name Quitzow, she tries to sit up a little. "Why would you think that?"

Butz thinks of Henning, who had mentioned Felix's name. And of Betty. Claire's sister.

"Did you notice anything unusual when you were working for Mr. von Quitzow? Maybe something small, something that didn't fit in with the usual routine?"

Merle's eyes scan Butz's face. For a long moment, neither says anything. Only the steady beep of some medical device fills the silence.

"I don't know who it was," she suddenly murmurs. "But I heard how he talked about it to Felix the first time. From the voice, it was a young man, early twenties maybe. We have a few editors that age."

"Talked about what?"

"He was upset, extremely upset . . . at first, I wanted to go into the room, but then I stopped at the door because I didn't want to interrupt." Exhausted, she sinks back onto the pillow, struggles to breathe. Just saying the words seems to be a strain. "Felix was winding the young man up, making him really crazy. He laughed in the young man's face, but the guy wasn't going to let Felix make a fool of him. He was dead serious. So serious I thought he'd go for my throat if I took one step into the room."

"What was it all about?"

"That . . . I don't know . . . that Felix was betraying his own ideas? Yes, that was it; that it was time to go back to what they'd intended to do at the start. Felix had lost sight of what it'd always been about—and he, the young man, I mean, was going to follow through on what Felix had started."

Butz gazes intently at her face.

"'Would you listen to this, Merle,' Felix called out to me through the door. I was still out in the reception. 'The kid's shooting off his mouth like you wouldn't believe.' I could practically hear the tears running down the young man's cheeks. He was so miserable because he was so committed—and Felix wasn't taking him seriously."

She coughs, turns aside, holds one spindle-thin hand to her mouth. Over and over, her wasted body shudders under the blanket. Butz stands and hands her a small plastic cup of water from her nightstand.

Merle reaches greedily for the cup, wants to pour the liquid between her parched lips. But at the sight of the water she is seized by a powerful choking spasm. She crushes the cup between her fingers and the water spills onto the bedcovers.

She has to prepare herself for death, thinks Butz. He can almost sense the Grim Reaper there in the room with them, looking down on her. Polite, diffident, merciless.

"Volker," Butz hears her whisper, and leans down to her. "I'm sorry . . . I didn't know I was infected."

"Ms. Heidt? Merle?"

She turns her face to him. Her skull, her forehead, seems caved in somehow.

"Wasn't he a colleague of yours? Volker Fehrenberg?"

Butz involuntarily closes his eyes, squeezing tight.

"I . . . I liked him," she rasps. "He came to Quitzow's office once or twice. He wasn't as stuck up as most of them. We got along well."

Fehrenberg. The first detective to investigate the murders of the women. Nadja in the parking lot, and the woman in the pit at the construction site, and Anni Eisler, whose body was fished out of the Spree by Butz's colleagues.

"I didn't know I was infected. I . . . I never would have . . . Volker was a big, healthy man, I . . . I slept with him."

"*You* infected Fehrenberg?"

Volker Fehrenberg, his body found in a car in the suburbs.

Merle wears a look of concern. She is clearly having trouble keeping her eyes open. *Yes, it was me*, she seems to want to say. But it is enough for her to look at Butz.

He lays a hand carefully on the blanket covering her. "Be calm, Ms. Heidt. It . . . wasn't your fault. You couldn't know."

Her expression brightens a little.

"You couldn't know you were infected . . ."

He sees her draw a deep breath.

"I think I want to sleep a little now," she whispers. She turns over onto her other side without waiting for Butz to reply. She places the palms of her hands together and pushes them under her cheek. Closes her eyes.

Butz straightens up. Her breathing grows more regular. He goes to the door, moving quietly, and listens. Can he still hear her breathing? Or has the sound already been extinguished?

He leaves the room without checking.

92

TWO YEARS EARLIER

"Can't you sleep?" Lisa rolled onto her back and stretched her right hand toward him.

Till pulled her close and embraced her warm body under the covers. "Don't you at least want to talk with him?"

"With Max?"

"He's really not doing well. This afternoon, at work . . . I've never seen him like that."

"Yes . . . yes, I can imagine."

"He was really wiped out. Like he hadn't slept for nights. I tried to calm him down but . . . he didn't want to listen. He seemed to be fixated on some ideas . . ."

Lisa didn't answer.

"Can't you go to him? It's like he's angry at me—probably because I'm working for Felix . . ."

She sighed. "You're right. Max really isn't well."

"We can't just let him go on like this. If we don't watch out he'll get into something he can't get out of."

Lisa said nothing.

"What does he do, holed up in his apartment like that, day after day? I think he's working on a manuscript, but has he shown you anything he's written?"

She shook her head.

"Shutting yourself up like that could drive you crazy."

"Yes."

"Will you talk to him?"

She turned to Till. "I've tried. I've tried for years, again and again. But . . ."

"But what?"

"It's never helped. He used to at least listen to what I had to say. But lately he won't even do that. He gets angry and shouts at me. He knows that something's not right, but he can't handle anyone even mentioning it."

Till pulled his knees up. "So, you don't want to try to talk to him anymore? What's that supposed to mean? That you're leaving your brother to his own devices?"

"What about Nina?"

"Okay, there's Nina . . . but you're his sister—"

"You're his best friend."

"And I'll go talk to him too. Like I said, he's pissed at me. But maybe there are other reasons for that—"

"Other than what?"

"Other than the fact that I work for Felix."

"Like what?"

Till thought about it. Various recollections came to mind. More than anything, he thought of how Max's father had taken him, Till, into the conservatory at the house back then, and asked him to look out for Max. Ten years must have passed since then. Till could not help wondering if what Max was accusing him of, what he seemed unable to forgive, perhaps came down to the fact that Xavier Bentheim had put more trust in Till than in his own son.

But he didn't want to talk to Lisa about her father.

"I don't know," he said. "We've known each other so long . . . so much water under the bridge."

The screams. The skull. The muddy tomb. Bentheim must have thrown himself at the door like a madman. *This isn't what I wanted.* Max's wide-eyed stare. *It was just stories.* The stuff about the hospital ward. Just stories. Max had made it all up. But Till had slammed the door.

He noticed how Lisa was looking at him. Bentheim had been her father too. Till had never admitted to her what happened down in the passages under Berlin.

"You have to talk to him, Lisa," he finally said. "Or he's screwed."

"I have talked to him, Till. A hundred times, a thousand times. I can't help him. He's not a kid anymore." Her voice was so low it was almost inaudible.

Till felt a tingling, prickling sensation spread through his body. How had it ever gone so far? He remembered how they had run through the garden together, all three of them, the day he first arrived at the Bentheim villa. How they had run down to the guesthouse in the garden, where Lisa disappeared into her father's workroom. He saw Max's face in front of him, a child's face, the slightly arrogant look.

Weren't you ever afraid of something you'd just read about? Wasn't that what Max had asked him, back then?

No, Till had replied. *Of course not.* But Max had known that kind of fear. His imagination had always seemed stronger than the reality he lived in.

"I've lost my connection to him," Till heard Lisa say, as if giving voice to a thought. "I know he's my brother, but it's like he's been through things that have changed him so much that whatever once connected us has been destroyed."

Till gazed at her face.

"All I'll do is make things worse. I would love to be there for Max. But he can't deal with it when I try to have a serious talk with him. It's like I'm hurting him just by wanting to talk to him."

Her eyes, big and dark, looked at Till through the twilight.

TWO YEARS EARLIER

Max was bent low over the top of his desk, utterly oblivious to everything around him.

The ballpoint in his hand flew across the paper. He was totally immersed in the world of his story. He'd been working since the sun went down. Thirty, thirty-five pages of cramped handwritten text were piled beside him. He'd kept all the notes he'd made in the last few months, and they fused now in the vision that had taken hold of him that evening, a vision in which, by some miracle, he knew what mattered, what to include, what to leave out. It was as if the moment for which he had been waiting so long had finally arrived.

He paused in his work, exhausted. All the groundwork, all the buildup—all of it—was perfect. Every word hit its mark, every plot point did its job, every chapter fit. It was like the outline for his text was being whispered directly into his ear by some superior being. Now all he had to do was guide it through its trajectory, find the climax, and reach the destination that everything was working toward. And then it would be done; once he reached that apex, it would give him sufficient strength to actually start writing the book.

Max set the pen aside and stood up. What he had managed today was not yet the text. It was just a sketch, a framework, the skeleton of the story he could finally write once the plan itself was complete.

He paced restlessly across the parquet floor in front of his desk. The climax . . . didn't the entire thing depend on that? He had to fulfill all of the promises he made along the way.

He stepped over to the window and looked out into the night. At the end of the street, the Spree glimmered darkly.

It was more than the climax of his text. It was the culmination of his entire life. Hadn't his whole life been spent preparing for this? It hit him like a bolt of lightning. Max realized that all the toil, doubt, and thought of his entire life up to that moment was a single colossus of preparation. A cathedral of human learning; human refinement was finally being crowned with the fruits it yielded!

The thought shook him a little and he leaned his head against the cool glass of the window. His text would invoke a reaction that would propel the reader along with it. The reaction would finally— in a single stroke—justify the *cathedral* of exertion that had made it possible in the first place.

Cathedral?

Max's forehead creased. A *cathedral of exertion*?

Confused, he straightened up.

A cathedral of exertion that *yielded fruit*?

No. That wasn't right . . .

A mountain of effort? No, no . . . the sum . . . ? Too abstract!

He sighed. The exact words didn't matter at all! He couldn't let himself be distracted now.

Max wrenched himself away from the window and returned to his desk. He glanced at the clock. Just before two in the morning.

He had the whole night ahead of him. And it was a good thing he did. He needed time, a lot of time, because he had a lot to do. With determination, he reached for his pen but then leaned back again. The climax . . .

He realized he was staring out the window. Outside, the traffic was slowly thinning. A few security lights cast a dim glow inside the office building across the street.

Max let the chair swing forward again. He picked up the pages he'd already written and scanned the lines, trying to get back into his characters' mindsets—at exactly the moment that they reached the climax of the story.

Tired, he let the pages drop again. Writing the first part of the outline had exhausted him. Wouldn't he do better to attack the finale with fresh energy? It was like being a professional athlete. First you warm up, then you go through a tough training regimen. But so much effort goes into the training that after only an hour or two the athlete can grant himself a break. Wasn't it just the same with Max? He figured he had already used his daily quota of energy. Perhaps he should take a break, recharge.

The thought caused a reflexive urge in him to stand up from his desk, but the urge was coupled with a suspicion that once he stood he wouldn't find the strength of will to sit down again. Once standing, it might be impossible for him to go back to his desk. Because once he sat down again, he would not be able to rise to his feet *again* without having put something meaningful down on paper! So, wouldn't he—if he stood up now and then sat down again—wouldn't he *then* be essentially fixed to his chair until he was finished? Regardless of what happened—no matter how terrible, agonizing, or unbearable it was—he would not be able to stand up again!

He took a deep breath. For a moment it felt as if the thoughts were cutting off his air supply. Another notion entered his mind:

What had he achieved today? He still hadn't started writing. All he'd done was revise the plan . . . again. And this time it was worse; he had not even managed to make it to the end of the outline. Not only had he not managed to finish it, he had not even managed to formulate the ending!

I HAVE TO SIT DOWN AND WRITE!

He shook himself, let his head sink. *Easy, easy. Settle down, Max. It's not so bad. You've got all the time you need. It's going well, it's coming along, you've already done a lot. Just keep plugging away at it.*

He leaned back. He was practically lying down in his desk chair.

I'll start today.

Exactly. That was it! Today he would start actually writing the story. No plan, no climax—just the first sentence!

Hastily, he stacked the handwritten pages together on the table and dropped them vertically onto the desk twice to straighten them into an orderly pile. He laid them flush along the right edge of his desk. Then he leaned down to the floor, where the open pack of writing paper lay, slid out a thin sheaf of pages, and placed them neatly in front of him. Finally, he picked up the pen and wrote a "1" in the upper right corner.

Title? Many different titles had occurred to Max, but he hadn't been able to choose one.

Okay, fine, that wasn't necessary just now. *Don't get bogged down!* On to the first chapter—or would there be different parts? He'd thought about that too. Many times. But he had not reached a concrete decision. Should there be chapters at all? He could just as easily write a single, long text. That was certainly possible, and maybe even advantageous!

He made an abrupt movement with his hand, as if to physically shoo these annoying, confusing thoughts away.

Page one.

He let his eyes lose focus, let his mind wander back to the notes he'd written. The scaffold, the plan, the blueprint of the book. Okay, he didn't have an ending yet, or a climax, a goal that everything moved toward. But he had the beginning.

Didn't he?

He had the beginning . . . but which way was he supposed to go if he didn't know his goal? How was he supposed to move when he didn't know in which direction to go?

Whatever, whatever . . . all that mattered was to take the first tentative steps. Later, if he didn't like it, he could throw it all away again.

And then again—the sheer, murderous urge to stand up.

"NO!" he shouted at the top of his voice. "I will start today! Today's the day. Today I will not stand up. Today I will not plan. Today I will write the first sentence, the beginning. It starts today!"

He breathed deeply, quickly, and lowered the pen to paper. Names and words raced through his head. Possibilities, implications—and always the certainty; no, not like that because of this, and not this for that reason, and that makes this a bad idea . . .

His shoulders felt like they were glowing red with heat. A piercing pain was stabbing up through his back and neck and into his head.

Lie down for a moment. On the floor.

He lay down before he could forbid himself from doing so. Nearly unconscious, he slid off the chair and lay with his face in his hands, his belly against the floor.

Max shivered.

He had to talk to Till. He'd call him, Till would understand. He wouldn't drink anything, wouldn't start mouthing off, wouldn't abuse Till, wouldn't justify himself. He just needed to meet with his friend. Till could help. Max would share his ideas with Till, and

Till would know where to start. Telling Till about it would make it clear in his own mind. Of course! He wasn't putting it off, he was . . . it was more complicated than that. Till had always helped him. When Till was there, Max could always calm down.

His legs were weak, but Max managed to pull himself together a little. Still on his knees, he reached for the cordless phone on his desk—and hesitated. The steel rod running up his back and into his head began to glow with heat again. His breathing grew quick and shallow, as if a pack of bloodhounds were after him.

Then he dialed a number. It rang. Someone answered, a voice. "Hello?"

The steel rod rammed upward from below, straight out through the top of Max's skull.

"It's me," he croaked into the phone, his hand convulsively gripping the receiver. "Let's meet."

TWO YEARS EARLIER

The next day, when Nina opened the door to her apartment, Max was standing there with his head shaved. He'd been out with Lennart.

"Weird," he grinned. "I wanted to meet up with Till, but I dialed Lennart's number instead." He laughed—and it sounded strange.

He talked rapidly, as if a dam had broken. They hadn't seen each other for a few days. Nina hadn't been anywhere near his apartment, and Max hadn't called.

"Have you had breakfast?" Max asked, peeling off his coat.

Nina was wearing a T-shirt and pajama bottoms. She hadn't yet showered, and she needed to get to work.

Max stepped past her into the small kitchen. He grabbed the kettle and filled it. "Just a cup of instant," he said. "Okay? Then I'll leave if you want."

She moved close behind him and ran her hand over his shaved head. It wasn't shaved completely smooth; the remaining millimeter of hair stood up like the bristles in a doormat.

"Why did you shave your head?"

He switched the kettle on, then turned to face her and grinned. "Do you like it?" It lent an unaccustomed hardness to his face, reminding Nina of a convict. "Does it make me look like a skinhead?"

She shook her head. He had the wrong face for it, too fragile.

Max took her hands and held them tight. Then he cautiously pulled her to him and kissed her. Nina leaned against his chest. It felt good.

Max stroked her hair. "I have to tell you about something, Nina."

She swallowed and let him go. She didn't want to be frightened and made up her mind not to take him seriously. He'd been out on another all-nighter with Lennart and probably didn't even know where they'd been. "About what?"

"It was a long time ago, but I can't get it out of my head."

Nina stepped to one side, not wanting to stand directly in front of him.

"I thought I wouldn't need to tell you about it, but now everything has to change."

He rubbed one hand over his bristly scalp. The water boiled, but Max ignored it. Nina reached for the kettle and poured the steaming water into a mug where Max had already spooned a little coffee powder.

"You know what?" she said, setting the kettle back on its base. "I don't want to hear it."

But Max seemed not to have heard her, because he reached for the mug, sat down at the table, and said, "It was a strange summer. Originally, I'd planned to go traveling with two friends, but they both backed out at the last minute, so I finally just took off with Quentin."

"Didn't you hear what I said? I don't want to hear it!" She was still standing by the counter. "It's Wednesday morning, and I've got a million things to do. You've gone and shaved your head and now you want to tell me about God-knows-what. I don't like this."

"No, hold on, just listen to what I'm saying." He sipped at the coffee and set the cup on the table in front of him. "I just took off. I didn't pack much. I figured if I needed something, I could buy it. Just driving through Poland took three days. Then there was the border to Lithuania—have you ever been there?" His gaze seemed to be directed inward somehow, like he was watching a replay in his head.

He had changed. What was it? What had happened? He always looked burned out and wired after a night with Lennart . . . but this time it was different. It did not seem like he had just pushed his limits, but more like something had found a way to get inside him. As if he had ripped open an abyss inside himself.

"We wanted to go as far as Petrograd, but the journey came to an end in Riga," he said. "Quentin turned back in Riga too . . . about three weeks before I left the city." He frowned, as if suddenly noticing her standing there for the first time. "Everything okay?"

She wanted to get out of the kitchen. Listening to him was pointless. The best thing she could do was leave.

But as she pushed herself away from the table, Max grabbed her by the arm. Nina flinched in fright. He had never before touched her with anything other than a caress.

"Stop it, Max."

"I'll let you go in a minute. Just listen to what I'm saying."

"Let me go."

He let her go. In two quick steps, she was out the kitchen door. But he was already behind her, and gripped her tightly at the hips. "Nina, wait!"

She spun around, her hand closed in a fist, and she punched him hard in the head—his hand closed around her wrist.

"Max, let me go!"

"I don't want to hurt you . . . but . . . you have to listen to me . . . I've been thinking about it the whole night . . . I have to tell to you."

Nina wrenched her hand free. "Out! Get out!"

He just looked at her. "Please, Nina—please." And suddenly, Max with his shaved head looked more like an unkempt animal than a man standing in front of her.

"The first night I was alone in Riga, I went out," he said. She looked at him with incomprehension.

"There are a few streets there where it's just one bar after another. Packed with people. Men and women from Russia, Lithuania, Estonia . . . and the Estonian women, you know . . . they . . . they're not just pretty. They're so attractive that when you see them, it just seems to get deep inside you . . . and some of them are just there . . . to get to know someone."

He had twisted his arms into a knot. Why didn't she just throw him out? But it was still Max, standing there. She knew she could throw him out if she truly wanted. But what then? Would he go back to Lennart? Or to his apartment? She had never seen him act this way.

Something had happened.

"Max, why don't you lie down in my bed and rest awhile."

His eyes were fixed on her face.

"I'll lay down with you if you want, and you can sleep."

He smiled. "Let me tell you about Riga, Nina. I'm nearly finished." He didn't let her respond. "Her name was Caitlin, she said. I met her in a restaurant. When I saw her, I thought maybe she's just a girl who's interested in getting to know a guy from Germany. Maybe she'd like to get to know me." He paused and seemed to brood on that for a moment. "After dinner, we went to a bar a few streets away. A few of her girlfriends were there. We had a few drinks and the atmosphere around us was fantastic. She sat in front of me and I thought, *You are such a pretty thing, Caitlin.*"

This was what she'd overheard him telling Lennart about, Nina suddenly realized.

"And then we left."

"Did you talk to Lennart about this? Just recently?"

But Max was so fixated on what he wanted to say that he completely ignored the question. "It was summer, Nina, and warm. So, I suggested going for a drive."

"Max, I . . ."

"She laughed and said, 'Yes?' She said it over and over, 'Yes, okay, but where do you want to drive?' 'Let's see,' I said. We didn't drive for very long, maybe thirty minutes. At first, we drove out of town along a highway. Then a bit later I pulled off onto a country lane. I thought she might get scared, but we were hitting it off really well. She was really wild and fun."

Nina stared at him.

"Then I stopped the car and took off her clothes. When she was naked, I . . ." He took a deep breath, shook himself. "I must have held her awkwardly. I was pretty drunk, I was excited . . . it was . . . like a little twig. I didn't know something like that could happen so fast. There was a crunching noise, you know? Like someone trying to get into my skull. It crunched and suddenly all the resistance was gone—and then she started to scream."

Nina sank back against the wall. "Why are you telling me this, Max?"

"It was an accident . . . I'm not even sure it was my fault. I wanted to take her to a hospital."

Nina's eyes were glued to the floor.

"I was bumping along this country road, and I thought to myself, *You've been drinking. A lot, in fact. You're drunk, in a car, driving to a hospital—you know what that means? In Lithuania?*

After you break an Estonian girl's arm? They'll keep you there, Max, I thought. *They'll take you to Riga and throw you in jail."*

Nina slid down to the floor and saw her knees before her eyes, but the image was blurred.

"I stopped. Right in the middle of the road. I leaned across her and pushed open the door on the passenger side, and I kicked her out. I didn't ask her if she wanted to get out or if I could drive her anywhere . . . she was screaming, and I opened the door and kicked her out. Out there, miles from the city. She held on. She looked into my eyes and there was pain in them, I could see that. It was late at night, and she knew we were in the middle of nowhere. I used my feet. I pulled back and I kicked her. Until she was out of the car. Then I drove away."

Nina put her hands over her eyes. She could hear herself crying, could feel the quaking of her body. This couldn't be true. Max would start talking again in a moment. He would say that it hadn't ended like that, that he had taken the girl with him after all, that he hadn't left her lying there in that road, miles from anywhere—but Max had fallen silent. She could hear him breathing.

"Nina?"

"No!" She jumped to her feet and ran into the hallway. She put her hand on the front-door handle. When she stepped out, the linoleum in the stairwell was cold under her bare feet—and then the door slammed shut behind her.

She flew down the stairs and was out in the street seconds later. It was a gorgeous spring morning.

Max was still in her apartment.

She would never see him again.

JOURNAL ENTRY

First, the dungeon at the train station, where the mother fed herself to her son.

Then the girl in the car.

Break her arm and kick her out.

Now the finale.

The things Malte showed me, the things I know from Max, the things Bentheim devised—I will leave them all behind.

It's time.

I'll do it.

Like I wrote about the father cutting off a piece of his own flesh.

Like I broke the arm of the girl in my car.

It's time.

The final step.

Time to finish what I've started.

TWO YEARS EARLIER

"Max?"

Till withdrew the key, closed the door behind him, and moved slowly through the front rooms.

"Max?"

It had been raining nonstop for nearly three days. The city looked like it would never brighten again. Puddles spread across footpaths and streets.

Till had pulled an old, dark-red baseball cap from the pocket of his raincoat and put it on as he stepped into the street. It had been a good half hour since Nina had called Lisa. About Max. She'd left him. She didn't want to go into details, but she had said enough; Max was a mess. When Lisa told Till about it, she suggested that they go together to Max's apartment to check on him. Nina's call had scared her. But she had a job interview that morning, so Till had offered to go see Max by himself first. Lisa had given him her key to Max's apartment.

As he crossed the Gotzkowsky Bridge, he saw that the fine rain had turned the surface of the Spree into a mesh of tiny craters and exploding reflections. Peering through the gray threads of rain, Till

could make out the brick church and the apartment block where
Max lived on the other side of the river. The windows were black,
the balconies jutting like rock spurs. He had thought about calling ahead, but Lisa had already tried to reach Max by telephone
without success.

What if he isn't home?

"Max?"

No answer.

Till made his way through the front rooms of the upstairs
apartment. The rooms were soaked in the dim morning light and
smelled like old food.

He finally found him in the bedroom.

Max was lying on the bed with his eyes open. He barely reacted
when Till entered the room.

"Hey."

He looked like shit. His face was so wasted that Till barely
noticed his shaved head.

Till sat on the edge of the bed, beside his friend. "Nina called
us. You had a fight, you and Nina?"

Max nodded.

And Till suddenly had the feeling that he might not be able to
pull his friend through this alone.

"I told her about Riga," Max said softly. "I lied to you, Till. At
Betty's wedding." He tried to smile, but there was no life in it. "It's
true. Something happened in Riga. It's not just a rumor."

Then Max told Till too.

"When I took off for Riga, I thought I could do whatever I
wanted," Max whispered, and his gaunt hand appeared from under
the blanket and reached out for Till's wrist. "Felix never stops talking about it. It's an illusion, you're not free, you just think you are.
Bullshit! I thought. I'm just going to drive where I want, pockets
full of cash. The girls would be falling at my feet—things would

not be controlling me; I'd be the one controlling them, me and my will . . ."

Till propped his elbows on his knees and hunched his shoulders.

"Felix can believe whatever he wants. I was different. His rules didn't apply to me. When Caitlin sat in my car . . . it was a kind of high, like I could pull her strings and make her move how I liked, like a marionette. *I* was the high roller, not a puppet stuck on someone else's strings! Caitlin was like a dream, Till. She had a white dress on. Straps over her bare shoulders. You should have seen her. She was . . . she was perfect. Her hair was blonde, dark blonde, full, and her eyes sparkled. Her mouth looked like some divine hand had shaped it from unimaginably sweet clay. She smelled—I can't say it any other way—she smelled like a flower. A delicate scent that grew stronger, bit by bit, as I pulled her dress off over her head and slid her panties off her hips."

His dark eyes were fixed on Till.

"She was *too* perfect. You know what I mean? Like when a picture is too beautiful, or when the taste of something is just too intense! You start to shake inside because you sense that everything you've ever experienced pales in comparison! When she turned around under me, she was naked, and when I bent over her with her backside against me, when she tipped her head back and stroked her hair forward over her shoulder, when she whispered to me while her body pushed against mine—it was like I was being shoved over a cliff. Somehow, I wanted to acknowledge that I'd never, ever, felt anything like that, and that I knew I might not be worth it. But I wanted to live up to the feeling, to be deserving of it—and I must have misjudged myself."

He fell silent. Till heard the rain rattle against the window, driven by a gust of wind.

"I don't even know if she made it back into the city from out there. Can you imagine what that was like?" Max whispered. "In the dark, with a broken arm. It had to be four or five miles to the next house."

Max's words felt like poison seeping into Till's body.

"The way Quentin does it . . . it's the only way to get past it," Max murmured. "To not be responsible."

"Seriously?" Suddenly, all the revulsion that had been building up in Till as Max talked, poured out of him. "What is it? Is this about you dissociating yourself from every boundary, every barrier—or is it just you shouting to the world about how free you are?"

"Isn't it the same thing?"

"So, show it in a good way! Are the only barriers the ones against pain? To stop you from hurting someone? Some barriers are just there because no one has the strength or the guts to go past them, and then there are the boundaries that aren't there to protect anything, but just mark how far people have come in their struggle to do something worthwhile. Why don't you tackle a boundary like that? Are you too weak?"

He stared at Max, his scrawny torso poking from under the blanket.

"Yes. I think that's it," Max said, his voice hushed.

"Now what?"

But Max didn't answer.

"Now you'll just lie here wallowing in the bullshit in your head and your own hopelessness!"

Max's shaved head tipped to one side. The bones in the back of his neck stuck out above his bent back like a skeletal peak. Till suddenly had the feeling that his friend was going to die right there on the bed in front of him.

"Come on, Max," he said after a while. His voice was quiet and cautious. He took Max by the arm, and when he didn't respond, Till pulled him up. He wrapped one arm around Max's hip, swung

Max's arm across his shoulder, and literally dragged him through the bedroom and into the bathroom. He stood in the shower stall with Max, ignoring the fact that his own clothes would get soaking wet, and turned on the shower.

At first ice cold, then warmer as the gas boiler sprang to life, and finally hot and strong, the water washed over them. Max's head was tilted back and his eyes were closed. The water streamed over the stubble on his head and the stubble on his chin and cheeks. Till squeezed shower gel over Max's head. The soap foamed white over his friend's naked body. He scrubbed him down, rinsed away the soap, and turned off the shower. Then he hauled him back into the bedroom. He jerked the filthy sheets off the bed, and laid Max on the stripped mattress, spreading the woolen blankets over him.

TWO YEARS EARLIER

When Max awoke, it was already dark. He could hear Till's muffled voice from the next room. He seemed to be talking to somebody at work, telling them he wouldn't be coming in the next day either.

The sleep had done Max good. For the first time in days, he felt like he could think straight. His head was in order again, and not just filled with a dull thrum and crackle.

He threw back the blankets and swung his legs over the side of the bed. On the chair by the wall lay a T-shirt, clean boxers, and jeans. Till must have put them out for him. Max quickly pulled them on and left the room.

Till was sitting at the kitchen table, a newspaper spread in front of him and a frying pan, still sizzling, beside him.

He looked up when Max entered the kitchen. "Scrambled eggs?" Till asked. Max nodded and sat at the table at a place already set for him, and watched as Till scraped eggs onto the plate. He reached for a fork but hesitated before eating.

"I don't have the slightest idea where to start," he finally said.

Till looked at him. "Maybe it's stupid, but I made a few calls just now. There's an organization in Berlin—for women."

Max looked up from his plate.

"They get involved when somebody has problems . . . with domestic violence, stuff like that. I asked if they needed help. They said sure, absolutely. They said they need everything: money, someone to run errands for them, to handle applications, represent them legally, clean their offices. If you want to help, you could go by."

Max placed the fork on his plate.

"I'll drive you down there," said Till. "If you like. I've taken tomorrow off. We'll check it out. What do you think?"

Yes, thought Max.

"And maybe you could drive to Riga sometime. Try to find Caitlin. But I can't come to Riga with you. I can't take that much time off."

Max pushed the plate away, leaned back, and drew a deep breath. He would donate money, he thought. All of it? Everything he had? And try to earn money somehow? Was that the answer?

"What do you think?"

"I could try to earn some money. I don't need that much to live." He kept his eyes down on the table. "I could live in one room and go to work." He looked up. "Or do you think I wouldn't find work?"

Till also pushed his plate back. "Aren't you working on a book?"

Something seemed to be twisting in Max's gut.

"You don't need to give it up completely," said Till, softly. "But maybe you ought to take a break."

The thought of returning to his desk, of going back to his notes, made Max dizzy.

After a while, Till said, "If it were me, I'd work for the women for a few weeks or months. Seriously."

"And after that?"

"And then I'd see. First things first, get out of this funk. Out in the fresh air. Things are sometimes clearer that way, right?"

Max noticed that both he and Till had the palms of their hands pressed flat on the table. He instinctively pulled his arms back and crossed them, deliberately changing his posture. "Okay. I'll take a break—but I still won't be any further ahead afterward," he murmured.

"With what?"

"With"—a shudder ran through Max—"my writing."

"What matters is the girl, Max. Caitlin. You can't get her out of your head."

"Fine, Till. Let's forget it all—stories, inventions, books—let's go out into the world." It felt almost as if the words were forcing their way out of his mouth. "I'll give away all my money, and we'll dive headlong into this city, into what Berlin really has to offer. Let's talk to the people, let's break 'em out of the rut they're in!"

Till looked at him with incomprehension. "Uh-huh? How do you see that working?"

"Right now, what matters most is that we just decide *that's* what we're going to tackle. We need to shake up the people of this city."

"But that doesn't get you anywhere, Max." Till shook his head. "You can talk to them till you're blue in the face, and all they'll do is laugh at you when you turn your back."

"While you and Felix turn the world upside down, right?" The words rang from Max's throat. And the pain exploded in his belly. "I loved you," he blurted. "But you're gutless, Till. You just threw yourself at whoever would take you in. My father, Felix. And Lisa, oh, yeah, Lisa."

Till had stood up as soon as Max started his tirade, but he remained by the table, his face dark and glowering.

"I learned to live with my father putting you ahead of me," said Max, turning on Till again. "I accepted everything being handed to me on a fucking platter, while you had to figure out how to get by in that home—and I put up with you suddenly being the favorite when you came to live with us. And why did that happen? Because you're smarter than me? Because your head isn't messed up with all the shit that's in mine?"

He slammed his fist into his stomach, and the fireball of pain that shot through him nearly knocked him senseless. "You think you're so sophisticated," he spat. His mind was racing, the words pouring out. "'Max is his own worst enemy,' you tell yourself. 'I'm smarter than that.' But taking orders from Felix isn't smarter, Till! You should hang your head in shame, letting him tell you how to turn the stories those poor bastards are cobbling together into some endless pigswill. Don't tell me what's good for me. Be careful you don't get sucked down in the mire you're working your way into!"

A wave of nausea hit Max. He gasped for breath, but he wasn't finished. "You want to carry on my father's work with Felix? I always hated my father. But I know one thing: you and Felix won't continue what he began with that crap of yours. The only way to go on with it is for one person to sit down and write what his conscience dictates!"

Till had turned to the door.

"Leaving?" Max shouted at his back. "Be my guest! But you know what? I'll tell Lisa about you. You've got my father on your conscience, Till—you won't poison my sister too!"

TWO YEARS EARLIER

Till read. The pages were written in a cramped hand and in some places seemed to have been written extremely fast. Max had done little more than sweep the pen across the paper. But Till had known Max's handwriting a long time, and he had little trouble deciphering the words.

When Max had screamed at him that he'd tell Lisa what happened to her father, Till knew what was at stake. He'd lose Lisa if Max went through with it.

So, he had turned around and, for the first time since they'd met ten years before, he deceived Max. "What if I tell you I know how much more honest it is to try what you're trying than what I'm trying?" It wasn't difficult for him to make that claim; there was actually something obvious about it.

He'd looked Max in the eye and added, his voice husky, "Let's give it a shot, Max. Let's try to get your writing back on its feet somehow. Maybe I can help. We can talk it over. We've got all the time in the world."

Max had looked at him red-eyed. "You think so?"

"Man, of course! Finally! That's the first sensible thing you've said today!" Till had shouted. "Have you got any notes? Anything I can take a look at?" And when he saw how Max's expression changed, he said, "No worries. I can imagine that everything's pretty confused. But first things first, we have to see what we've got to work with."

Max had stood up and crossed the rom to Till, who was still standing at the door. "You mean you'd really be interested?"

Till laughed. "Of course!"

Then they had gone to Max's study together. Once inside, Max handed Till a box filled to the brim with unbound sheets of paper, and told him he would wait for him in the downstairs apartment.

That was nearly three hours before.

All the contradictory beginnings and sketches, the changing names and dates, the diagrams and lists that covered the pages in the box . . . Till had started going cross-eyed long ago. He was feeling wiped out from the fight with Max—the things Max had said to him. It was only his thoughts of Lisa that kept him going. He saw her in his mind's eye. And he saw Max throw in her face the thing that Till had kept from her all these years. And he saw her face, which had always looked at him so affectionately, suddenly harden and the love in it vanish, never to return.

It could not happen.

Till picked up the pages lying on the table in front of him and stuffed them back into the box. He knew that Max trusted him, regardless of how thoughtlessly and furiously he yelled at him.

And it was this trust that Till would use now to save Lisa's love for him.

Beyond the windows, as Till made his way down to the apartment beneath, the first gray light of morning was starting to appear.

Max was lying on the burgundy sofa, asleep.

Quietly, Till crossed to the window and opened it. The fresh spring air of the disappearing night streamed in.

"Max! Hey!" Till dropped into the armchair opposite the sofa. "Hey!"

Max's eyes opened. It took him a moment to orient himself.

"Everything okay?"

Max ran both hands over his eyes, over his shaved head. "I'm glad you're here, man." He sat up.

Till nodded. "I read through your notes."

Max slumped back in his seat as if to signal that he knew how bad it was. "And did you get anything out of it? I mean, it's a complete mess."

"Hey, sure, I understood some of it." Till thought for a moment before going on. "It reminded me of Poe's story, 'The Tell-Tale Heart.' You know the one? Where the guy telling the story assures us all the way through that he's sane. But in the end, *through* the story he's telling, he shows that he's anything but."

Max took the blanket that he'd spread over himself and slung it around his shoulders. "Yeah. Great, right?"

"Something like that is what you've got here . . ."

Max drilled his tongue into the inside of one cheek, looking thoughtful.

"Yeah?"

"Yeah . . . yeah, maybe."

"And this detective? We get to know him while he's investigating a murder, don't we?"

"Yeah . . ."

"Exactly. So, we spend the whole time waiting for him to catch the killer. And it's only at the end that we figure out that he's been faking it all along—us included. That he hasn't been solving a puzzle, he's been putting one together; that he hasn't been getting closer to the killer but is actually the killer himself and has been covering his own tracks!"

Max cast a glance at Till, obviously worried about what his friend thought of the idea.

Till leaned back in the armchair and laid his head on the backrest. "It's crazy."

"Crazy how?"

"I mean, did you really think you could pull it off?"

"What?"

"Making the reader believe that. Making them follow an investigation right to the end, only to figure out in the last sentence that what they're reading is more thriller than detective story . . . that it's more a story about a murder than about solving a murder."

"Well, you'd have to plot it all out in advance, of course, but that's why we're here now," Max replied, defiant.

"Hmmm . . ."

"What?"

"I'm sorry, but it won't work."

"Oh. Really?"

"Yeah."

Max frowned. "Why not?"

"Max, what you've been thinking about here, it's a concept, a theory. But no one could write it." Till let his arms drop onto the arms of the chair. "Not me, anyway. As sorry as I am to say it, I can't help you with this."

Max looked at him, downcast. "So, everything we said earlier no longer applies? Just like that?"

Till exhaled. For a while, he sat back in the armchair, not moving, his eyes fixed on the wall at the other end of the room. Then he looked quickly at Max. Max seemed to be lost in thought, sunken somehow, like his cheeks, forehead, and chin were telescoping into each other.

"Can I tell you something, Max?"

Max didn't move.

"Your father once told me that the most important part of writing is that the writer has a certain personality, a certain integrity."

Max's face seemed to fold together a little more.

"After reading what you gave me, I don't think you have the right personality. I don't think you have what it takes to write anything good."

Max's eyes hung dully on Till.

Till straightened up a little. "I'm not saying that to piss you off," he said. "I'm telling you that as a friend, okay?"

Max sat very still, like a little kid who doesn't understand why he is being yelled at. Till spoke very calmly. "You trust me, don't you?"

Max's bottom lip jutted forward like a boy's, and he nodded.

"You're not good enough, Max. That's the reason why it's not working. It's not a question of concentration or the hours you put in. It's not about the ending, the effort, or the hard work. Your character—who you are, Max . . . Max Bentheim—you're too . . . too broken. Do you know what I'm saying?" Sympathetically, Till looked him in the eye. "Perhaps it's your father's fault. Back then, those talks you had, the arguments with him, maybe he's the one who broke you." Till paused, thought for a moment or two, went on. "But it doesn't matter how it happened—it's who you are, plain and simple. I don't think you're doing yourself any favors by throwing yourself at this book like a lunatic."

The left corner of Max's mouth twisted upward as if trying to smile. But it didn't happen. "Stop, Till. I got it."

"Okay. I can stop."

Max didn't take his eyes off him. After a while he asked, "Did you really mean all that?"

Till pinched the bridge of his nose. "What you did with the girl in Riga. The way you talk when other people are around. What you did with Irina. Doesn't all that make you think?"

Max didn't move.

"When I came here yesterday morning, you were finished, Max. Totally exhausted. Why?"

Max gave himself a shake. "I'd been trying to write. I've been trying to write for years, but it's never worked. I've never managed to do it."

"And?"

"I can't get past it."

"Past the fact that it isn't working."

Max nodded.

"The writing's just the surface, Max. It's what you'd like to be able to do. There are not many who can write—it's not so bad if you're not one of them."

Max gazed at the floor.

"You have to admit that your writing skill hasn't come far. It's not an easy pill to swallow, I'm sure. But . . ."

"But what?"

"But what I'm saying to you goes deeper. I'm not saying you have to give something up that you've only imagined you could do. I'm saying that as a human being, you're fucked. You're a degenerate. You sicken me."

"I . . ." Max didn't finish the sentence.

"You sicken me, Max. It's true. This is not just something you're telling yourself. *I'm* telling you. It's not some bitter insight you think you believe but really just flirt with. It's the truth."

Max shook his head. Timid, hesitant. "Look, Till, I . . . it's been a long few days; I . . . I just need a little rest, I think."

"You want to sit here in your apartment and brood. Alone and with nothing to get you up and about again. Doesn't the very thought of that make you feel sick?"

"You're just saying this, aren't you? Because of Lisa. So I don't say anything to Lisa."

"You can tell Lisa anything you like. Lisa gave up on you long ago."

"No, she didn't." Now his top lip was trembling.

"Ask her. Tell her whatever you like. Ask her sooner rather than later." Till fished in his pocket for his phone. "Right now. Why not?"

Max's eyes widened.

Till held out the telephone in his direction. "I'm your oldest friend, Max. You can trust me. I'm telling you this to help you. I thought we could work on your text. But it's useless. So I have to help you another way."

"By abusing me."

"I'm not abusing you. I'm telling you the truth."

"And then you'll go and leave me sitting here."

"You'll cope."

"How's that supposed to help me?"

"You just gotta swallow it, Max."

Max let his head hang, but kept his eyes directed upward. Till thought he could see Max listing heavily, as though he'd been dealt a blow he'd never recover from. "Can you help me, Till?" Max's voice sounded like it had when he was a young boy. "Take back what you just said? Please. Can you do that? Can you say it isn't true?"

"You're a piece of shit, Max. You know it. I know it. It's the truth. No one can change that. It's about time you sickened yourself like you sicken the rest of us." Saying that, he stood, stepped in front of Max, raised his foot, and pressed the sole of his shoe against the face of the young man who'd once been his friend. Then he straightened his leg.

Max's eyelids squeezed down over his eyes. Till pressed down with his foot, pushing Max's body into the sofa. Then he pulled his foot away, turned, and left the room.

98

TODAY

The sky tears open, a gash two hundred miles long. The split reaches from the distant horizon and goes over her head, disappearing beyond the buildings on the other side of the street.

The gap seems to bleed. Globules of dark violet. Pink droplets ringed by orange coronas. Yellow light. Yellow waves, black at the core, explode, erupting bluely, discharging tiny, pale-blue clouds that flow and merge with the yellow washing over everything.

Claire's head is tilted back and her mouth is open. She stares up into the sky. She is wearing a helmet and holding on to Frederik, who is driving the motorcycle. She wants to ask him to stop. She wants to show him the splendor of the colors, the explosions in the sky. But instead, she just holds on to Frederik and lets the slipstream blow her hair back.

But if the sky is bleeding and dissolving away in explosions of color, how long can it be before everything flows together in a tremendous vortex?

She squeezes Frederik even more tightly.

What does it mean? Is it the end of the world?

The facades of the buildings reflect the eruptions of color. The glass in the windows reflect the red-orange globules, and the rush of the wind in Claire's ears is drowned out again and again by the honking of horns, the squeal of brakes, the clang and clatter of sheet metal.

All of Berlin seems to be in motion. It seems to Claire that every motor in the city has sprung to life. As if the rattling pistons, revving cylinders, and spinning wheels have joined forces in a concert of machine noise.

Automatically, her thoughts turn to Butz. She hasn't spoken to him since their last phone call, when she'd been in front of Frederik's building.

Butz.

She hasn't said good-bye to him.

She hasn't told him about Frederik.

She hasn't told him she's leaving him.

What will he think? Will he come looking for her? Shouldn't she let him know that it's all okay? That he doesn't have to worry about her?

She sees Butz's face in front of her. His sunken cheeks, stubble, and short, gray hair.

I'm sorry, Butz, she thinks. *But you'll get by without me.* And she imagines him returning to their apartment, hanging his coat on the hook, and trotting through the rooms. Looking for her, but filled with the certainty that she's no longer there.

She hears a thrum, a rumble and crash beside her, and when she turns her head to the side she sees another building collapse just as they are speeding past.

It isn't just the first or the second. It's the entire street.

A chain of catastrophes that seems to Claire like some kind of magnificent show, perfectly timed for Frederik and her as they shoot along the broad avenue on the motorcycle. Each building collapses at exactly the moment they pass by. Apartment blocks, office blocks, stone facades five, six, seven stories high, falling in on themselves. It's as if they are perfectly wired by some demolition maestro, like the maestro himself is pressing the button, triggering the disintegration of the next building just at the moment they draw level with it.

"Frederik?" Claire is shouting at the top of her voice just to overcome the noise, the slipstream, the roar of the collapsing buildings. But he doesn't seem to hear her.

Oh, let's stop for a moment, it's so beautiful, she thinks.

But Frederik just keeps on driving. He threads his way into a roundabout, shifts gears with his foot, speeds away with a twist of the wrist; and Claire leans with him, into the curve.

Above them, the rain starts to fall. The yellow streaks change color, dark blue now, beating down on them.

On the seat in front of her, Frederik seems to melt into a steel-blue wedge, racing over the asphalt. It's as if man and machine have melded together. For a brief moment, she feels that she is no longer sitting behind him on the saddle; instead she is hovering above, watching him race on alone while she herself drifts away, up into the air, high above the streets and buildings.

Higher she climbs, high into the sky that is shot through with the shining blue-black streaks of the rain. Higher and higher, all the way to the gash in the sky that has spread to cover almost the entire span of the heavens.

Until she tumbles into it.

Frederik feels Claire's embrace change. It is no longer a loving embrace that speaks of her feelings for him; it is the crush of a cramped muscle.

He winds back the throttle and lets the motorcycle roll to a stop at the side of the road. The buildings along the road stand side by side, solid and intact.

He wants to get her to a hospital as fast as he can, but he doesn't want her to fall from the seat. Ever since she fell in the storage unit in the basement, something has changed about her. At first she broke out in a sweat. Then she grew feverish, euphoric, and then finally despairing.

Frederik turns back to her.

The visor on her helmet is fogged.

"Claire?" He pulls at the arm she has wrapped around his waist.

"Everything okay?" He reaches out and flips up her visor. What is staring back at him from inside the helmet turns everything on its head.

She said it herself, the last time she had spoken coherently. *Everything is transforming.* And Claire is no longer with him.

But neither is she completely gone.

Carefully, he removes her helmet. Her eyes are dull and her skin waxy. Her lips are pulled back, baring her teeth.

VIDEO RECORDING

Here, okay? That's not bothering you, is it?

Is it?

I'll just put the phone here on the desk.

Like sooooo . . .

And it'll record what we—

What?

Soon, Irina, soon . . . one thing at a time.

Sit down. D'you want something to drink? No?

I know you have to go. But just be patient a bit longer.

Ha ha.

Why am I laughing?

Just wait.

Look, let me get straight to the point. I want to have this on film because I think Felix—

Yes, Felix von Quitzow . . .

Hold on, let me finish.

That Felix, with his project—

What do you have to do with that?

WAIT just a minute . . .

Right, I let myself be won over by Felix because I believed in what he was doing here—in his original idea.

But what he wants to turn it into, his famous "second step"—I won't be part of that!

No, don't get up, sit a little longer—

I'M NOT FINISHED!

HEY!

The door's locked. What, do you think I'm totally stupid?

Come on, what's the point of that?

You think you can scratch through an oak door with your fingernails?

It's senseless.

. . .

Irina, how many times have we slept together?

What? You know I'm stronger than you. I won't let you go. I choked a dog, Irina. I broke a woman's arm and another . . . I crushed another's windpipe while I was coming inside her.

But that was just the first step.

MY first step.

My second step is you!

Does that burn?

It's just a scratch, Irina. It's your arm, I know, and yes, it's bleeding, but it's just a graze . . .

I have to scratch open your skin, Irina. It isn't that . . . how can I put it? . . . it isn't that I enjoy doing it . . . but I have to do it.

It's the consummation.

The consummation. It's how I achieve what Bentheim sketched out in his books.

The consummation of the knowledge that we are not free but are parts of a whole that's rolling in slow motion through the universe— no, the whole is the universe!

So, yes, I don't just want to scratch you—what I rub into the wound, that's what matters!

Your brain will fester. Once the virus has made its way up your spine, your head will burn like the sun rising in the desert.

Your mind will transform from a doubting, twitching little maggot into a FORCE OF NATURE!

You will attack others if they so much as annoy you with a glance. Because you will be rabid.

TODAY

"I never understood it, Till. You were just gone." Lisa is leaning close to him. She speaks quickly, softly, but the words are precisely articulated.

Till knows exactly what she's talking about. Two years earlier. He was just gone—from one day to the next.

Her gaze moves beyond him into the depths of the restaurant. The entire place seems to hum, buzz, tremble. Every table is taken, groups of six, twelve, eighteen guests, groups of guys in business suits, groups of families, friends. It's like the weeks leading up to Christmas, when the city vibrates with the hustling, bustling, jostling crowds, everyone swept up in the holiday mood.

Till leans back a little.

It was Felix's suggestion to come to this place. He was in high spirits when they came back down from the rooftop into the apartment where Lisa was waiting for them, and he had invited Till to get something to eat with them. Till could think of no reason to turn down the invitation—there was only room in his head for one thought: *Felix was right.* If Till did not want to destroy Lisa, he would have to set her free.

They'd barely entered the restaurant when an acquaintance of Felix called him over to his table. Till and Lisa sit alone, staring at each other.

"I fell into a hole, Till," Lisa says. "I couldn't understand why you left. We'd only just begun. I waited ten years for you, until Betty's wedding, until you were finally back in Berlin. Then what happened? We were finally together, and then you were gone again!"

Till sees how tense she is. "Felix told me that something happened between you and Max—that day two years ago, the day you disappeared." Her eyes stayed on his. "I didn't just lose you that day, Till. I lost my brother too. He was never himself again after that."

He hears the words in his head: *Let her go, Till. Don't you see how she's looking at you? She aches for you . . . she loves you . . . she thinks the two of you belong together. Don't let those feelings ruin her. Let her go, let her find happiness somewhere else.*

His voice is hoarse when he finally replies. "I don't love you, Lisa. I never have. I wanted to be part of your family. I was blinded by the wealth, the luxury, the style. I did anything I could to not have to leave that house. I was only fooling myself, telling myself that I'd fallen in love with you—but none of it was true."

She can't comprehend what he is saying. Her skin is suddenly tight over her cheekbones, her pale eyes seem chiseled into her face.

"Maybe I wanted to love you, Lisa, but I was never able to. You were always honest, always open, but that was wasted on me. When we slept together two years ago, I had to think of Nina or Irina just to . . . to do it."

He knew that what he was saying rang false, but at the same time, Lisa was stunned by the impact of his words.

This is the only way—he has to rip himself out of her, to erase himself from inside her.

He had broken Max because he feared that Max would reveal their secret to Lisa—that he would confide in her that Till had killed their father. How could he think he would be able to keep it a secret from her forever? He'd been guilty not once but twice. He had killed her father and destroyed her brother. Felix was right. He had to set her free.

Till's eyes are turned down to the empty plate in front of him, but at the edge of his field of vision he sees Lisa stand. He glances up at her. She is standing beside her chair and looking down at him.

It is the Lisa he has always loved. He will never love anyone like he loves her. He can see that she is burning. Her entire view of the world has twisted. She has relied on him since they first met, and now, suddenly, she believes it was all a mistake.

She turns away. Till watches her as she moves with uncertain steps between the tables and toward the exit.

There are no tears in her eyes. He knows from her face that what he said robbed her of the possibility of crying.

He has rejected her.

He no longer stands in her way.

THE FUNERAL

Even when Till steps up to the freshly dug hole and he looks down into the damp, shaded rupture in the earth, when he sees the wood at the bottom of the hole, the flowers that have fallen on it, the dirt tossed down . . . even when he reaches for the trowel in the bowl beside him, lifts it, and turns it over the hole, hears the rattle of dirt on the coffin . . . even then, he still can't believe that down there, beneath that wooden lid, there is anything other than *nothing*. He can't believe that there is no hollow space, no black empty hole. He can't believe that a body lies there, with arms and legs, a torso, a head. He can't believe that inside that box—still recognizable—is the face, the eyes, nose, mouth he knows so well, that are so famil-iar. Those features his own eyes looked at so many times, that he has known since he was eleven years old. The eyes, nose, mouth of the boy he loved perhaps more than any other—the eyes, nose, mouth of his friend Max.

Till gazes down at the lid of the coffin and can't comprehend what it actually means. He tries to tell himself that Max is . . . But he fails. All he can feel is the incomprehension that comes from his friend no longer being there. What is he?

Dead?

Till doesn't realize he's crying. He doesn't notice the tears on his face, falling on his jacket, on the ground, into the grave in front of him where he still stands. His legs are shivering. He senses only vaguely the way his shoulders heave, the shaking of his body, the dull sparking of his brain.

Max is dead. Alone. In a filthy hole in the earth.

Till hadn't seen him since that last time he went to Max's apartment.

SIX WEEKS EARLIER

"Come on. It's Thursday night, the city's packed. Why don't we go grab a drink somewhere?" The young man stroked his three-day growth without turning away from her pretty blue eyes.

"Want to come along?" Lisa looked over to the desk beside hers, where her colleague Jenna was leaning back in her chair.

"When? Now?" Jenna raised her eyebrows.

"Why not?"

"Lisa, babe, I can't!"

Lisa felt Enrico, beside her, heave a sigh of relief. She'd already turned him down twice—couldn't he take a hint?

"Enrico, it's like this . . ." But that was as far as she got.

"Wait, stop!" Enrico laughed. "You can't do that."

Depends what you mean . . .

"If you turn me down now, I can't ever ask you out again." He grinned, which looked good on him. "So, invitation retracted." Then he looked at Jenna, who'd been listening curiously. "And before I even think about trying again, I'll ask Jenna about you." He turned back to Lisa.

She had to smile. Fair enough. She didn't want to demoralize him completely. After all, she liked Enrico. He was smart, good-looking, and in her first months at the newspaper she'd learned a lot from him.

"What would be the point?" asked Jenna, throwing herself into the fray. "Talking to me first, I mean." She sipped at the plastic cup in her hand. "If we're gonna talk, then we're talking about me!" She let the back of her chair snap forward and grabbed a second plastic cup from a drawer. "You want a drink?" She glanced at Enrico, who was still standing beside Lisa's desk.

It's true that Jenna hadn't been as helpful at the beginning as Enrico, but Lisa appreciated the fact that she wasn't shy when it came to saying what was on her mind. Even if what she had to say wasn't particularly flattering.

"Oh, yes." Enrico pulled over a free chair with his foot and flopped into it.

Jenna reached for the bottle of sparkling wine parked on the floor beside her desk, filled the plastic cup, and handed it to Enrico.

"You too?" She nodded at Lisa.

"Why not?"

The wine fizzed in the cups. It was nicely chilled and dry. Jenna had kept it in the editors' fridge all afternoon. She had a long article coming out in the morning edition, and she'd cracked the bottle just after the deadline to celebrate.

"Why are so many people still here?" Lisa looked around the large, open-plan office.

Okay, it wasn't the *New York Times*, but as far as Lisa was concerned, there was no better paper to work for in Germany. Normally at this time of the day the ranks of editors and reporters were starting to thin out, some of them off to evening events, others finishing work for the day. But today, most of the desks were still occupied.

"Is it because of the sale?" Lisa glanced at Enrico.

"Could be." He sipped at his cup. "Treibel, at least, is pretty fired up."

Treibel. The most important man in the building. Not a single major article made it into the paper without the editor-in-chief picking through it. And Lisa couldn't even start researching anything without getting the nod from Treibel first.

"So, have the Swedes bought it now?" Lisa set the toes of her pumps on the top edge of the filing cabinet under her desk. She'd heard that a Swedish energy group wanted to take over the paper, but she didn't know if there was anything to the rumor.

"Treibel's probably worried that he's going to be fired by a Swede tonight." Enrico grinned. "He wouldn't be the first editor-in-chief to get the chop after his paper got sold."

"Oh, come on," said Jenna. "What I heard points in a completely different direction—"

"Yeah, I heard that one too. But I don't believe it," said Enrico, interrupting her. Lisa could hear that Jenna's remark made him uneasy.

"So?" Lisa leaned toward Jenna over the arm of her chair, but kept her feet on the filing cabinet. "What did you hear?"

"That it's not some anonymous power company that's bought the place. It's one man—with something very specific in mind."

"Aha! What, exactly?"

Jenna shrugged. That was all she knew.

"Seriously?" Lisa said, intrigued. "Somebody's bought the shop but no one knows who it is?"

"Wait and see." Jenna leaned her head back and laughed her most infectious laugh. "Unless I'm mistaken, the new owner's supposed to be getting a guided tour through editorial. Today."

Today? That's why they're all still here!

Just then, Lisa heard a murmur run through the room and saw the door at one end of the big office swing open—the editor-in-chief's door.

A small troop of employees marched in led by Treibel. Hot on his heels were several suits that Lisa had seen down on the lower floors: the people in charge of advertising, marketing, sales—all the financial matters of the publishing house, which owned a slew of other companies besides the newspaper.

And in their midst was a face Lisa knew well.

The clear, shining gaze. The huge eyes.

Utterly changed.

He looked twenty years younger. His concentration lent his finely chiseled features an almost hard edge.

Felix.

What was he doing here?

Felix was deep in conversation with Treibel, but Lisa was too far away to catch anything of what they were saying.

She stood up quickly. Automatically.

She hadn't seen Felix for nearly two years, not since they'd parted on the street outside their apartment.

"Everyone, I'm going to keep this short. Nice to see you all still here." Treibel had stopped at the first desk. He continued. "I'd like to introduce you to Felix von Quitzow." Most of the journalists stood up from their desks and turned to the group who'd just entered. Treibel nodded to Felix, who was just then shaking his head because one of the men he'd come in with had leaned over to say something to him. "We are happy to announce that Mr. von Quitzow has bought the concern. And I would like to say that we look forward to working with him and his team to ensure our paper is equipped with what it needs to meet the challenges of this ever-changing world," Treibel continued with his usual corporate mumbo jumbo.

But Felix, who had also turned to the assembled staff, seemed to be scanning the journalists, all of whom were looking at him attentively, for one particular face.

Lisa's heart skipped a beat.

And then his eyes locked on hers.

SIX WEEKS EARLIER

It was cold when Lisa stepped onto the street.

Cold, damp, dark. The city seemed to be crouching in wait for her like some kind of predator. A mosaic of shiny, black surfaces with lights moving and blinking between. The passersby were faceless, reduced to backs, legs, clacking heels. In the distance, Lisa saw a train rattle across the overpass that crossed Friedrichstrasse, on the other side of Unter den Linden. She turned the collar of her raincoat up and began walking in the direction of the train. She wanted to get home. It was late, close to midnight.

Felix and Treibel hadn't spent much time with the journalists. They'd moved on without letting themselves get dragged into any deeper discussions. Lisa guessed that, as the new owner, Felix wanted to see the rest of the place. And even though they didn't return to the journalists' office, Lisa hadn't been able to shake the feeling that Felix was nearby. In the end, she couldn't put off going home any longer and had picked up her coat, shut down the computer, and left the building. Home—the little apartment she'd found for herself after she moved out of Felix's.

She walked along Friedrichstrasse past the closed shops. The pavement was still wet from a brief shower earlier that evening. Behind her, she heard the rumble of a diesel motor. A taxi lumbered slowly past, its wheels almost twisted from decades of service in the city. The tires made a kind of crackling sound as they carved through the thin layer of moisture that still clung to the asphalt. Lost in thought, Lisa watched the car's taillights, the red glow as the car pulled away—then she noticed another car, parked at the curb about twenty yards ahead and facing her. Its parking lights were on. A sedan. Shiny and dark blue, it looked coiled and sleek as if ready to pounce.

Lisa glanced at the windshield but could make out nothing on the other side because the glass reflected the shine of the streetlamp between her and the car. She noticed that the rear door on the driver's side was open, and simultaneously realized that something was wrong.

Instinctively, she slowed her steps.

She could see something beneath the open door.

Two arms.

Bare forearms, the hands flat on the pavement, the nails sharpened to points and polished. The fingers spread, crooked, tensed.

A woman's arms. Bare, slim. Something cultivated about them.

Lisa stopped. Her heart was thumping.

The woman's head had to be directly behind the door itself, but she couldn't see it.

Was she sick?

Lisa's eyes darted back to the windshield again.

The reflection had moved. She could see through the glass, into the car.

There was no one behind the wheel. But behind the headrest on the passenger side, she could make out someone's profile. Cut off by the shadow, but looking toward the woman who was supporting herself with her hands on the road.

Lisa drew in a sharp breath through her nose and skirted a few steps to one side, putting the display window that extended out from a shop between her and the sedan. She couldn't stop looking at the door of the car; behind it, the woman with the bare arms moved her small, spread-eagled hands a step forward, like a dog moving on its front paws. Then Lisa could see her back as it protruded from the car. A bare back, stretched out, arched and doubtless goose-pimpled from the cold. The woman's head was turned back, probably talking with whoever was inside the car. But what Lisa saw of her head was no face, no profile, no hair, no bare scalp. Instead, she saw only a strangely smooth, shiny surface.

Then the woman slid completely out of the car and onto the curb. The motion was fluid as she pulled her legs from the backseat and rested her knees on the pavement, maintaining her crawling posture. And Lisa suddenly recognized what it was that enclosed the woman's head like a giant fist: a pink rubber mask that seemed to have holes for neither eyes nor mouth. Instead, where the holes should have been, were full lips and bright shining eyes, printed onto the plastic with photographic brilliance. The printed features had thin leather bands sewn over them that stood out slightly from the mask. The bands gave the impression that the sensitive organs and openings beneath had been sealed off behind an unbreakable barrier.

A shoe appeared below the edge of the door.

Lisa looked up, and she saw a figure rise to its feet behind the door.

Felix.

Wasn't he still in the building?

What was he doing with this woman?

With a click, the car's trunk sprang open, and the masked woman slipped inside it like a cat.

Felix slammed the trunk and the latch clacked firmly in place. Then he slowly turned around. Lisa stood leaning against the display window, less than ten yards behind him. She knew he must have seen her.

For a fraction of a second, she had the impression of a hairless tentacle jutting out of the collar of his coat, a swollen blood vessel along one side and its tip twitching in her direction.

She bumped against the wall behind her and saw the oversized eyes turn on her. And without meaning it to happen, a little sigh escaped her, the sound of it like a caress to her ear.

SIX WEEKS EARLIER

"So, you know him?" Treibel let his hands fall flat on the desk. "I thought so!"

Lisa leaned back in the chair on the other side of Treibel's desk and crossed her legs. "I can't see what difference that makes."

Treibel had called her into his office the following morning and broached the subject immediately. He'd found out that the newspaper's new owner, Felix von Quitzow, also published the work of her father, Xavier Bentheim. Did Lisa perhaps know Mr. von Quitzow personally?

She would have preferred to keep her association with Felix to herself. But to do so seemed somehow deceitful. So she had simply said yes, she did. But she did not feel obliged to give Treibel more detail than that.

"You know, Ms. Bentheim," the editor-in-chief began, rather hesitantly, "for us, and I mean for the survival of this newspaper, it would, of course, be of great interest to know exactly what the new owner is planning to do with it."

Yes, that much was quite clear.

"There's an agreement with Quitzow that guarantees our editorial independence, but still . . ." He moved around the desk and eased into the second armchair on the other side, next to Lisa. "Still, I find myself wondering what's going on in his head. I mean, he can't seriously believe he's going to make money with this old rag, can he?" He looked at her quizzically.

Don't ask me what Felix is planning, she thought, but she kept it to herself. She patted the armrests lightly under her hands.

"I'm sure I don't need to tell you this, Ms. Bentheim, but it would naturally be invaluable to your fellow journalists if we could all . . ." Treibel smiled at her, and Lisa realized he was doing his best to be charming, "reap the benefit from your acquaintance with Mr. von Quitzow."

"Mmmm?" she leaned toward him, over the armrest.

"Maybe just a chat?" Treibel smiled. "Do you think you could manage that? We have the perfect rationale: Mr. von Quitzow has bought the paper that employs you as a journalist. You want to meet up, but my God, not to interrogate the man!" Treibel stood up again. He seemed strangely worked up. "No, just a meeting, just because of the old tie between you and Mr. von Quitzow."

Lisa gazed at the tip of her shoe on the foot crossed over her knee.

The previous night it had been impossible to simply turn and walk away when Felix had looked at her. It felt like minutes passed as they looked into each other's eyes. Then a shadow had cut between them, and the contact was broken—no, not a shadow, but a young man in an immaculate suit, his hair cut very short, making a beeline for the car. Felix had turned away from her, sat back inside the car, and allowed the man—his driver—to close the door behind him.

Barely daring to breathe, Lisa could only watch as the driver started the heavy sedan, swung it around in a screeching U-turn, and roared away.

"You know what?" she heard Treibel say. "I was actually supposed to be meeting Mr. von Quitzow this afternoon. But now I've got a better idea."

Oh really?

"*You* meet him instead. He didn't want to meet with me anyway. I just pushed the point until he finally said yes. Now I'll do him a favor and surprise him with you, Ms. Bentheim. You can pay him a visit in my place. Call it a kind of inaugural visit, purely as a courtesy. I'm sure he'll appreciate it. And once you're there, you can use the opportunity to find out what he's planning, which is what really matters to your colleagues, after all."

Treibel was suddenly standing very close to her chair. He leaned down until his thin-skinned, gaunt face loomed next to hers. "Our fate is in your hands, Ms. Bentheim."

Felix had looked younger, much younger, Lisa thought. How old *was* he? His entire body had emanated an odd inner tension.

"What do you say?"

She still felt the piercing look of the man who'd been standing by the heavy sedan. There was desire in there, a brutal craving that she feared might suddenly have changed into something else the moment he let that woman—so strangely concealed and revealed at the same time—out of the trunk again. Changed into something else, because the woman with the black band around her neck was not Lisa.

Or would he want to do the same things with her, with Lisa, that he did with the woman in the mask?

104

SIX WEEKS EARLIER

When Lisa stepped out of the subway car, the air around her felt as if it had grown even colder. The rain hit her like thin needles, like tiny grains of hail that only melted when they hit her skin.

After her talk with Treibel, she'd gone home briefly to change. Then it was back on the subway and onto the train to Mitte. Treibel told her that Felix's offices were no longer in the massive stone building, the top floor of which she and Felix had once called home. They had moved across the road into a recently constructed, modern glass-and-steel edifice. The subway station was still the same.

Stadtmitte.

She waited impatiently at the exit until the evening crowds parted enough for her to slip through. She held a folded newspaper—specially bought for the purpose—over her head as a slight protection from the rain. The tight skirt and the high-heeled shoes she was wearing meant crossing the street was more an act of tottering than walking. She felt the rainwater splash her legs. Her hand, clamped on the newspaper, was getting cold.

When she reached the side street where the two publishing buildings were located, she bypassed the old stone palace on the left and hurried across the street to the entrance to the shimmering, pale-blue box rising on the other side. Through the glass facade she could blurrily make out the various floors of the building. Desks were pushed up to the glass all the way along the front, and Lisa could see employees in their offices, potted plants adding a touch of affectedness and luxury.

The front doors slid open before her with a hiss. She lowered the newspaper, felt her wet hair clinging to her head. Behind the reception desk, a perfectly made-up blonde, her lips pursed, looked at her.

She was expected. Treibel had phoned ahead and informed Felix's office that Ms. Bentheim would be standing in for him at the meeting. A silvery elevator whisked Lisa up to the sixth floor, where she was met by another young woman, this time a petite brunette with her hair pinned up. She was exceptionally attractive, the lines of her face partly hidden behind heavy tortoiseshell glasses. She introduced herself as Quitzow's personal assistant, and led Lisa to a lounge with a glass wall providing a view out across Gendarmenmarkt all the way to the Konzerthaus.

"Would you like a water, perhaps? Coffee? Champagne?"

Lisa thanked her. "No, nothing, thank you."

"Then I'll come back for you in a moment. Mr. von Quitzow is still in a meeting. But I'm sure it won't be much longer."

"Wonderful."

The assistant left the room. Lisa's hand went up to her damp hair. She was feeling rather like a soggy poodle. But the luxurious interior invigorated her, and she sat down in one of the low, white club chairs. Outside, the rain was hammering furiously against the heavy glass. The thunderstorm looked like it could wash away the entire city.

Now and then, from the corner of her eye, she caught sight of employees hurrying along the corridor that led back to the elevators. As they hurried by, obviously keen and focused, they gave the impression of being well aware that they worked in one of the most exclusive companies in the city, perhaps even the country. Everything about the place seemed to be telling her how privileged she was to even be allowed to be there—but also that she could be out on her ear any moment if she failed to live up to the demands of the place.

What was she supposed to say to Felix when he finally had time to see her?

She sighed. She should never have let herself be talked into this! How could Treibel even consider loading the responsibility for the entire staff onto her shoulders? And she was supposed to try to get something out of Felix without telling him what she was actually after? What was Treibel thinking?

"Ms. Bentheim?"

Lisa shot to her feet.

The assistant was standing at the entrance to the lounge and smiling at her.

"This way."

Lisa's heels clicked across the marble floor and came to a stop in front of a large double door made of flawless walnut.

"Ready?"

What the hell? Of course!

Lisa nodded and the petite woman pressed down on the door handle. The door swung wide.

"Ms. Bentheim to see you, Mr. von Quitzow."

Lisa felt the blood drain from her face.

She was looking into an enormous hall, remarkable less for its height than for its depth. Endless surfaces of light stretched across the ceiling and floor, and all the walls were made of glass. In the middle of this flat box of windows and light stood an enormous oval table with what must have been forty people sitting around it: young men who seemed to want nothing more than to get on with the meeting, women around forty in elegant business outfits, and older management types who looked like they'd stepped out of their airplanes only that morning, having flown into Berlin from London or Moscow.

"Ms. Bentheim!"

Lisa stepped into the hall.

"What can I do for you?"

Felix had stood up from his place at the head of the table. The eyes of everyone there, without exception, were on Lisa.

"I'm sorry, I really didn't want to interrupt . . ." said Lisa, at a loss for words.

"No problem, Ms. Bentheim." Felix had sat down again without offering her a chair. "What brings you here? We can interrupt our meeting here for a moment." With a smile, he swept his eyes around those present.

"Mr. Treibel asked me to give you his apologies," Lisa stammered.

"But of course. Like I said, no problem."

He set this up on purpose! Felix called this meeting deliberately just to make me look like an idiot in front of everybody!

"Ladies, gentlemen?" Felix turned to his gathering. "Let's break for, say, twenty minutes?"

Murmurings. Chairs pushed back on the Plexiglas floor, papers shuffled. Some of the attendees began quiet conversations as they stood and gathered their things.

But no one looked at Lisa. Not even Felix, who was immediately surrounded by a half dozen of his team, looking like a circle of curious boys. One young man literally kneeled next to him.

Lisa cursed herself. Never in her life had she felt so awkward and stupid. As the first of them passed her, her legs began to shake, and she feared that she might collapse on the spot if she didn't sit for a moment. With her wet raincoat across her knees, she lowered herself onto one of the now-empty chairs and laid her hands, still ice cold, in front of her on the tabletop, also cool.

When the last employee left the hall, Felix leaned back in his chair, a smile playing on his lips.

"Treibel sent me," Lisa blurted. "I'm supposed to find out what you're planning to do with our paper." He knew her far too well. How was she supposed to fake anything? "I should have told him I didn't want anything to do with it, that he couldn't hide behind me."

"Treibel?" Felix seemed almost surprised.

"Our editor-in-chief? The one who introduced you in the editorial office yesterday evening?"

"What would I care about Treibel, Lisa?"

She had to swallow.

"Is that really all that matters to you?

Words. Scraps of memory. The resonance of uncountable touches.

"You left me, Lisa." Felix's voice was no more than a whisper. "Don't you have anything to say about *that*?" His eyes pinned her in place. His chiseled mouth was closed, the muscles of his jaw straining. "You hurt me, and now you stroll in here and start telling me about Treibel?"

Suddenly, it was all there again. The unrelenting nature, the superiority he had always radiated. Felix was nearly thirty years older than her, and he had not wasted those years.

"After everything, you have the audacity to show up here and act like nothing ever happened?" Felix had risen from his chair and moved over to the wall of glass. He stood looking down on to the street below. "What do you want from me, Lisa?"

For Lisa, it was as if their encounter had opened a floodgate that had been closed for a long time.

She had never really been able to handle him. That was why she'd left him and gone to Till. To Till, who had listened to her, with whom she could talk, with whom she could make herself understood—as equals. To Till, whom she hadn't seen since that night two years earlier, when he'd gone to find Max.

"I wanted a child with you, Lisa. Remember that?" Felix had turned to her again and his eyes shone. He took a step toward her, and for a moment she had the crazy idea that he would lean over her, wrap one arm around her waist, caress her with the other. "You never told me what you thought of that, Lisa. All you did was run away!"

All the friendly nonchalance he'd afforded her in the circle of his colleagues was gone. The scorn and agitation pouring out of him now—which had to be rooted in her physical presence—charged the air around them.

"Didn't you let me go, Felix?" Lisa heard herself reply, her voice strangely raw. "That night, just down there . . . I got out of the taxi, do you remember? We talked. I was trying to . . . I was trying to figure out what I wanted. But you suddenly turned away. You tapped in the code for the door and left me standing there—suddenly, it was all over." She could hardly believe she was saying these things. Hadn't Felix turned his back on her to clear the way for Till? "Isn't that how it happened?"

He stood in front of her as if he was nailed to the floor. Lisa took pleasure in the way his eyes devoured her. Could it be that she was equal to him? In contrast to two years earlier, when she felt completely at his mercy?

She was suddenly overtaken by the memory of a summer day many years earlier. The memory of swimming in her parents' pool and Felix appearing from nowhere. How he'd looked at her with the same eyes that were looking at her now. How he had watched while she toweled herself dry. How then, as now, she sensed this man was consumed by his desire for her. It was this desire that had always frightened her.

"Come with me." He reached for her hand. His touch like an electric shock. "I want to show you something."

She let herself be led from the chair to a door set into the glass wall. Felix impatiently jerked open the door in front of her.

Cold as ice, the rain whipped inside.

SIX WEEKS EARLIER

On the other side of the door, a narrow steel bridge stretched across to the stone building on the other side of the street. Heavy steel cables were all that held the bridge in place. No roof, no walls. Just bolted, riveted rails running along both sides. The lightly constructed bridge connected the buildings at the sixth floor. Lisa had first noticed it a few months earlier, but hadn't paid it much attention.

Felix pulled her through the door. Below, Lisa could see the evening traffic—cones of light from headlights sweeping around the corner, pedestrians hurrying along the sidewalk, alone and in pairs.

"You'll want to see this," Felix called to her over the rain, releasing her hand and walking ahead of her; the bridge was too narrow to allow them to cross side by side. "It's in my old study. This is the quickest way."

Lisa placed one hand on the chilly metal railing, the only thing that protected her from the void below. Strong gusts of wind whipping along the street set the steel construction swaying. She stopped, and the noises of the night washed over her.

"Lisa?"

She looked up.

Felix had already reached the other side and was gesturing for her to follow him.

She looked down again, taking care that the heels of her shoes did not get caught in the holes punched in the steel plates that formed the footway of the bridge.

"Did you really think I'd let you play with me like this?!"

At first she thought it was the wind howling through the stony towers and oriels of the old company building. But it was Felix, shouting back at her over the storm.

She looked up, terrified, and saw him staring at her. A blast of wind cut through her raincoat and dress and blew her hair aside. It was true. She had been playing with him. In her mind's eye, she saw the voluptuous white body of the masked woman, the way it arched when Felix pulled the collar tight.

As she looked across at him, there was a clang, a rattling noise. Felix had grabbed hold of the steel handrail and was shaking it. A strange feeling overcame her, as if her stomach had come loose in her abdomen.

A hard crash jolted through the steel structure she stood on—and she found herself staring into the abyss on her right; the handrail was gone.

Felix had pulled it out of its anchor point with a jerk. It swung down and around, then back again, locking into place vertically below the bridge. Lisa instinctively gripped the railing on the other side with both hands.

"Let it go, Lisa."

Go back—how far onto the bridge was she? Turn around? In high heels, with one rail gone?

Felix kicked hard at the central section of the handrail, the part she was holding onto. A crashing noise, and her hand released the rail.

She swayed. A jolt—the bridge rang and vibrated as though it might fall apart any moment.

Bitterly cold, slippery from the hours of icy rain, the bridge, its handrails gone, stretched away in front of Lisa like a steel track to the stone building across the street. Looking down, Lisa saw her shoes fixed on the steel surface of the bridge—and left and right nothing but seventy feet of space between her and the road below.

Her legs failed her. She sank onto the metal plate she was standing on, and her arms closed around the rivets and beams that the bridge was built from. Her breathing came shallow and fast as she pressed her cheek to the wet steel. It felt to her like it was burning.

THE FUNERAL

He can see Lisa standing next to her mother, the two of them in front of the row of conifers that are rising skyward. Lisa's dark-blonde hair shimmers against the black jacket she has thrown over her shoulders. She looks more beautiful than Till remembers her ever looking before.

They haven't seen each other in two years, but Till is too dazed, too numbed by everything that's happened, to even talk to her.

He takes a few steps back from the grave. Now Nina is there, staring down. Farther left, Julia Bentheim has her arms around both Lisa and Betty. With her shoulders high, Julia seems drawn in on herself, her face somehow distorted. The three women stand so close together that they seem to be holding each other up.

Soon, soon he will go to them. But right now, he is too overwhelmed.

It feels like just yesterday that he spoke to Max in his apartment for the last time. After that final confrontation, Till had returned to Toronto and his old life. He had thrown himself back into completing his thesis, drifting through the days like a sleepwalker.

Being back in Berlin feels like an awakening, a shock that drags him back to life out of his deathlike exhaustion.

This time it wasn't Lisa who'd contacted him, as she had about Betty's wedding. This time, Julia had written. "No doubt it would have been important to Max for you to be there," she had penned on the newspaper announcement of her son's funeral.

The news had hit Till like a fist in the face.

Since that last day, he'd heard nothing from Max. He'd suspected, feared, dreaded that things would not go well for him. He'd heard through acquaintances that Max had left Berlin and moved somewhere south. But Till had never imagined that the next time he would come to Berlin it would be to bury Max.

"Till?"

He turns. Nina is next to him.

His arms open as if by themselves, and he pulls her to him. Nina's forehead is warm against his throat. He feels the way her slim body practically sucks up the embrace.

"Till, I . . . I've wanted to talk to you for so long . . ."

He holds her tightly.

"But suddenly you were gone. You weren't in Berlin anymore. The word was that you and Max had a fight. And . . . I didn't know how I could . . . by phone, or by email—"

"How what, Nina?" Till lets her go. He leans slightly to be able to look her in the face. Her eyes are red, and she keeps her head low, as if she doesn't want him to look at her.

"Till, I . . ." She breaks off.

Till's eyes come to rest on the part in her dark-brown hair. Max had been crazy about her. There was no one he ever cared about more.

She lifts her head and her dark eyes are directed at him. "I . . ." she whispers, "I mean, Felix and I . . ." Her voice grows raw and she stops again.

Felix?

Till looks past her to the others present at the funeral. It's true, he can see Felix standing at the back. Till had noted his presence earlier, briefly, but that was all. "Back then, Felix asked me . . ." Nina moves very close to Till as she speaks, and he can smell the delicate scent she is wearing. "He asked me—" But instead of ending the sentence, she interrupts herself. "He wanted something from Max, you know?"

"From Max?"

"Yes."

"Nina, I'm sorry but I don't understand—"

"It was about his father's books. Felix had plans back then, and he wanted Max's permission to use what his father was writing, but Max didn't want to sell him the rights."

Till nods. He remembers Max telling him something about that.

"Felix started pressuring me. Do you understand? He thought he could get to Max through me. He thought he could go through me to get Max to do what he wanted."

Till has to concentrate to follow her hurried words.

"But I didn't want Felix to come between us, between Max and me," Till hears her whisper at his throat.

"Yeah. Yeah, I think I know what you mean." Max hadn't wanted Felix using his father's books for his own purposes. Till can remember Max talking about this. It was in the room behind the theater, where those people were gambling. "But that was all so long ago. Why . . . I mean, Max is dead, why are you telling me this, Nina—"

But she doesn't let him finish. "Felix kept on and on at me. He didn't care at all. Anything was fair game, anything for him to get what he wanted. I told him he should go to you, Till, if he wanted something from Max. I pointed him in your direction, to distract him from Max and me! I put him on to you, Till!" Her pretty eyes are shining. "Or Felix would never have let go. He wouldn't have stopped until what was between Max and me was ruined. I know it wasn't right, but Max meant the world to me back then." Her eyes search his face.

"Max mentioned once that there was something between you that bound the two of you together. Some experience, something you both went through . . ."

"Mmm?"

"I told Felix that, Till." Tears are flowing down her face now.

The funeral, the memory. It all seems to come crashing down on her at once. Almost as a reflex, Till strokes Nina's cheek, wiping away a tear. For a moment he feels a strong urge to simply kiss her. But she goes on whispering.

"I told Felix that there was an experience in your childhood that you never spoke about to anybody. Max had basically told me as much. And I'd hardly got the words out of my mouth . . . and I could feel the way he latched onto that. He wanted to know more about it. It was clear instantly that he was thinking about how he could use that to get what he wanted from Max."

Till feels his temper worsening. There was only one experience in their shared childhood that they never told anyone about. What happened in the passageways beneath the city.

"Then Felix went to Max and told him you'd said something about this experience. But it wasn't true, Till. He only said it to upset Max and to set him against you. He knew the easiest way to weaken Max was to drive a wedge between the two of you . . . to damage your friendship."

Till exhales. *Felix?*

But Nina is already continuing. "All that mattered to Felix was making the two of you enemies. I'm so sorry, Till," she says. "I should never have said anything to Felix. But I wanted him off my back. And that was wrong, terribly wrong. You were always so important to Max. The conflict between you two practically tore him apart."

Once again, Till sees his friend sitting in front of him on the sofa in the living room. He sees him saying he'll tell Lisa everything. He sees Max's eyes, full of hate, boring into him, and how everything about Max signals that he's prepared to carry through on his threat.

Felix had engineered it all. He wanted them to argue.

And Felix, just as he'd intended, got what he wanted.

SIX WEEKS EARLIER

Something was swinging softly.

But it was not the icy steel bridge.

It was something soft, white, warm.

Lisa stretched. Her head bumped against something hard. She opened her eyes. She was lying on her side and staring into beige and blue. Farther away, something red blinked.

She was lying across the backseat of a car.

Dazed, she looked down at herself. A woolen blanket covered her, and she remembered herself as child, sleeping on the backseat of her father's Jaguar.

Slowly, she sat up. The motor was silent, but the night still slipped past the windows.

The driver's seat was empty. She was alone. One window was down. She focused her eyes and looked out through the windshield. Bit by bit, the individual impressions coalesced into a picture.

She had fainted out there, on the steel bridge. Now she could see Felix standing at a balustrade in front of the car. On his right rose a low steel tower; beyond that sparkled dark-blue water.

It was still night, and they were moving. But it wasn't the car she was in that was moving. It was the small ferry the car was on.

Lisa pulled the blanket closer around her. She knew exactly which car this was—she had seen it when she encountered Felix on the street close to the newspaper building. He must have carried her to the car and laid her inside after she fainted. Where were they going? She looked beyond Felix, out over the water. They were on a lake, gliding toward the shore, an embankment that sloped up behind a thin strip of beach.

Farther back, a brightly lit mansion perched on the summit of a small hill. A shimmering chain of lights led from the dock they were heading toward—where a second ferry was just moving away—up to the mansion. Lisa could make out several people on the dock. Clearly they had just disembarked from the other ferry.

Lisa saw Felix turn in her direction. He smiled, and ducked his head a little to look at her through the windshield. He waved to her.

When she waved back, he walked from the balustrade to the car and pulled the driver's door open. "How are you feeling?"

Only now did she remember what happened on the bridge. He had dropped the railings—she could have fallen! How dare he put her in this car?

But all she said was "good."

He sat behind the wheel.

"Where are we?"

"We're nearly there. A small party, some friends," he said. "I thought you might enjoy it. If you like, you can change into something fresh." From the passenger seat he took several large paper bags and handed them back to her. "Or you might catch a cold."

Wasn't this all wrong? Shouldn't she simply get out, take the ferry back, find a taxi? Her hands reached into the first paper bag and came out holding a dark-green dress.

"Better hurry. We'll be there soon," he said, turning the key in the ignition. The engine sprang to life.

In the next shopping bag, she discovered blue silk lace underwear, smoother and more supple than anything she had ever touched or even seen.

"Don't worry. The windows are tinted. And I won't turn around."

The ferry slid up to the dock with a slight bump. Lisa saw the door open in the tower on the right in front of the car, and a man stepped out. He threw a rope to another man, who was waiting for the ferry to dock.

She pulled the undershirt she was wearing over her head. The things she'd had on earlier had been soaked in the rain and someone must have taken them off her—she didn't want to think about who.

The dress felt like a caress against her skin. She found shoes in the bags too, but Lisa preferred to pull on her own shoes again; they were laying in the footwell behind the driver's seat. This was all wrong, all wrong. But she had to have dry clothes if she didn't want to get sick. And she would give everything back to Felix later.

The car trundled quietly off the ferry and purred past the other passengers, who were now making their way on foot along the narrow road toward the house on the hill. A few moments later, gravel crunched under the tires. Felix pulled up in front of the entrance. Flaming torches created a maze of shadows and reflections on the front of the building.

Lisa had finished getting dressed. Felix opened the door for her. "You look incredible."

They climbed moss-covered stone steps to the entrance. The double front door stood open and she could hear music, low and muffled, coming from inside. The building was from the eighteenth or early nineteenth century. The lobby seemed designed to do nothing but delight visitors with its extravagant luxury. A red-carpeted stairway led in a broad sweep to the second floor. Lisa could hear the sounds and voices of the guests coming from all sides. The visitors seemed to have dispersed into the various halls and wings of the house.

The glitz of the lobby, the looks she attracted, the puzzled smiles that her appearance conjured on the faces of the other guests . . . it all made Lisa feel somewhat intoxicated, and she was glad that she had accepted the dress that Felix had given her.

While Felix airily greeted the people approaching them, they made their way from the lobby into an adjoining mirrored ballroom. A broad sweep of windows opened onto a garden, its park-like landscape a patch of dark green cut from the darkness by the light of scores of flaming torches. On a raised platform at one side of the ballroom, two violinists and a pianist were playing. Two couples twirled playfully in a dance, the remaining guests stood around in groups, chatting.

"Quitzow?"

Lisa turned her head and saw Henning's father approaching. Farther back, she recognized Treibel and his wife. Confused, she released Felix's arm. Being seen with him made Lisa feel uncomfortable. And in clothes that he had bought for her, to boot! Someone moved between her and Felix, and she used the opportunity to put a little more distance between them.

She strolled across the room, toward the windows and the garden outside. Behind her, she heard Felix greet Henning's father. A waiter offered her a tray with flutes of champagne. She accepted a glass, sipped, and relished the crystalline, almost glittering feeling of the liquid in her mouth and throat. Refreshed and with the champagne in her hand, she stepped through one of the glass doors into the air outside.

In front of the ballroom stretched a terrace paved with stone. Lisa stood and looked out over the garden, specially decorated for the night's festivities. Gas patio heaters kept the cool of the evening at bay. Out here, too, the guests had gathered in little clutches: women in evening dresses, gray-templed men with long-legged dogs at their side, smartly dressed children in blue or white outfits running among the adults. Broad beds of gravel offset the drop between the house and a pond that marked the lowest point of the garden, a good two hundred yards from where Lisa was standing.

Lisa was trying not to focus her thoughts, but she sensed that only one of them was really tangible: *Felix*. That thought, in particular, she did not want to let in.

She walked down the long steps into the garden. As she did so, she felt the soft fur of a dog sweep by her leg. Off to her left, she had noticed thirty or forty guests gathered at a kind of rail. They seemed to be watching something on the other side. Smiling, she watched the dog run ahead of her and push between the legs of the people at the parapet. What was it so curious about? Lisa joined the spectators and peered over the shoulder of a shorter woman who was standing at the balustrade.

On the other side was a sheer, fifteen-foot drop into an oval depression perhaps a hundred feet across, the walls carefully constructed and all topped by the stone balustrade. It was an arena that must have been built at the same time as the mansion. It reminded Lisa of the aesthetic of grottos and decorative ruins of that era. She pushed through to the front, laid her hands on top of the stone parapet, and looked down into the pit.

In the middle stood a young man, naked but for a cloth wrapped around his loins. He held a long staff in one hand, its end split into two points. In the other hand was a wooden shield protecting his upper body. But his eyes were not on the spectators above him. They were on an animal moving silently around the pit wall. A panther, glossy and black, its fine whiskers shivering in the torchlight.

"Are you sure you want to watch this?"

Breathless, Lisa spun around. Felix had touched her arm. She didn't know what to say.

"The panther has no chance," Felix said. "The man is in costume, but he knows what he's doing. He'll kill it."

Lisa felt tears rising in her eyes. Why would anyone do such a thing?

Then Felix pulled her to him, his lips touching her ear. He led her away from the parapet, perhaps more supporting than leading. "Just say the word, Lisa, if you want me to put a stop to it. Say it, and the animal lives."

"Can you do that? Please?"

He pulled her closer. "Soon. Soon I'll tell them to stop. Just another moment, now that you are finally with me."

She felt the way her body pressed against his, how her touch only served to increase his desire.

"I can't stay away from you, Lisa, but . . . maybe it was the right thing for you to turn your back on me. Maybe . . . definitely . . . I know I shouldn't want you like this." His arms held her tightly. "I'm a danger to you, Lisa, but I can't get you out of my head." His hands moved lower, caressing, clasping the curve of her backside through the sheer material of the dress.

And the more menacing his words, the more she felt her body forming to his.

"I want you, Lisa. But I know it's dangerous for you to be with me."

It was as if she had no choice; she succumbed to it, willingly, feeling at the same time, deep inside, how wrong it all was.

TODAY

Butz is sitting at a table by the window.

He'd looked up when the restaurant door opened. Now, he's watching every move she makes, but the woman ignores him completely.

She's probably in her early thirties, wearing a kind of coat he hasn't seen in Berlin for at least twenty years. A fur coat. And not some shabby pelt that looks like it's been mothballed too many years in a wardrobe, and it doesn't look fake. No, she's wearing a silky smooth, thick, warm, soft fur coat, the kind of coat Butz would have loved to reach out and stroke.

She walks past him to a table farther back in the restaurant, where a young man in an unbuttoned shirt is waiting for her.

It is the slightest of movements, a flick of her hip, a casual swing of her arm. But it causes the heavy fur coat to open down the front as she turns to show it off to the young man. Her skin is pale, almost shining, a quick flash through the gap, the curve of her breasts, the camber of skin down to her navel and beyond, where it is bisected by a broken black line: the elastic of her panties, sheer around her hips and tapering to a tiny triangle between her thighs.

Butz catches his breath. She has her head turned back to watch her companion's reaction. But she has to know that her coat swung open for a moment, that she is revealing her nakedness to Butz too. She has to know that his eyes caught that strip of skin between her breasts, framed by the sides of the coat. His eyes travel up past her throat. She turns her face in his direction, and Butz's eyes fix on her full lips, which—noticing the pull she has on him—she parts slightly, revealing a row of pearl-white teeth.

And then the moment is gone. She turns around and sits at the young man's table, keeping the coat on and not wasting another moment on Butz. All he has to look at now is her back and the back of her head, her hair pinned up casually, expertly.

"My colleague will be here in a moment. Would you like something to drink in the meantime?"

Butz looks up as if startled out of a dream, and into a waiter's sweaty face. "Um . . . maybe just some water . . . yeah, water would be good."

The waiter leaves and Butz leans back. When he arrived five minutes earlier, he was told that the waiter who'd agreed to meet him would be a little late but shouldn't be much longer. He glances at his watch. Just after six. Are they just stalling? Or is the guy really going to show up?

Butz had dropped by the police garage earlier that afternoon to look at the car they'd found Fehrenberg's body in. The forensics guys had gone over it and had found no clues to indicate who had taken the body out of Fehrenberg's apartment—or why. But Butz couldn't get it out of his head, and he had wanted to see the car for himself. The car had been reported stolen, and the police were assuming that it had been taken for the sole purpose of driving to Fehrenberg's apartment. It was clear where the corpse had been lying on the carpet in the trunk. But no matter how deep Butz dug into the car, he could find nothing to point to a motive, or anything that would help them reconstruct what happened.

But just as he was about to leave the garage empty-handed, another vehicle caught his eye. Just a few parking bays away was Fehrenberg's official car. Fehrenberg had parked it in the garage before he'd signed off for vacation. And it was still there, just a few steps from the one someone had laid his body in, the one the technicians had brought to the garage. It was in Fehrenberg's other car—the official one—that he found the business card for the restaurant he is sitting in now.

It wasn't difficult to figure out why Fehrenberg had a business card for the restaurant in his car.

He'd been there as part of the murder investigation.

Butz had been through all the official investigation paperwork he could find, although Fehrenberg had destroyed his own notes and records. He'd been handed the case two weeks before he was due to go on vacation; it concerned a young woman who had turned up dead in the women's restroom at a restaurant. Half naked and choked to death, jammed between the toilet bowl and the wall of the cubicle. The cops had been able to determine that whoever did it probably fled through the window in the entry section of the restroom. And also that a number of the guests—and the waiter who'd been on shift that evening—had seen him.

The killer.

The man who'd entered the restaurant with the murdered woman. Who'd sat with her at a table before they both disappeared to the toilets in back, one just after the other.

A young man. Midtwenties. That's how the witnesses had described him. With eyes only for the girl.

"Didn't the other cop already tell you everything?"

Butz turns. Behind him, a scrawny, rather unhealthy looking man is approaching. This must be him. The waiter who'd served the killer and the young woman.

"I wanted to hear it from the horse's mouth."

The waiter casts a glance beyond Butz, as if to make clear that he really has no time for this. "Look, mister," he croaks, his voice raw, "I already told your buddy. If I were you, if I wanted to know where the guy who strangled that girl came from, I'd go down to the motel at the end of the street and talk to them. The Comfort."

Fehrenberg had talked to some other officers about the case just before he went on vacation. He hadn't mentioned the Comfort to them. Or they didn't tell Butz about it, at least.

"You served them, right?" Butz looks intently at the waiter. The man's austere face shows clearly just how little interest he has in working in this restaurant, and how little interest he has in being interrogated about the dead girl yet again.

"Yeah."

"So, what makes you think they came here from the Comfort?"

The man narrows his eyes. "It's not like they were the first. How long have I been waitin' tables here? Since ninety-four? How many couples like them d'you think I've seen? They meet down that way, at the end of the cross street, they go to the Comfort, and if they get along, afterward they go get something to eat—and that's here." He leans forward. "Sometimes I can even smell it . . . if they've already done it, or if they're going to." He straightens up again. "Makes you want to vomit."

JOURNAL ENTRY

As if anesthetized.

As if risen from a crucible of molten steel.

Tempered.

But still alive. Uninjured. Undamaged. Untouched.

Despite what I did.

Like walking through a wall of flame without getting burned. And walking out the other side.

Hardened.

Alive and energized by walking through the flame.

A new person.

No more fear, doubt, hesitation.

Forging ahead. A new self, breaking out. Toughened. Mature.

An unleashed force, hungry for direction.

Unstoppable, resolute. Stronger than ever before.

The skin—

Really? That's it? That's all I can think of?

AAAAAAAHH!

Her skin.

The skin of the girl in the department store. When you stripped it, touched it, stroked it.

The curves, the warmth, the sounds, the movements—touching the skin . . . It felt like a pearl, a pearl made of . . . of flesh, sex . . . from another world.

Her body, how it pushed back, resisting me until I overcame her.

AAAAAAAHH!

There are no people anymore! Just bodies, maggots, sightless limbs, twisted mouths, blind stumps. There are worms, amphibians, gnarled swellings—glands, folds, lumps, lips, entrails and openings, coils, gristle, bulges, things distorted, contorted, crushed.

It is a disfigurement, a deformation, a soiling. But not decay. No. It is the birth of a raging, hateful force, squandering, smearing, driving out anything of beauty.

A force that I set free. A force that is inside me, that drove me to pull down her panties, that drove me to touch her, made her stretch and curve against me, that drove me to plunge into her with a motion that felt for a moment like it would never end.

THAT'S IT?

That's what lies at the bottom of the hole I've climbed down into?

Nothing but the hunger, this unbearable desire, to again feel a young woman's naked, hot body squirming and yielding under mine? Lust making the world around me burn?

TODAY

Small men with tanned faces, fluorescent jackets, steel-toed boots. Men inside the tiny cabins of versatile little excavators. Men sitting high up in the seats of trucks lumbering along dirt tracks. Images of concrete pillars jutting into the sky, supporting a massive concrete slab high in the air—a six-lane, sometimes eight-lane, roadway.

Autobahn images.

Pictures taken at night, time exposures stretching the headlights into long, thin trails. Or in daylight, the rush-hour jam, cars bumper to bumper, three or four side by side in each direction. Where the men and women sweat inside their steel boxes, where they battle tooth and nail for every inch they can get. Images of a gray strip that winds its way completely around the city and where, in the course of any day, tens of thousands of cars circle the maze of buildings and streets, the jumble of pipes and tunnels, signs and walls, men and machines, that are all tangled together in the middle.

Pictures of the Berliner Ring.

Claire had been working on it for two months. Again and again, she had talked about it with Butz, telling him how with the images of the Ring she wanted to capture the true nature of the beast—the nature of the city itself.

So, they had gone driving around the Ring. Surrounded, sandwiched, cars in front, behind, on every side, each one moving at a different speed, each one a terrible threat to all the rest if the driver dared to spin the wheel.

"Can you put on the blue light?" Claire had pleaded. "Just for a moment, for me?" Her eyes full of promise.

With the siren wailing and blue light flashing, Butz had raced along the Ring. Dynamic, speed-blurred shots of cars swerving aside came out of it, and Butz had risked his job. Claire had squatted on the passenger seat, every muscle in her body tensed, the window rolled down and her camera aimed outside, clicking off shot after shot as they sped between the other vehicles. Butz had heard the shutter clatter, and Claire shouting at him, urging him to drive faster, switch to the fast lane, now over to the emergency lane.

He stretches his legs in front of him. The back of his seat is adjusted back a little, and he stares out through the windshield, into the dark.

He found the pictures from the Ring on the desk in Claire's room. Just this morning, before he went to the LKA garage.

He can't get them out of his head.

In one of the images, he saw part of Claire's face. She was wearing sunglasses, the wind driving her hair into her face. And she was beaming, so thrilled to be flying along with the siren wailing.

He has not seen her since finding Micha.

He has not spoken to her.

There was a message on his cell phone's voice mail that morning. "I'll call as soon as I can. Everything's okay." He didn't wake up when the phone rang. He must have been too exhausted.

He straightens up in his seat a little. It was only a matter of time before she left him, anyway. He props his elbows on the steering wheel as he thinks of the last time they slept together. Claire had already been somewhere else in her head; he shouldn't have touched her.

He looks out through the side window of his car, looks at the restless glow of open flames flickering outside. Now and then, sparks spray into the sky, shooting up from the tips of the flames. The fire is burning in a steel drum, and the glow of it backlights the silhouette of a woman standing beside the drum. She is wrapped up like a Christmas gift. Bows and buckles, bits of bare skin. A piece of candy. Something to snack on.

He's just come from the Comfort.

They remembered Fehrenberg's visit well. Butz's colleague had asked about a young man and a girl, and the woman at reception vaguely remembered them being there. But like most of the guests, they'd paid cash up front, so they weren't entered in the register. The receptionist backed up the waiter; the two young people looked like they'd just come from the street with the fires in the fuel drums. Butz knows that pretty much anyone going to the Comfort would come from there, from the street that ran through the underpass below the Berliner Ring. If he wants to find out who the girl was, he'll be better off asking around down there.

Butz parks his car in a lot beside the street. Once, it had been a decent suburban street connecting Berlin with Bernau. Part of it runs under the route of the Berliner Ring, but the houses along it haven't had families living in them for years. Now, the pimps who run the girls at the drums have set up their offices there. An entire street gutted and settled by people that Berlin's respectable citizens prefer to avoid.

Butz's eyes are on the candy girl beside the drum. She has crossed her legs in their thigh-high boots into an X, her cell phone at her ear, one shoulder high. A pair of headlights glides toward her, slows, stops. She puts the phone away and leans down to the passenger window, her ass protruding steeply.

Butz spent the entire evening in the houses, tussling with the guys who watch over the women out here. He showed them pictures of Fehrenberg, pictures of the crime scene. But it was a waste of time. It was obvious that the pimps wanted as little to do with the cops as possible. Butz finally ran across a stocky, bald guy who said he'd already talked to Fehrenberg about the dead girl in the restaurant. She wasn't one of his girls, and he didn't know who'd been taking care of her. But he could recall that Butz's colleague had pushed the same picture under his nose that Butz was just then showing him: the toilet cubicle in the restaurant washroom, and the dead girl slid down beside the porcelain bowl.

"But you know what?" the bald guy grumbled, and his eyes shone, strangely watery. "Seemed to me your buddy—what was his name?"

"Fehrenberg. Volker Fehrenberg."

"Yeah, him. Seemed to me he was more interested in our girls than in his case!"

Candy girl, behind the headlights, climbs into the black car crouching there in the night. The car's lights shift upward slightly as the car approaches, the light sliding over Butz as it turns. His eyes follow the vehicle as it pulls past him, but behind the mirror-tinted windows he can't make out anything.

The flames in the drum still flicker.

Fehrenberg had been poking around in the restaurant asking about the dead girl. What was it in his investigation that had led him all the way to the office of Felix von Quitzow? His inquiries into the restaurant case and Fehrenberg getting to know Merle Heidt, Quitzow's secretary; these things took place just before Fehrenberg went on vacation. But what was the connection? Had the restaurant case led Fehrenberg to Quitzow? Or was it pure coincidence?

The engine howls when Butz turns the key in the ignition. He's pressed too hard on the gas.

Seemed to me he was more interested in our girls than in his case, he hears baldy's needling voice. Is that what it was? Was it Fehrenberg's obsession with women that had set him on his downward spiral?

Butz's car idles in the gravel parking lot, the engine ticking. Everyone in the office knew what Fehrenberg did to shake off the stress of the job: every once in a while, he'd take off to the most out-of-the-way corners of the city for the temptations to be found there. He'd return to the job again looking a little hollow-cheeked, but with the ominous rumblings he'd been emanating before taking off settled down, at least for a few weeks.

Butz shifts into first gear, then changes his mind and slips it back into neutral.

He can keep on asking questions here until he finds the pimp who'd been running the murdered girl. But would that get him any further? Would it put him on the murderer's trail? No, it wouldn't.

There is only way to get to the murderer; he has to try to finish Fehrenberg's investigation. And that had led Fehrenberg to Merle. But Merle is dying. Infected by the rabies that is spreading fast.

Butz presses his hands to his temples. Every fiber of his body tells him he's on the verge of understanding how it all hangs together. What connects the death of the woman in the parking lot, the death of the woman on the construction site, and the deaths of Anni Eisler, Fehrenberg, and his own assistant, Micha.

He can sense that he's *this* close to the answer. But at the same time, it feels like he's a mile away from putting it all together. Because he has no idea which way he's supposed to turn. And the choice of directions seems endless.

Grimly, he shifts into first, presses the accelerator, and turns out of the parking lot. He rolls through the underpass under the Ring and turns right onto the on-ramp.

Fehrenberg is the key. Butz has no choice. He has to try to get behind his dead colleague's mask. And to the best of his knowledge, there's only one person in this world that Fehrenberg trusted.

He'll sink his teeth into her. And he won't let go until she's told him what she knows.

Fehrenberg's mother.

TODAY

Till remembers:

Flickering.

A hum. A buzz. A thrum.

Splinters of light.

Cold pain, arcing through him.

A naked body. The skin pulled up by inches—by the hooks driven through her tissue. The naked dead body of a woman, hanging on steel cables from the ceiling, slowly, slowly revolving.

A sound like wings beating.

"Till?"

His mouth is dry. Dry like someone's been holding a blow dryer to his mouth for hours straight.

He is lying on his back on a mattress in a dim basement room. In front of him are the tips of a split tongue, moving, one tip to the left, one to the right . . .

He blinks.

The tongue is pushed aside. A scar-face appears in its place.

Water—I have to drink something . . .

Till's eyes roam across the ceiling above him. His sides are burning, like lines of gasoline set alight. Then the blanket slides off, and he is looking down at his own body.

His arms are sewn to his torso, his legs stitched together.

"Hey? Is anyone there?" A voice breaks through the other sounds in the room. A pack of small figures seems to be milling around the foot of his bed.

"Well, Till? What do you think? Like it?" It's Felix, staring at him through the room's dim light.

Till's nerves jangle. The screams overlay his thoughts like treacle . . . he can't think straight. Then his memory returns with terrifying clarity.

It's only been a few hours. It was in the restaurant where they'd gone after Max's funeral.

"No more stories, no more lies!" he screamed at Felix.

He'd waited until Felix went to the restroom in back. Then he'd gone after him.

"You talked to Max about me! Were you trying to make us fight? Did you want me to fight with him?"

Felix, standing in front of Till, was leaning back against the sink. He looked pale. It occurred to Till that they could hear him out front, in the dining room, but he didn't care. He couldn't hold back; he didn't want to hold back any longer. Nina had told him the truth, standing by Max's grave.

"What did you say to Max? What did you tell him I told you?"

Felix was watching him, sizing him up, trying to figure out how far he'd go—when Till's arm suddenly shot out. He put all his weight, all his strength into the blow. His knuckles rammed into Felix's cheek, and something flashed in Till's eyes. He was far too adrenalized to hold himself in check. The force of his punch pulled him forward, and he saw Felix's head whip around. Felix tumbled back, slamming into the sink. His hands clawed at the cold porcelain.

"You got 'em, didn't you? The rights to his father's fucking books. You did it. But you killed him! He couldn't deal with it!" Till was out of his mind. "You're the one with blood on his hands, not me—"

He threw himself on Felix and dragged him to the floor, went to slam his knee into Felix's ribs, and if he broke some of them in the process, then tough! He needed to get rid of the guilt racking him for what he'd done to Max, and to make Felix pay for setting them against each other.

And that's when the pain exploded in the back of his head. Till jerked one hand up to his neck and realized he'd been hit. Then the second blow landed, propelling him forward, over Felix, until his head was over the sink and he threw up.

At the same time, Till heard voices behind him and realized vaguely that someone was helping Felix up from the floor. He swung around, took one step—and collapsed.

Felix contrived to get him into that basement.

Till feels a scream escape his throat as he brings his legs up to his chest, pulls his thighs apart. He feels the stitches in his legs stretch and jerks his elbows outward, breaking apart the sewn skin.

Then he's standing.

He hears the clamor from the man behind the wall and sees in his mind's eye the animals starting to feast on the rat man back there.

You can't let him die back there, Felix! They're eating him. They're digging into him! Can't you hear him screaming?

Through the dim light of the basement he sees Felix throw his hands in the air.

"Now!" Felix shouts, and he spins around, grabs the handle on the wall, and hauls on it.

Just a machine. The screams are just recordings. There's no one in the hole behind the wall. The rat man—he doesn't exist.

But the scratching, the sliding, the scrabbling, like thousands of spiders scrambling across a mirror—he's not imagining that! It's real. In horror, Till hunches back against the bare cement wall and sees them crawling toward him, sniffing, scratching, scavenging. Hungry.

What boils up from the tunnel, the furred bodies, the claws groping at the cement floor, the sharp, bright eyes—none of it is imagined. It is a flood of animals. An endless pack of rats, the first few rodents now at Till's feet.

He runs, stumbles, moves on, the blood dripping from the torn stitches in his sides. Through the tunnels that wind their way under the city—the tunnels he'd passed through with Bentheim once before, many years earlier.

He follows the scar-faced man who has rescued him from the animals, moving through the one-time Chinese fast-food joint in the green-tiled subway tunnel, taking the steps up to the square, moving until they reach an apartment and she opens the door for him. Lisa. Till had seen her earlier, standing with her mother at the funeral, but he hadn't spoken to either of them.

Now she is standing in front of him, her hair hanging loose, her lips parted very slightly, her hands reaching out to him.

Everything inside Till is pushing him toward her. It's been so long since she was with him. He wants to embrace her, undress her. He wants to pick her up, carry her to a bed, let his lips explore her body, the body he has missed for so long.

TODAY

An imposing apartment building from Berlin's Gründerzeit. Apartments with ceilings fifteen or eighteen feet high. White plaster facade, richly decorated window frames, the corner of the house designed as a tower. Its highest window no doubt offers an amazing view over Kurfürstendamm.

Nikita, it says on the directory, but when Butz presses the button, nobody comes to the door. So, he rings the bell for a lawyer's office on a lower floor—and gets lucky. The door buzzes and Butz pushes it open.

A steep marble stairway leads up to an entrance hall big enough to build a house in. On the ceiling is an extravagant fresco of a woman warrior riding a chariot. The floor is crafted from different types of marble, and has a long red carpet across it that looks like Wehrmacht liaison officers might once have marched across it. In the center of two curved staircases is an elevator, built into an iron cage forged in the shape of rose tendrils.

Butz climbs into the elevator, struggling through the two sets of double doors.

Nikita.

There it is again, in the same ornate script that was on the bell panel outside. Beside it is the "3" button.

On the third floor, opposite the elevator, looms a heavy entrance door of dark-stained timber. There is no bell. Instead, there is a heavy brass doorknocker, which Butz lifts and lets fall. The sound of it reverberates flatly in the rooms beyond.

Merle had brought Fehrenberg here. That's what Fehrenberg's mother had told Butz.

When he had rung the woman's doorbell, she was clearly pleased to speak to someone who had known her son and worked with him. She said she knew the name Merle Heidt, and that her son had told her he'd met her at Quitzow's firm.

"He liked her," Fehrenberg's mother said, her open, heavy face lighting up like the moon. "She's something special, he said."

She had asked him into her living room and served him coffee. Butz sat down on her sofa and began stirring his coffee with an ornamental teaspoon. Fehrenberg's mother sat facing him. "This Merle took him with her to a club." Mrs. Fehrenberg's eyes were fixed on him as she said it, and the corner of her mouth twitched.

"To Nikita," she whispered. "Merle took him into Nikita. Do you know that place? Can you imagine what it's like in there?"

Butz furrowed his brow. He might have heard the name of the club at some point, but he wasn't sure.

"He told me about it. Volker always told me everything. And it all seemed a bit strange to him too."

Why had Merle Heidt taken Fehrenberg to Nikita? Butz made some calls. The police were aware that it was a brothel, but the place had never really drawn much attention.

What did Merle want from Fehrenberg? Or did someone make her take him there? Was Fehrenberg's visit to the brothel the reason behind the removal of his body from his apartment?

Nikita.

Heavy and immovable, the solid oak door looms in front of Butz. No one responds to his knocking. He steps back and scans the door, his eyes coming to rest on the bottom edge. Something shimmering, glinting. Butz leans down and runs his fingertips over the carpet, which reaches all the way to the threshold. The carpet is made of red sisal with a herringbone pattern—and it is wet where it butts against the door.

"Hello?"

He straightens up again and hammers at the door. Water is seeping from the other side.

"Hey!"

He looks to one side and sees a second, lower entrance that also leads off the landing. That door is slightly ajar. Butz is there in two steps and pushes the door open.

A long, dark corridor opens on the other side—at the far end glows a brightly lit hall. The corridor is covered in one long pool of water that ends where it laps against the threshold. The entire apartment is flooded!

Butz moves quickly along the corridor, the water splashing under his shoes, until he is in the hall at the other end, where he turns.

The splendor, the flamboyance, the luxury of earlier days. Excessively ornate, the room seems almost stuffy: velvet furniture, heavy wall decorations, a larger-than-life-sized ebony wood figure with a turban on its head and a golden bowl in its outstretched hands in one corner, like a scene from the *Arabian Nights*. Behind a counter the light is scattered by countless mirrors and filtered through a multitude of bottles in different colors. The floor has been constructed from green, dark-blue, and red stone slabs. Right now it is under a half inch of clear water.

"Hey!"

Doesn't anybody know what's going on here? Butz notices a white bowl standing on a low platform in the center of the hall. A tub, a basin—what is it?

Quickly, he crosses the room to a passage that leads deeper into the building. He can hear the hiss of escaping water coming from that direction.

Red, black, violet, and glowing-white single rooms lie beyond the doors that Butz opens as he makes his way down this second corridor. Abandoned, untidy, excessively decorated rooms, the decor obviously designed to spark lust in even the most lifeless soul. The doors all have small viewing windows set at eye height, some of them curtained. And all the doors are unlocked—except one. Butz stops. He turns the handle, braces himself against the door, but it doesn't open. Because of the water flowing along the corridor, the small window is misted. He wipes it clear with his forearm. Why, of all the doors in here, is this one locked?

Through the cleared patch on the glass, he is able to see dimly into the room on the other side. He can make out a window opposite the door, half covered by a transparent curtain.

What . . .

Butz runs both hands over the little window. Did he see a shadow flit past the window?

"Open up, everything's flooded!"

A form, a silhouette . . .

The shadow seems to have turned its head toward him.

"I can't leave you here. Butz, Berlin police. Open up!"

The shadow glides away to one side.

He turns his head to protect his eyes from flying shards, and there is the tinkle of breaking glass as Butz's smashes the small window with his elbow. Then he reaches one arm through the window, feels for and finds a latch below the door handle, and turns it.

He swings the door wide and steps through.

Water flows from the corridor, past his feet, and into the room. The figure has retreated in front of him, back to the bed. It is a woman, but . . .

Confused, Butz takes a step toward her. Her torso, arms, legs, hands, feet . . . she looks almost doll-like. Only her face is not hidden by the black, shiny synthetic skin that clings tightly to her body, completely covering it. But even her face seems strangely inanimate and artificial. The hollows of her eyes, the small nose, the high cheekbones, the chin, even the hair—everything so symmetrical that it jars him.

"What's the matter with you?" he asks.

But she doesn't answer. She just looks at him, her puppet face turned in his direction.

"What's going on here? Everything's flooded!" He can't stop himself from running his eyes down over the artificial black skin, beneath which the curves of her body are clearly visible, and seductive.

She crouches like a cat on the dark-red sheet that covers the bed.

Can't she speak?

"Come with me. You can't stay here. I'm calling the fire department."

"No," he hears her quiet answer, and her voice sounds pure and clear.

"What?"

"I can't leave the apartment."

"Nonsense! Why not?"

"Are you really from the police?" She has laid down on her back, but her face is still turned toward him.

Butz reaches into his pocket and pulls out his badge. "Everyone's left, there's nobody else here. Don't be afraid."

Has someone tattooed her, perhaps? Butz had seen that a few years earlier during a raid: that girl had been marked—on her face too—to make it essentially impossible for her to lead a life outside the apartment where she was forced to work.

"You don't need to be afraid. You'll be taken care of."

"I can imagine."

"No, not the way you think. You can rely on my colleagues—"

"You're talking about something you know nothing about."

"What was going on here? The whole place is flooded . . ."

She rolls herself up on the bed, her black-clad body glistening on the blood-red sheet.

"Where are the women who worked here?"

But she doesn't answer him.

"Merle Heidt? Have you heard that name?"

"Merle. Of course . . ."

"She came here with a colleague of mine, Volker Fehrenberg."

Butz sees the way the woman tilts her head back to look at him. "Many men are brought here."

"Brought here?"

"The only ones who get in here are the ones brought by the girls. Quitzow wants it that way."

"Quitzow? He runs Nikita?"

She has turned her head down again.

Butz looks at the floor. More water is flowing around his shoes into the room. He can hear the hissing of the water coming from farther back in the apartment. He has to report this—but something holds him back. Right now the water damage is not important . . . but this woman . . . she might know something . . .

"It was like a wildfire," he hears her murmur. "When I first heard about the symptoms, I didn't let anybody into my room. I can't afford to get sick. At the start, we thought it was just headaches. Until the pills stopped having any effect on the symptoms."

She stretches one arm and lays her head on it. "You should have seen them . . ."

"Merle Heidt was the first." The rabies. She's talking about the rabies.

"No, Merle wasn't the first. The first was Irina. It started with her. They say Irina's ex-boyfriend was the one who infected her. That's what I heard later. I don't know why he'd do something like that . . . I didn't know him. The others said he'd been under the influence of Felix for years. But when he infected Irina, he did that all by himself."

The water is flowing freely into the room. Butz reaches out his hand. "Come with me. It's too dangerous here. A short circuit or something . . . you could get hurt . . ."

But his voice fades as he sees her fingers flick at the pull of the zipper that runs the length of her smooth black skin.

"Do you think I'm exaggerating?" She clasps the zip with her fingertips. "I told you, I can't leave the apartment." Slowly, very slowly, as if not wanting to rush things, she opens the zipper, which runs from the side of her hand to her underarm, down her side, over her thigh, all the way down to the tip of her delicate foot.

"Wait—"

"You're not listening to me. I can't just throw myself at the mercy of the first police officer who comes in . . . after they . . . I mean . . . don't you see that? I know the effect it has . . ."

There is a whispering sound as the zipper glides over the curves and hollows of her body, and the two sides of her skintight suit split apart.

Butz's mouth is dry, his eyes locked on the lengthening triangle of snow-white skin revealed as the zipper slides down.

He has to get to Quitzow's offices, he has to find Irina's boy-friend—but Butz's thoughts are muddled, he can't think straight as he watches her strip.

No tattoos, it's . . .

"Do you see what I mean?" he hears her whisper. With one hand she pulls off the skin suit, which clings to a thin film of sweat on her body.

"But . . ." his throat feels blocked. "That's . . . NO! . . . that's beautiful."

"You think so?"

But his lips are already moving over the skin that she has released from the suit. And unable to stop himself, he finds himself sliding between the arms reaching out to him from the bed, feels his hands slip under the artificial skin, peeling it away from the body beneath, modified for no other purpose than to please him.

THE FUNERAL

Lisa is only able to see the cemetery through a veil. The pines, the footpaths, the bells, the people, the looks, the flowers, the earth, the gestures, the words, the tears.

She was out on assignment for the newspaper when word reached her. Max was dead.

It's been ten days since then.

She speaks his name to herself, but she can't see him in front of her. All she sees in front of her is the veil, blurred by the morning procession.

The speeches in the church. The waiting. The coffin.

I let my brother die.

She stands a few steps away from the hole they've dug and watches as the wooden box is lowered into the earth. How can they bury someone without making sure he has some way to get out again? How can they lay somebody inside a wooden box and pile tons of earth on top?

Till is there. She can see him standing farther back, among the pines. She hasn't seen him for two years, but her thoughts are elsewhere. For Lisa, it's like she's been riding flat-out on a motorcycle, and crashed. As if her body has hit the asphalt at a hundred miles an hour.

I let him die.

Wasn't that true? Wasn't she supposed to keep looking after him? Why didn't he make it? What happened inside his head that made him destroy himself like this? What kind of incomprehensible, self-destructive mechanism had him in its grip?

The previous summer, Lisa had gone to see him one more time. Her mother had given her the address. Max hadn't lived in Berlin for a long time, more than a year.

"Why Rome?" Lisa asked her mother. But Julia had not been able to give her an answer that made sense. He likes how old the city is, Julia said, but Lisa couldn't believe that was the real reason. Her mother added that he liked the warm climate down there.

Was that the reason? Or was there something else that Max could only get from Rome, something that made him want to go live in a city where he knew nobody?

So, Lisa had flown to Rome. She took the airport shuttle downtown, and then found a taxi to take her to the address her mother had given her. The rickety Fiat seemed to rattle through the burning, deserted streets forever. It was August, and everybody in Rome had apparently left the city to lie on the beach or hide away in the cool of the mountains.

But Lisa jolted through the streets in the taxi, away from the city center, away from the pink and ochre apartment buildings, away from the concrete *palazzi* that crowded the suburbs in their hundreds—in their hundreds of thousands—escarpments of cement and tile crowned by forests of antennas, the narrowest of sidewalks in front, crammed with parked cars. Uphill, downhill, past the walls of enchanted villas now engulfed by the outskirts of the city, past overflowing trash containers that looked as if they were emptied only rarely, past the dilapidated steel shutters of the grocery stores and car repair workshops that had set up shop on the ground floors of the buildings.

When the taxi driver finally stopped, Lisa looked out her side window. She saw two run-down apartment buildings. A dusty, rutted road led between the apartment buildings and up a low hill behind them. The driver refused to risk his wheels on the unpaved track, and so Lisa had no choice but to get out and walk. She paid the man and set off between the apartment buildings, carrying her wheeled suitcase.

Behind the apartments that fronted the street were four or five single-story houses huddled together on the hillside. They looked like they were from Cicero's time. Sweat was running down Lisa's back as she dodged potholes on her way to house number 5A. That was the address she had from her mother.

The front door stood open and Lisa stepped into a cool front room, which was cut into two halves as if by a knife; one bright half, where the sun beat mercilessly through an opening in the ceiling, and a dark half lying in shadow. On the shaded side were three boys, maybe eleven or twelve years old, casually kicking a half-inflated plastic soccer ball. They took no notice of her.

"Max? *Cerco* Max Bentheim?" she said.

The boys stopped kicking for a minute, smiled, and nodded toward a dark doorway that led deeper into the house.

The house was undecorated, the walls bare. The floor was tiled, which helped to keep at bay the murderous heat that was frying the city. The windows were closed in the room that Lisa entered. But the sun and heat still filtered in through the cracks, making the room shimmer a little.

A colorful but forlorn combination of cheap furniture was strewn around the room. Through another door she could see a mattress on the floor; a sheet, twisted into a bundle, lay beside it. In one corner a TV was on but switched to mute; playing was a game show that looked like it had been recorded in the 1980s. A dark band flickered across the screen at regular intervals.

Max was not home. But at the table was a young man, not much more than a boy, perhaps eighteen or nineteen years old. He was sizing Lisa up, simultaneously curious and hostile. After she explained that she was Max's sister, and he had managed to get over his surprise, the young man told her that Max was away. He was good-looking; beneath his shining, unkempt hair his eyes were large and dark. But there was something about his face that bewildered Lisa and instinctively made her wary. She did not dare to ask him what he was doing at Max's place.

What was she supposed to do? Come back later? It seemed unlikely that she'd manage to catch Max just when he happened to be home. And she had no cell phone number for him.

She decided to wait inside the little house for her brother, and sat on one of the chairs at the table where the young man was already sitting. Plates with remnants of spaghetti, empty bottles and unemptied ashtrays all vied for space on the tabletop. Lisa thought better of propping her elbows there.

After a while, the young man stood up and went outside. She sat upright in the chair for another hour before falling asleep. The slam of a door woke her.

Lisa blinked in the direction of the room where the children had been playing. Her shirt clung to her back, her neck hurt from falling asleep sitting up. The sun hadn't quite set, but the heat had gone out of it. The light outside was mostly blocked by the closed shutters, and the room was nearly dark.

But she recognized him immediately.

Max had stopped at the threshold and was standing there, looking skinnier than she remembered. His hair was cut short and his light, faded-blue linen suit hung on him loosely. But it was his face that startled her. Even as a boy, Max's face had been sharp-edged, chiseled, unable to hide the conflicts fighting inside him. But those hard lines had deepened now; he looked almost spooky.

"Max."

Lisa stood up. She'd wanted to call and tell him she was coming but the house had no telephone.

And then she was hugging him. She felt his arms around her—but there was no strength in his embrace.

"What a surprise . . ." he seemed to be having trouble keeping his eyes open.

"How are you?" The words nearly choked her. What was he doing in Rome? Who was the young man she'd met earlier? What had happened to his face?

But she didn't want to show the alarm she felt at Max's appearance, and began giving him a cheerful rundown of what was going on in Berlin.

They sat at the table. Max had his face to her—but his eyelids sagged repeatedly. With what was clearly a huge effort, he opened his eyes wide again. But then the pupils beneath seemed to roll up with his eyelids, and Lisa was left looking at the whites of his eyes for a moment before his pupils slowly emerged again from under the lids.

She had never seen anyone look so tired.

It was obvious that he only wanted one thing—to sleep. Should she leave him alone? Go to a hotel and come back in the morning? Or stay? But where? There was no guest bed, no armchair—was she supposed to lie on the bare floor?

She stood up suddenly. "Maybe I should find a room somewhere close, and tomorrow we can look around the city a little?"

Max stood too, and nodded. He embraced her then turned away.

Only now did Lisa realize that the young man who had been there earlier must have returned while she slept. He was lying on the mattress in the next room. Feeling out of place, she watched Max pass sluggishly through the doorway and sink onto the mattress, into the young man's arms.

When Lisa returned to the house the following morning, the front door was locked. The kids she'd met the day before were now playing soccer in the road. But when Lisa asked them if they knew where Max was, they just shook their heads.

For three days, she went back to the house. For three days, she knocked on the locked door. Then she found a taxi to take her back to the airport.

She never saw Max again.

He is lying in the oak coffin that they have lowered into the earth. She loved her brother more than anyone in the world. But she had not been able to save him from his death wish.

TODAY

"Till, do you know why I set the rats on you?"

They are standing in front of the restaurant. Lisa is gone, but Felix is still there.

"I want you to work for me again," Felix says. "But not in the office. This time, I want you to write for me. That's why I took you down there. I know that the only way to write in a truly compelling way is to experience certain things for yourself. Only then can you make a reader addicted to what you're telling them. That is what I need from you, Till. Your job is to get them hooked, to addict them to the fictional universe!"

Till looks at him. The fictional universe. How many times had he talked about that with Max and Felix the last time he was in Berlin?

"See the car parked over there?" Felix nods in the direction of a black limousine double-parked across from the restaurant. "It's waiting to take us to a house I own in the south of the city. It's all ready, Till. I've set up a room for you. You'll have everything you need."

Till sees himself and Max creeping into Max's parents' living room and climbing up the bookshelf. They'd spent the entire night reading through his father's books and puzzling over what Bentheim was working on down in the guesthouse.

"One critical section of the fictional universe is almost complete," Felix was saying. "That's what I want you to do for me—finish this first section. You knew Xavier Bentheim, you know Lisa better than perhaps anyone else, and you and Max were inseparable. I want you to finish writing the heart of the fictional universe for me, Till. I want you to set the cornerstone in place. The cornerstone of *Berlin Gothic*."

TODAY

"If free will doesn't exist—and I'm dead serious about this, Till—*if free will doesn't exist*, then what? What happens if it's an illusion that we are able to choose freely? What does it mean that we are only discovering that fact now, discovering that it's an illusion? What does it mean if we are only now ready to take that seriously? If today is the day when we are finally no longer able to ignore this discovery, Till? What if we can't continue as we always have before, because we suspect, we sense, we *know* we can't keep going on like that, that we have to react to this new knowledge? How are we supposed to act?"

The limousine took them south of the city, to a house on a lakeshore. Felix walked ahead of Till into the living room. Its broad windows looked out onto a clearing in the woods. A staff person brought coffee for them and they made themselves comfortable on sofas in front of an unlit fireplace.

"If I'm supposed to write for you, if I'm supposed to put the cornerstone in place," Till says, "then I have to know where you are going with the fictional universe."

Felix agrees. "It is very simple," he says, choosing his words with precision. "To understand what I'm planning, you only have to ask yourself one question: *What is it that we want to do?*"

Till's face betrays his confusion.

"That is the question that interests me," Felix adds, and sits up straighter on the sofa. "The question that I'm convinced we have to take seriously. So seriously that I refuse to take on anything else as long as this question remains unanswered. We have to think about what our goal is, our goal as . . well, as humanity, Till! We have to come to a decision about where we want to go, Till—and then, only then, can we take the first step. But where can we possibly go if there is no such thing as free will? Can you see just how much this question lies at the heart of what makes us human?"

Till crosses his legs, exhales. "So?" he asks. "Do you have an answer? To the question of where we want to go?"

Felix just looks at him for a few seconds, apparently thinking about how to put it. Finally, he replies, "Things keep going, right? It doesn't matter what we think or believe. The world keeps turning, the human race develops. Cities push higher into the sky. Countries sink into floods as the sea levels rise. Wars rage over bits of land. It is the whole that keeps on going, that keeps developing. The whole, of which you, I, all of us are just parts. The universe, Till. Creation. Being!"

Everything.

Bentheim talked about the same thing, Till thinks. When they were wandering through the passages under the city together.

"Everything, Till. Everything there is. There must have been a point where it all started. They call it the big bang. Have you ever thought about that?"

"About the big bang?"

"The moment the universe was created. What caused the big bang?" He gives Till a moment to fully digest the question before continuing. "If, by definition, the big bang is the moment of creation, and there was nothing before the big bang, what could have possibly caused it? Just trying to think about this kind of thing hurts the brain, doesn't it, Till?"

Yes.

"There's only one way I can get my head around it, Till."

Only one way.

"Everything there is," Felix says, "was created by the big bang, and the cause of the big bang was the Creator. Whatever we imagine such a Creator to be."

The cause of the big bang was the Creator.

"It's enough to know that the one attribute of the Creator is that He caused the big bang. *Being* is His opus." Felix's eyes are boring into Till's. "The Creator is the author of being, Till—like the author of a book is its creator."

Till's lips part slightly.

"Before the writer begins to write his book, it doesn't exist. But once he has begun, we are able to more or less enter the world of the book. We can experience the world that the author has made."

Yes, I know.

"The author of this book world that we are able to experience created it. And if we are aware of this process of creation, then we have been given a clear opportunity to discover more about the process by which the Creator must have brought *being* into being. Because the Creator created everything there is in the same way that an author creates everything that we experience when we read a book. Right?"

Yes.

"Now listen, Till. This is where the key mental step comes in. The step that shows us what it is we want to do once we've realized that free will does not exist."

Till hears the crackle in his throat as he swallows.

"Can you follow what I'm saying?"

"Yes."

"Do you want to know what the key mental step is?"

"Yes."

"This is it; in his book, a writer can make the characters he's created speculate about him. And in exactly the same way, the Creator gave us the possibility to speculate about God."

Till has the feeling that he is sinking into the sofa he is sitting on. But he clings to Felix's words as if they might stop him from disappearing between the cushions.

"And not just that. The author can not only have his characters speculate about their creator but also write himself into the book as a character!"

Yes?

"You probably don't get it right away, Till. But, for me, that's what it's all about. That's the point I will insist on as long as I can still breathe, the one thing that I will not let go." Felix's face tenses. "The point for which I will smash this world like a melon thrown from a tower."

Till envisions the melon's red flesh splattering across the asphalt.

"Ask yourself this question, Till," he hears Felix go on. "The relationship between the characters in a book and the author who invented and wrote them . . . isn't that exactly like the relationship between humans and God? Can you see the similarity between the two?"

"Yes, yes . . ."

"But if we have no free will, Till, if we are just parts of God's creation—can there be a more exalted, a bigger, a more beautiful calling for us than to meet God?"

Meet God. The words rumble in Till's consciousness like a dam has broken. He feels something when he hears them, but he cannot form an image in his mind.

"Do you understand? Meet God? It has never happened before, but why shouldn't it be possible? Only because it's never happened? There are many things that once never existed, but today they do! How do we know that it isn't possible to meet God? God the Creator, God who made everything! If we can only find the way! Can you imagine a more breathtaking goal?"

"No."

"Neither can I. And I am absolutely convinced that it's not just me who thinks this way. I'm not crazy. Objectively speaking, this is the most important, the most sublime goal that could ever be realized by a human being. That is the goal toward which we must work, Till."

It is the goal we must work toward once we've understood that free will is an illusion.

"And it isn't some crazy goal; it's not some carrot on a stick, forever out of reach! Even if that's what it seems like now."

We can meet God—and that's not a crazy goal?

"How?" Till asks.

Felix laughs and jumps up, stalking energetically through the room—talking all the while.

"How? That is exactly what I want to talk to you about. It's the goal I have dedicated my lifework and my resources to. It is the only goal worth working for, Till. It is the only goal left standing once it becomes clear that you have no free will. We lost sight of the goal when this unparalleled aberration of humanity took hold, when the free-will illusion started its victory parade . . . and humans began to glorify something that never even existed. The moment we understand that free will doesn't exist, the true goal reappears. The goal of meeting God."

"But *how?*" Till can't hold back any longer. "How are we supposed to do that?"

The enthusiasm that he has worked himself into with his words seems to spur Felix on. "It happens in two phases, Till. The first is to understand that we are living a lie when we believe in free will." He stops and fixes Till with his gaze. "It's not about chasing personal happiness or getting rich or sleeping with as many women as possible. Those are all aberrations caused by the fallacy of free will. Root them out! Done. But just because we have no free will does not mean that will itself doesn't exist. It isn't that everything is meaningless! This brings us to the second step: to understand that we are parts of a creation that could only have happened because the Creator wanted it that way. His will gives *being* its meaning! His will is to us like the will of the writer of a book is to his characters! Do you see what I mean?"

The will of the writer.

But Felix is still talking. "The characters in a book aren't free. Whatever they do, plan, or carry out, it all leads to whatever objective the author has in writing the book! So, what is God's intention with *being*, Till?"

How is he supposed to know that?

"What does a writer have in mind with his book, Till?"

"He wants to tell the reader a story."

Felix is silent for a moment, but watches Till keenly. Then he nods. "He wants to tell the reader a story—that's exactly it, my boy."

Till doesn't flinch from Felix's gaze.

"Exactly. That's our ace in the hole, that's the card we have to play to get to our goal."

"Our goal . . ." Till hardly dares speak the words, "of meeting God?"

Felix nods. "It's always the same train of thought, Till. God as the Creator of being—and human beings as His characters. And if we're wondering how we humans might be able to meet God, then we have to consider how the characters in a book might manage it, might manage to meet their writer. That's the key!"

Till narrows his eyes to slits.

"Can the characters in a book meet their writer? Can they leap out of the book, climb out from between the covers, clamber across the writer's desk, and up his sleeve until they're perching on his nose?"

"No."

Felix smiles. "No, they can't. But the writer can write himself into the book, right? And if he writes himself into the book, then the readers can meet him, can't they?" His face reveals the tension, the excitement, inside him. "Think back to the days of the Romans, right at the start of our calendar. Sandals, gladiators, crazy prophets . . . got that?"

"Okay . . ."

"Think about the story of Jesus. Let's forget the question of whether the story's true or not, or if Jesus is the son of God. Just think about the *story* that's being told. Didn't God, according to the *story*, write Himself into being just like a writer writing himself into his book? By making contact with the people as Jesus?"

In his mind's eye, Till sees the cross standing high on Golgotha. It's an image created from hundreds—thousands—of paintings, overlaying each other, all of them depicting the same motif.

Felix reaches out with both hands, as if to draw Till's attention back to him again. "As His creation, as His characters, we certainly can't climb out of the book He's written, can we, Till? But He can write His way *in* to us. Am I right?"

"Yes . . ."

"So, the question that we face has to be: How can we get Him to write Himself into being? How can the characters in a book get their author to write himself into their story?" He waits for Till to answer, but Till is still trying to get his head around what Felix is saying. "Right?" Felix suddenly bellows, and Till jumps in surprise.

"Sure . . . of course . . . that's . . . it's right . . ."

Meet God—the very thought makes Till feel like his heart is fluttering inside his chest.

"Now, Till," says Felix. "How could the characters in a book get their author to write himself into the book?" He pauses dramatically before continuing. "When we find an answer to this key question, we'll know how we can get God to step into his creation! When we find an answer to this question, we'll know what we have to do to reach our goal, what we have to do once we've realized that the belief in free will is a delusion!"

TODAY

The trees at the edge of the woods stand serenely, leaves rustling in the wind and glittering in the sunlight like a sequined dress.

But down below, among the trunks, over the soft forest floor . . . they come. The first of them. More follow behind. The swish of their feet through the fallen leaves mingles with the rustling of the leaves overhead. They say nothing. They exchange no looks. They don't stop. They don't run, they don't fall, they simply keep going—out of the twilight under the trees, out onto the bright clearing where the house stands. There is a group of three—maybe four—dozen figures; pale, emaciated, their faces are dull and apathetic.

Unswerving, they move toward the house. When they reach the glass fence that surrounds it, the hands they press to the glass leave steaming traces behind.

116

TODAY

"If God made the world like a writer creates the world of his story—if we assume for a moment that God is a God of creation, as people have thought for thousands of years, regardless of the language they use to talk or think about Him—then we've got a toehold on understanding the will behind His creation of *being*."

The hidden will.

"We have to ask ourselves one question: Why does the writer write his book? The answer to that gives us a clue to the question: Why did God create being?"

"He wants to tell a story to the reader."

"Exactly! He wants to tell a story to the reader. Which leads us to a question that takes us an important step further in our own undertaking: If God is the author of being—who is His reader?"

Till feels a smile forming. It was a question that had never occurred to him.

"For me, this is a crucial question, incredibly important. We begin to understand something about ourselves once we understand God to be our author. But how are we supposed to imagine this author, this creator, without being able to talk to someone able to perceive his work?"

"We can't."

"That's the point! We might as well think that God created His work for himself just to see how it turned out. But this still means there has to be someone to read or perceive the work, right?"

Till rubs at his temples. But he's thinking *yes*.

Felix takes a step in Till's direction. He stands directly in front of him. "We've said that we humans are God's characters. Maybe He didn't exactly plan or design us, but He created the *being* that we are part of. Now think about who God created His work for. God must have wanted to have a particular effect on the one who was supposed to perceive that work in the same way that a writer wants his book to affect the reader in a particular way. Maybe to make him think, or to frighten him, or simply to make the book something pleasing, right?"

"Yeah, sure, but—"

"So, shouldn't it be possible for us, as God's characters, to act in such a way that God has to write Himself into His book, into being, in order to please the one who reads His work?"

Till inhales sharply, holds his breath. He feels suddenly that they have reached the heart of what Felix has been trying to tell him.

"This is the God machine," Felix nearly shouts. "This is how it works! Can't you see the incredible power of that?"

Till feels all the notions, the concepts, the terminology, the understanding—everything he took for granted—all of it pouring out of him, receding like the turning of the tide.

"We are God's characters—He is our author. But it depends entirely on us, Till, to determine how exciting God's work is for its readers—whoever they may be. It depends on humans—who are the characters! God's 'book' can be exciting or not. It all depends on what we do."

"Yes . . . yes . . ."

"What do we want to achieve?"

"We want to meet Him."

"Exactly. But as His characters we can't get out of the book, out of being. But He can reveal Himself to us, He can write Himself into the book. By recognizing us as His characters. And when He does this, we gain power over Him, Till. We gain power over God! The first time this notion entered my head, it stuck there, and I couldn't sleep for three weeks."

Power over our Creator?

"By creating His work, God was pursuing a goal. He wants His work to please someone, even if that someone is only Himself. So this gives us two possibilities: Either God's work achieves His objective, meaning it is as He would like it to be, as good as a book is that pleases its reader. Or His work does not achieve its objective. It's as bad as a book that the reader doesn't like. But as characters, we determine what the work is like, how the story goes—by the way we act. This gives us the power to influence whether God achieves His goal or not!"

Felix has to stop to catch his breath. Till can see that he has reached the core of his thinking.

"This puts something in our hand that we can use to force Him to reveal Himself to us. If we do things that make it so His work can only succeed if He writes Himself into the story, then He'll do it. Because He wants His work to achieve its objective."

The God machine.

"It's the God machine, Till. Do you see what I'm saying?"

Yes.

"And throughout all of it," Felix is nearly bubbling over with words, "we have no free will. Everything that I'm trying to explain here is how we *have* to act. This may be just a glimpse into the future. Maybe I'm just the first to express it. But it is easiest to understand if I say how we're supposed to act, how we have to behave to make God write Himself into being, so that being—as a performance, if you like—pleases God Himself . . . or whomever!"

Felix's agitation has infected Till.

"By putting everything, as God's characters, into making God reveal Himself, then, for the 'readers' of *being*, things will get boring if God does not reveal Himself. Can you see that? As far as I know, no one has ever described it like this, Till, but it's clear—it's the laws of dramaturgy that will reveal God to us in the end. In all these millennia, no one thought of this! But it's time—it's time to see things as they are!"

He doesn't wait for Till to respond. He starts pacing the room again. "Picture this: human beings all stand and stare at one spot and wait for Him to appear there. All of us, standing silently, waiting, looking at this place." Felix stops pacing, his eyes on Till again as if Till's seat is the spot he's talking about. "Boring to the bone to watch, right? So, God's work is boring. Then there's only one thing left for Him to do: appear exactly at the spot where all of us are staring! And that is why I need the fictional universe! That's the hidden meaning!"

Till's heart is pounding. This is what it's always been about for Felix—what he was hinting at in countless conversations that Till and Max puzzled over as kids. It's what Felix and Bentheim were cooking up the whole time. All along, they wanted to force the Revelation!

"We get the people addicted, Till. We give them a fictional universe from which they can never escape. They lose themselves in it because they find everything they want in there, everything they are hungry for. We give them love, sex, friendship, horror, fear, hope, fulfillment, meaning, and once they lose themselves in the fictional universe, we never let them go. And then we make them see that, together, they will constitute a God machine if all of them wait for God at a particular place. We align the people, Till. We coordinate their feelings, their thoughts, their wishes, their cravings, and, as God's characters, we get them to force God's Revelation! The fictional universe is the God machine. As human beings, we will be doing no more than bringing God's will to completion, the will He has already put in place in His creation. He wants to reveal Himself—and I, you, we, *we* are carrying out His will!"

TODAY

The first of them have started climbing the glass fence. They climb onto the shoulders of the others and pull themselves up the glass. But it is smooth and a coil of barbed wire spirals along its top.

Some fall. Others press their noses flat to the glass and stare at the house set in the clearing no more than two hundred yards beyond. Behind its windows are two men. One of them is small and wiry and has his eyes fixed on the other, who is younger and looking up at the first man. The two men are so absorbed in their conversation that they notice nothing of what is going on outside.

TODAY

"You must understand that I don't want to impose my will on the Creator, Till. It's *crucial* you understand that. It's rather that I . . . that we, if you decide to help me . . . are more like chosen ones, the ones who make the will of God a reality."

Felix flops into an armchair. He seems drained—somehow hollowed out—by his speech.

Could it be? Till's head is spinning. *Could it be that Felix is right? That the God machine works?*

"In all of human history, we have never been closer to the Revelation of God than we are today, Till. I'd stake my life on that. I'm not just some bad guy forcing my sick, overinflated will on the world. I'm not the Joker from Batman, Till. I want to save the world from the diseased instincts of the truly evil. It's not *my* will that I want, it's the will of God! And those who oppose the will of God are setting themselves against the *being* taking place around them."

He sinks back in his chair. "If you resist, you are the villain, Till. If you don't help me, you become the bad guy."

Till also feels completely drained. He's glad that Felix has stopped talking.

They sit in silence for a while.

"So, I'm supposed to write the fictional universe for you," Till finally says, trying to pick up the thread again. "I'm supposed to write it in a way that makes people more and more addicted to this universe, more and more dependent on it, obsessed with it, wanting it more and more, wanting to be part of it . . ."

"That's why I set the rats on you, Till. I know you're a good writer. I've put a lot into trying to make you the best."

"Why me, Felix?" *Am I really the right one to be working on something this big?* "Why have you put so much into *me*?"

"I need the best, Till. And I know you can be that."

"But how, Felix? How do you know that?"

Felix's eyes bore into his.

TODAY

Claire shudders. When she thought about Butz it was like being stabbed.

Who is this? This man whose arms she is lying in on the sidewalk? Where is Butz?

She feels the way the man's arms tighten around her, and the memories come pouring back.

Frederik . . . it is Frederik.

She is lying in his arms on the sidewalk. In front of her, for miles and miles, stretch identical apartment blocks from another era. A monumental street, looking more like Moscow than Berlin.

"Better?" He looks at her. "I'm taking you to the hospital, Claire. But you have to let me carry you. You're not well."

She looks at his lips. Feels repelled. She knows she isn't well.

Take him with you, she hears herself whispering, inside. Then you'll be together. Then you won't be alone anymore, Claire. And it's not so bad, is it? The colors! That orange, that green . . . remember the green you saw? Isn't it worth it? Maybe he'd like to see that too!

She curls up in Frederik's arms, turns her face up to his, and kisses him. She sees again the way he softens when she looks at him—when suddenly, in front of them, the slabs of the sidewalk open up.

The concrete plates—they must weigh tons—are hurled high in the air, as though they've been hit by a battering ram from below. Claire watches them turning in the air in slow motion, sees them hit the ground and break apart with a loud crack. Pieces of concrete spray in all directions, and she throws one arm in front of her eyes to protect herself.

But the noise continues. From beneath her elbow, she sees the street before her tear open from one side to the other. Two hundred yards—maybe three hundred—to the apartment blocks on the other side.

The things surge up, pouring out of the gap, crawling over one another. Their faces are strangely formed, as if they are overgrown with muscle. They well up from the newly formed crevasse like blood from a fresh wound.

Claire feels her lips separate from Frederik's. In her fright, she is clinging to him, melting into him in fear.

Her eyes follow the figures streaming out onto the street like lava from a volcano. Or is this only a fever dream?

She feels how Frederik's fingers seem to grow, to lengthen, even as the wave of creatures pours toward Alexanderplatz, where the tower juts high into the evening's dark-violet sky.

TODAY

"The light one. Yes, the raincoat." Lisa reaches for the trench coat that the waitress hands her, knocks the heavy curtain at the restaurant entrance aside, jerks open the glass door, and steps out into the open air.

She takes a deep breath.

The little street outside is buzzing with activity. Pedestrians dodge around her, and the street is backed up with cars that can't get around a double-parked delivery van. In the distance, she can hear the traffic on the main road.

When we slept together two years ago, I had to think of Nina or Irina just to do it.

She is moving then, stumbling in the direction of Friedrichstrasse. Everything around her seems to have come crashing down. It's not a city around her—it's a black morass. Her life is a mire.

She sees Till's eyes in her mind's eye. *I wanted to love you, Lisa—but I never really did.*

Her shoulders stiffen to concrete.

He never loved her? Till, whom she has known since she was eleven?

No. He told her that just now. That he wanted to love her, but couldn't.

Like a wounded animal, she hurries on. A creeping feeling begins to insinuate itself in her, a feeling she had never before believed could be true. Has she suppressed the same feelings about Till? That she never really loved him either, only wanted to? Is that why she went back to Felix again just six weeks earlier? Had Till and she only wished they loved each other? In reality, was she drawn to a man like Felix, and Till to girls like Irina and Nina?

Or could there be another reason for Till's rejection . . . something other than not loving her?

But what? Why would he lie to her about this? And if he is lying, is it worth wasting her thoughts on him?

"I told them it was Konstantin Butz. That I was there when it happened and saw him shoot through the windshield. I told them there was nothing to look for and they didn't have to tape off the place. All they had to do was ask their buddy Konstantin Butz."

"And?"

"They said they'd already spoken to him. It was self-defense. Henning had threatened Butz's life and he had to defend himself."

"And is that true?"

Betty stares straight ahead while she steers through the traffic. Lisa is not sure if Betty is really in any condition to drive, but at least it seems to distract her and calm her down.

Lisa had tried to reach Claire first, but her phone was turned off, so she called Betty, who came into the city to pick Lisa up. It was only when Lisa climbed into the passenger seat that she discovered what had happened. Betty, her face strangely stiff, told Lisa everything. It was like she had switched to autopilot as some sort of mechanism to protect herself from losing it completely.

Lisa turns and looks out the side window. Passersby on the sidewalks, drivers in other cars, people waiting at traffic lights or gazing at the screens on their telephones.

The cloud rising around the base of the tower on Alexanderplatz. What happened at Betty's house. What Till told her in the restaurant.

What the hell is going on?

For a moment, Lisa has the strange impression of the city as a sleeping tiger on the verge of waking up and attacking her. But she can see none of this in the people passing by outside her window. No one is screaming, no one is waving their arms around, no one is running around in the street. At first glance, everyone looks like they always have. But . . . that man, back there, leaning forward and charging ahead? And the woman he rushes past, speaking into her phone, screening her mouth with her hand?

Or is it the sound of the jackhammers, the arc welders, the construction workers, tearing up the street in three different places that is making her so nervous? Is it the honking of horns, the blinking traffic lights, the distant whine of a siren, the way a cyclist suddenly flashes past her window?

"It's everywhere . . ."

"What?" Lisa jumps a little and looks at Betty. *Did she say something?*

"Butz . . . what happened to Henning . . . all this craziness . . . can't you feel it?" Betty has not taken her eyes off the road.

Oh, yes, Lisa can feel it too. Or can she? Isn't everything like it always is—everything business as usual?

"Henning suspected something like this. He said something was going to happen."

"Really?" Lisa turns and looks straight ahead.

The traffic has stopped. A man in a fluorescent police vest is blocking the street. They can't go straight. One driver has already begun to turn around. Betty eases the car to a stop.

"Henning couldn't talk to me about it," Betty says. "But Felix seemed to know that something was coming."

Felix?

The traffic has come to a standstill. Drivers are getting restless, honking their horns. The officer on the street gestures to a patrol car at the side of the road, signaling them to block the street with their car.

"So, what did Henning say?"

Betty's blue eyes look over at her. To Lisa, her little sister looks exactly like she did two years earlier. Lisa automatically thinks of talking to her sister just before her wedding, in the back room at the church. She remembers how Betty had said that she would prefer to marry someone like Felix.

"What did Henning say, Betty?"

"Felix is planning something . . ." She breaks off. "I don't know what it is. But Henning said things were completely out of control. That Felix had gone way too far." Betty's fingers are clawed around the steering wheel, and she is leaning a long way forward. "I . . . I'm scared, Lisa. I don't know what I'm supposed to do—" she turns to her sister. "Do you remember, just before I got married? I . . . I didn't want to marry him, Lisa. But you persuaded me. You told me I should do it."

"Yes . . . yes, but—"

"I thought I could rely on Henning, that he'd make sure that nothing bad happened—"

A loud horn cuts through Lisa's thoughts. She turns forward again. The car in front of them is pulling away, the traffic jam dissolving.

"Drive!"

But Betty just clings to the steering wheel.

"Drive, Betty! Drive, for God's sake. Felix said he'd be at his house in the south this afternoon. That's where we're going! We have to talk to him. Henning's dead. Don't you get it? You're not imagining anything! It's not something that'll go away if we just wait long enough. Something's going on—and Felix knows what it is!"

TODAY

The path through the forest looks familiar.

Till stops and looks around. The house where he'd been talking to Felix is out of sight. He's been walking for twenty minutes—excited, confused by what Felix has told him. He has to get some distance. Be by himself. Calm down. But it isn't working. There's a buzz in the air . . .

Till keeps walking.

The wind hisses through the treetops overhead. Hasn't he walked down this path before, back when he was a boy? Till had not taken notice of the route as he drove to the estate with Felix, but they'd been heading south.

And suddenly, he knows.

Instinctively, he starts to trot, then faster, stumbling over the leafy ground. He sees a low fence between the trees, runs along it to the entrance . . .

Many of the graves lie outside the fence line. Maybe fifty or sixty altogether. But Till knows one of them all too well. It's the second time in two days that he's been to a cemetery. But this is not where Max is buried. This is the cemetery where they buried his brother. His real brother. Armin.

He sees the headstone in the last row, just in front of the wall that forms the rear boundary of the small graveyard in the middle of the forest. The grave has not been tended for a long time. A small pine tree has taken root there, and a tarnished vase stands empty on a flat stone. Grass has grown over it, surrounding the dark headstone, and the stalks move slightly in the rising breeze.

"Armin Anschütz" is written on the headstone.

He was sixteen years old.

Till doesn't feel his knees sink into the soft earth covering the grave. How long since he last came here? Ten years? Twelve?

"Armin." And all the strain, the fatigue, of the last hours comes crashing down on him.

TODAY

Till doesn't know how long he's been sitting like that, there on the moist grass covering the grave, when his head finally starts to clear. He's been staring at the ground, seeing but not seeing the grass, the vase, the stone. He feels the moisture that has soaked through his pants, but he does not stand.

The images of the last day and night are tangled together in his mind, a stream of disconnected scraps. He sees the naked woman suspended from the ceiling down below the city, her body turning slowly in the hot air. He sees Lisa standing next to him in the restaurant, Felix with him on the roof.

And he sees the graves of Armin and Max. Sees Max laughing with him in the Bentheim house, sees them running along the hallway to the foyer, and then up the stairs to the top floor. He sees himself as a boy, sitting at the breakfast table with Max, Lisa, Betty, Claire, and their parents, sees Bentheim talking to his son. He sees himself coming back to Berlin for Betty's wedding, sees himself talking to Max and Henning and all the others at Irina's party. And sitting in front of the café with Lisa, telling her about the thesis he'd been writing in Toronto two years earlier.

How could everything have gone so incredibly wrong? When did he lose track of his own life? When did he lose Max? Was their fight the moment when his own life went off the rails? Or was it earlier? Back when he slammed that door on Bentheim, deep beneath the city? Slowly, slowly, the memories seep through; Till's conscious mind springs restlessly from one to the next.

Wasn't it Max's hatred of his father that drove Till to slam that door? But the hate . . .

Till buries his face in his hands.

Max's hatred of his father—wasn't it Till who fanned the flames, who really got it burning? Hadn't Bentheim shown that he had more confidence in Till, that he trusted him more than Max—his own son?!

And now Felix wanted him to write the fictional universe, the universe that Max's father was the first to sketch, the universe Bentheim had told him about before they'd gone down into the passageways under the city.

Berlin Gothic.

A story about disease, animal testing, Haiti—a story about an invasion.

Access, zone, core. Till hears Max saying the words. They were sitting in the gambling den behind the stage where the girls were dressed in animal costumes, and Max told him about what he'd uncovered in his father's boxes. Just like Max had shown him the notebook twelve years earlier, the one he'd stumbled across in the basement of the guesthouse in the garden. The book with the notes of the man who'd traveled to Haiti with his sick wife, hoping to find a cure . . .

Berlin Gothic.

A story about a spreading contagion.

It's like a fist of steel suddenly punching Till in the ribs. He gasps for air, feels his forehead clammy with sweat.

The unrest hanging over the city—Berlin seems to be shivering . . .

But it's not the start of spring, not some change in the weather. It's something else. Something that leaps out at you as you walk through the streets, something you feel you can reach out and grasp.

Earlier, just as he was leaving Felix's house, he passed the kitchen, where a radio was playing. The announcer was saying that cases of rabies were being reported and spreading rapidly. The sick were being kept together in one hospital in the north, the voice on the radio said, but no one knew for sure if that would be precaution enough to stop the disease from spreading.

Dizziness, hallucinations, sleeplessness. Delirium. An infection of the brain, a virus that spreads through the spinal cord until it reaches the brain.

A virus that attacks the brain, robbing those afflicted of their self-control.

A coincidence? Was this just some weird coincidence?

That now, *right now*, with Felix banking everything on making his plans a reality, putting all his power into pushing ahead the work on the fictional universe, that a virus was running rampant and causing events in the fictional universe to happen in real life?

Never! There's no way that it's just chance!

Berlin Gothic was the story of a disease that turns human beings into creatures with no will of their own. Bentheim had told Till that much himself. *Berlin Gothic* was the story that Bentheim told Till about in the garden.

And what was happening now in Berlin—the spread of the virus—was exactly like the story. It was Bentheim's story coming true.

The story that formed the base of Felix's fictional universe.

No . . . it was no coincidence!

When Till had heard the voice on the radio, he knew it couldn't just be chance. He returned to the living room and confronted Felix.

It's exactly what Bentheim was talking about, Till said. This was exactly why Bentheim chose to write a story about an epidemic that dissolved human will: he wanted to write about a world where the illusion of free will no longer dominate!

Felix had conceded that Till was right, that was the reason he was interested in Bentheim's manuscript. *Berlin Gothic* was ideal for what Felix had in mind. But the fact that rabies was spreading in real life . . . that had nothing to do with Felix. How could it? No! Till had met that particular nutcase himself—

Which nutcase?

Quentin! Quentin! The same Quentin who argued at Irina's party two years before that if the illusion of freedom was stripped away, all that was left was the descent into evil. And Quentin had been following that course ever since, like a man possessed. But Felix had never shared that crazy obsession. For Felix, it wasn't about Quentin's descent. It was about the God machine.

Till lies on his belly on his brother's grave, his face pressed against the back of his hands.

Quentin. It was Quentin who'd spread the disease, the culmination of his descent into evil. But Felix knew about it. He conceded that much. He knew about it, and perhaps he could have stopped Quentin. But he didn't.

And why not?

Because the spreading disease was exactly what Felix needed for what he was planning. Because it meant the people would be more strongly drawn to his fictional universe. When it turned out that what was happening had already been written in the universe, readers would be even more fixated on it!

Felix also admitted that he didn't just let it happen. He did everything he could to block anyone trying to stop the infection from spreading. He'd sent someone after the girlfriend of the detective in charge of probing the first deaths—Claire. He'd had bodies disposed of before the cause of death could be determined—all to give the disease as much time to spread as possible. And to hinder the investigation, to stop the detective from finding out what the real reason for the deaths was . . .

Till feels himself choking, like he's gagging on a chunk of bread stuck halfway down his throat.

Quentin had triggered what was plaguing the city. The tribes Till had encountered beneath the city, Quentin had spread the virus through them. It was just a question of time before they overran everything.

Berlin is going under, something whispers inside Till. *The people will be buried beneath the rubble in the hundreds of thousands. This city is cursed—it's been destroyed before, and now it's happening again.*

Suddenly, he thinks he hears something.

Is that it? The screaming, the raging of the masses? The crumbling, crashing walls?

The city is going under, he hears in his head. *And you're to blame.* He presses his hands over his ears, but he can't shut out the voices.

What drove Quentin to go so far? Till remembers the way Max repeatedly mocked Quentin. But where did the animosity that burned in Max—and that he turned on Quentin—come from? The animosity with which he derided Quentin at Irina's place and outside the club?

It came from the fact that ever since Till arrived in the Bentheim family, Max had given up any hope of ever living up to his father's demands!

Max couldn't stand his father's contempt. His despair grew as he saw how his father respected Till, listened to Till, encouraged

Till—and even asked him to look after Max! That was where the bitterness had its root, and that's what made him turn his rage remorselessly against anyone that crossed him. And against Quentin and himself—until he was destroyed.

The memories were still fresh in Till's mind. The way Max ridiculed Quentin at Irina's place in front of everyone. Because his father wanted another boy to be his son, he took all the self-loathing he felt and dumped it on Quentin. He hit him with all the cruelty, all the callousness he could muster. He robbed him of any shred of self-respect as surely as the last shred of Max's was snatched away the moment Till showed up.

It was Quentin who released the chaos, the disease, the despair, the death on Berlin.

Quentin.

But it all came back to Till. He was responsible for what happened to Max. And for what Max did to Quentin.

And if it's true? If what Felix secretly hopes is true? What then? What if the downfall of the city speeds the creation of the God machine?

TODAY

Till gets to his feet and knocks the dirt from his knees.

Nothing to hear but the rustle of the leaves overhead.

His brother's been dead for twelve years. "See you," Till murmurs. He turns away and makes his way slowly between the gravestones toward the exit. He tips his head back automatically—he can hear something approaching.

A moment later, it's deafening. A roar like a mountain crashing down on top of him. Then Till sees them through the crown of branches. Helicopters. First one. Then a swarm of them.

Till stumbles out of the cemetery to the clearing at the entrance.

The rotor blades flicker in the sunlight like the wings of giant robotic dragonflies. They fly low over the clearing and away in the direction of the city center, six or seven of them.

Till watches them until they are beyond the trees and out of sight.

What the hell is happening in Berlin? Is the plague spreading faster than anyone imagined? Are they being overrun? Is it like a storm surge that will swallow the city in a matter of weeks, days—hours?

He runs back along the path through the forest.

Is he really to blame for what's happening? His arrival at the Bentheim's house set it all in motion. But is Max at fault for being the kind of person he was? Did he have the chance to be anyone else? Is Till to blame for Bentheim putting him ahead of his own son? Is Quentin to blame for his slide into evil?

Is anyone to blame for anything? Or is it that everyone is innocent of the things they do? How can anyone be guilty of *anything*? Suddenly—and maybe for the first time—Till no longer understands what the word *guilt* means. Could Felix be right in saying there's no such thing as guilt? That one is the way one is, and one does what one does? With his arrival at the Bentheim's house, Till was certainly the cause of what happened, but was he to blame for that?

To avoid stumbling, he looks down. Steps over a root.

And doesn't that mean that Felix is right to push ahead with his God machine project with all the resources at his disposal? Isn't he right in using Quentin's insanity to set his machine in motion? And doesn't Till then have to do everything he can in the hope that one day, in the far-distant future, the machine achieves its goal?

TODAY

When Lisa and Betty reach the Bundesautobahn, it feels like all the mayhem back in Mitte simply falls away. The freeway is so empty it's almost spooky, and Betty's car hums smoothly along the six-lane autobahn, heading south. At the Funkturm, Betty swings right, curving onto the AVUS, and keeps going.

"Have they stopped?"

Lisa, who has stretched herself out in the passenger seat, now follows Betty's gaze ahead. They are rapidly drawing nearer to a clutch of cars on the roadway ahead.

"Looks like it."

Betty eases off the accelerator.

Some of the cars are actually sideways, and farther ahead a delivery van seems to be completely turned around.

"Careful!" Lisa lays one hand on her sister's arm.

It's an accident. A couple dozen vehicles are involved, and everything about it tells Lisa that the police and ambulances should have been there long ago. But there's no one at the scene at all. Just the cars, strewn across the roadway.

"Just drive through," Lisa murmurs. The cars, the silence, the strange lifelessness of the accident scene . . . it's making her uneasy.

Betty turns the steering wheel, sliding the car past the first vehicles standing there, doors hanging open, scraped and dented sheet metal, oil leaking onto the asphalt. Lisa sees a BMW ahead. There is something dark sticking to the steering wheel, as if the driver's head slammed into it at the moment of collision and split open.

"Dead end." Betty nods ahead through the windscreen.

Two cars are so wedged together that they can't squeeze past.

"Are they crazy? This should be sealed off." Lisa sits forward in her seat and looks out through the passenger-side window.

They have pulled up in the middle of the knot of vehicles, some of which are seriously damaged. The trees of the Grunewald, stretching along both sides of the AVUS, are no more than twenty yards away.

Betty has opened her door. Lisa turns to her. "Stay here. I'll take care of it." She opens her own door and climbs out.

Outside, it's sunny, agreeably warm, and the air carries the pollen and scents of the forest around them.

Lisa nods encouragingly through the windshield to Betty. Then she approaches the two cars blocking their path. The door of the BMW, which has rammed into the side of the car in front of it, hangs ajar. Lisa pulls it open.

She raises her arm instinctively and buries her nose in the crook of her elbow. A reek of disinfectant and iron hits her almost physically from inside the car.

"Everything okay?"

Without turning around, Lisa signals to her sister with her hand: *Sure, sure. No worries.*

She takes a deep breath and leans inside, reaching for the steering wheel. It turns easily, and the key is still in the ignition. Lisa turns the steering wheel so that the car will roll out of their path, then braces herself against the doorframe and tries to push the car backward.

It doesn't move.

She jams her sneakers into the asphalt and throws all her weight into it. A grating noise, then the car starts to roll.

Well, what do you know!

Now that it's moving, it's easier. The BMW rolls slowly into the car behind it with a dull crunch.

That should get them a little farther. Perhaps it's enough to get them all the way through. Lisa stands on tiptoe, looking over the cars toward the open autobahn at the far end of the accident scene—and stops short.

Just past the last car, the autobahn goes into a curve, half hidden by a truck and trailer rig. Lisa can see into the gap between the truck and the trailer and—what is that? Is something moving down there?

She glances back at Betty, who is looking questioningly at Lisa through the side window. Lisa signals to her to wait.

At the end of the trailer, a figure has appeared. Big, awkward, a silhouette, but even from this distance it looks dirty, unkempt. One figure, and behind it three more, no, thirty more now, all as vague and absent as the first, lurching and trudging their way along the autobahn, as if about to fall over their own feet with every step. But they don't. They keep on coming.

Straight toward Lisa.

Lisa turns to Betty. She waves her hands at her sister: *DOWN! GET OUT OF SIGHT!*

She can't shout out, she can't run to her sister. She can only do it with hand signals, or those things will see them both.

Betty understands. Her head disappears, and a moment later her car looks like just another one of the empty ones involved in the accident.

Lisa drops onto the asphalt. Crawling into the BMW is out of the question; the dark crust on the steering wheel is too horrible. She pushes herself across the rough tarmac and squeezes under the car, between the tires on one side, lying there on her stomach so she can see out between the front wheels.

The feet of the things—a cohort of ragged shoes, destroyed pumps, mud-crusted sneakers, worn-out slippers—barely clear the ground, more dragged than lifted. Looking beneath three cars, Lisa can see the shoes shuffling in her direction. She can already hear the sound of it, the slow, heavy noise of the soles mixing with the twittering of birds off in the trees.

And when they reach her?

Lisa holds her breath.

Schschsch schschsch rrrr rrrr hchchcrr hchchcrr . . .

The feet, the legs of jeans, the boots, and the bare and sandaled ankles pass Lisa and the tires surrounding her. If she stretched out her hand, she could touch the filthy pants, the shredded socks lumbering past . . .

None of them says anything, but Lisa can hear the figures breathing. She feels her heart beating in her throat, and the sweat gathering on the asphalt beneath the palms of her hands, trickling down the skin under her arms, down her back.

Schschsch schschsch rrrr rrrr hchchcrr hchchcrr . . .

Then the last pair of shoes passes by and the sounds recede. Cautiously, Lisa turns her head to see which way they are lumbering. From beneath the chassis of the car, she can see the collection of shoes and legs moving off, heading toward the city. They must be at Betty's car now—but she can't move, not yet!

Schschsch schschsch rrrr rrrr hchchcrr hchchcrr . . .

The dragging, shuffling, scraping, trudging moves away. The buzzing in Lisa's ears fades.

Iiiiep iiiiep iiiiep . . .

What's that?

A low squeaking sound has mixed with the muffled, now distant, footfalls. An even, rhythmic squeaking noise.

Iiiiep iiiiep iiiiep . . .

Lisa pushes herself silently out from beneath the BMW and raises herself onto her knees on the asphalt. She looks back and can still see the backs of the creatures. They have left the cars behind and lurch on, heading into Berlin. She looks at the car where Betty has hidden herself.

Iiiiep iiiiep iiiiep . . .

Is it moving? Betty's car?

Now Lisa can see it clearly. Betty's car is rocking, rocking lightly from side to side!

Ducking low, she runs to the car. The back door—it wasn't open a minute ago, was it?

"Betty." Lisa just whispers the name, but the whisper sounds to her like a scream. Then she's at the door, looking in.

She can't believe what she sees.

"What . . . ?"

Her sister is crouched on the backseat, her forearms propped on the headrest in front, her legs folded under her. Her face is turned toward Lisa, her head tilted back, her eyes no more than slits. But her mouth is open. Behind her towers one of the figures, inconceivably huge. And the gurgle coming from its mouth mixes with the whimper that comes high and clear from Betty.

Frozen at the sight of the two of them like that, wedged together, Lisa looks at the creature's hand. In one motion it snaps the elastic and tears away the panties stretched tight across Betty's plump thighs. She can only stare at Betty's T-shirt, which it pushes up with huge paws before grabbing her sister's hips and pulling her hungrily, hard, onto it. So hard that Betty's breath is forced out of her, her eyes squeeze shut, and she uses her hands to push herself down onto the backseat, impaling herself on it as far as she possibly can.

Lisa realizes that her breath is coming in gasps, that she wants to throw herself at the two of them, to stop this from happening—but she can't move.

Her arms collide with something, suddenly, and she is awake, distraught, her face covered with a fine film of sweat.

"What . . . ?"

They are on a road in a forest—trees all around! Lisa's head lolls, her eyes sticky with sleep, still drowsy.

Betty is beside her. At the wheel. Flashes a quick smile at her, and then concentrates on the road ahead.

"We're nearly there. You must be so exhausted."

Lisa straightens up.

She fell asleep! In the passenger seat, while Betty was driving.

"See? There's the gate. We're in luck, it's open."

The gate to Felix's country estate.

TODAY

Till's eyes fly across the text.

Berlin Gothic.

He is sitting in the room that Felix has set up for him in the house. In it, he has stored all of the fictional universe produced so far. Some of it from Xavier Bentheim himself, some of it from Felix's employees. All of it available on the huge monitor on the table in the middle of the room.

Infection.

Access.

Zone.

Core.

The words that Max had used back then, in the gambling den at the theater, when Till had talked to him about the fictional universe of Felix and Max's father, it all comes back to Till.

Access—that was the start of it all; Max had told him that. In the first part, what Bentheim had called *Access*, a boy gets caught up in life-changing events, yes . . .

The second part was *Zone.* In the *Zone,* the boy discovers how far the infection has already spread.

And in *Core*? In *Core*, the boy had worked his way through the *Zone* and into the *Core* in order to find out who was controlling everything!

Spellbound, Till clicks through the files. Is there a connection between the rabies outbreak spreading in the city, and the infection in the fictional universe, in *Berlin Gothic*?

Forget the subplots—they're of no interest—get past the secondary settings. He ignores the fringes of the fictional universe, the spin-offs written for teenagers, horror freaks, sex addicts, or whomever. The main thread, that's what's important. The story that Xavier Bentheim himself put into words. The story of the epidemic.

As Till reads feverishly through the swathes of text, it feels like a screw is being turned deeper and deeper into his head.

Yes, there's a disease in the book. And a circle of friends in Berlin, and a writer of puzzling manuscripts. There's a Max in the book, a Quentin, a Malte, a Lisa, and . . .

Reading it makes his guts physically hurt.

A Till.

Berlin Gothic.

A Till, who runs away from a home for children and finds refuge with a family—the Bentheim family—where he makes friends with Max, the only son, and falls in love with Max's sister, Lisa.

Till's hand sends the mouse skimming across the desk as he scans through the files, the extracts, the overviews and summaries. He jumps from paragraph to section, from chapter to volume, from thread to thread. His brain processes names, dates, and places. He skims dialogue, registers key words. He's beyond the passages that Bentheim himself wrote and is deep into the newer parts of *Berlin Gothic*, following the story of the virus.

In the book, too, Till is to blame for Quentin releasing the disease. Guilty and innocent at the same time. Is it Till's fault if Max can't come to terms with playing second fiddle to him? No!

But it's his arrival in the Bentheim household . . . Yes! Of course! And it also happens in *Berlin Gothic*.

". . . and yet, his appearance in the Bentheim house is what finally leads—even if indirectly—to the outbreak of the disease."

The type blurs before Till's eyes. Anyone reading the story would have to admit it—but . . . isn't it true that *Berlin Gothic* actually delivers exactly what Felix expects of the fictional universe? That it destroys the illusion of free will?

Till—the Till in *Berlin Gothic*—can't do anything to stop things developing the way they do. In the end, he's the one who sets everything in motion, but it all happens without his direction. He can't choose *not* to be superior to Max. Till is an affront to Max by virtue of his very existence. He can't do anything to not be guilty!

Can he?

No, comes the scream from inside Till, the Till sitting at the desk. *It's not true that I just imagine I'm free! Max was the one who was right—not Felix! I won't let Felix confuse me. Max is the only one who did the right thing! He did everything he possibly could; he used all the strength he had to defend himself from Felix's ideas about the illusion of free will. He stuck to his belief that he was free. Even if it led Max to hell in Riga, he was right to insist on his freedom. And he was right to insist on it, because it's the most valuable thing we have!*

Till's eyes drift back to the screen in front of him.

I don't care what the Till in the book thinks—I won't give up my freedom! he thinks.

Or . . .

And Till feels a new thought creeping up on him.

Or is what I'm thinking now already written somewhere in this book?

Then . . .

He feels his chest constricting.

Then he isn't free—and it makes no difference how hard he fights it.

Suddenly, Till feels his eyes closing and his thoughts turn *upward*—he turns to the one who must be writing him, if he is being written.

Lead me on the true path.

He listens in the blackness spreading before his closed eyes, listens in the infinite, flickering dark points that make up the blackness.

Can you hear me?

Yes. I hear you, Till.

Till feels the hairs on his arms stand on end.

Are you the one writing me?

Yes.

Then lead me on the true path. The words wander like ghosts through Till's mind, without him having to seek them out.

Did you understand the God machine?

Till swallows. *That people are supposed to focus entirely on the fictional universe?*

Some already are.

They're already reading Berlin Gothic?

Yes, Till. They want to know if you and Lisa get together. They want to know if the city gets destroyed. That's the point of the city's destruction, Till—the people gaze into the universe and wonder if the city will be saved.

Till's forehead creases with concentration.

*Do you see how the one for whom the fictional universe—*Berlin Gothic*—was created is watching you even as you sit there, listening to something?*

Till hardly dares to draw breath.

The Berlin Gothic *reader asks me what's happening with your character, this Till. He isn't doing anything anymore, the reader tells me. He's just waiting. Till is waiting for you to do something—and the reader means* me, Till.

Till waits, listens, his eyes shut.

Can you hear me, Till? Do you understand what I said?

I hear you. But who are you?

I'm your author, Till, your Creator. I'm Jonas Winner.

TODAY

Till is bathed in sweat as he is jolted out of the vision. Through the broad picture window that looks out onto the clearing in front of the house, he suddenly sees them groping and scrabbling out of the earth. Mud-smeared, filthy, decaying—in the hundreds. The *thousands*.

A flood of moving beings pouring up from the soil, out of the shafts, the trenches, the canals that lead through the hidden city— the city he'd wandered with Bentheim, and where Bentheim's bones must still lie. Likely not far from the remains of the two dogs Till could not choose between when he was a boy.

Had they let them live?

He jumps up from his chair and races through the stone foyer to the back door. Outside, he runs down the steps and across the clearing on the side, where none of the creatures have yet appeared. The edge of the forest shimmers green ahead of him like redemption.

Till has no idea where Felix is. He hasn't seen him since they spoke earlier, and hasn't seen anyone else in the house since he retreated to the study to look through the fictional universe.

He doesn't know where he's supposed to go; he doesn't know if he would be better off barricading himself in the house or if he should call for help. He can't think clearly or logically; he runs in a panic without direction. He just runs, pursued by the horror descending on the house. Behind him, he hears a cracking noise, creaking and splintering, but he races along the path through the forest and doesn't turn back. He sprints between the trees, ducks under branches, feels leaves and twigs whipping his face, past the cemetery, deeper into the woods.

And suddenly he feels like a small boy again, eleven or twelve, racing mindlessly, trying to outrun a horror, but suspecting all along that the horror is one he won't be able to escape, because it's not something chasing him. It's something already inside him.

TODAY

It's all still there.

The side wing, a semicircle that stretches around the courtyard and houses the dormitories on the ground floor. The refectory with the cross on the wall and benches screwed to the floor. The playground equipment between the tall pines, the pine cones littering the sandy ground, the bleached plastic toys—some split and broken—inside the wooden boards that make up the walls of the sandbox.

Brakenfelde.

Abandoned.

Till hasn't been here for twelve years, not since that early evening after Armin died when he just kept running, out through the fence into the surrounding woods, on and on through the underbrush, faster and faster, before Dirk could catch him. Dirk. Till had tried to tell him that something was wrong with Armin.

Brakenfelde.

The home where he'd once lived—the first home he could remember. The place where he'd spent perhaps the unhappiest times of his childhood.

Brakenfelde, where his brother, Armin, hanged himself in his room.

When Till ran along the forest path, past the cemetery where Armin lay buried—he knew where he was. The clearings and paths, the depressions between the trees, the places where he'd run as a child, the hollows and gullies where he and Armin and their friends played hide-and-seek, Cowboys and Indians, and soldiers.

The clearings and corners of the forest stretched around the children's home on all sides—around the home that Till had fled that desperate night.

Brakenfelde.

Less than twenty minutes on foot from Felix's house. They were neighbors! The children's home where Till grew up before the Bentheims took him in was next to the house of Felix von Quitzow—the man who'd done everything he could to get his hands on Xavier Bentheim's work.

TODAY

"I haven't seen you for so long, Till. Come over here, into the light . . . that's it."

It wasn't far. As a boy, it felt like a trip around the world, but now it took less than two hours. A two-hour march through the forested, hilly, sandy landscape on the southern edge of Berlin. Two hours on foot from Brakenfelde to the Bentheim house.

The cul-de-sac, the veranda with the massive columns, the stairway curving up to the porch. It's all still there. Not as freshly painted as it had been, not as well maintained, but all the more intriguing for that. The trees were older; the thickets and hedges were denser and obscured the view into the garden more than they had.

When Till arrived at the villa, the front door was locked. Nobody opened it when he rang. He walked past the main house and into the garden, where he saw the glass door into the living room standing open. Without a second thought, he stepped inside. He noted the smell—a mix of wood and freshly washed clothes— an odor that seemed not to have changed at all over the years. From the living room, he went into the hallway, searching through the entire lower floor, but saw nobody. He found her upstairs. Julia Bentheim.

"It's how he wanted it, Till. He said it would be good for you." Till is aware that she is watching his expression intently to see how he reacts to this news.

She lies in her bed, gray-haired, somehow slightly shrunken, although she can't be much older than fifty.

She had everything she needed, she'd told Till when he asked how she was. He could see the pleasure on her face, her joy at having him there. She was just feeling a little tired and had laid down for a moment to rest.

He sat on the edge of her bed and told her where he'd come from, speaking slowly at first, then faster, more hastily. How was it possible that Brakenfelde lay so close to Felix von Quitzow's house? Not much more than a fence separated the two properties.

She looks at him now. She gazes up at him from her pillow, and perhaps for the first time it occurs to Till how alike Julia and Lisa are.

"Felix wanted you to be strong. Strong, and with an iron will, strong enough to finish what he and Xavier had started. He had no faith in Max. He thought he was unstable and unfocused."

Till stares at her.

"I wasn't supposed to let you out of my sight, Till. After the death of your brother, he did everything to make sure that someone was keeping an eye on you all the time. He didn't want anything to happen to you. Even after you ran away from Brakenfelde, you were never really alone. When you suddenly jumped in front of the car, I just couldn't brake fast enough. I was terribly frightened, and so relieved when Trimborn told us you were all right."

As Till listens to her, he has the sense of his entire life breaking apart like some delicate, dreamed object falling to dust the moment he wakes up.

"So why didn't you ever . . ." his voice is heavy, but he keeps his eyes on the face he is so fond of. "Why didn't you ever tell me anything about this? How could you keep it from me?"

He can see she is getting upset. "You were such a marvelous, healthy boy, Till." Her eyes are soft and she has taken his hand in hers. "I had the feeling . . . I don't know. Max was unhappy, and I worried about him all the time. But you? There was something carefree and happy about you, and I thought I'd destroy that by telling you who your father was."

Felix.

Felix von Quitzow is his father. Felix had given him and his brother up to Brakenfelde in order for them grow up in a children's home. To make them tough, to make them equal to the task that Felix envisioned for his sons. One day, they would have to carry on with the plans that he had started. To continue the fictional universe—in exactly the way Felix had explained to Till earlier. Felix knew back then that the machine he saw in his mind's eye would only achieve its goal after many generations had worked on it. But it was also clear to Felix that the machine could only work if everything in those succeeding generations was done exactly right. If every new brick in the wall of the fictional universe only served to increase the level of addiction until, eventually, everyone was sucked into the vortex. And to make sure his descendants were up to the task, Felix sent Till and Armin to Brakenfelde—which was supposed to toughen them up, not leave them soft or weak.

But Armin had not made it.

TODAY

"What have you done?" Lisa screams. "What were you working on all that time with Henning and the others?"

She had seen Felix crossing the lawn toward them as they drove onto the grounds. She had thrown open the door, jumped out, and run toward him.

"Lisa, listen to me . . . this is about a lot more than what you or I want, it's—"

"About what? What could possibly justify what you've done?"

She hears something smash, sees the faucet attached to the wall of the house rip away, the hose fly through the air, the water shoot into the air in a steep fountain. "The city, Felix . . ." she blurts. He doesn't even turn to look at the faucet.

"Things couldn't go on like they were, Lisa. We had to set a goal, something to get beyond the centuries of confusion."

He must be mad. She sees his gleaming eyes, hears a car door slam behind her. Her eyes move past Felix to the carport beside the house, to his car parked there, listing slightly—

The earth—the earth beneath the car has given way!

"What kind of goal? Are you out of your mind?"

She watches as his car slides into the gaping hole that has opened up beneath it. And she feels the lawn under her feet start to vibrate.

"What's happening, Felix?"

Even as she says it, something is pushing up through the grass beside her: an animal, a rat, a weasel—no—it's an *arm*, the fingers like kinked thorns, like they want nothing more than to dig into Lisa's leg and drag her down with them into the loam. Then the earth next to the arm breaks open and a creature pushes through, rising at Lisa. The next moment, she is on the ground and kicking at its eye with the spiked heel of her shoe.

Lisa hears the slippery noise as the heel sinks into the creature's eye, and sees its other eye trained on her, its hair hanging over its forehead. Its chest rises out of the ground and the claws on one hand grip her ankle. With the other hand, it pushes itself up, working its way out of the lawn, intent on attacking her. But the heel in its eye holds it down. It blinks its good eye, and Lisa jerks her leg free, feels the heel slide out and she turns her head away, not wanting to see what her shoe has done to the vulnerable organ.

Around her, everything is going crazy.

It's like she's lying on a raft with sharks snapping all around her.

The ground, the grass—the entire property must be completely hollow underneath. Everywhere she looks the earth is sliding, subsiding, opening up, and she sees heads, limbs, arms, hands like talons shooting out of the soil.

The Last Judgment.

The resurrection of the dead.

Did Felix build this house on top of some old cemetery?

Or are these things breaking out of old passages running underneath the land?

The creature that grabbed Lisa's ankle rises out of the ground as if pushed by powerful springs under its feet. It's a man, Lisa can see that now. A man who is no longer in control of himself.

She sees the dirt fall away from his decaying clothes, sees his one intact eye lock onto her, his arms spread wide to grab her. She pushes herself up off the ground and starts to run, just managing to slip between the hands, which clap together empty behind her. Then she sees Betty's car turn between her and the house—the passenger door flies open and she races toward it! Felix has opened it from inside and grips the steering wheel tightly in his left hand.

Everything is seething and convulsing; it is as if the entire property is boiling.

Lisa sprints to the car. Her head bangs hard against the edge of the roof when she jumps in and one foot is still dragging along the sandy driveway when Felix hits the gas. With a yelp, she pulls herself completely inside the car; the door slams shut as the car whips around. A crater opens up in front of them and Lisa feels Betty's hands digging into her shoulders from behind her. She is thrown sideways when Felix jerks the wheel to one side, and she is pressed into the seat when he accelerates. She sees the columns that frame the entrance rapidly approaching, hears the smash when they sideswipe the gatepost—and braces herself against the dashboard to stop herself from being thrown out of her seat by the abrupt motion of the car.

TODAY

Till sees Felix's face closer than he has ever seen it before. So close it makes him ill, so close he feels like a tomcat with its teeth sunk into another cat in battle. He feels Felix defending himself, feels his hands clawing at Till's hair, but Till is younger than him, stronger, more agile.

He was standing at the window looking out over the garden, his back to Julia, when he saw them coming. The car rolled into the cul de sac—and the lawn and the surface of the road began to move.

As soon as the car stopped in the driveway, a young woman jumped out and hurried past the koi pond to the house. Till was so distracted that he hardly recognized her, even though he'd seen her as a girl in exactly the same place twelve years earlier—and not a day had passed since then that he hadn't thought about her a hundred times.

"Mom? Mom!" Lisa's voice rang through the house as she raced up the stairs.

"Till!" Lisa didn't waste any time greeting him. He knew she hadn't forgotten what had taken place just hours before in the restaurant, but she had no time for that now. "We have to get out of here!"

They helped Julia out of the bed, then all three of them ran down the stairs, along the hall, and through the front garden to the car waiting in the driveway, its motor running.

Till helped Julia into the backseat, next to Betty. And as he straightened, he saw Felix, now out of the car.

For a second, they eyed each other. Till had the feeling he was seeing this man as he really was for the first time. And a moment later, he was on him. Till reached between the arms that Felix had thrown up in defense and hoisted him off his feet, as though he were ripping a small tree out by the roots.

"You let Armin die!"

Till is blind to what is going on around him. He doesn't hear the rumbling, the drone that becomes a shrill hiss, the piercing shriek. He doesn't see the road they're standing on being torn apart, doesn't see it open up like a mouth—or that the teeth in the mouth are the living things emerging from the hidden city below. It's a mouth as big as the abyss that Bentheim described when Till eavesdropped on him in his workroom in the garden.

The entire driveway splits open, as if a water main has been washing away the earth beneath for weeks. Beyond the drive, a fissure continues through the front yards of the other properties. Till hears the noise of cracks opening in the walls of the houses.

He feels Felix's hands clawing at his cheeks, sees the torsos of the figures as they climb up from the cleft torn in the asphalt. They are still held by the earth, still half buried. The ground they are trying to free themselves from keeps giving way and they slip back, sinking deeper, only to start working their way up and out again.

With a burst of strength, Till hurls away the floundering body he holds in his hands. He feels like he's being scalped, Felix's clawing hands taking great chunks of hair with them. For a moment, the scream that escapes Felix seems to drown out the confusion and turmoil that surrounds them. Till sees Felix's face, sees his body twist as he flies through the air, sees him land among the bodies in the fissure and slip down among them, his face reflecting his horror, his left arm and both legs already out of sight, going down among the flailing creatures, his head following until only his right hand is visible, curled like a talon. Then that, too, is swallowed in the crush of bodies.

EPILOGUE

Berlin falls. Like it did once before, when the bombs dropped from the sky and laid waste to the city. When the terrible dingy metropolis was turned into a carpet of fire.

Butz strides in the direction of Alexanderplatz. Where he stands now, there is nothing to see of the pandemonium in the bowels of the city. Only the people passing by seem more frantic than usual. Fewer cars are on the road—a tension seems to cover the entire city like a gigantic bell jar.

He dragged himself away from the woman in Nikita, called his colleagues, and entrusted her to them. Then he went to Quitzow's headquarters.

The building was almost completely abandoned when he got there. He'd spent practically the entire day firing questions at the few remaining staff. All that Butz knew was that he was looking for the former boyfriend of a girl named Irina. But that was enough. He managed to find an employee who knew he could only be talking about Quentin. And everyone knew Quentin. Butz finally tracked him down in a cellar deep below the formidable building.

When Butz saw Quentin, he realized he'd met him once before, a few years earlier, at a birthday party of Claire's. He remembered only that Quentin had made no special impression on him.

Quentin was curled in a ball on a mattress in a corner of the cellar. It almost looked as if he'd lain down to die. To Butz, he appeared emaciated, wasted, driven to the limits of his powers by the demons he'd released inside himself.

"We shone a light," Quentin stammered. "We shone a light into the abyss, where nobody was willing to go."

Butz pried out the piece of paper Quentin had been holding in his fingers and read what was written there.

He's asking about me already. It won't be much longer before he's down here, down here with me—then he'll find me. I'll be lying on this mattress, he'll be standing in front of me in the doorway.

Why did I tell her my name was Max? When her hand opened the buckle on my belt, when she sat on my lap in the toilet?

Was I afraid I couldn't bring myself to . . . kill . . . her? Was I afraid she might discover my real name and give me away if I didn't find the strength to squeeze the life out of her?

It's done. I've reached the bottom of the well. I've completed the descent into evil.

Do you hear that?

His footsteps on the stairs?

It's time.

The moment has come for me to bring my account to an end.

May this record never get lost. Or all the pain, all the lust, all the burning heat would have been for nothing.

The door handle is moving. Time's up.

There he is!

Farewell.

Butz pulls off his raincoat and throws it over his shoulder as he paces along the street. It's hot in the city. Summer has begun. But summer's not the only thing causing the heat. To Butz, it seems like the opening of the subterranean parts of the city is letting the heat out, a fire that must have been building up among the cables and pipes and tunnels beneath the city, and that perhaps can never be eradicated from the earth here—even when the forests have begun to appear again, thousands of years from now, sprouting among the ruins of the walls that will be half buried in the earth.

He could have smashed Quentin against the wall, but he did not touch him again. Quentin was still very young; the thoughts in his head that had pulled him in one direction as if on a string for years were now marching in place. Now that he had reached his goal, there was nowhere left for them to go. It was clear that Quentin would never recover from what he'd done.

Butz called Quentin's location into dispatch and left him there alive. The entire city was already a cauldron boiling over.

He stops, holds his breath, listens. Again and again, squadrons of helicopters pass overhead, droning across the slot carved out of the sky by the buildings on either side of the street. A tang of singed rubber hangs in the air.

He almost believes he hears them screaming, hears them bellowing and whining, raging and crying. The inhabitants of Berlin, stoic and hounded, hard-nosed and gloomy, are trying to get on with their lives, whatever battle, whatever insanity might come crashing down on them.

Butz is one of them. He has always thought of his city as ugly, scarred, disjointed. But he loves Berlin, even if he doesn't really know why.

He won't abandon the people here. He will stay with them and try to help, try to get them through the chaos that has once again descended on the city.

• • •

When Lisa looks into the rearview mirror, she sees the reflection of the sea of light covering the night sky.

In front of her, the autobahn stretches in a straight black line, and piece by piece the car chews up the broken line down the middle of the road.

In the passenger seat beside her, Till has slumped to one side and fallen asleep. Earlier, she drove her sister and her mother back to Betty's place. A guard at a checkpoint had assured them that Betty's house was well outside the main danger zone. The two women wanted to stay there until the situation resolved. But Lisa and Till decided to leave the city.

Lisa leans forward and turns on the radio. It emits a crackle, and soft music fills the car.

She had slept with Till earlier, just after they'd passed through the city limits. They stopped in a parking area and wandered into the woods—and simply lay on the ground there.

Lisa placed her head on Till's stomach and listened to him as he spoke. He talked about when, so many years ago, he came to their house for the first time. And while he spoke, Lisa saw it all in front of her: Max, Betty, Claire, her mother, their carefree life—and her father, whom she lost not long after that. At first, Lisa could not comprehend what Till was trying to tell her. But at some point, she began to understand.

Till was the one responsible for the disappearance of her father. It was no coincidence that he vanished and never came back just a few weeks after Till had been taken into their family. Till had locked him in a dungeon as they were wandering through the hidden passages under the city.

Lisa listened as Till told her about the things they had discovered in her father's workroom in the guesthouse in the garden, and about what Max and he, as children, had believed as a result. She lay on the forest floor and listened to his voice while he told her that he was guilty not only of her father's death but also for her brother falling apart.

And at some point, Lisa stopped listening to Till's words, stopped trying to find the sense in them that she wanted—and gave herself over to what she felt for the man she was lying against.

She took his hand and laid it on her body, felt the way he touched her and caressed her, until desire carried them both away.

The white line in the middle of the road passes steadily. She can still feel Till's body against hers, and she knows that the day was favorable. She took no precautions against getting pregnant, and she is sure that Till would not have wanted her to.

Max.

If it's a boy, they will name the child Max, she thinks. And Claire if it's a girl. Lisa has a feeling she will never see Claire again.

A crackle on the radio, and the music fades.

A voice replaces it, interrupting the program, but Lisa can't understand what the voice is saying—the words are smothered by static.

Then the only sound in the car is a steady hiss that mixes with the low thrum of the motor.

Night.

All she can see are the twin pools of light that flit ahead of her over the asphalt.

She drives on, but the world around her falls away.

ACKNOWLEDGMENTS

THANK YOU!

Berlin Gothic originally appeared from August 2011 to June 2012 as a seven-volume e-book. I was still working—feverishly!—on the last books in the series when the first had already been published, a process that has no doubt left its mark on the series.

First of all, I would like to thank Anne Middelhoek for discussing every book in great detail with me before it was released. I'd also like to thank Gabriella Page-Fort and Sarah Tomashek at AmazonCrossing for their fantastic support and Edwin Miles for the amazing translation. And a special thank-you goes to Numi Teusch and Penelope Winner, who never stopped supporting my endeavors.

Finally, I would like to thank everyone who was there to help in the days when I was practically living in my study, possessed by the need to tell the story to its end within the time frame I'd already announced. To all those who actively accompanied the original publication of *Berlin Gothic* with e-mails, posts, tweets, reviews, and commentary: your encouragement, enthusiasm, and participation were simply great! I can only wish the same for any author struggling with a manuscript, and would therefore like to dedicate the book to you:

Angelika O., Ingo R., Melanie K., Claudia P., Stephanie R., Heide C., Petra K., Hans-Jürgen C., Harry K., Dietmar S., Angelika S., Johannes P O., Miriam D., Maria Carmela K., Lydia S., Chris K., Franziska B., Max H., Kyra C., Tom B., Liane L., Sebastian B., René W., Claudia T., Jan K., Ke Le, Sandy S., Kerstin F., Martha F., Leander W., Gaylord A., Hilke-Gesa B., Uwe F., Claudia P.-D., Marc P., Roland S., Ansgar B., Mandy M., Julia B., Michael H., Dietmar J., Marion D., Bianca H., Markus H., Heike T., Sabi N., Eva W., Renate A., Joachim M., Natalie S., Yamäs R. S., Maria Z., Rainer L., Nunu Na, Uwe L., Jay Cee, Melanie M., Elfrun K., Katja M., Sandra Z., Joanna M., Helmut R., Karin M., Corvus Semimortuus Genesis, Sandra R., Erin W., Johnny B. Redröm, Michael K., Jeannette J., Claudia S., Juergen M., Felix P., Salina F., Nic Pe, Bettina W., Andreas A., Anne H., Felicitas M., Alexandra B., Thomas S., Norbert S., Stephanie F., Frank W., Helga T., Christian S., Ute K., Stefanie R., Michael B., Jürgen K., Alois F., Hubert K., Simone S., Franziska S., Cindy W., Egon B., Jessica K., Helmut K., Monika K., Markus G., Henryette S., Manuela M., Brigitte B., Jennifer Sch., Micha Mc B., Bernadette H., Benjamin H., Elke V., Carmen V., Thomas M., Benjamin H., Ni Zi, Romina L., Florian K., Melanie S., Bianca B., Dirk J., Beccy Nur B., Markus B., Cornelia P., Sina Bin Ich, Gerd W., Is'n Witz Oder, Daniel F., H. Manfredowitsch, Miriam K., Kerstin I., Elke M., Silke L., Cosi Ma D., Heiko B., Stefan E., Angelika W., Ka Ro, Sandra L., Johannes G., De Storemönsch, Vanessa R., Thomas H., Holger G., Lee L., Marko S., Claudi G., Ralph B., Michael K., Götz R., Yvonnsche E., Karen R., Michael J., Jens R., Jean De W., Peter T., Axel St., Anja W.-J., Martin G., Silke B., Thomas W., Michaela M., Julia K., Corinna M., Mortem Custos, Torsten K., Frank B., Markus F., Markus T., Jes Si, Anja S., Julia B.-von B., Gordon M., Heike

B., Renate Th., Philipp K., Ralph Th., Thomas B., Till Moepert, Thorsten D., Peter B., Rupert M., Sophia H., Marcel B., Matthias S., Dana K., Anja M., Claudia S., Sandra N., Jenny Lee S., Irene L., Martin H., Anderl R., Katja Sch., Anke F., Cora S., Patrick R., Rene Z., Diane G., Andrea O., Simon Lukas S., Corina von Oben-Herab, Rüdiger E., Jens H., Veronika H., Sabine H., Xander Morus, Tom H., Thorben M., Karin B., Yvo K., Olga O., Sabine H., Annika U., Daniel W., Heike K., Joerg F., Barney K., Rp K., Christian B., Marco P., Ewald G., Torsten W., Oliver R., Philo C., Richard N., Kit, Alice K., Paul M., DavidGr14870366, literaturjour, umbrellabros, yovisto, ZwirblerRoman, grastisbuch, masterhare, leselink, wir_lesen, Smugacienia, FrankM., maganius, MatthiasZ., AffToolsTips, kayst., followeleboo, qbinmedia, RenateH., MartinaG., Gerlasi, nebelwanderer, s_meury, _NeneLovesBooks, ebokks, jrhernandez_org, SIVerlag, DuftDoppelpunkt, Stories, IrmaOndra, KKrause1990, Buecher_Wiki_2, forumzukunft, fraulaube, ComputerWissen, Ausgehandelt, gerhard222, LiteraryWalk, AndreasR., justii67, axelh., zellintelligenz, aKaren_autorin, SWestend, _XinXii, Alexandra71, hanna_hm, pommersche, SeinUndWerden, DarkPoets, rolfvonm., ana_S., schriftart, buzzaldrinsblog, TM20_de, HeikeK., eBookSonar, fiftyfiftyblog, ZeitRauber, ThrillerKiller1, leselust, e_book_news, comm_cationista, HeresLynx, virenschleuder, Mareike H., buchfieber, Krimilady, krimiblogger, Thariot, serpensz, sarianas, Ivyesque, KrimiKiosk, eLiterati_de, ebookmarketingz, BBAndMore, Michael L., MopedDriver, Jan27K, Andre_W., zochiii, MagistraFaust, BorisMaggioni, Andreas P., Marc_M., Amaro B., Regenu V., Phoebe H., Daniel Daniel, m_cz, 1QUrsu, jochenjochen, mmatting, Teipudon, seanwriter67, PagePlace_de, Patrick N., Emily B., buechermonster, divingcoffee, KnaurVerlag, emuatberlin, jazzecho, Prinz_Rupi, rundumkiel, Helmut_P., Ebookgemeinde, MartinH., rolfst., Irrenazt, darktom, Anik H., Frank M., kamerapaul, Xieldan,

Floris, josef.e., pe.b., thaysenf., fmthiele., lehmann.b., Polly-W., alex, alexander.sch., thilo.r., markus.fr., Gernot.H., tweety.d., corinnast., best.driver, k.guger, peters-m., k.unterthiner, jens.w., tj_sch., chrisb., thomas.l., LeonieP., tom.p, sillesw., ley., loef., weg. simone, shildebr., aileen.e, peter.ch.m., nc-br., axel.m., dagmar.s, markus_s., dietlindp., r-grz., christian.g.b, mark, e.schwarz, Izzi, Dieter H., Alfred H., anke frank, Iassm., Daniel W., Caludia S., vheimbuch, Tobias L., Barbara M., @koeller_koeln, Andreas P., Taetowierter, Uschi H., Uwe K., Jörn-Uwe Dr., Karin Müller, Heike, Kai E., Björn Schreiber, Gunnar M., Guido B., Isabella B., abraxas, Franziska E., Andrea Ö., Peter St., Roland K., Uwe Ridinger, Cecile E., Maria K., Sören K., K. Reinbold, hellclimber, Philipp B., Leuneam Remeark, Sven Matthias, R. Uebelhöde, buchreport, D. Lenz, O. Zille, Daniel Gr., K. Köcher, David Gray, Harry O., Ina F., Veronika B., Werner Sch., Stefan M., Sebastian H., Ileana G., Mirjam H., E. Hartmann-Wolff, Edwin M., Gabriella P.F., Jeff B., Renate W., Matthias W., Peter A., Anselm M., Werner W., J. Klingelhöfer, Miriam H., Johanna K., Daniela P., Gisella P., Christian, Viola, Jonas, Monika, Chrissy, Jay F. Kay, Linda, Anja, Teipu, Jasmin, Hakan, Azraelle, Tom, Noldolus, Sandra N., Caro, Matthias S., Pageturner, Berni, Peter Z., Klaus M., Destiny, Peter Hostmaster26, Fank H., !Undercover, B. Samantha, Thomas R., Katzenpfad Nokzeit, Jörg Eichholz, Tom S., Frau Iffi, Sophia H., Heide M., Cora S., Karin M., Uwe R., sterntaler, Jens, Walter, S. Heil, HPeter, Georg M., M. Bieski, Nicole K., Melanie S., Offene TB, Johannes G., Silke L., Julia N., Mark B., Angi K., Silke B., Nathalie F.-M., Louis Z., Karin M., Lydia Z., Egon B., Jennifer S., Daniel S., Caroline B., X- reader, ASR Gmbh, Thrillme, Skirad, webmaster und SEO, chris, Salina F., Sylvia R., Natalie, Melanie K., Maria C. K., Chris Karlden, Cyrus/\Virus, Blackanni, Bettina M., Johannes C., EvelynAutsch, A. Pförtner, Toby, Me R., Sabine H., Bianca H., Dietmar S., Caroline B., Jana C., Guth P., Silke

B., Elke V., Yvonne E., Oliver R., Silke W., Melanie M., Martha F., Claudia F.D., Christoph R., Nicky Ta, Jasmin K., Petzi, atarijunge, Stefan B., Aant T. Nhi. Part II, Oliver W., Ann-Kathrin Sch., Marco Sk., Kiki I., Marion Sch., Martin R. R., Ulrich Sch., Dennis R., Andreas M., Bri MI, Sabrina J., Birte A.d.B., Katharina B., Bianca H., Tanja S., Stefan L., Stefan E., Verena S., Nina F., Nadine K., Ebulon W., Dunja Maria A.-G., Thomas Kr., Ieasy Sch., Goran L., Regina M., Nicole N., Manfred R., Daniel Sch., Harvey N., Markus H., Oliver M., Anne J., Kurt H., Razorblade Gran Torino, Ka Ti, Mirjana R., Kay St., Jassy P., Nadja T., Ute S., Simone St., Rigna Folk St., Dubba J., Mareike M., Heike B., Miriam G., Angelika K., Angela S.-D., Nina G., Jürgen F. K., Marcel Z., Miracle B., Dagmar M., Jana Ch., Be Rit, Heike H., Rebecca L. Z. J., Sascha B., Monika B., Eva D., Frank H., Kathrin W., Hui Buh, Thomas L., Hannjo R., Martin S., Anja K., Melanie F., Monika R., Nadine K.

More about *Berlin Gothic* and my other books can be found at: www.jonaswinner.com

ABOUT THE AUTHOR

Born in Berlin in 1966, Jonas Winner lived in Rome and the United States before moving back to his home city to study philosophy. As a reporter and a television editor, he shot documentaries and covered cultural affairs. His experience informed his work on screenplays, and several of his detective stories and thrillers have aired throughout Europe. He released his debut novel in 2011, followed by the seven-part *Berlin Gothic* series, which became one of Germany's first e-book bestsellers. Winner lives and writes in Berlin.

ABOUT THE TRANSLATOR

Photo © Ronald Biallas, 2012

Born in Australia but widely traveled, Edwin Miles has worked as a translator, primarily in film and television, for more than ten years. After studying in his hometown of Perth, Western Australia, Edwin completed an MFA in fiction writing at the University of Oregon in 1995. While there, he spent a year working as fiction editor on the literary magazine *Northwest Review.* In 1996, he was shortlisted for the prestigious Australian/Vogel Award for young writers for a collection of short stories. After many years living and working in Australia, Japan, and the United States, he currently resides in his "second home" in Cologne, Germany, with his wife, Dagmar, and two very clever children.